To Andrew
For being there to catch me

PETER NEWMAN

The Ruthless

HARPER
Voyager

Harper*Voyager*
An imprint of HarperCollins*Publishers* Ltd
1 London Bridge Street
London SE1 9GF

www.harpercollins.co.uk

First published by HarperCollins*Publishers* 2019
1

A catalogue record for this book is available from the British Library

ISBN: 978-0-00-822903-0 (HB)
ISBN: 978-0-00-822904-7 (TPB)

Typeset in Sabon LT Std by Palimpsest Book Production Limited,
Falkirk, Stirlingshire

Printed and bound in the UK by CPI Group (UK) Ltd, Croydon CR0 4YY

MIX
Paper from
responsible sources
FSC www.fsc.org FSC™ C007454

This book is produced from independently certified FSC™ paper to ensure
responsible forest management.

For more information visit: www.harpercollins.co.uk/green

PROLOGUE

She had been elsewhere, between lives, formless and timeless. There was a sense of hanging above angry water, of shapes sliding under the surface, of shadows rising to feed, hungry, yet unable to break through to where she hung. She both feared the shapes and was drawn to them. But when she tried to go down to them, something held her up: unbreakable strands threading around and through her. Where she herself was neither light nor shadow, these strands glowed blue and violet, glimmering like crystal. Together they were a tether connecting her to the world beyond, to a platinum sphere, her anchor. This, she knew.

And so she had watched the shadows swirl and throw themselves against the divide, pressing against it, bending it, but unable to push through. On instinct, she tried to reach out, sure that if she could touch whatever separated them, it would part for her. However, the bands of light that protected her also fixed her in place.

The shadows could not reach her any more than she could

reach them, but they could whisper, and the sounds they made walked slow through the non-space, inching their way upwards. Though she had no bones in this place, no flesh, no blood, no limbs, the thing that remained had something of her senses, and she turned towards the whisperers, straining to listen.

Words came, trickling into her consciousness. Secret words, forbidden ones. The kind that excited her. Yes! This was true. Recalling something of her old nature sharpened her resolve. She was a hunter of secrets. She was a hunter of demons.

This time, like the times before, she told herself that she must remember what they said, that she must hold on to what she learned. It was important.

The voices were not as one. Some feared her, some hungered for her, and others made senseless noise that buffeted, making her rock from side to side, like a pendulum of glowing wires, or a hunk of meat on a rope.

But it was not meat that the shadows hungered for. They wanted memories, the very pieces that made up her soul. If they could tear one away, it would leave a space. Tear a second and the space would grow, becoming a burrow in her heart for them to hide inside.

There was a change above her, a tightening of the blue-violet strands, and she knew from experience that she would soon leave this place and become herself again, whoever that was.

The shadows sensed it too, redoubling their efforts, pressing so close that she was able to make out features, teeth and torn edges, ragged holes that allowed glimpses of muscle bunching naked inside.

She could feel a tension now, a pull at her back accompanied by the desire to rise. But a new noise made her resist and hold where she was.

Tucked within the writhing mass of shapes was a smaller, more human one, crushed, crying out, over and over: 'Pari!'

She knew that name. For it was her own. She knew the voice of the one crying out too. Someone dear, someone she loved. Peering closer, she saw his face bubble up from the darkness, set like a pimple on the back of some great beast.

The features belonged to Arkav, her brother. But that was impossible! Arkav was in a young body, very much alive. He could not be here. Could not be here and there at the same time. Unless some part of him had been lost between lives, bitten from him when he had last hung in this place.

Their gazes met, and he called out again, begging for her help.

She fought to go to him but the strands held her tight, making her feel like a prisoner. This too, was truth. *I am a prisoner,* she thought, and knew this had long been the case.

Then Arkav's face was blocked out by the rush of shadows, of hungry mouths and the screeching of something tearing, of the distance between her and the angry dark shrinking in the blink of an eye.

The strands of light grew tight about her, like a fist, and she was rising, as fast as the chasing shadows, then faster, leaving them and her brother behind.

This time, she told herself, *I will remember.*

CHAPTER ONE

Pari came back to the world slowly. Everything was black, muted, unreal, and her mind felt fuzzy. There were things she needed to remember. Something about her brother? Yes, that was it. The details skipped around the edge of her consciousness, still close enough for her to grasp, but other things were fast taking her attention.

There were straps around her arms, legs, body and head, holding her tightly in place.

There was something in her mouth that held it open, and a textured shape was pressing down on her tongue. Somehow she knew it was a mesh, and that it held a Godpiece, the anchor that kept her soul from drifting free between lives.

At first she'd thought she was in darkness, but someone stood over her blocking the light, close enough that the fabric of their clothes fell across her like a veil, tickling her nose as their hands worked at the strap behind her head. After a few moments it was removed and the obstruction in her mouth slipped free.

4

The other straps remained in place.

When the figure stepped away from her, a room of stone was revealed, windowless and grey, with pillars, well spaced, that spiralled slowly from the outer wall into the centre where she lay. Cool air brushed her naked skin, and she saw there were seven strangers moving around her, their robes whispering as they walked. The sound tickled a memory in her mind of something important. She had recently heard whispers that carried a hidden meaning. What was it?

Each figure carried a crystal-tipped wand that glowed, providing the only light in the room. Odd bulges moved within their robes, as if stunted limbs grew from their middles. Masked faces watched her, each one divided down the middle, black on the right, white on the left. One of them, she could not be sure which, spoke: 'One woman is welcome here. Are you that woman?'

Pari worked her mouth as her brain snapped fully awake and put all of the pieces together. *It isn't just a question, no, it's a test. This is a rebirthing ceremony. My rebirthing ceremony. And not my first – I've been here before. Many times.* She could feel certainty rising within her and with it, knowledge.

I am Deathless.

The thought rang in her mind, powerful and true. She had died many times but had always come back. So long as her blood remained in the world, be it a son, daughter, grandchild or someone who sprouted from that line; her soul would have a new home to go to.

I am Deathless.

An image came to her of a castle – her castle – floating high above the forests and rivers of the Wild. And within the castle, faces; of her hunters and servants, guards and Story-singers, Cutter-crafters and attendants. Not just one set but legions of them, getting older, being replaced.

She had ruled over them for generations. The sky-born who shared her castle, and the road-born below, scattered in scores of settlements, all hugging the Godroad, all facing the Wild.

I am a Deathless of House Tanzanite. And she knew that there were others in the house, all with their own castles and peoples and sprawling bloodlines. And she knew that House Tanzanite was one of seven, and that they were all united in a duty to hunt the demons of the Wild and stand guard over humanity. But that did not mean they got on, nor agreed on all things. Pari grimaced as she recalled just how true that was.

The robed people surrounding her were the Bringers of Endless Order. They had pulled her soul from wherever it had gone between lives and put it into a new body. Now they were testing to see if they had been successful. Whether they had truly hooked a human soul or had brought something else into the world.

She flexed her fingers and toes to see if she had a full complement, and that they would move to her will. To her relief, the digits obeyed. Sometimes a vessel sustained injuries, and sometimes the rebirth was not a complete success. Pari had heard stories of Deathless that only had partial control of their bodies, where the soul was misaligned, allowing a demon to slip into the cracks, gaining power over a hand, an elbow, or worse, the jaw.

The Bringers watched her closely. It occurred to her that she still hadn't answered their question.

'I am Lady,' she began, then stopped. The voice that issued from her throat was unfamiliar. High, girlish.

Seven masked faces leaned closer at her hesitation, no doubt searching for signs of possession. If she made a mistake, innocent or otherwise, they would assume the worst, declare her abomination, and end her.

She cleared her throat. 'I am Lady Pari Tanzanite.'

'Lady Pari Tanzanite is welcome,' replied one of the Bringers. 'If you are she.'

'If,' hissed the others.

'If you are she,' continued the first Bringer, 'you will prove your humanity. Look at yourself and tell us what you are.'

Her body was more petite than her usual preferences, however there was some tone to the muscles, suggesting a reasonable level of fitness. Golden tattoos glittered against her sky-born skin, one for each significant death she had experienced. The nature of the tattoos and their frequency were decided by the High Lord of House Tanzanite at the end of Pari's lifecycles. This was unfortunate as Pari's relationship with High Lord Tanzanite was cordial at best.

She did not need to look to know that there was gold ink on her shoulder, just as she knew there were gold spots on the pads of her fingers and a single mark on her lower lip. She looked anyway. It was not above the Bringers to place false marks to confuse, or her High Lord to have added a new one to make a statement about Pari's previous life.

But there was nothing obvious. If there were any new tattoos, they were tucked somewhere out of sight.

'I feel the marks on my fingers and remember my first life, where I had touched a lie and refused to let it go, even though it burned me.'

The Bringers did not react, watching her with a searing intensity.

'I see the mark on my shoulder and remember my fourth life –' she frowned '– and the poor fortune that ended it.'

Again, the Bringers remained quiet, though she suspected they had shared some look at her expense.

'I feel the mark on my lip and remember my fifth life, and the power of an expressive face.' Which was a polite way of saying that when she needed to, she could pout people to death. It was still up for debate whether High Lord Tanzanite thought this was a good thing.

'What is the name of your high lord?' asked one of the Bringers.

'What is the name of your Deathless brother?' asked another.

'Priyamvada is the name of my High Lord. My Deathless brother is Arkav.'

In her first life she'd had another brother who had lived a normal, single life. To her horror she found his name evaded her.

'What is wrong with him?' asked the Bringers together.

Pari's full body shiver was constrained by the straps. 'Pardon?'

Only a single Bringer repeated the question: 'What is wrong with him?'

She sighed to herself. *Here is the test.*

Arkav had not been himself for several lifecycles now. Her once flamboyant, confident sibling had become prone to dark moods and bouts of misery. More than once, he had cut himself. She had done her best to hide the full extent of this, as had her house, but the Bringers had secret ways. They knew things. It was more than possible they had discovered her secrets.

It was also possible that this was a trick question, designed to get her to bluff. There was no way to know for sure.

A third possibility occurred to her. At a rebirth ceremony, the only ones allowed inside were the vessel, the Bringers of Endless Order, and the Crystal High Lord of the Deathless being reborn; in this case Priyamvada Tanzanite. The last she had heard, her brother had been taken into the High Lord's care. Perhaps the question about Arkav was being asked for the High Lord's benefit. Perhaps Priyamvada was lurking behind one of the many pillars, observing.

It did not matter. If Pari failed the test, her brother was doomed. And besides, Pari had grown rather fond of herself over her lives. 'Nothing is wrong with Arkav,' she replied, enjoying the way the Bringers leant back in surprise before adding: 'that I cannot fix.'

There was a pause and then the Bringers stepped forward as one, the gemslight from their wands dazzling. She tensed in preparation, even though there was nothing she could do to defend herself. When they stepped away, the straps had gone from her chest and limbs.

'Lady Pari Tanzanite is welcome,' said a Bringer.

'Welcome,' echoed the others.

One by one, they left, pausing to nod to her as they did so. She caught a glimpse of peridot eyes within one of the masks, too bright, and was sure she knew them. It was assumed that the Bringers never left their sanctum, save to perform rituals, but masked as they were, no one knew their identities, they could walk freely across the land and never be recognized. They could have lived among the Deathless in secret all these years and no one would know.

Pari had never liked the Bringers. They held too much power for her liking. *Their incredibly sinister appearance doesn't help either. Just what are they hiding under those robes?* She suspected the answer would be unpleasant, but that only piqued her curiosity.

When the last of them departed the chamber was plunged into darkness. She sat up on the slab and stretched, relishing the ease of movement. Her last body had lived to a ripe old age, and she had not been kind to it. To sit up, simply to think something and do it was such a joy! She swung down from the slab and, seized by the urge, jumped up and down several times.

Navigating from memory, she felt her way around the circular chamber, past the inner pillars, to the outer ones, until she found the wall. From there it was a simple matter to follow its gentle curve. As she walked, the stone was cold underfoot, but the chill did not reach her joints.

A voice from nearby sapped the happiness from her. Female, deep, cold: 'Lady Pari.'

Pari dropped to her knees. 'High Lord Priyamvada, you honour me.'

There was a pause, and Pari felt the rebuttal before she heard it. 'No.'

Well, she thought, *at least I won't harbour any illusions of false affection.*

'Your boast to the Bringers. You stand by it?'

'Of course,' replied Pari. To lie to the Bringers of Endless Order was a crime. They both knew it. *My High Lord just wants to make it clear that I'm in her trap.*

'Good. House Tanzanite needs its Deathless in good order, and it has missed Lord Arkav's full attention.'

'I would see him.'

'He waits for you with Lord Taraka.'

'Lord Taraka? Is there business?'

'Yes. Prepare for it.'

'At once.'

Primyamvada had been ancient when Pari first became Deathless and was by far the oldest of their house. She used her words sparingly, and never went anywhere on a whim. Pari's instincts told her that something else was going on. Her nature led her to ask what it was.

'While we are alone,' answered Priyamvada, 'know that this is Arkav's last chance. He must add to his legacy or lose it entirely.'

Pari nodded, the gesture lost in the dark. 'I understand.' There would be many others vying for the chance to become Deathless. If Arkav was cast out, his Godpiece would soon find a new home.

'Know too, that if he goes, you will follow.'

'Forgive me, High Lord, but that I do not understand.'

'Really? You have left me no choice. Either you will see that Lord Arkav is fit to serve the house, or you have defiled this sacred chamber with your lies.' She heard the sound of the High Lord moving away. 'I am fond of your brother. It would be a great sadness to lose him.'

'Yes,' agreed Pari.

The great stone door groaned as it opened, spilling light into the chamber. She caught a glimpse of Primyamvada's silhouette shaking its head, and then she was alone.

There were three exits from all Rebirthing Chambers. One

for the Bringers, a second for the Deathless, and a third for abominations. This last one was set into the floor at the far end of the chamber, and led to a sudden drop from the bottom of her floating castle all the way down to the chasm below.

She had used the third once before, in the castle of Lord Rochant Sapphire, and sworn never to again. Even so, it was with great reluctance that she stepped through the second door. She had a feeling that whatever was coming would be far from pleasant.

Sa-at hunched down within the branches, making himself as small as possible. He did not want the people below to see him because he knew they would be scared and run away.

It was rare to see Gatherers from Sagan this far off the path. There were eight of them, doing their best to fill their heavy bags with berries, nuts and yellow funghi. They always travelled in groups and they always moved quickly, nervous faces darting, jumping to every sound. Unlike Sa-at they wore thick clothing and heavy gloves to protect themselves from scrapes and cuts. Even in the daytime it only took the slightest scent of blood to wake the things of the Wild.

The dense canopy hid the suns from sight but by the glow of the leaves, he could tell it was moving from afternoon to evening, and that Vexation, the stronger of the red suns, was dominant.

'Come on,' said one. 'We should be getting back.'

'Just a bit further,' said another.

'We got a good haul,' said the first. 'Why risk it?'

'See this?' One of the hooded figures pointed to something on the floor and Sa-at leaned out from his hiding place for a better view. Branches shifted under his stomach to support his weight, the leaves stretching to form a veil between him and the group below. Sa-at had made many pacts with the nearby trees. He fed them whispers and little pieces of his kills, and in return they sheltered him.

Not every part of the forest was his ally, in fact many of the trees hated him, but even they tended to leave him alone.

Sa-at did not know why.

From his new position, he could see a little better but the thing the group were looking at still eluded him.

'It's a creeper,' continued the speaker. 'If we follow it, it'll take us right to the mother plant and we can bleed it for Tack.'

There was a brief debate which Sa-at observed with interest. Because of its rarity, Tack was extremely valuable. Usually, the hunters were the only ones that dared go deep enough to find it.

'Think of it!' said the one leading the argument. 'One haul would keep us all for a year. We could repair the fences, or we could buy a tame Dogkin to pull our barrow. Or . . . '

The opposition's point was simple. They could get lost if they went deeper. They could die, or worse.

One of the group had a habit of waving a hand as she talked, making little circular motions like a whirling leaf when it fell to the ground. Another clasped their hands in front of them, as if they had just caught a baby Flykin and wanted to shake it to death. They spoke too fast for him to follow all of the words, but he could see that some were worried and some were greedy, and that the majority wanted to press on. He also enjoyed copying their gestures.

When the Gatherers had moved away, Sa-at sprung from

13

the branches, flinging out his arms so that his coat of feathers flew out behind him. For the few seconds it took to land, his face was split by a joyous grin, then he rolled across the floor to come to a stop where the group had chewed up the ground with their heavy boots.

The creeper vine sat there like a bulbous tongue stretching from the dark of the trees. He stayed in a crouch, folding his arms behind his back as he inspected it. The skin of the creeper was pale, suggesting it had not yet fed. It had not inflated either, laying flat and lumpy where it should be firm and round.

As he pondered this, a Birdkin flew down to join him. At least, it looked like a Birdkin. Its body was only slightly smaller than his head, and covered in feathers of the same black as those that made Sa-at's coat. He knew it was also a demon, and that this made people afraid.

Sa-at did not know why.

'Crowflies!' he said.

'Sa-aat!' it screeched back.

He pointed at the creeper with his nose. 'Wrong?' he asked.

The Birdkin hopped closer and turned its head, regarding the creeper with one of its glistening compound eyes. It twitched one way, then the other, then opened its ivory beak.

Sa-at reached out a hand. His little finger was missing, and sometimes the old wound became itchy. When that happened, or when he wanted to be close to Crowflies, he pressed the scarred knuckle into the Birdkin's beak.

Crowflies' neck jerked, as if it were about to vomit, and then he felt the proboscis stir from inside, peeking out to prick his skin.

14

A flurry of images brushed Sa-at's mind – a vision of the world as Crowflies saw it, a fractured mosaic. The colours he saw were strange, the reds brighter, the greens darker, and shadows no longer matched the things that made them.

The Gatherers' footprints stood stark amid the dirt, and among the human ones Sa-at was now shown others that had been there recently, a succession of small round holes, as if someone had poked their fingertips into the dirt again and again.

Spiderkin? wondered Sa-at.

Crowflies gave a twitchy nod. They had dragged the creeper here as a lure. No doubt there was more than just the plant waiting for the Gatherers.

Sa-at made a cage with his fingers. *A trap?*

Another nod from the Birdkin.

The people with the funny hands will be eaten?

And another.

Sa-at pulled a face. He didn't like the idea of the people being eaten. He saw Spiderkin all the time but he rarely got to see people. He wanted to see more of them. Maybe there was a way to stop the Spiderkin's trap . . .

As soon as he'd had the thought, Crowflies stiffened, unhappy.

'But,' protested Sa-at, 'they'll die.'

Crowflies gave a shrug of its wings.

He pulled his hand free, sucking the end of it as he stood up.

'Sa-aat!'

He was being warned not to go.

'I'm going.'

'Sa-aat!'

He paused for a moment. Crowflies was his friend, his only real friend in the Wild. The Birdkin had brought him food and drink until he was old enough to hunt. It nursed his injuries, watched his back, taught him. Everywhere Sa-at went, Crowflies was there like a winged shadow. Deep down, he knew it was trying to protect him.

But then he thought of the Spiderkin wrapping the Gatherers in bladesilk. In a week or so he would come by this part of the forest again, and find eight skeletons stripped of everything save the hands and feet.

If he waited another week, the hands and feet would be gone.

The maimed skeletons would hang for a few more after that, and then vanish. Sometimes, much later, he'd see a fragment of bone attached to one of the trees like a trophy, and be certain that he'd seen it before.

His stomach turned a few times and then he started running.

Behind him he heard several squawks and felt the feelings behind them.

'Sa-aat!' (*Annoyed.*)

'Sa-aat!' (*Go if you want, I'm staying here.*)

'Sa-aat!' (*Exasperated.*)

A little smile tugged at the corner of his mouth as he skipped between a tangly mass of bushes. Despite it all, Crowflies would come. *It always comes.*

The trees gathered closer in this part of the Wild, shutting out the day. Great strands of web ran taught between them. Where it rubbed against the branches, deep grooves were made, red fungus sprouting from it like raw skin. Fat shapes sat within the canopy, their legs bunched together to conceal their true size. Sa-at knew the signs and quickly guessed at their number.

The Gatherers did not.

A couple of them made a token effort to keep watch, though they had no light to penetrate the gloom, and were of little use. The others were clustered around a green trunk, as wide as a broad-shouldered man, with pale yellow veins running like marble across its surface. Several creeper vines were coiled at its base.

As he got closer, a nervousness began to grow within Sa-at. He felt something he did not have a name for – a desire to impress. He skidded to a stop and paused. He had very rarely seen people and had never spoken to one before.

One had spoken to him however, when he was tiny, a man called Devdan. Sa-at learned many words from him. He had been kind for a time, and then he had stopped being kind. Sa-at remembered the man's hands on his throat, and then the threat of fire and sharp things. He had been tiny but the memory was vivid in his mind, like a body preserved in amber. These people seemed kind too, would they try and hurt him as well?

'I see something!' said one of the Gatherers, and they all turned towards him. They carried simple weapons, knives and long poles of wood. One carried a sling, that they proceeded to load.

Sa-at had never seen a sling before and was briefly distracted by the excitement of something new. The promise of the unknown made the hairs on the back of his neck tingle.

'What is it?' said a voice from the back.

'Looks like a person.'

'Ain't no people here but us.'

'Said we shouldn't have come!'

'Is it a demon?'

Sa-at tried to think of something to say but the excitement and nerves had made him too fizzy, so instead he took a careful step forward.

As one, the group stepped back.

'Don't look it in the eye!'

'Don't let it touch you!'

Behind them all, moving smooth and slow, the first of the Spiderkin slid down until it was level with the Gatherers' heads. Upside down, its legs opened like bony petals, tensing to strike.

Sa-at finally found his voice. 'Run.'

'Did it say something?' asked a Gatherer.

'Don't listen to it!' said another. 'Don't let it get close!'

A second Spiderkin slipped down next to the first, a third and fourth close behind. These were the scouts, the fast ones. Their job was to slow down the food for their queen.

'Run!' he repeated.

'Don't listen!'

He did not understand why they were still standing there. The new Spiderkin flexed open as well, the little mouths tucked in their bellies oozing with drool. They were ready. He did not understand why it was so difficult to communicate with these people. Crowflies always understood what he said and all the meanings underneath.

With arms spread wide, Sa-at let out a wild cry and ran towards the group, desperate to get them to move.

The Gatherers cried out in alarm and the Spiderkin paused to assess the new threat. The sling spun round three times and a stone whizzed past Sa-at's shoulder. He kept running.

The Gatherers fell over themselves trying to retreat, stumbling directly into the Spiderkin.

There was a flurry of legs and screams as the Gatherers tried to flee. They had finally realized the danger, but instead of running back towards the lighter area of the forest (which would have taken them past Sa-at), they ran away from everything, moving randomly off into the dark.

Seven vanished into the forest, but one was grappled by a Spiderkin, his legs kicking wildly as it began to ascend.

Sa-at used his momentum to leap, grabbing the Gatherer's boot as it thudded into his chest. They swung, spinning on the end of the strand, the Gatherer dangling from the Spiderkin's legs, Sa-at dangling from the Gatherer's. Their arc took them into the path of other strands, tying all four together, and sending the other three Spiderkin into a frenzy.

The Gatherer shrugged off his satchel, getting partially free. A last leg was hooked under his shoulder however, and he fought desperately to unhook it. A droplet of saliva fell past them to the floor. That meant the Spiderkin's mouth armour had pulled back. All the Gatherer had to do was punch it there and he'd be let go.

'Hit it now!' urged Sa-at.

However the Gatherer was too busy screaming to notice.

As they swung towards a tree, Sa-at kicked off from it, spinning them faster. If the Gatherer had been caught by one of the big ones it wouldn't have mattered, they would both have been taken to the lair. However their combined weight and motion was too much for it to hold, and the Spiderkin let go with a hiss.

The next thing Sa-at knew he was on the floor. Before his thoughts could catch up, he was on his feet. The Gatherer was doing the same.

'Run!' Sa-at urged.

This time, there was no hesitation. The Gatherer did as he was told.

'No,' Sa-at called after him. 'Not that way!'

But the Gatherer was too busy screaming to listen.

After a moment's frustration, Sa-at followed him, leaving the Spiderkin to stab at each other as they untangled themselves.

CHAPTER TWO

The Gatherers had run blind, stumbling between the trees in a haphazard fashion. Each was guided, by twisting paths and prodding branches, until they had all been brought back together. Then, gradually, the Wild had funnelled them deeper into its heart, to places that even Sa-at avoided when the suns went down.

When the first of them stopped to double over and pant, the others followed suit.

Sa-at watched them from a distance, curious to see what they would do next. Crowflies had caught him up during the pursuit and had settled itself on a nearby branch.

Each member of the group gave their name to prove they had survived the encounter, and each time the rest of the them would smile and reach over to touch the arm of the one who had spoken. Sa-at liked that. He wondered what it would be like to be smiled at in that way. As the last one announced themselves and was welcomed, he copied their smiles from his hiding place and reached out a hand in their direction. None saw, save for Crowflies, who did not care to comment.

'Sa-at is here too,' he whispered, and then, so as not to feel lonely, he touched his own arm.

'I think we're not far from . . . ' gasped one of the Gatherers. 'Or maybe we're near . . . I think . . . no. I don't know where we are.'

'We need to get home.'

The others were quick to agree but none of them were sure which way home was. Another discussion started, quickly turning into an argument. Sa-at listened with interest, eagerly devouring the new words. He was particularly intrigued to know that some of the Gatherers had more than one name.

That woman likes to turn her hands and speak.
Her name is Hil.
Hil's other name is 'Great Idiot'.
The man who clasps his hands is Rin.
Rin's other name is 'Dogkin's Cock'.

At one point it looked as if the group was going to split up, with one half going with Hil and the other with Rin. However, when Hil claimed to recognize a mossy chunk of rock, they stopped arguing. And when she said they were not far away from a path she knew, Rin told her to take the lead.

She's wrong, thought Sa-at. *They're going the wrong way again.*

Crowflies pointed at the group with a wing and made a derogatory noise.

'You don't like them?'

He received one of Crowflies' looks, where the Birdkin

slowly tilted its head to one side as if Sa-at had said something ridiculous.

He watched thousands of tiny reflections of himself shrug in the Birdkin's eyes. 'They're funny. I don't want them to die.'

That earned him another look.

The Gatherers were too tired to set off immediately. They agreed to take a short rest as it would be the last they could dare on the journey home.

Sa-at pulled himself up onto a thick branch and settled next to Crowflies. What would be the best way to help these people? He tucked his arms in and let his chin rest on his knees. This was a problem that would require thought. He knew they were afraid of him. Perhaps he could chase them out of the forest. However, it would be difficult to herd them over a long distance. And what if they scattered or decided to fight?

While he pondered the problem, he listened to the Gatherers' chatter.

'Did you get the Tack, Rin?'

'Right here.'

There was a cheer, followed by a question, tentative: 'You're going to share it with us, right?'

'Depends on whether you called me Dogkin's Cock or not!'

They all laughed at that. Sa-at was not sure why.

'Rin?' asked another. Sa-at realized it was the one he'd saved.

'Yeah?'

'I lost me bag back there. I got nothing.'

'Don't worry, Tal. Important thing is you're alive.' There

was a chorus of agreement. 'You and yours won't starve neither. We'll all share a bit of our take.' Rin looked round at the rest of the group. 'Won't we?'

There was a second round of agreement, though Sa-at thought it was less enthusiastic than before. 'You checked yourself again yet, Tal? Still no blood?'

Tal raised an arm and examined his armpit. 'Don't think so. It's sore though.' He pushed his finger through a new hole in his jacket and, after wiggling it around, showed it to Rin with relief. 'No blood!'

'No blood,' Rin confirmed, and a sigh of relief passed round the group.

'We better go,' interrupted Hil. 'Vexation's the only strong sun in the sky today, and it isn't going to wait for us.'

An idea popped into Sa-at's mind as the Gatherers stood up and put away their rations. He kissed the leaf of the nearest tree, leaving a little of his spit behind, and scrambled up the trunk. It did not fight him, though it did not help him either.

Crowflies watched, bemused, as he heaved his way into the upper reaches of the tree. As soon as he arrived, he grabbed a branch and pulled it towards him, creating a breach in the canopy.

A shaft of Vexation's light, richly red, punched through.

'Look there!' called one of the Gatherers.

They rushed to the gap and Sa-at held himself still, hoping not to be noticed. 'It's worse than I thought,' said Hil. 'By the angle of sunlight, I'd say we only got a few hours. We're further off than I thought too.' She blew out a long breath through her lips.

'Think we can make it?' asked Rin.

'Be tight.'

Rin nodded. 'Will be if you take the wrong way again, you great idiot.'

There was a warmth to the words that took away their sting. Instead of getting cross, Hil squeezed his arm, changed direction and started walking.

The group followed her on the ground, and Sa-at followed them in the trees, walking the tangled pathway of branches. Whenever Hil seemed to be going off course, he pushed the leaves aside to let Vexation's light guide them.

For hours they trudged. Fear kept them at a good pace, and soon, Sa-at was struggling to get ahead of them. But keep ahead he did, until they reached a part of the Wild where the trees thinned a little and his help was no longer needed. He watched them from a high branch. Though most wore similar clothes, he could easily tell them apart. As each one passed by he gave a little wave. None of them saw.

Fortune's Eye and Wrath's Tear had already set, and Vexation was low in the sky. Hil looked up – straight past Sa-at – took a quick bearing, and hurried on. Nobody said anything. They could all feel the change in the air. Soon, night would fall and the Wild would stir in earnest. Grim-faced and determined, the Gatherers kept going, all of their attention on the floor at their feet. The forest had not started to move yet, but it was only a matter of time.

Perhaps that was why they did not notice that only six of the group were still following Hil. Sa-at noticed. He had been counting them as they went. He turned on his perch, scanning the nearby area for any signs of the eighth Gatherer.

There! He saw that one of the group had stopped further back, like a lone reed swaying in the breeze.

He slipped silently from the tree and circled round so that he could approach from behind. Their breathing sounded laboured and they were making unhappy noises with each exhalation, as if in discomfort.

Sa-at was just trying to decide whether to risk talking to them when they fell over.

He watched them for a few moments, and when it was clear that the Gatherer wasn't going to move, he crouched down nearby and rolled them onto their back.

It was Tal, the one he'd helped before. There were no obvious injuries, no reason why he had stopped. *Maybe he's tired?* Sa-at sniffed. Something didn't smell right. Another sniff and he had located the source. He lifted Tal's arm so he could get his hand into the man's armpit. The stink of fear-sweat made him wrinkle his nose. Did all people smell this bad? His own armpits made a smell sometimes but it was nothing like this. In fact, Sa-at quite enjoyed smelling himself at the end of the day.

He found the hole in Tal's jacket and worked it wide until he could get his hands in for a feel. In the middle of Tal's armpit, he found a stud of scar tissue, about the size of his middle finger, which was also the same size as the tip of a Spiderkin's leg. Tal groaned when he pressed it.

On the other side of the scar tissue would be a tiny strand of web. Attached to the web would be an egg, floating inside Tal's body. When night fell, the egg would hatch and the baby Spiderkin would call to its queen to collect it. Sa-at ran a hand through his hair. He did not want Tal to die.

With a flutter of wings, Crowflies landed next to him and pushed his hands aside with its beak for a closer look.

'Can you get it out?'

Sa-at held his breath while Crowflies inspected the entry point. After a few moments, it nodded.

'Will you?'

Crowflies looked from Sa-at to Tal and back again as it considered the question. Eventually it hopped over and tapped Tal's thumb with its beak.

'No. He needs his thumb.'

Sa-at watched the beak hover, then tap an index finger.

'No.'

This time the beak came to rest on Tal's eyelid.

'No!' Sa-at tugged at Tal's earlobe. 'This bit?'

Crowflies shook its head.

'What about both of them?'

There was a pause, then Crowflies nodded. It worked its head into the hole in Tal's jacket, paused, then stabbed into his armpit. Sa-at saw the Birdkin's throat swell as its proboscis thrust out.

Tal called out in pain and tried to twist away but Sa-at held him down while Crowflies worked.

The red-tinged sky faded to grey and then Crowflies pulled back, something trapped and wriggling within its beak. The Birdkin regarded the thing's tiny legs with interest. There was a crunch and a small but audible pop, and the wriggling stopped. Crowflies tipped its head up and swallowed.

'Did you stop the blood?' asked Sa-at.

Crowflies gave him a look.

'Thank you.'

He turned away while Crowflies took its due, only turning back when the wounds were pinched closed. Both earlobes were gone, snipped away so smoothly it was as if they were never there. Tal was groaning and muttering to himself, though his eyes were only half-open. It seemed as if his body were awake but his mind still lurked in some dream. He allowed Sa-at to pull him up and lead him stumbling the way the group had gone.

It was fully dark when they reached Sagan.

There was a space where there were no trees and the ground was scorched black by old fire, abandoned land that bridged the gap between the edge of the Wild and the fences and fields where Sagan began. Lights burned orange along the tops of the fences, and as Sa-at pushed Tal towards them, he heard people shouting.

'Over here! I see Tal! I see Tal!'

More of the lights began to move, until they had picked Sa-at from the darkness. He squinted his eyes against the sudden glare and waved. Tal raised his hands over his face and groaned.

'He's in pain! And what's that feathered thing next to him?'

Sa-at tried to think of something to say but, again, the words would not come.

Others were speaking though. 'Something has him!'

'Don't let it take Tal!'

There was movement at the fence, though Sa-at couldn't make out what it was. He wanted to say his name the way the Gatherers had back in the Wild. That he was Sa-at and he was safe. And then they would smile at him and touch his arm. He wanted it so badly but he could not find the words. It was as if all the breath for speaking had fled his body.

So instead he smiled and gave Tal a gentle push towards

Sagan. The young man managed several awkward steps before tripping and falling over.

'It's killed Tal!' shrieked a voice.

'Get it!' shouted another.

A stone landed in the dust by Sa-at's feet. Then another. He held up his hands in surprise and felt something sharp smack into his palm. It stung and he cried out.

'Good shot, Rin! Keep at it.'

He took a step back as another stone hit his shoulder. That stung too, and his eyes pricked with tears.

Fear overcame shock, making him turn and run. The stones and shouts followed him, back across the barren ground and into the dark of the Wild.

Satyendra strolled across the courtyard, slowing as he reached the centre. On cloudy days this was his favourite place in the castle. An open space as far from the oppressive walls and the hated crystals as it was possible to be.

It would be even better if there was nobody else here.

He was good with people, but they brought out the worst in him, and he often wished he had been born elsewhere. A quiet settlement on the edge of a Godroad, or one of the watchtowers on the border where he'd only have the land-scape for company. Within the confines of Lord Rochant Sapphire's floating castle, privacy was hard to come by.

Some of the apprentice hunters were playing 'snare the demon', a game in which one person was the titular demon and had to get from one side of the courtyard to the other. The other players were the hunters, and their job was to grab the demon. If three hunters got hold of the demon at once, they won.

When they saw Satyendra they called out to him, begging that he join them. It had always been like this. As the Honoured Vessel for Lord Rochant Sapphire's next life, he was special, elevated above the others. Everyone wanted to sit next to him at mealtimes or pair up with him while training. He was an auspicious being, a lucky charm, and they loved him for it.

Almost as much as he loathed them in return.

Apparently, he had impressed even as a baby. He was born under the same alignment of the suns as the Sapphire High Lord, Yadavendra, and had impressed the man so much, that he had been gifted with a name of equal status and length as the other high lords. Clearly, Yadavendra had low standards. As best Satyendra could tell, he had been honoured for not crying. His mother always went on about how quiet and brave he was as a baby. *How ridiculous. They praised me because I did nothing. That's no achievement. Perhaps they're hoping I'll be just as quiet at the end, when I'm sacrificed for the good of the house.*

And with the next proper alignment of the suns only a day away, the end seemed far too close for comfort. He had to find a way to postpone.

One of the apprentices moved into his path. Though he'd known them all for years, in his head he referred to them by feature rather than name. This apprentice was called Pik, but he had dubbed them *Nose,* for obvious reasons. 'Want to play, Satyendra?'

He buried his irritation deep, and put on a mask of reluctance. 'I'd love to but Story-singer Ban is expecting me.'

'Just one game, please.'

'Please!' echoed the other apprentices.

'I don't know. He won't like it if I'm late. Lord Rochant was known for his punctuality.'

His primary duty as an Honoured Vessel was to be like a mirror to Lord Rochant in thought and deed in order to enable an easy rebirth. It was implicitly understood that everyone in the castle was supposed to assist him in this, and for years Satyendra had been using it to his advantage.

As he expected, the apprentice hunters backed off, disappointment plain on their faces, and, for a delicious moment, their shared sadness washed over him, like the scent of cooking from another room, making his mouth water. A secret part of him stirred, and demanded to be fed.

I should move on, he thought. *Ban hates it when I'm late, and if I play, I'll need to win.*

There was a terrible pressure in being Lord Rochant's Honoured Vessel. For it seemed Rochant had been hatefully good at everything: flying, tactics, lawmaking, diplomacy, hunting, art. His legacy was like a shadow that dwarfed Satyendra's achievements. How was he supposed to match somebody with lifetimes of experience? Somebody known for their wisdom. Who never lost.

It was impossible. Better to sidestep the issue of the game entirely and go to his lesson.

He walked on a few paces, pretending reluctance, before stopping. It was too late. He wanted to feed. Needed to. He would play and win and make them sad. Then he would drink it in. The plan had already formed, any flaws hidden by an irresistible need. His back was to them now and he could not help but lick his lips in anticipation.

'Could I play the demon?' he asked.

31

'Of course,' they replied, a little eagerness returning to their eyes.

He made a show of thinking it over. 'I suppose I could stay for one game, but it would have to be quick.'

The apprentices rushed to their starting positions, spreading out across the courtyard, while Satyendra walked to the far wall.

'Ready?' they asked.

'Yes,' he replied, then, as they started to run towards him, added: 'No. Which demon am I going to be?'

The apprentices stopped, confused. One of them said, 'What?'

'I need to know which demon I am.'

Though the game did not normally require the demon to be named, all of the apprentice hunters had grown up being taught about the inhabitants of the Wild. Suggestions came thick and fast:

'Be one of the Red Brothers.'

'Be a Watcher!'

'Be a Kindly Father!'

'Be the Stranger!'

'Be Murderkind!'

Satyendra shook his head. 'No, I'm going to be the Scuttling Corpseman.'

'But, the Corpseman is dead,' replied Nose. 'Lord Vasin killed it.'

'No he didn't, he cut off its arm, and anyway, this is a game so I can be who I want. Be careful though,' he warned, 'the Corpseman kills any hunter it catches alone.'

While they were digesting that, he started running down the left side of the courtyard, and with a whoop, they came after him.

The Ruthless

Most of the apprentices were full grown, with adult frames that hadn't yet filled out, and faces that still contained an echo of childhood. At seventeen, Satyendra was not the fastest nor the strongest of them. He was small like his mother, but he had her steel, and one other advantage. For Satyendra was different. Not just because of his status but because of something deep inside him, something fundamental. He didn't understand why or how, but he knew, in a way that he never articulated, that something inside of him was twisted.

As far as he could tell, the majority of people in the castle did not lie. It did not even occur to them. For Satyendra, deception was a part of everyday life. Every pleasantry was a lie. Every smile. Every kind word. It was a daily necessity to keep his secret. A lifetime of practice had made him the best deceiver in the castle.

And so, in the game, he lied. As he approached the first pair of apprentices, his body told them he was going left, and when he went right instead, they were wrong footed. He used the same trick on the second set. The third set were expecting a feint, they watched his eyes instead of his body.

They might as well scream their plans at me, so bright is it on their faces.

He told them with his body that he was going left, but hinted with his eyes that he was going right.

They believed his eyes, and he sailed past them.

Too easy!

He was halfway across the courtyard when he heard his mother's voice from one of the upper windows. He was being called. Pretending not to hear, he put his head down and ran for the finish.

Chunk, one of the older apprentices came charging up behind him. Satyendra tried to weave to throw her off, but she was so much bigger and so much faster that it didn't matter.

All he had to do was keep going a little further. The wall grew larger in his vision. Under the clouds, the sapphires set in the stones seemed dull and dark.

Just a few more steps!

The more it looked as if he was going to win, the more he could feel the frustration of the other apprentices, like a dam about to break. He wanted the sadness underneath, he needed it.

As his pumping arms swung out behind him, he felt a hand close on his wrist.

'Got you!'

No!

Chunk pulled him backwards, away from the wall. His fingers had come tantalizingly close, another inch or two and he would have won. They skidded together, both working hard not to fall or get their legs tangled.

Satyendra could feel his momentum being stolen and it enraged him. He had to win!

'I've got him!' she called.

He twisted to get free but her grip stayed firm. When he tried to drag her towards the wall she simply leaned back and he was unable to shift her weight. The other apprentices were running over. If any two of them got their hands on him then he would lose the game. Their frustration had vanished, their sadness become like a memory of mist. His hunger clawed at him.

His mother's voice called again, louder this time.

Neither of them paid the Honoured Mother any attention. Chunk grinned at him and he grinned back.

He was still smiling as he pressed his foot against the side of her knee and pushed. Braced as her leg was, it was easy for him to pop out the joint.

Her smile vanished into a scream.

The mix of surprise and pain was heady, and Satyendra drank it in. Their suffering like a physical thing, nourishing. Around him, everything came into sharper focus. He felt more alert, more alive. It was as if he'd been in a desert and forgotten how sweet water could taste. A part of him knew that this was going to make trouble down the road but when the rush was on him it was hard to care.

Her grip on his wrist was still strong, the shock making her squeeze even tighter. It didn't matter. His strength grew as hers waned, and he broke free easily and took the last step to the wall.

While the apprentices were gathering around Chunk he touched his fingers to the cool stone. 'I win!' he declared.

When he turned back the others were staring at him. Most were dumbfounded but three were advancing with violent intent.

They look angry, he thought. *Angry enough to forget the rules.* Perhaps they were going to actually strike him this time. *Let them try!* He thought, *I can do anything!* Though bolstered by another's pain, he knew that the odds were not in his favour. Behind his bold smile, a worm of sanity crept in, telling him he should apologize or beg, anything to stop the incoming beating. His fear smothered the rush, and the closer they got, the more he wished that he had not put himself in the corner of the courtyard.

His mother's voice cut across the scene, half speaking Satyendra's name, half singing it, stretching out the sound into several long notes. The apprentices froze in place immediately as the word seemed to bounce from the walls. Even the sapphires laced throughout the structure began to hum softly, setting Satyendra's teeth on edge.

He hastily took his hand from the stone. 'I am here.'

His mother seemed to glide towards them, her icy expression capped off with a delicate frown of displeasure. 'What is the meaning of this?'

Satyendra assumed a respectful pose. 'We were playing hunt the demon. The other apprentices didn't like that I won.'

'He only won because he cheated!' exclaimed Nose, pointing at Chunk who was still groaning on the floor. 'Honoured Mother Chandni, look what he did.'

'Did you hurt her, Satyendra?'

'Yes.'

Chandni shook her head. 'The hunters will be most displeased to hear that.'

'No they won't.'

Her expression grew colder still. 'What did you say?'

'I said they won't be displeased to hear what I did. If anything, they'll be displeased with—' Satyendra struggled to recall Chunk's real name and resorted to gesturing instead, 'the way the other apprentices behaved.'

She made a point of looking at all of the surprised and outraged faces before turning back to Satyendra and folding her arms. 'Explain.'

'Of course, mother.' He looked at Nose. 'What did I say before we started?'

'That you were supposed to be having a lesson.'

Chandni nodded to herself. 'You knew you were late and yet you still agreed to play. That makes it worse.'

Satyendra narrowed his eyes at Nose. The boy was such a dung head. 'After that. After you'd begged me to play and I'd agreed to one,' he glanced at his mother, 'very quick game.'

'Um, you asked which demon you should be.'

'Yes, and after that?'

'You . . . ' Nose looked up and stared hard at the clouds as if he could make out the suns twirling behind them. 'You said you wanted to be the Scuttling Corpseman.'

'And what does the Corpseman do?'

'Oh! You said it kills any hunter it catches alone.'

'Exactly. As Lord Rochant says, only a foolish hunter engages a demon alone. That's why in the game it takes three of them together to tag the demon and win. If we had been in the Wild for true, she –' he pointed at Chunk '– would be dead or taken. She failed once because she thought to take me alone. She failed twice when she let her guard down, and she failed a third time when she allowed me to look into her eyes.'

The other apprentices nodded at that, and some space opened between them and Chunk.

'And the rest of you,' continued Satyendra, 'all failed for not keeping up with her. You should have anticipated her charge and supported it. You let the demon win. When Lord Rochant returns through me, he will expect better than this. We must be ready for that day, mustn't we, Mother?'

'Yes. We must strive to be worthy of our Deathless Lord.' They all hung their heads, though a few still looked angry.

'And you, Honoured Vessel Satyendra, need to get to your lesson at once, we've wasted enough time here.'

'Might I help my friend first? She is in pain and you have often told me that I need to learn the line between perfection and cruelty.' Chandni stared hard at him, and Satyendra kept his face innocent and dutiful. 'I try only to be as firm and fair as Lord Rochant would be.'

'Very well.'

'Thank you.'

As his mother returned to the castle, Satyendra crouched next to Chunk. 'I'm sorry about hurting you before and I hope you can understand it wasn't personal.' He looked into her eyes, watching the way his lie slipped into her ear and down to her heart as easily as sweetwine.

'But you smiled at me,' replied Chunk, sniffing up some of the teary snot threatening to spill over her top lip. 'You tricked me!'

'Yes, which is just what the demons of the Wild would do; trick you into letting down your guard. You know the rules: Don't let the demon get close, don't meet its eyes, don't listen to its voice.'

'But . . . '

'But nothing. The Wild is unforgiving. Our people rely on the Deathless and their hunters to keep them safe. We have to be perfect or we fail. You have to be perfect.'

'You're right,' she sniffed.

'I am. And I forgive you.'

He felt her twinge of indignation, tasting the moment it fluttered into suppressed anger and shame, all of her feelings served to him on a platter of background pain. It was so good his mouth began to water.

What is wrong with me? Why am I like this?

He put his hands on either side of her knee. 'This is going to hurt,' *and suns save me I am going to enjoy it,* 'Brace yourself.'

'Okay,' she replied.

'One. Two. Three!' He gripped harder, feeling her tense in discomfort, drawing out her anticipation for a shade longer than necessary, then popped the joint back into position. Chunk screamed, and Satyendra dropped his head forward, letting his long hair curtain off the rapturous smile.

His blood sang with her pain, his skin rippled with it, the hollow lethargy that usually dogged him replaced with energy and happiness, boundless.

So good!

Under pretence of checking it had gone in properly, he manipulated Chunk's swollen knee with his fingers. Shivering with the pain elicited from each prod.

Out of the corner of his eye, he noticed Nose was staring. As he looked up the boy jerked his head away too late, too abruptly, to seem casual. *Did he see me? Really see me? Does he suspect?*

'That should be fine now,' he said to Chunk.

'Thank you, Satyendra.'

'You're welcome,' he replied, standing up with reluctance. There was more to milk here but he dared not risk it. 'Hopefully they'll have your back next time.'

Aware that he was already late, he said his goodbyes quickly and jogged off to his lesson with the Story-singer. Running felt good. He needed to work off some of the rush before sitting with Ban. The old Story-singer wasn't the strongest willed in the castle, but he was no fool either.

As soon as his back was turned to the apprentices, Nose had stared openly, not realizing that his suspicious reflection could be seen in the crystals around the archway.

You see me, Nose, thought Satyendra as he passed through the arch. *But I see you. Maybe you're not such a dung head after all. When I'm done with you, maybe you'll wish you were.*

CHAPTER THREE

A bath was waiting for Pari when she reached her chamber, as were servants. The former topped with petals, the latter armed with brushes. A swift and thorough cleaning followed, while Pari tried to collect her thoughts. Always after a rebirth came the horrible feeling of having forgotten something, and this one was no different.

As the servants towelled her dry, Pari considered her body anew. She had asked to be given her granddaughter, Rashana, as a vessel. A perfect match both physically and in temperament, Rashana would have led to an easy rebirth. However, as punishment for going to the Sapphire lands in secret and without permission, she had been given Priti instead, her great granddaughter. Shorter, sweeter, obedient to a fault. The type of girl that would not know an original thought if it struck her in the face.

If the vessel's body was like a jug, then Pari's soul was the water. And if the jug did not have room for certain of Pari's qualities, then they would spill over the edge and be lost.

However, unlike a jug, a vessel could be reshaped, and Pari had seen to it that one of her people visited Priti in secret to complete her education. In the years while she was between lives, he had been working quietly to encourage rebellious thoughts. His name was Varg, and unlike most of the servants, he was not known to the High Lord or any of the main staff. At least, he should not be. She'd had him go in disguise under a false name just to be safe.

Given the ease of her rebirth, she could only assume that Varg had done well. The calluses on her hands suggested her great granddaughter had enjoyed some clandestine climbing, as well as knife work, and she could only guess at the other terrible things he had taught her.

It's a start, she thought. *Though my arms look like they could use some more work.*

She would have liked to be a few inches taller too. Such things shouldn't matter, but they did. She made a mental note to have the platforms on her shoes adjusted accordingly.

Silk was wrapped around her, tight on the arms and legs. Over this was draped a violet gown with loose sleeves and high shoulders that curled to points. A layer of gem-studded jewellery was added to that, and her face was painted; gold around the eyes and mouth, subtler tones elsewhere, smoothing the lines on her face and the youth of her skin, obscuring the age of the body to let the Deathless soul shine through.

A woman sang for permission to enter and Pari gave it. She was dressed in the uniform of a majordomo, tanzanite studs flashing at her throat. Her arrival automatically dismissed the other servants, who hurried away as she bowed deeply. 'Welcome back, my lady.'

Pari looked at her full face blankly. 'And you are?'

The woman laughed in delight, sounding briefly like a common child from the settlements below. Pari looked closer, noting that the woman's skin was made up, that beneath it she was pale for a sky-born. She had clearly spent many years in the castle but had not started life there.

'Wait,' she added. 'I know you . . . Don't tell me.' A number of names skipped through her mind. 'It can't be? Ami? Is it you?'

The woman clapped her hands. 'Yes, my lady.'

They embraced, carefully so as not to upset Pari's outfit. 'My dear Ami, it is a delight to see you again. Look how you've grown! You were a slip of a girl the last I saw you.'

'The cook and I are the best of friends,' she replied with a smile.

'It is always wise to be on the cook's good side. I take it you've come to enjoy our food.'

'Oh yes. So much better than what I had before. The Sapphire don't know what they're missing!'

'Spoken like a true Tanzanite.'

Ami lifted her chin. 'Thank you, my lady.'

'Inform the High Lord that I will be with her shortly. And send Sho to me, I need to know what I've missed.'

'I . . . ' Ami's face folded in sadness. 'Forgive me, my lady, but Sho is no longer with us. I have taken on his duties in accordance with your wishes.'

Pari looked again at Ami's uniform, taking it in truly this time. So strange to see someone else in it. She had had many majordomos over her lifecycles, but for the last three, they had all been Sho or Sho's mother. 'Of course you have, I remember now. Tell me, did he die well?'

'Oh yes. He was surrounded by family. They sang him on his way at the end, and we all took part. Even the crystals in the castle joined in.'

Pari closed her eyes, imagining what it must have been like. Tanzanite crystals grew throughout her castle, most of them clustered at its base but some wound through the upper floors and laced the walls. It was their power that kept her castle in the sky, and her people had long ago learned to sing and play music that resonated. It was seen as a good omen when the crystal sang back. 'I wish I could have been here.'

'Sho wished this too. He has left you some final words.'

'Where did Sho get his hands on a message crystal?'

'I don't know, my lady.'

Pari smiled. 'He always was a crafty one. Bring it to—no, it had better wait until after the meeting. Do I look ready to face High Lord Tanzanite? Be honest.'

'Yes, my lady.'

Pari nodded, feeling the statement to be true. In the Unbroken Age, it was said that there were those that could read the soul inside the body and know another's intent even before they did. Pari had spent lifetimes trying to master the art, with limited success. She had developed instincts, senses for what another person might feel or do, but they were vague, and often hard to interpret.

'How long have I been between lives?'

'Sixteen years, my lady.'

'Sixteen! I was told it would be fifteen years at most.'

'Lord Taraka said there were complications with your vessel that had to be smoothed out.'

'Ah.' *I wonder if that was the fault of my meddling or something else.* 'Is Varg here?'

'Yes, my lady. He is camped with the courtyard traders to keep out of Lord Taraka's sight. I know he is eager to speak with you.'

'I'm sure he is. But he will have to wait. Is there anything else I should know before I meet with the other lords?'

Ami frowned as she considered the question. Clearly there were a lot of things and Ami was struggling to filter them. *She's still too easy to read,* thought Pari, adding it to her list of things to attend to.

'Never mind, Ami. If it isn't on fire then I will deal with it after the High Lord. Have the others arrived yet?'

'They are all waiting for you.'

Pari pursed her lips. She was tired from the rebirth but the High Lord was forcing her to attend before she had fully recovered. It was a low tactic. 'Was this gathering overseen by Lord Taraka, by any chance?'

'Yes, my lady. How did you guess?'

'Bitter experience.'

Ami wisely made no comment, instead summoning servants to collect the back of Pari's gown. It was time to face her peers.

The gentle flow of conversation ended as Pari entered the room. Ordinarily, she would have greeted the other Deathless Lords as they arrived, and granted them permission to enter. Ordinarily, it would be she, the Lady Pari, sitting in the chair opposite the door rather than her High Lord. However, on the day of a rebirthing ceremony, the usual laws were put aside.

She tried not to be hurt that of the six other Deathless that made House Tanzanite only three had bothered to attend her.

'Lady Pari, welcome back to the realm of life.' High Lord Priyamvada had stood, and the other two immortals followed a beat after. As was her preference, the High Lord had taken a tall body with an ample frame, the bright gold-violet of her gown a broad block of colour. It made Pari feel as if she was looking at a fortress rather than a person. Priyamvada's high hat became a turret, and her full-lipped mouth a spout for dropping acid on any foolish enough to get too close.

Armoured in paint, that face gave nothing away. A golden tattoo sat like a star on her forehead, commemorating an old death wound gained long before the rest of the house had their first birth.

'Thank you for holding my walls and my lands while I was gone,' Pari replied. 'Thank you for watching my people and keeping the Wild from their doors.'

Priyamvada gave a slight nod, and sat, allowing everyone else to do the same.

Once Pari's gown had been properly arranged, the servants bowed and slipped away. She tried to catch Arkav's eye but he was staring at the floor, his mind elsewhere. Despite the skilled work of his tailors she could see he'd lost weight, sharpening his features in a way she did not like.

Why does he ignore me? It's as if none of us were here.

Lord Taraka indicated a desire to speak. His body had thickened during her absence, and he too was doing his best to compensate for living in a shorter vessel than his previous lifecycles. The many crystals around his neck tinkled delicately as he moved, before settling again on his bare chest. He was sometimes known as The Holder of Whispers, a literal title as well as a metaphorical one, for each crystal captured any words spoken nearby, and Taraka could make them speak at a touch. It was his job to keep a permanent record of oaths, agreements and indiscretions, to be dug up at the worst possible time. He also did a good line in secrets, holding dirt on everyone in the house save Priyamvada herself.

After he had received a nod from the High Lord, he began. 'Allow me to add my personal welcome to that of the High Lord, Lady Pari. Your new body suits you well.'

'You are too kind, my dear Taraka.' *One day, I'm going to enjoy making you suffer.* She gave him her best smile to better disguise her thoughts.

'Though I have brought Lord Arkav here so that he could witness your auspicious return, I regret to inform you that he cannot stay.'

She glanced at Arkav but he remained oblivious. 'May I ask why?'

'We are sending him to the Sapphire lands to carry out an investigation.'

'With what authority do we investigate another house?'

It was Taraka's turn to smile. 'Some laws are universal, superseding even a High Lord's right to govern. When High Lord Yadavendra of the Sapphire destroyed his sister's Godpiece, he broke a sacred rule and weakened his house, and all of us, forever.'

The major houses, Tanzanite, Sapphire, Jet and Spinel, each held seven Godpieces, while the minor ones, Ruby, Opal and Peridot, held three. Thirty-seven Deathless in all, spread out like a net to protect as much of the land as possible. Yadavendra's action had reduced that number to thirty-six and left a gap that could never be filled.

'Has there been a trial yet?'

'The Council of High Lords has requested Yadavendra's presence on several occasions, but he has not come. At first he sent representatives, then messengers, and now, silence.'

'For a time, we have been content to wait. House Sapphire was given a generous period to deal with its own affairs but that is drawing to a close. I understand Lord Rochant Sapphire's rebirth is imminent. If his return does not lead to them taking action themselves, it will be upon us to act, lest more Godpieces be lost.'

'Forgive me, but the Sapphire High Lord's crime happened during my last lifecycle. How could we have stood by so long?'

'It is not our way to rush into things.' She winced, knowing that he was making a comment about her recent conduct. 'There was much grief within the Sapphire, we had to let it run its course. We had hoped that Yadavendra would do the right thing, given time to reflect.' Taraka sighed. 'He has not.'

'There's rushing into another house's business,' said Pari, 'and then there's procrastinating, and quite frankly we should have—'

Primyamvada's eyebrows twitched as if contemplating a frown and Pari took a breath. 'Apologies. The rebirthing has sapped my manners. I meant to say that I find it hard to believe so little has been done.'

'We could not commit to anything until the other houses had also taken a stance,' replied Taraka. 'For that we needed all of the other High Lords to discuss the matter internally, to debate, to question. You know how these things drag on. Yadavnedra's stance is unprecedented. To counter it, we needed to be of one mind. That accord has taken time. Understand, Lady Pari, that you were not the only one awaiting rebirth in this period. And there have been other concerns. The Wild stirs on the Ruby borders, worse than we've seen in a long time. One of their Deathless has been sent between lives, and their High Lord labours under a severe injury.'

'Sent? Wounded? You mean by things of the Wild?'

'I'd have thought that went without saying. In her wisdom, our High Lord has ordered the remainder of our Deathless and their hunters to aid the people of House Ruby.'

So that is why the rest of the house did not come to welcome me. 'The threat must be bad indeed to send so many.'

'It is. Which is why we cannot afford to have the Sapphire implode on us. Lord Arkav is going to see how things stand there and, if necessary, demand that High Lord Yadavendra return with him to face trial before the council.'

'But you can't!' Taraka put a hand to his mouth in a gesture of surprise, and the High Lord's eyes flicked to Pari. Even Arkav looked in her direction, though he seemed unfocused still. 'Yadavendra was willing to exile his own sister. He allowed his people, his innocent people, to be taken by the Wild. There's no telling what he'll do to Arkav.'

Taraka laughed as if she'd said something funny. 'He wouldn't dare. To harm a Tanzanite would be an act of war. In any case, even if Yadavendra did his worst, we would simply bring Lord Arkav back again. There's nothing to worry about.'

But Pari knew better. She had seen first hand that there

were ways to hurt a Deathless, leaving the kind of scars that followed you from one life to another. She thought of Lord Rochant Sapphire, bound, broken, and alone.

Priyamvada fixed her with a look. 'Lord Taraka misspeaks, though he is right on one count: Lord Arkav has nothing to worry about, Lady Pari, because you will be with him.'

This is her plan. Either Arkav will bring back High Lord Sapphire, or our sacrifice will be a rallying cry for the other houses, and she'll be able to replace me with a new, more pliable Deathless. How convenient.

There was an awkward silence that nobody else dared to break. Eventually Priyamvada stood. 'We will leave you and your brother to catch up, Lady Pari.' She glanced at Arkav. 'I don't need to tell you how important this is.'

'No.'

'May the suns illuminate your path.' And with that, Priyamvada walked out, Taraka following behind like a chastized Dogkin.

She smiled broadly at him as he passed, savouring the way his face puckered like the arsehole of some ancient goat. When the sound of their footsteps had faded away, Pari turned back to Arkav. His silence was like a knife in the guts. She'd known that the brother of old was long gone, his calm and confident nature lost to sullen moods and wild displays of anger, but that was preferable to the absent figure that now sat in front of her.

'Dear Arkav, what has become of you?'

When he didn't reply she collected her gown as best she could and moved round to him, lifting his chin with her finger. 'Arkav?'

He blinked at her, but there was little reaction in his face.

She opened her arms to him. 'Arkav, it's Pari. I've come back for you.'

Something stirred within him, as if only his body had been awake before. 'Pari?'

She felt her eyes itch with tears as she nodded. 'Yes.'

'Pari!' he exclaimed as she pulled him close. 'You're so far away.'

'Not any more. I'm right here.'

His arms tightened around her and his voice trembled like a child's. 'I was afraid. You disappeared and then when I tried to find you the servants lied.' His voice became steel, 'They lied!' Then childlike again, 'I went to Priyamvada and she took me and held me in a room and wouldn't let me go, and then you died and it was so long that I wished I was dead too.'

'Why would you wish that?'

'So we could be together. I don't trust the others.'

Pari gave him a squeeze. 'Nor do I.'

'I'm so tired.'

'Yes.'

'Can we sleep now?'

'Yes. Everything is going to be better.'

He drew back from her so that he could look into her eyes. For a moment he seemed just like his old self, as if the Arkav she'd come to know was a cloak and he'd cast it away. 'Do you promise, sister? I don't want to be this way any more.'

'I promise.'

As soon as the words were uttered, his eyelids fluttered and he settled himself against her. Seconds later, he was asleep. She stroked his hair, just as tired as he was but unable to sleep in her current position, and unable to move without disturbing him.

Thoughts danced in her mind, jumbling one another. *Why haven't the Sapphire sorted themselves out yet?* There were plans she was aware of, secret ones, that should have resolved all of those problems by now. *Why is Yadavendra still in power? What has Vasin been doing all these years? Why hasn't he taken control?*

She supposed, as with most things, she was going to have to go there and sort it out herself.

CHAPTER FOUR

Lord Vasin Sapphire arced swiftly across the sky. Below him, the Godroad glinted red as the sunlight of Vexation and Wrath's Tear played across its surface, the gold of the first sun, Fortune's Eye, dulled and bloodied. As he crossed over it, the energies of the Godroad sparkled against his crystal wings, lifting him, like the hands of a parent, gentle, taking him to new heights.

And he was ready to rise. Ready to act.

It is finally time.

The lands of House Ruby were among the least hospitable he'd visited. A vast forested swamp, punctuated by little islands that, often as not, turned out to be the shells of some Wildborn monstrosity. The Godroad provided the only thread of sanity in the landscape, and House Ruby's settlements clung alongside, standing proud on long wooden stilts.

Lately, the swamp had begun to rise. Nobody knew the cause but Vasin suspected his own house's failings were to blame. Attacks from the Wild had become bolder and more frequent. It felt as if an unseen hand were manipulating the demons in some way. Not like a commander with an army, but a shepherd, driving their demonic flock in the same direction.

Away from us. Each of our borders and beyond, but never in our own lands. First they pressed the Tanzanite, then the Spinel, and now the Rubies. It cannot be coincidence.

An odd movement in the water caught his eye, and he banished his worries for another time. Movements in the water were common, but not in the middle of the day, for the greater a thing of the Wild was, the less it liked the glare of the suns. He circled slowly, always coming back over the Godroad to regain height for the next pass. The swamp water was too cloudy to see shadows in, but whatever it was swam close to the surface, its ridged spine making a mountain range of ripples.

Vasin wore his sapphire armour, his second skin of living crystal, and he had his spear, but that was all. He was alone in the sky, without his hunters in a land he did not know.

Though he loved to fly alone, Vasin hated to hunt that way. *Without spear sisters and spear brothers, a hunter soon becomes the prey.* A memory surfaced of his encounter with the Scuttling Corpseman, of his flight through the trees, and how close it had come to destroying him.

Mindful of past mistakes, Vasin continued to circle, gliding lower but keeping a healthy amount of air between himself and the water. There was definitely something there. It too was being cautious, roving up and down alongside a short stretch of Godroad. *This gets stranger and stranger. It comes in the day, it comes close to the Godroad, and it comes to a place where there are no people.*

It briefly occurred to Vasin that perhaps that last fact was not true. After all, he was there. Perhaps it was looking for a chance to snare a Deathless. He dismissed the idea as nonsense, but levelled off just the same and adjusted his grip on his spear, sliding a thumb over the trigger in readiness.

As he watched, more details of the thing were revealed. It was long, a kind of Lizardkin, with pronounced ridges running from nose to tail. At first he thought it had branching limbs, like a living, writhing tree, but he soon realized it was carrying other creatures that bucked and kicked in its grasp.

The Lizardkin lifted its body from the water, revealing a wide snout, circular, covered in scales that glittered. Vasin could not help but drop a little closer, and realized that each scale was an eyelid, and that the glittering was actually the thing blinking, blinking, blinking, hundreds of times with its whole body. He knew that beneath the surface its body went on, the great belly brushing the silt at the very bottom of the swamp. For he'd recognized it now, the Story-singers had told him of this creature and it was dangerous, a true power of the deep Wild: Quiverhive. *But what is it doing here?*

Quiverhive stuffed the squirming thing it was carrying into its mouth, but instead of feeding, it tilted its head backwards, and spat.

For a horrible moment Vasin thought he was the target, and banked away, diving to gain speed before pulling up on the far side of the Godroad.

He was safe.

But he had never been in danger.

He recognized the spat creature as a Murker, one of the lesser perils of the Ruby lands. One legend had it that

Murkers were created from the reflections of vain people. That those who looked too long into the Wild's waters left a piece of themselves behind. Another legend had it that when an unwanted baby was drowned in the swamp, its body would turn into a Murker when it touched the bottom.

This one was typical of its kind. Like a short and rubbery child, with grey-white skin and webs of gauzy flesh lidding nostrils, ears, eyes, and flapping in the spaces between fingers and toes.

It wailed as its arc took it onto the Godroad, circling its arms as if trying to arrest its motion and reverse away. With a wet smack, it landed, and immediately, there was the smell of burning. For nothing of the Wild could endure the Godroad for long. All demons feared it with good reason, and this Murker was no exception.

It flailed and tried to roll itself clear, but Quiverhive had pitched it into the centre of the Godroad, and within seconds it was too blind with pain to think. Each movement only enhanced its suffering, and so it rolled back and forth, disintegrating before Vasin's eyes.

He wondered if he were witnessing some kind of execution. Though he did not understand the intricacies or the factions, he knew that the powers of the Wild often fought amongst themselves.

Quiverhive stuffed a second Murker into its mouth and spat it after the first. To Vasin's amazement he saw it follow the exact same arc and land on the other Murker's still twitching corpse.

Before this one had a chance to die, Quiverhive spat a third Murker, to make a stack on the first two. Vasin watched and Quiverhive watched, the scales flipping open and staying that way, as if it strained to see the details.

The first Murker had been reduced to a few chunks of ash that were already being dispersed by the wind. The second was dying, its struggles enfeebled, its skin aflame. The third was also dying but slower, partially shielded by the bodies of its fellows.

With a full body convulsion, Quiverhive propelled itself forward and up, forcing half of its bulk out of the water. Until its snout came to rest on top of the third Murker.

The creature grunted and squirmed as it was crushed beneath Quiverhive's weight, but Quiverhive kept still, as if holding its breath.

Vasin found he was holding his. He was witnessing the impossible. Since the end of the Unbroken Age, the Godroads had been a safe haven for humanity and had formed an impassable barrier, hemming the demons within.

No more.

It is on the Godroad! How is it not burning?

He was sure he'd been noticed, but Quiverhive seemed unconcerned by his presence. When the Murkers began to crumble, it slithered back into the swamp, the myriad scales rippling, flipping over, the eyes tucked away once more. Mouth closed, it turned and drifted off, sinking slowly back beneath the surface.

I must tell the Rubies, he thought, wheeling back to his original course. *I must tell everyone.*

The trees had thinned out then vanished entirely, leaving a vast swampy lake that stretched out in all directions. Or rather it left two, as the great mass was split down the middle by the Godroad, a shining red path that cut through the yellow-brown. Vasin raced along it, diving again and again to keep his speed up. Each time, the energies of the Godroad would gather under his wings, growing brighter before exploding outward, catapulting him onwards and upwards.

Ahead, the castle of the Ruby High Lord sat heavy on the horizon, the crystals glowing bloody in its base and lower walls, like a tooth fresh-plucked from a giant's jaw and set in the sky.

He was unsettled by what he'd just witnessed, and glad for the warming caress of the suns on his back. Unlike his own castle, the Godroad did not work its way up towards the entrance. Instead, the Godroad came to a stop beneath it, and chains had been run from its edge to the castle, allowing cages to be winched up and down.

Vasin let himself drop lower, until he was skimming only a few feet above the Godroad, then, as the guard station rushed towards him, he tilted his body so that his wings were vertical, turning them into brakes. Still going at some speed, he touched his Sky-legs to the road in a single bounding step, letting them absorb more of his momentum. The long curved blades of his Sky-legs flexed and flicked him up again, but not as high as before. As he came down he took another step, shorter this time, then another, until he came to a bouncing stop before two of House Ruby's guardians.

Where he was covered from head to toe in armour, they were dressed in simple tunics that came to the knees, no doubt imported from his own lands or those of House Opal.

He held out one hand, palm up and open, and rested his spear on the ground, the crystals embedded in the base chiming softly as they clinked against the Godroad. 'I am

Lord Vasin of the Sapphire Everlasting. I come as a friend to share your burdens, and I come as a hunter to share your enemies.'

The two guardians saluted him, but slower than they would have in previous years, and a wary look passed between them. Vasin waited for the proper response, saddened at the cool reception, but not surprised. *This is what we get for turning our backs on our neighbours.*

'Be welcome, friend,' they said at last, their tone bitter. 'Be welcome, hunter.'

He watched as one of the cages was lowered down, swaying from side to side.

'Is your High Lord in residence?'

Another look passed between them and Vasin's heart sank along with their expressions. Then, the older of the two women replied. 'High Lord Anirika was sent between lives two days ago.'

'I'm sorry.'

'The Toothsack came with the higher water and attacked Raften. Even though she was injured, our High Lord flew out to meet it.' There was pride as well as sadness in the woman's voice. 'The Toothsack was banished back to the swamp and Raften is safe again. But . . . '

She trailed off and the two women became sullen, accusing. If he had only come sooner. If House Sapphire had acted in accordance with the traditions, this could have been avoided.

'Again, I am sorry. Is anyone in residence? I have urgent news.'

'Lady Anuja sits on the throne during the High Lord's absence. She led a hunt this morning. They have yet to return.'

'I am sorry to have missed it.' His statement was genuine enough that he saw them soften a little. 'And another hunt in the High Lord's lands so soon? Can you tell me the details?'

'Fourboards sent out the call for aid. They made the sacrifice last night and set loose their tributes at sunrise.' The guardian shook her head. 'Six tributes they sent, Lord Vasin. Not three. Not four. Six. Can you believe such a thing?'

Every hunt required tributes. They were the bait used to lure the things of the Wild out of hiding. Each would bear a light so the hunters could find them, and a fresh cut, so the demons could too. Many tributes did not survive, but those that did were elevated among their peers, any past crimes or failings forgotten. It was one of the ways road-born could come to the attention of the Deathless, and be taken to one of the floating castles as servant or hunter. Alternatively, tributes could enjoy positions of power or influence among their peers.

Six tributes will be impossible to manage, thought Vasin grimly. *They'll be spread too far, and that much blood will bring every demon from miles around.*

'These are strange times,' he replied.

'Strange indeed!'

'I wonder what they will do if all six survive.'

'Little danger of that I fear, Lord Vasin. The Wild is bold these days.' Her voice cracked, betraying the fear lurking beneath the words. 'Never known nothing like it, nor has me mother, nor hers. Have you in your many lives seen this before?'

He thought about Quiverhive and the Murkers being spat

onto the Godroad. He thought of the Scuttling Corpseman sparing his mother, even allowing her to sever its arm and take it as a trophy. *They all think she sold us out to the Wild when all along it was Lord Rochant.* 'No,' he replied. 'Not like this.'

'Aye,' she agreed. 'These are dark days. Six! It's just not right.'

The two guardians grabbed the bottom of the cage as it came down and guided it in. It was a simple design: one edge of the square base had a bench carved into it, another had a set of posts for tying animals to. Vasin stepped inside and the guardians closed the door behind him.

A signal was given, and the cage began to ascend in slow rhythmic jerks.

He liked the Rubies. They were direct but in a warm, honest fashion. It was refreshing not to be constantly worrying about how he was coming across, or what it was the other person was really saying. He realized he was looking forward to seeing Lady Anuja again. She was the youngest of her house, like he was, and that gave them a certain understanding. *And we both know what it's like to be out of our depth.*

As the cage got higher, he could see the way the currents became more violent further out. Directly beneath the floating castle was a whirlpool, and he knew that at the bottom there was a crack that led deep into the earth and beyond. From it, alien mists rose, like ethereal hands of purple, yellow and green. Something of the whirlpool's frenzy caught them, swirling them together, blending the colours briefly before they faded. The further away from the crack they rose, the harder they were to see, and by the time they reached above the level of the swamp, only slight distortions in the air were discernible to the naked eye. It was the essence in the mists that caught the crystals in the base of the castle and kept it buoyant, like a boat, bobbing on invisible waves.

Because of the interaction between essence mist and whirl-pool, the currents spiralled rather than floating straight up. Were it not for the chains that held it in place, the Ruby High Lord's Castle would be forever spinning. As it was, the castle made a slight twist to the left until the chains tightened, pulling it right again, making it seem to Vasin as if the whole structure were a huge head, subtly shaking in disapproval.

Servants met him at the top, escorting him to the Chrysalis Chamber, where he could remove his armour. It was always odd to enter the chamber of another Deathless. They were sacred places, where the crystals that made their weapons were grown and shaped. Each chamber had a bond with the Deathless that used it, deepened by time and blood. The Ruby High Lord's Gardener-smiths muttered to themselves when he arrived, clearly unhappy. It wasn't ideal for him either, but as he had come alone, without entourage, he had no choice but to endure their moaning.

Half of the outer walls were made of glass, capturing and focusing the sunslight into the chamber, the other half was studded with rubies that the Gardener-smiths would harvest when ready. A section of the chamber had been hastily curtained off, no doubt to stop him from seeing the new armour they would be growing for the High Lord's next lifecycle.

They fear that a glance from a Sapphire might taint the crystals somehow. Gardener-smiths are all the same, so fussy and superstitious. He knew that his own would be most unhappy that his armour was going to be touched by foreign hands.

For all that, when he stood in the ritual position, they moved quickly enough, and in a way that he recognized, taking each piece of his armour in turn, checking it for damage, before cleaning it and placing it carefully on a stand. Vasin never liked coming out of his armour, or, as he thought of it, *coming down.* The crystals had his blood in them, and were grown and regrown over the years just as his bodies were. When he wore it, he felt connected to his deeper self, and drew confidence and strength from it. He was elevated literally and spiritually.

Out of the armour, he felt a lesser being, like he was half-asleep. And when they unstrapped his Sky-legs, he immediately missed the sense of potency in his stride.

A bath followed, then food, drink and a sleep on scented cushions. Long flights were as exhilarating as they were exhausting. He awoke to a servant singing for permission to bring biscuits and water, and he stayed conscious just long enough to consume them before drifting back to sleep. By the time the message reached him that Lady Anuja had returned and awaited his company, the suns had set, and he felt refreshed.

He touched the ruby embedded in the nearby wall. It was warm under his fingertips, having bathed in the suns through the day. At his command it began to release the stored sunslight, illuminating the room and giving it a vermillion tint.

A servant sang for entry and was waved inside, Vasin taking an instant dislike to the way the man's eyes darted over his things. A slightly irreverent tone of voice, too, no outright rudeness, but unmistakably souring, like a tiny piece of grit buried in a hunk of bread. The servant helped him dress, wrapping the silk tight on his arms, legs and body, before covering him with the long gown of deep blue that he'd brought. He hated that he did not know the servant. It made him feel vulnerable. *What if this one is spying? They may just be displaying a fashionable dislike of the Sapphire, but what if they wish me ill?* The thought was impossible to shake, particularly when the servant was touching his face with paint, and highlighting his eyes and lips in gold. *It would be so simple to kill me. Poison on the face paint. A thrust of their brush into my eyesocket. I wonder if High Lord Yadavendra would be cruel enough to add such a death to my legend? I wonder if he would deign to bring me back at all?*

Sixteen years ago he had been shocked to realize his own staff had been subverted and swapped for those loyal to his brother. The problem was sorted out, now, but it had left him suspicious of anyone he didn't know. Unconsciously, the index and middle fingers of his right hand curled into a hook, ready to strike the servant at the first sign of anything threatening.

'Does Lord Vasin wish me to do his cheeks?'

'Why wouldn't I?'

'We have many visitors to the castle at present, all with different needs. Our Tanzanite guests have been dusting the cheeks, while the Opal favour bold dots. One of the Peridot Lords likes several small dots that give an angular rather than circular impression. It's a new thing, so I'm told. I have not had the honour of serving any of the Sapphire. Would

Lord Vasin be kind enough to direct me as to his fashions?'

'The Peridot may have fashions, but Sapphire ways do not change.' It was all he could do not to roll his eyes. The minor houses could be so strange, sometimes.

'I see. Our own lords and ladies are the same. They only ever ask for the lightest brush upon their cheeks. What might the Sapphire way be, Lord Vasin?'

Having never been asked the question before it took him a moment to formulate an answer. 'You know, accentuate the cheekbones, in a way that's striking but elegant.'

'The cheekbones. Yes, my lord. Anything else?'

'Yes, of course there is.' Though in that moment he couldn't remember what it was. He was a Deathless, he shouldn't have to think about things like this. 'But that will do for now.'

'Very good, Lord Vasin. Are we to be expecting any more of your noble house? Or any of your esteemed servants?'

He wants to know if it's just me or if we're sending more aid. Either the Ruby have become even more informal than I remember or this one is asking for a beating. 'If any more of my kin are coming, you will be informed.'

Vasin put just enough disapproval into his tone that the servant carried out the rest of his preparations in silence. *In another lifecycle I'd have struck him for his insolence.* He took a moment to appreciate how his self-control had developed and ordered the servant to escort him to Lady Anuja. *Not only did I not raise my hand, I didn't even raise my voice. Mother would be proud.*

CHAPTER FIVE

Honoured Mother Chandni brushed her long hair, slowly, almost fearfully. The shutters on her window were closed, as they always were when she prepared herself, holding the room in a permanent state of grey.

Here, alone, she dared to consider how bad things were.

On the surface, all was well. Lord Rochant's castle ran smoothly under her leadership, arguably better than it ever had. Many saw her as a hero, including High Lord Yadavendra. Thanks to her, Satyendra had been saved from assassination, and Lord Rochant's line preserved.

Since then, under her guidance, Satyendra had grown into a fine young man, intelligent, quick, sharp eyed, a perfect vessel for the best of the Sapphire Deathless.

Except, Satyendra wasn't perfect.

And she was no hero.

As if to prove the point, the brush caught in her hair, making her wince and curse her clumsiness. *Will I never get used to using my left hand?* She shot a glare at her right, sitting dead and useless in her lap. She could work the fingers, of course, even get them to hold the brush, but without feeling it was impossible to sense resistance or the shifting of the brush in her grip.

A tiny scar still remained from the assassin's needle, a single white dot, innocent, in the centre of her palm. The poison from it had stolen all sensation, from the tips of her fingers to just below her bicep, and would have taken more had it not been for the quick thinking of Rochant's cook, Roh, and Chandni's own sacrifice to the Hunger Tree. On her right hand, the nails of her middle finger and thumb had never grown back.

Proof of my betrayal.

It was forbidden to deal with the Wild, but Chandni had done so twice.

The first time to stop the spread of the poison, an act of desperation. The second was even worse, an offer of another's life in exchange for Satyendra's.

And I bear the proof of that too.

She put the brush down on the table and ran her hand behind her head until she found it, a different kind of softness nestling within her hair. Sprouting from the base of her skull was a feather, long and black. Over the years she'd tried trimming it back, cutting it off, once in a desperate rage, she'd pulled it out by the shaft. But whatever she did, however extreme she'd been in her self-surgery, she'd find it sprouting there again, good as new, the next day.

Two dealings with the Wild.

Two marks of shame.

She should have told Lord Vasin when he found her. She should have told High Lord Yadavendra. But she didn't because Satyendra needed someone to hide his imperfections until such time as he'd grown out of them.

At least, that was how she justified her crime to herself.

The truth was she couldn't bear the thought of being judged any more than she could bear Satyendra being cast out. And beneath that was another truth: she wanted to be there when Varg came back.

Tucked away out of sight in her chambers was an old piece of cloth, and wrapped within it were pieces of a mosaic. Each fragment had arrived quietly, discreetly, pushed into her hand by a travelling merchant who visited the castle the same time each year. Together, the pieces made a picture of two people kissing: a bearded man and a long-haired woman, their lips pressed together in a smile, with a large white Dogkin sleeping nearby.

Fifteen pieces sat within the cloth. Fifteen units of time. Only one gap in the mosaic remained, and it had not escaped her notice that both the merchant and Pari's rebirth were due any day.

The last piece was coming, already on its way, and Varg with it.

She still wasn't sure what she'd do when he arrived, but the thought of him, the fantasy of him, had given her a much-needed escape.

And though the wait had been agonizing the years had passed with a strange swiftness. Normal life had muted the reality of her time in the Wild. She'd taken to wearing gloves in public and plaiting her hair so as to tuck the feather from sight. The precautions had soon become habit, almost natural. From a lesser servant, such behaviour might have raised suspicion, but she was above reproach, a model

Sapphire. Rather than garner criticism, she'd generated new fashions among the sky-born.

A footstep, close, too close, broke her from her reverie, and she span round in her seat, putting her back and the feather to the wall.

'No need to be afraid,' said Satyendra, clearly delighted to have caught her out. 'It's only me.'

'It's not becoming for an Honoured Vessel to creep about like that. Suns! How many times have I told you to sing for entry like everyone else?'

Satyendra smiled at her, but she did not feel reassured. In the half light his expression was ghoulish, and memories of his face – his other face – rose up from the depths. She had only seen it once, when he was a baby and they were on the Godroad returning home from the Wild. It had been enough: the image was seared into her mind forever. 'And how many times have I told you I'm not like everyone else. I don't like singing.'

'That's not the point and you know it. You should announce yourself, not sneak into other people's chambers like a thief.'

The comment seemed to bounce off him without impact. 'It's very dark in here, Mother. What are you trying to hide?'

She took a moment to compose herself. Satyendra had a way of being able to get under her skin like nobody else. 'I'm assuming you came here for something other than to torment me.'

He fell silent then, his dark eyes glittering with hurt, and into that silence poured guilt. She was letting her temper get the better of her and it was most unbecoming. None of this was Satyendra's fault. It wasn't right to take out her frustrations on him. He'd come to her for help and she was pushing him away. She forced down her other worries to give him her full attention. 'I'm sorry. Let's try this again. You wanted to talk. Is it about the rebirthing ceremony?'

'Yes.'

'Tell me.'

'I think we need to postpone.' She took a breath to dispute this but he was already pressing on with his argument. 'I don't know the legends well enough yet, and I need to get better at hunting and strategy and understanding the flow of trade. There's so much still to learn and I have to be perfect, Mother, you know that. Nothing else will do. I'm Lord Rochant's only chance to return so I have to get it right. So you have to send a message to High Lord Yadavendra and tell him to call off the Bringers. It's too soon for the ceremony.'

'This is really worrying you, isn't it?'

He nodded quickly and she could see his eyes welling up. The sight of it choked her heart. 'Come here,' she said, opening her arms, and he flew into them. 'Oh my poor, sweet Satyendra.'

'I'm not good enough. I'm not ready. Don't let them take me away.'

She stroked his hair as he sobbed, so long, so like her own, and it struck her that this might be one of the last times she would be able to comfort him. There was a pain in that thought that she wasn't sure she could endure. Would postponing the ceremony be such a terrible thing? It would give her more time with her son, and it might make the rebirth smoother. *How can I advocate sending him to his death? I know it is a great honour. I know it serves Lord*

*Rochant and the house. But now the moment is here I . . .
How have the other Honoured Mothers and Fathers done
this in the past?*

She soothed him with gentle sounds and cuddling, as she
had when he was a baby.

Eventually, he lifted his head to look at her. 'Will you tell
him?'

'You mean Yadavendra?'

He sniffed and nodded.

'He's the Sapphire High Lord, it's not my place to tell him
anything.' As Satyendra's face began to crumple again, she
added, 'But we can ask him, together.'

'When?'

'As soon as he arrives. He's already on his way.'

Pari felt the change in territory before they reached the
official border. The Tanzanite lands had a lot in common
with their Sapphire neighbours, both contained their share
of woodland, threaded through with rivers and lakes. In
their own way, both were beautiful. However, her home
landscape was more varied, with open plains and hillsides
breaking up the relentless forest, whereas here she saw
densely packed trees in every direction, like some vast green
flood that was only thwarted by the upper reaches of the
mountains. Though her own forests were certainly dangerous
– the Wild was the Wild no matter where you were born
– it was less aggressive somehow.

Once, this view had been tinted by her love for Lord
Rochant Sapphire. Now that had been ripped away she saw
it in all its menacing glory.

They travelled with only two carriages, one for herself

and Arkav, the other for their staff, all competent, but none dear to her heart. It was too risky to take someone who might get hurt or used against them. *I wonder if our High Lord was thinking the same when she chose us for this venture.*

'I think High Lord Primyamvada is worried about me,' said Arkav. 'She tries to hide her feelings but I see them. I frustrate her.'

'No you don't.'

'I do, and that's okay. She's only frustrated because she cares.'

'About you, maybe,' muttered Pari.

Arkav didn't argue, just quirked his lips in such a way that, for a moment, it was like truly being with him again. Pari sighed and turned back to the window. The Godroad had been slowly shifting in colour as they travelled, going from bluey-violet, to dark, then lighting up again, pure-blue, dazzling.

'You're worried about me too,' said Arkav.

'I was worried. But now we're together again, I know things are going to get better.' She took his hand and squeezed it.

'Why?' he asked.

'Because I'm not going to rest until they are.' When he didn't respond, she squeezed his hand more firmly. 'Do you understand? We will get through this.'

There was no reaction. It was as if a vital part of her brother had withdrawn to places she could not follow.

They were truly entering Sapphire lands now. Pari could see a simple wooden tower had been constructed next to the Godroad, allowing those stationed there plenty of warning when visitors approached. However, no structures survived long in close proximity to the Godroad's energies and the nearest legs showed signs of repeated repair.

How typically Sapphire to stubbornly endure rather than build somewhere more sensible.

Despite her sneer it dismayed her how easy it was for the Sapphire to police their lands. Everyone but the brave and foolish used the Godroads. Traders and Story-singers would have to come this way. Those that needed to deal with the Sapphire for survival, and those that needed to travel through on the way to other houses would first need to gain permission from the tower.

That's a lot of power to have, I hope it hasn't gone to their heads.

It had been some time since a Deathless from another house had paid the Sapphire a visit and she wasn't entirely sure what kind of reception they were going to get. A guard stepped up onto the Godroad in front of their carriage and ordered them to stop. She was sure that at least two more were in the tower.

As the carriage slowed she looked at Arkav. He remained locked in his thoughts. It would be up to her to lead things.

She opened the door of the carriage as the guard marched over. They looked young and inexperienced, but to Pari everyone looked that way. 'You may approach,' she said.

'I don't need your permission,' came the blustered reply. 'Who are you and what is your business here?'

Pari turned her head so that the young woman could admire her profile. 'See for yourself.'

The guard took in her fine clothes, her dark sky-born skin,

the golden marks on her lips, and paled. 'I . . . we weren't told to expect you.'

'Ah well, let us be on our way and I won't hold you responsible.'

Pari could see her thinking about it, minute shifts in posture and expression telling the story of surprise becoming fear becoming pride, so she was disappointed rather than surprised by the reply.

'No, Tanzanite, I asked you your business.'

'And I ask if the lofty Sapphire have forgotten their manners?'

Small dots of pink appeared in the white of the guard's cheeks. 'I'm here with the authority of High Lord Sapphire and in his name I say who comes and goes. Me! And if you don't answer my questions you'll have to sit here till you rot or go back home. I don't care which.' Several guards had appeared at the top of the tower, bows held casually, yet prominently in their hands.

'I'll take that as a yes,' said Pari.

'What?'

'Clearly, you have forgotten your manners and clearly nobody's taught you any history or you would know better than to claim authority here.'

'What are you talking about? This is Sapphire land!'

'No it isn't.'

'Yes it is!'

'No,' Pari replied, smiling a sweet smile and pointing at the nearby trees. 'That is Sapphire land.' She pointed at the tower. 'That is on Sapphire land. We are on the Godroad, and the Godroad runs through your lands and mine, and the lands of all the Crystal Dynasties. It was built before even the first Deathless took breath and though it is our duty to protect it, it is also our right to use it. No one house claims ownership. No High Lord. No one.

'So, by all means, patrol your dirt tracks and pathways, but do not think anyone has the authority to block me using any part of the Godroad, for I am Deathless, and you, road-born, you most certainly are not.'

There was a pause as the guard tried to process this. After a moment she looked back to her fellows who all stared back, their blank faces doing the equivalent of a shrug. One or two of the bows disappeared from sight.

Pari waited for the guard to realize that she was alone and in trouble.

'I . . . ' she began. 'I . . . '

Pari lowered her voice. 'I would advise apologizing, using my proper title, and then getting out of our way as quickly as possible.'

'I'm sorry, Lady . . . '

'Pari. Of House Tanzanite.'

'Lady Pari of House Tanzanite.'

'There. Much better.' She gave a little wave of her hand. 'Now, off you go.'

The guard backed away, head bowed low, and the carriage set off, swiftly leaving the tower behind. Pari gave one last regal wave to the stupefied guards and sat back in her seat to find Arkav was staring at her.

'What is it? Something on my nose?'

'You lied. There is no law that separates the Godroad from the rest of the land.'

'I think lie is a bit harsh. The law is unclear. I thought my interpretation made a lot of sense.'

'It's wrong.'

'Careful, Arkav, rigid thinking has always been an issue for the Sapphire, but never for us.'

He turned to look at her, suddenly, intensely present. 'No, I mean this is all wrong. The way they talked to you, the way they made you act, it's all wrong. It never used to be this way.'

'I agree. Yadavendra's a fool to arm children and tell them to hassle every poor soul on the Godroad. If I didn't know better, I'd say he wanted to provoke a war.'

Arkav continued to stare at her. 'The Sapphire are broken, like me. Are you going to fix them too, Pari?'

And what else could she say, looking into those sad, bleak eyes, but: 'Yes.'

The last time they'd met had been less formal, but while her mother was between lives, Anuja was acting as High Lord of her house, and so they observed the proper protocols.

At the doorway to the throne room, Vasin stopped while the servant sang of his arrival. Anuja's attendants sang back that Anuja was here and ready to receive him. Only then did he step forward, planting himself on the threshold.

'Lady Anuja Ruby, hand of your High Lord, I stand at your door and ask that it might be opened. I stand within your walls and ask that they might shelter me. I stand with a hand outstretched in friendship, and ask that you might take it.'

Anuja was seated on a wide padded couch. She too was bound in silk, white, a high-necked gown fitted over it, with broad sleeves cuffed in Wrath Tear red, and lined in Vexation's darker shade. Had he not known it was there, he would have missed the hint of gold on her cheeks. Her left eye was unadorned to make the golden legend around her right blaze in contrast. It struck him as odd that she had not risen to greet him. *Perhaps the servant had been instructed to be disrespectful, a prelude to the true insult.*

And yet when she spoke, her voice was warm. 'Lord Vasin Sapphire, sky master, Ruby-friend. Fly to me as you did on your last visit and you will find my hand is ready to clasp yours, tight and true.'

She raised her hand and he strode across the room until he stood before her. Still, she did not rise, so he bowed as he took it. They locked eyes as well as fingers.

Vasin was never the best at reading faces but even he could see how tired she looked, the fierceness of gaze that he usually admired seeming to quiver like a nervous candle.

Anuja gestured for him to sit, and the servants arranged his gown around him before turning back his sleeves. Then they placed a selection of dumplings on a low table between them, and poured two glasses of sweet wine before retreating to the edges of the room.

'I was sorry to hear about your mother,' he began.

'Thank you. We sorely miss her strength.'

'Were you there when it happened?'

'No, we always leave one behind in case the worst happens.' There was a bitterness in her words, and Vasin remembered that the last time the Ruby High Lord had gone travelling, Anuja had been left behind, the High Lord taking her older sister.

'I've never seen the Toothsack with my own eyes,' she continued, 'but I hear it was a great battle. Our Story-singers are already preparing a work to honour it.'

'I hear the Toothsack was wounded but not killed.'

A little of her normal spark returned. 'Much like your own encounter with the Corpseman, yes?'

'Yes.'

'Like us, the things of the Wild have a way of coming back.'

'Speaking of that, may I ask how quickly your mother and sister will begin their next lifecycles?'

She made a short gesture and the servants left the room. 'Actually, I was hoping to talk to you about this very thing.'

'Me?'

'Yes. I wanted to ask your advice.'

'Lady Anuja, I am not known for my wisdom. But,' he added hastily, 'it's yours if you want it.'

'My mother has prepared a vessel for her next lifecycle but the next auspicious alignment is over a year away. Normally, I'd wait, but with things as they are . . . '

'What's the alternative? Even we need the favour of the suns.'

'There's a partial alignment coming in two weeks.'

Vasin frowned. A partial alignment would place the rebirth at risk. To even consider it Anuja must be desperate. He asked, 'Can we talk as we did before, as friends?'

'Please. I'd like that. Acting as the High Lord's hand is . . . tiring.'

'I believe it and I want to help. How bad are things here, really?'

She sipped at her wine, prompting Vasin to do the same. 'The Toothsack didn't just take my mother, any more than the Wild took my sister; it decimated our hunters. The ones we're fielding now are barely more than apprentices.

78

Normally, a successful hunt silences the Wild, but the Toothsack's attack seems unrelated to the other troubles.'

'Have you had any trouble from Quiverhive?'

'No. We've had Murkers, and at least one Weeper. And all kinds of rumours. My people are afraid, Vasin. They're jumping at shadows, seeing all kinds of things that aren't there. That hopefully aren't there, I mean. We don't expect the Toothsack to return any time soon, but just in case I'm making sure that no Deathless hunts with mortals alone. That's possible at the moment with support from the other houses, but they won't stay here forever.'

'House Tanzanite sent three Deathless, didn't they?' Anuja nodded and he continued, 'Was Lady Pari among them?'

'Last I heard, she was between lives.'

'Still?'

'I believe she'll be undergoing a rebirth any day now. Do you need her?'

'Not exactly.'

The gold around her eye flashed in the gemslight 'You're hiding something from me.'

It was true. He was. But much as he wished to confide in Anuja, some secrets were too dark for their budding friendship. 'I'm sorry.'

There was a pause and they both sipped from their drinks.

'Well,' she said. 'I am still glad you came. Please don't take this the wrong way, but I was hoping House Sapphire would send at least two Deathless so that I could relieve some of the others. And where are your hunters?'

'I'm afraid I'm all you've got.'

She digested this for a while. 'The last time you came to us without escort, you were here as messenger. It made sense for you to fly alone for the sake of speed. This time you are here to hunt. It makes no sense to hunt alone.'

Vasin kept his face neutral.

'Could the great House Sapphire not spare any of its hunters to support you?'

'My High Lord believes they are all needed at home.'

'How are things in your lands?'

He wanted to just come out and say it: he hadn't been sent. He'd come alone so that no others would suffer for his actions. 'Things are quiet. High Lord Yadavendra would tell you this is only the case because we are being so vigilant.'

'Yes, I have heard many tales of how vigilant the Sapphire have become. We had thought your wingless hunters a passing fashion but they seem to have lingered. No tales of battles against demons have reached us, but there are many stories of harassment suffered by any house traders not flying a blue flag. Perhaps you could make sense of them to me, Lord Vasin?'

'Would that I could.'

'Houses Spinel and Jet have their own problems. They have told me so, and I understand. But Houses Opal and Peridot have sent one of their Deathless to our aid, while House Tanzanite has sent three, each with a full flight of hunters at their back. Your house does not reply to my mother's messages and then sends you alone? Unannounced?' She looked at him but he could not meet her gaze. 'This, I do not understand.'

'I'm sorry that my house hasn't provided proper aid. I'm . . . I'm going to make it right.' They locked eyes again. He didn't say the words out loud. Didn't need to.

'Go carefully, my friend. But don't take too long. The

other houses are poised to act. If not for the Wild, we'd have done so long before now.'

'Please get them to hold off a little longer. If there is outside intervention, he'll go to war. My family is proud, I don't know if they'll tolerate outside interference.'

'I'm not the Ruby High Lord, just her voice while she's away. My mother wants Yadavendra gone and as soon as my hands are untied, I intend to see her wishes met.'

'Understood.'

'You mentioned Quiverhive just now,' said Anuja. 'Why?'

'I saw it on the way here.' He relayed the events in as much detail as he could. 'At first I thought it was simply using the Godroad as a means to kill the Murkers but it was more than that. It was experimenting.'

'Experimenting? Testing the power of the Godroad is more likely. Looking for a way to cross and finding one. By the Thrice Blessed Suns! This changes everything. Our whole society rests on the sanctity of the Godroad.' Anuja went to take another drink but her cup was empty. She set it down with an angry clink. 'It must have come when I was hunting at Fourboards.'

'You don't think that's a coincidence?'

'No. It's being tactical, Vasin. I don't like this at all.'

'Me neither.'

'I think I'm going to bring mother back early. House Ruby needs her wisdom, now more than ever.'

'If it fails, does your mother have a backup vessel?'

'Yes, but it's not the best match. A grandson. I'd have to play it safe and slow if it came to that. Eight years I'd say, maybe more to get him ready.'

Vasin wanted to rub his temples, but to do so would smear

the paint. A headache was starting. His mother would know what to say. She always knew. But until he could restore her, he was on his own. 'I think you should wait, I'll stay as long as you need and support you. We could hunt together.'

He smiled at her but she didn't respond in kind. 'No, we can't.' She lifted her gown to reveal bandages and several splints, all conspiring to hold together a shattered leg. 'The hunt at Fourboards was brutal. There were too many tributes. I and the Deathless from Opal and Peridot flew together, but their hunters were tired from travel, and mine weren't ready for something on this scale.' She sighed. 'Six tributes was a mighty amount of bait and the Wild was hungry. It sent many mouths. More than our hunters could field. I . . . '

She fell silent and lowered her head, and the shadows grew darker under her eyes.

'What is it? You can tell me.'

'I haven't mentioned this to anyone else, I didn't want to appear weak or like I was making excuses. I'd told myself I was imagining it, but after what you've told me about Quiverhive I'm not so sure.'

'Tell me.'

'The thing is, my people got the worst of it.'

'You fought the biggest demon? The biggest group?'

'No. Well, yes, but that isn't it. The Wild singled us out, came for us above the others. Vasin, they singled me out. When I landed, they came for me, and me alone. It was like they knew I was coming. How can that be?'

'I don't know, I thought all but strongest of the Wild feared us. Surely they were easy prey for you.'

'We slaughtered them, but they didn't seem to care.'

Vasin's headache got suddenly worse, as if trying to match his sense of foreboding. The odd behaviour described at Anuja's hunt seemed to chime with Quiverhive's activity. 'I think this was another experiment,' he said. 'They tested the Godroad, and now they're testing us.'

CHAPTER SIX

Vasin followed the servant, trying to order his mind for what was to come. He was being led to a night gathering of House Ruby's guests. This would be in part to discuss the business of the hunt, and in part to posture, to politic. It was Vasin's chance to solidify the quiet work of the last sixteen years, and gain allies against Yadavendra. It was also a chance to fail long before the inevitable confrontation with High Lord Sapphire.

Nerves flew like angry hunters in his stomach.

The strangeness of his environment didn't help. House Ruby was more sparing with its gemslight than he was used to, leaving patches of the narrow corridors dark. He noticed the individual rubies were not all cut to the same size. Some were a few millimetres thicker than others, and some stood slightly taller. You had to look to see them, the differences minor, but to his eyes, the imperfection was telling. The ceilings were too low, too cramped, and he had the absurd sense of them pressing downwards, trapping him.

Despite the late hour the castle seemed empty as he travelled, and this too disturbed him. A Sapphire castle always had guards at stairwells and key corridors. As much as he hated that – the feeling of always being watched was one of the things that drove him into the sky after all – he also found it reassuring.

They arrived at a room Vasin had not seen before, and he heard laughter echoing through the arched entrance. The servant waited for it to fade and then sang to announce his arrival and request permission to enter. Vasin felt a brief pang of fear that he would be rejected. Ridiculous, irrational, but in the moment, impossible to ignore. It was soon refuted by Lady Anuja, who gave permission, prompt and clear. The servant showed him inside.

The room was of a reasonable size, heptagonal, and filled with long, low seats, puffed up with cushions. Each chair was accompanied by a tiny squat table with drinks and small baked treats.

He saw three Deathless faces turn in his direction, smiles slowly fading from some shared joke.

Here we go.

Lady Anuja was sat opposite the doorway, artfully positioned. Her stiffness and discomfort dressed as regal posture, with the cushions carefully constructed around her to support her injured body. All signs of fatigue were gone from her face. 'Lord Vasin. Ruby-friend. Sit, relax, be welcome.'

'Thank you,' he replied with a bow, noting the raised eyebrows and pointed look that passed between the other two inhabitants.

'This,' continued Anuja, gesturing to her right, 'is Lord Lakshin of House Opal.

He saw a slight, delicate man, his body most likely coming to the end of its prime years. There was a studied poise about him, that struck Vasin as too rigid to be comfortable. The Opal tended to keep to themselves, and he knew nothing of Lakshin beyond a name. This in itself was odd. Most Deathless were known for something, even if it was embarrassing. No legend was visible either, which would be fine if Lakshin was in his first lifecycle, but he wasn't, suggesting mediocrity. And as everyone knew, there was no such thing as a mediocre Deathless, at least never for very long.

Anuja pointed to her left. 'And this is Lord Quasim of House Peridot.'

Quasim was in a young body, well muscled, but already showing signs of a fast life. The legend of a previous lifecycle had turned both of his ears gold, along with the knuckles on his right hand. Vasin wondered what the tales behind them were. He'd heard the Story-singers praise Quasim's courage and humour but he also recalled his mother making a barbed comment about the man going through three lifecycles in the time most Deathless enjoyed one.

He gave a bow of respect to them both. 'A pleasure to meet you.'

In the red light, their faces seemed like statues, their eyes hidden in bloody shadows. Neither of them bowed nor saluted, though their heads tilted in the barest form of acknowledgement. It stabbed at his pride, making his fists clench within his long sleeves, but he couldn't blame them for being angry. After all, House Sapphire had all but slammed its doors on everyone else.

He went and took a seat, pondering the best approach as the servant poured him a glass of wine.

This has to go well. If I can win them over, I gain two more voices that will support my challenge when it comes.

'I'm afraid I bring bad news.' And he told them of his encounter with Quiverhive.

Anuja looked grave as he spoke, Quasim puzzled, as if still waiting for the punchline to a joke, and Lakshin shook his head in disbelief. 'A demon *on* the Godroad? Unharmed?' He shook his head a second time. 'Impossible. Perhaps you mistook its closeness for contact, as you say, you were high above it.'

'I know what I saw.'

'Did your hunters see it also?'

'No.'

'Your entourage then?'

Vasin's heart sank. 'No . . . I travelled here alone.'

'Then you will forgive me if I trust centuries of experience before the report of one Sapphire Deathless.'

There was a brief and awkward silence. All four of them filled it by sipping from their drinks.

Quasim leaned forward. 'Lady Anuja tells us you are most nimble in the sky, Lord Vasin.'

He gave a nod to Anuja in recognition of the compliment. 'Then I hope I prove worthy of her words when we next fly together.'

Quasim grinned. 'She says you're almost as good as me!'

Anuja rolled her eyes but said nothing. Her silence seemed out of place, given that she acted as the High Lord of her house. It troubled him.

'Perhaps,' Quasim added, 'you would be interested in pitting your wings against mine?'

'Perhaps,' echoed Vasin. 'But I am more interested in how

my wings might serve my friends. I've heard a little of how things are here, but not from you.'

'Things are hard,' said Quasim, still grinning. 'And glorious. The Wild throws ever more at us, and we prove more than a match for it.'

'I hear the most recent hunt had six tributes.'

'Aye! And they drew out a mighty horde for us to fight.'

'What was it like?'

'It's hard to describe,' said Lakshin. 'You really had to be there.'

Another insult. He kept a tight grip on his pride, reminding himself that he needed the Opal onside. 'I'm here now and I don't intend to be idle. If there's anything you can tell me, it would be appreciated.'

Lakshin scowled and Vasin wasn't sure if it was at the memory or the imposition. 'These aren't like normal hunts. They start the same way of course, but the moment we take wing, things change.'

'Forgive me,' he glanced at Anuja. 'But there's nothing normal about sending six tributes.'

'It's true,' agreed Lakshin, also glancing at Anuja. 'May I?' She waved consent and he continued. 'In the hunt before, Fourboards made its sacrifices and sent out two tributes, as is the tradition.' Lakshin looked out of the window towards the distant, glittering lights below. 'Neither of them made it more than twenty paces into the Wild before they were taken. Can you believe it? It was so sudden our hunters never even found the torches.' He shook his head, still disbelieving. 'The following night was a long one for the people of Fourboards. Murkers came right up to the fences. In the end, they were driven off but by then they'd managed to break one of the supporting stilts and an entire house fell into the swamp.'

'They attacked the settlement itself? You're sure?'

Lakshin seemed annoyed at the interruption. 'What of it?'

'I thought Murkers only attacked living things.'

'They were, the house was full of living things.'

'Yes, but to bring down a structure like that . . . '

'Please. They're beasts, the house was between them and food so they attacked it. It's no different to when the Toothsack ate part of Raften.'

Vasin frowned. He wasn't convinced, and nor it seemed, was Anuja. Lakshin seemed to consider the matter closed and carried on.

'In response to the attack, the elders of Fourboards called another hunt and upped the number of tributes to six.'

'And did these tributes get through?'

'Oh they got through,' said Quasim. 'It was incredible. Imagine it, Lord Vasin. All that blood in one place crying out through six wounds. They called every demon in the swamp.'

'Incredible?' snorted Lakshin. 'It was the height of idiocy. There we were, three Deathless, all backed by hunters, and it was all we could do to not be overwhelmed.'

Vasin was surprised when Anuja didn't respond to this criticism of her people. *Perhaps she agrees with him.* 'I don't think idiocy is the same as desperation. By the sounds of it Fourboards needed the second hunt to succeed.'

'You don't throw out a thousand years of tradition because of one anomaly!'

'What other choice did they have?'

'To endure. The traditions are there to protect us all. By

breaking them, Fourboards put us all at risk. Surely you of all people should understand that?'

Vasin took a deep breath as he imagined hooking his fingers into the Opal's lower jaw and ripping it out. He kept his hands by his sides however, and his voice light, 'That's why I'm here, to honour our friends in House Ruby.'

Lakshin's eyebrows lifted. 'I look forward to seeing it, Lord Vasin. Now, if you'll excuse me, my lady, it's been a long day.'

Quasim stood up as well. 'A glorious day! Fourboards is safe once more, and the Wild will take time to recover from the beating we gave it.'

As will Lady Anuja, thought Vasin. *As will we all.* It troubled him that despite all they had seen, Lakshin and Quasim were still behaving as if everything was normal. As if tradition and skill alone would be enough to see order restored.

'A toast before you leave,' announced Anuja, raising her cup. She did not stand, and so the other two Deathless were forced to sit and collect their drinks. 'To days shared. Be they long, glorious, hard or joyful. Let us endure them together, as friends, always.'

'To days shared,' they said. Then toasted, stood, bowed, and left.

'I should retire too,' said Vasin. 'Leave you to your business.'

She held up a hand. 'In a moment. First tell me you can hunt with them.'

'Of course. The question is whether they'll hunt with me.'

'They will hunt wherever and with whomever I chose, until such time as their High Lords call them home.'

He thought about her words. *She states that they will follow her orders, yet makes a point of asking me as an equal, as if I were here as a High Lord rather than subordinate. And this after inviting me to join their gathering, calling me Ruby-friend in front of her allies. She knows I move on Yadavendra and is giving her support.*

On impulse, he knelt before her and took her hands in his. 'Thank you. I won't forget this, and nor will House Sapphire.'

She inched closer, wincing with the effort, sliding her hand down his wrist to clasp it. For a time they held eye contact, and Vasin was glad of it.

'The Wild is changing, my friend, and we must change with it. The Sapphire must heal and be better than they were before.'

'We will, I promise.'

She squeezed his wrist. 'And I will hold you to it.'

A new day was dawning and word had reached them that High Lord Sapphire was coming with it. As soon as Chandni left her chambers, she stood straighter, any worries banished from sight. Her majordomo's robes were perfectly fitted, their edges crisp, the studs of sapphire bright at her collar. Gloves covered her scar and any awkwardness with her right hand, and her feather was trapped within a braided cage of her hair. Unmanaged, it would pool around her feet. As it was, the bottom of the braid swung against the back of her calves.

She made her usual tour of the castle, pleased to note that everyone was where they should be. The other staff acknowledged her, and she exchanged a quick word with each as she passed. Usually these were banal comments on the weather or the way the castle was sitting in the sky that morning. In a couple of cases she would stay longer, enquiring about the health of a family member or whether a requested tool had arrived. She worked her way through the castle, past the legs of the sapphire giant that stood astride the main entrance. Mid-thigh they vanished into the ceiling, his lower body, upper body and head each on a different floor. The guards standing between his feet saluted as she went down into the kitchens.

A rich symphony of scents greeted her as she descended the stairs, accompanied by the familiar clatter of pots and plates. Once, long ago, she had run down here, assassins hot on her heels. The memory remained fresh in her mind, reborn every time she came this way. She forced herself to slow down. It had become a point of pride to use every step, and savour the fact that it was at a pace of her own choosing.

In most other places in the castle, her arrival would prompt a flurry of salutes or bows, but here in the kitchens, everyone was engaged in their tasks: kneading dough, chopping herbs, cleaning the never ending supply of dirty plates. Here, and here alone, Chandni tolerated it. For though she was in charge of the castle, the kitchens were Roh's domain.

A thick slab of sapphire protruded from a corner of the room, the air around it shimmering with heat. Energy from the suns fed the crystals beneath the castle, the warmth and light carried up through the walls like blood through veins. Here, the sapphire had been shaped flat with shallow depressions for placing pans and plates, and during the day something was always cooking on them.

She made her way over to the old cook, who was busy stirring a pot of thick sauce. 'Good morning, Roh.'

'Big day today, Honoured Mother.'

'I trust you have something special prepared for the High Lord's dinner.'

'That I do, that I do. And I've got his favourite soup ready for lunch. You know our High Lord, always early.'

It was true. Not in the way that Chandni was early. She liked to arrive with time in hand, to ensure she was present at the appointed hour. For her it was about respecting others and being precise. Yadavendra, on the other hand, would be shockingly, monstrously early. It was one of the reasons Chandni had already dressed in her best clothes, as on a previous visit she'd still been changing when he'd arrived. The frantic rushing, the panic, it had made for some of the worst hours of her life.

Never again, she'd sworn to herself. *I'd rather go out into the Wild.*

The throwaway thought brought back true memories of the Wild, and she shuddered. And then, straight after, came memories of Varg. He'd been thrown into her life so suddenly, and then left it the same way. He'd made the Wild bearable, and he'd been devoted to her in a way that nobody else was. The staff here were all loyal, but they were loyal to her as a tool of House Sapphire and Lord Rochant. Varg was loyal to her personally.

Even though he serves Lady Pari, he wants to be with me.

She thought of his gruffness, his strength, his appalling language, and had to suppress a chuckle. Then she thought of other things, the ease at which he blushed in her presence, his hands massaging her feet, of them wandering elsewhere, his promise that he would pay off his debts to the Tanzanite and come to her. That had been sixteen years ago.

It was fantasy of course, but it was her fantasy, the only one she had, and she clung to it.

'I imagine you have a lot on your mind, Honoured Mother, what with the High Lord on his way,' said Roh.

The blood grew hot in her face. 'Oh . . . yes. I'll leave you to it.'

Roh hummed an acknowledgement and went back to her business, while Chandni made her way out quickly.

Any thoughts of Varg were long gone as she reached Satyendra's chambers. All was quiet in the corridor outside save for the swish of fabric as the guards saluted her. She acknowledged them and paused at his doorway to sing for permission to enter. As his mother, she didn't have to, but she did it anyway, to make a point.

There was a pause, not quite long enough to be rude, but awfully close, before Satyendra replied: 'Come in.'

The atmosphere in the room was strange, tense. Satyendra held a tablet of glass in his hand that held details of Lord Rochant's life. He was doing a good impression of studying it, carefully ignoring the other boy in the room.

Pik was three years younger than Satyendra, a cousin on her side of the family. Though they shared a similar body shape, the boy had none of Satyendra's sharpness, and without Mohit's blood, the blood of Lord Rochant, there was little to distinguish him. Only her patronage allowed him to keep his privileged spot in the castle. Pik's face fell when he saw her, and he went back to cleaning the room.

She inspected his work and frowned. In a castle full of

high-achievers, what might pass for adequate elsewhere appeared sloppy. 'You've missed a spot.'

'Sorry, Honoured Mother. I haven't got to the left side of the room yet.' He picked up his sponge and hurried past her.

'I'm not talking about the left side of the room.' She pointed to the place he'd just left. 'There? Do you see?'

'Oh, sorry' he replied, hurrying back. 'Sorry.'

'Calm down, Nose,' said Satyendra. 'Nobody cares about one speck of dirt. That's not why you're here, is it Mother?'

'No, and call Pik by his proper name in future.' She walked over to the wardrobe, and pulled out Satyendra's cloak. 'Are you ready?'

'I suppose so.'

She held the wardrobe door open as Satyendra climbed inside and waited for him to manoeuvre himself behind the clothes there before shutting it. She heard him sigh through the frosted glass.

'Don't come out until you hear the knock.'

'I've done this before, you know.'

'Stay quiet and we'll be back as soon as we can.'

He didn't reply and she put her hand on the door as if to communicate the things she couldn't say. Then she turned and held out Satyendra's cloak to Pik.

Without meeting her eyes, the boy took it and put it on.

They left together, moving quickly through corridors. Aside from the guards, the place was quiet. Chandni allowed herself a slight nod. *As it should be.*

From a distance, with the hood up, Pik passed easily for Satyendra. Chandni spoke as they walked, giving the impression that the two were discussing important matters,

Honoured Mother to Honoured Vessel, and that they were not to be interrupted. That would be enough to keep most away, and she'd taken steps to make sure that the few others with the authority to approach, like Roh and Ban, were occupied elsewhere.

Despite the meticulous planning, Chandni knew that it would only take one piece of bad luck for her deception to be uncovered, especially on a day when the High Lord was visiting. She may as well worry about the castle falling from the sky for all the good it would do.

Not even I can plan for Yadavendra.

However, no High Lords ambushed her, no one moved out of place, and she and Pik arrived safely at the Chrysalis Chamber.

Sunlight poured in through the glass wall, a physical force sparking sweat and slowing thought. She wondered what such intense conditions must do to the Gardener-smiths' minds.

Entering, they were confronted by an imperfect form of blue crystal assembled opposite them on a stand. This was the replacement set for Lord Rochant's armour. The previous set had vanished around the same time the Deathless had been kidnapped, its whereabouts a mystery. There was armour sufficient to identify the body and limbs, but there were gaps the sapphire had not yet been coaxed to fill, and while it was approximately the right size, it did not yet seem to live in the way a finished suit did.

When Lord Rochant was reborn, he would don this armour. Each piece was grown alongside its vessel so that it would fit perfectly. The trouble was that contact with the crystal seemed to cause Satyendra physical pain. His skin would pale and bubble, losing its colour, and his face would—

No. None of them could stand that. She hoped that when Lord Rochant's soul took residence it would purge all traces of the Wild from the body, and all evidence that her son had been corrupted. Until then, however, the armour still needed to be grown and so Chandni had come up with another solution: Pik.

Only one Gardener-smith was here and she didn't look happy about it. As Pik began slipping off his clothes, she came over to Chandni, rubbing her hands together like a nervous Flykin.

'How much longer?'

'This may well be the last time. The High Lord is coming. If he is happy with Satyendra then the rebirth will happen immediately. Wrath's Tear is in ascendance and we don't want to miss the opportunity.'

'And if he isn't happy?'

'Then it will wait until he is.'

'But—'

Chandni's scowl cut her off. 'Our arrangement hasn't changed. I've always provided appropriate substitutes for the fittings and you have been well compensated for your understanding, not to mention my discretion over your own failings. I have not betrayed your secrets, I am sure you can do me the same courtesy.'

The Gardener-smith glanced at Pik. 'The size is right, for now anyway. This lad will outgrow yours in another year.'

'In a year this will be well behind us.' *Please let it be behind us.*

'But what about the bond?'

It was seen by the Gardener-smiths as a sacred triangle: the Deathless soul, the perfect vessel, and the crystal skin. Each was connected to the other and together they were strong. 'This boy shares my blood, that will have to be enough.'

The Gardener-smith grumbled but picked up a bracer from the stand and placed it carefully on Pik's forearm. Then, with a false nail on her little finger, she pricked his hand, touching a daub of blood to the crystal to wake it.

It felt wrong to stay and watch, and so Chandni retreated to the entrance of the chamber. She hadn't been there long when a young guard arrived at speed. It was a few moments before he could speak but she already knew what he was going to say by the manner of his arrival and the strained look in his eyes.

'Honoured Mother, High Lord Yadavendra is here. He wants to see you and Lord Rochant's Honoured Vessel immediately.'

'Tell him we are just having a fitting and will be with him shortly.' She gave a moment of silent appreciation to Roh. 'Tell him we have food prepared and will send it to him while he waits.'

'Forgive me, Honoured Mother. The High Lord is aware of the fitting. When I say he is here, I mean he is following right behind. The captain knows how much you hate surprises so he sent me ahead.'

Her heart began to thud heavily in her chest. 'Give the captain my thanks. Now guard this door and don't let anyone in until we're ready, not even the High Lord, do you understand?

'Honoured Mother?'

'Do as I say!' she snapped, and rushed back into the chamber.

When his mother had left, Satyendra counted to a hundred in his mind, making sure to pause between each number. One of the many annoying things about being an Honoured Vessel was that it was hard to go anywhere without being noticed. And nobody could know what he was about to do.

He pushed himself off from the back of the wardrobe and listened through the door. There were no sounds and no shadows visible through the frosted glass. He opened it a crack and listened again before stepping out.

From under the bed he pulled out a simple grey cloak with blue trim and some trousers. The cloak he'd stolen from Pik on a previous visit, and the trousers he'd traded for with one of the apprentice hunters. He changed quickly, pulling the hood as far forward as it would go, then practised walking up and down a few times. He allowed his head to dip a little and modified his stride to make it slower, mimicking the way he'd seen Pik move.

If those idiots in the castle were willing to believe that Pik was him, then it would be easy to reverse the illusion. There were risks, certainly, but Satyendra rarely got to roam about the castle freely.

The guards outside looked surprised when he emerged from the room. 'Finished already?'

He didn't reply immediately, not wanting to appear too clever. When he did, his voice sounded almost identical to Pik's usual whine. 'No, forgot my sponge.'

They laughed at that. 'Better hurry then. When the

Honoured Mother gets back, she'll expect everything to be spotless.'

'Yes,' he agreed, and turned away.

Once out of their sight, he made his way quickly towards the lower-mid level of the castle, where the apprentice hunters slept. By now all of the apprentices would be training, leaving the rooms free for him to explore. Each one contained four bunks and a single gemlight. Sacks were slung from each end of the bunk, containing their possessions. Satyendra moved between them, searching for things he might need.

If the High Lord can't be put off, this could be my last chance.

A knife took his fancy. The handle was carved from wood, highly polished, with settings for gemstones. Even unfinished, it would be desired in the markets.

He already had a knife stashed away, but it was a blunt one stolen from the kitchens. This one was much nicer. He tucked it away and continued to rummage, taking anything that might help him effect an escape, along with anything he liked the look of. He was far greedier than normal, and more reckless.

They'll never suspect me as the thief, and even if I'm caught what can they do? I'm too important to exile or hurt.

With his treasures hidden within his cloak, he made his way towards one of the quieter areas of the castle, a little courtyard that had once been used by Samarku Un-Sapphire to cultivate a rare type of flower called Dawn's Blush. Since Lord Rochant's arrival it had been abandoned and left to grow wild.

Why the courtyard hadn't been maintained or repurposed

was not spoken about, but Satyendra liked to think it was an act of pure pettiness. A little shoot of spite in Lord Rochant's otherwise perfect record.

Whatever the reason, the resulting neglect had led to the creation of Satyendra's favourite hiding place. Nobody else went there, and it was easy to slip within the net of tanglevine and become anonymous. Years ago, when he had faced up to the idea that the rebirth ceremony could not be put off forever, he had begun preparing for the day he might have to flee the castle. This meant gathering supplies: clothes, food, tools, all the things he'd need to survive alone on the road.

The problem was he'd no idea what those things were. Apart from his adventures in the Wild as a baby, he'd never left Lord Rochant's floating castle.

His mother was coy about that time, but he'd gleaned that road-born who ventured outside of their villages had to wear special clothes, and that they covered their feet, face and hands at all times. When he had exhausted his patience with her, he'd turned to Story-singer Ban, asking about hunts and travel, and then attacking the old man with questions. However, this proved frustrating, as the Deathless were not troubled by simple issues like needing to eat or sleep outside, and if they were, the practical details were dropped in favour of a 'higher truth'.

Armed with some meagre facts and his imagination, Satyendra had set about gathering what he thought would be needed. Over time, he strategically started to lose things: tops, trousers, even boots, until he had an impressive stash tucked away.

He carefully opened up his hiding place, adding the knife

and the other new acquisitions before covering it all up again and slipping back towards his room.

When he arrived the guards seemed relieved to see him, as if they were expecting someone else, someone worse, and there was a strange vibe in the air as he travelled, a tension that made his mouth water.

Yadavendra is here, and he was both cheered and appalled at the thought. It was easier to feed that other part of himself when the High Lord was around which also meant it was harder to resist. He'd told himself in the courtyard when he'd dislocated Chunk's knee – the pop still resonated deliciously in his mind – that it would be the last time. He tried to remember that he could also enjoy other things, like his mother's praise. He resolved to resist. To stay focused on the matter at hand: to cancel the rebirth ceremony or escape the castle.

But on the way back to his chambers, when the plan played out in his mind, he could not banish other thoughts – of using his influence to make others suffer – nor deny how they made his stomach grow warm.

The Gardener-smith carefully attached the plate to Pik's chest.

Chandni looked back to the entrance of the Chrysalis Chamber. She couldn't hear Yadavendra yet, but she could feel him getting closer. If he arrived before Pik's disguise was complete, all of her planning would be for nought. 'Get the next piece on, quickly now.'

'The crystal needs to be woken first, then I'll prepare the next piece.'

'Put it on, now, or I'll do it myself.'

The Gardener-smith shook her head, muttering darkly, but

she complied. 'It isn't the way it's done. No, we always place the pieces right, then wake them. That's how it's supposed to be. That's how it's always been.'

'I don't want to do this,' said Pik.

Chandni leaned in close to the trembling boy. 'Listen to me: High Lord Yadavendra just wishes to see the armour. All you have to do is stand there. Bow when he enters, bow when he leaves. You can do that, can't you?'

'I don't want to lie to the High Lord.'

'You'd bow to him whether you were in the armour or not, wouldn't you?'

'Yes.'

'So you're not lying, you're being respectful.'

'What if he talks to me?'

The contents of Chandni's breakfast bubbled uncomfortably in her stomach. If Yadavendra talked to Pik they were finished. 'I will occupy the High Lord. If he asks you something directly, nod or shake your head, and if you absolutely have to say something, keep your answers short.'

Pik's head began to shake in time with the Gardener-smith's. 'I can't.'

'You can and you will, because if you don't, the three of us will be sent into the Wild. Do you *know* what happens to boys like you in the Wild?'

Did he know? She knew. A sudden memory of her fight with the Whispercage came into her mind. It had taken her baby from her. She corrected herself. *Tried* to take him . . . there had been a moment when the Whispercage had lifted Satyendra from her lap but she had stopped it. The thought of what that monster would have done if she'd failed was too much to bear.

The sound of many boots could be heard outside the chamber, making all three of them jump. 'Get the helmet on!' urged Chandni.

'But the helmet is always last,' replied the Gardener-smith, stubbornly trying to cling to some scrap of tradition. 'I haven't done the gauntlets or the wings yet.'

'Just get it on for—' a curse sat on the tip of her tongue. Not a mild one like 'suns' either, the kind of salty phrase that she'd reprimanded Varg for many times. The kind she never, ever used. 'Just get it on,' she repeated, and hurried over to the entrance and down into the main courtyard.

Yadavendra, High Lord of the Sapphire, could be seen striding across it. Both he and his hunters were still garbed for flight, their wings flashing in the sunlight. Sky-legs empowered each step, giving them a gliding, bounding gait. There was something both magnificent and terrible about the sight. As ever, Yadavendra was dressed in his armour. Most Deathless would have theirs removed upon arrival but he did not. In fact, she struggled to recall the last time she had seen him without it.

Compared to Chandni he was a towering giant, sharp edged, and glinting. In his hand was a golden staff, tipped with a sapphire blade, that swept dangerously back and forth as he approached.

The lone guard that she'd asked to hold the entrance had already stepped aside. Chandni made a mental note that he was not fit for promotion and bowed low, placing herself directly in Yadavendra's path, like a pebble before a tidal wave.

He didn't stop until he was virtually on top of her, his armoured bulk blocking out the suns. His hunters settled in a semi-circle behind, more like soldiers before a battle than guests in friendly territory.

'Hail to you, Yadavendra, greatest of all the Sapphire,' she said. 'In Lord Rochant's name, I welcome you to his home and thank you for honouring us with your presence.'

'Honoured Mother Chandni,' he replied. 'It pleases me to see you. I hear only good things. These lands endure, this castle thrives. You do Lord Rochant credit. When he returns, I will tell him so.'

'Thank you, High Lord.' She looked up at him. 'Were the currents in your favour?'

'They were.'

'Do you or your hunters require refreshments after your long journey? My cooks would be delighted to provide for you.'

'In good time, yes.' He gestured with his staff for her to move and she had no choice but to comply. In her mind she pictured the Gardener-smith shuffling about, no doubt doing everything in its proper order. *What have I become that I am angry at a fellow Sapphire for doing things in the right way?* She doubted Pik's helmet had been attached. *I need to keep Yadavendra talking.*

'How may I serve?' she asked as she stepped to one side.

'I wish to see young Satyendra. He's inside, yes?'

'Yes, and I know that he's very excited to be able to see you again.'

The smile inside Yadavendra's helmet was genuine as he strode past her. 'Good.'

There was little to do but follow in his wake and hope for the best. She didn't like the idea of leaving the hunters in the courtyard, armed and unattended. There was a restlessness about them that made her nervous. Perhaps it was simply that she didn't know them the way she knew Lord Rochant's hunters. Or perhaps it was that they were an armed force within her walls that she could not control.

They stepped inside, the sudden heat taking her breath away. The Gardener-smith had fled to the corner of the room, and Pik was caught mid-turn as he'd gone to follow her. In his armour, he looked like Yadavendra in miniature, save that Rochant's shoulder plates and bracers were shaped differently. They were less elaborate than the other Sapphire Deathless. Some believed it was to show he was unlike them, coming from a different bloodline, but Chandni believed the armour reflected the man: elegant, minimalist, direct.

She gave silent thanks when she saw Pik was wearing his helmet.

'Satyendra,' said Yadavendra, 'Come here where I can see you.'

Pik complied. The boy was not used to walking in Sky-legs and wobbled slightly as he approached.

The High Lord tutted and glanced at her. 'Rochant is always steady.'

'I'm sure it is just his excitement getting the better of him. You know how much he adores you.'

'Yes,' he agreed, 'we cannot hold a boy's love against him. Indeed, it shows he is ready, a true match for Lord Rochant's devoted soul. Now, Satyendra, do as I do.'

He stretched out his arms, luxuriating in the magnified sunslight. As the sapphire plates on his body drank in the energy they began to shine.

Pik hesitated until Chandni glared at him. Then, the boy

complied, lifting his arms. As the crystals on his armour began to glow, the places where the armour was unfinished were highlighted, becoming patches of black.

Yadavendra tutted again. 'Your Gardener-smiths have some work to do, Honoured Mother. Are you sure they're up to the task?'

'I admit their progress has been slow but with so much riding on this rebirth they're being especially conscientious.'

'Understandable,' he mused. 'But not acceptable. Perhaps we should have them replaced.'

Though the Gardener-smith's head was bowed, Chandni could still see her imploring look. 'Please, High Lord, I am sure that they will redouble their efforts.'

'They'd better. I expect the armour to be joined and alive by the time the Bringers arrive.'

'It will be, I promise.'

He nodded, appeased. 'I will take that lunch you offered me, Honoured Mother. Satyendra can dine with me, so that I might better assess his readiness.'

Pik's squeak of terror was just audible over her reply. 'My guard will escort you to your chamber and I will have Satyendra changed, prepared and sent after.'

Yadavendra paused. For a moment, she was worried he would deem the idea of needing to change unnecessary. After all, he seemed to live in his armour. 'As you wish, but your guard can stay where he is. I know this castle far better than he ever will. Which reminds me, with the rebirth so close, we must take extra care to protect Satyendra. As such, my hunters will provide an escort for him.' He turned to Pik and waggled his finger in what was presumably supposed to be a friendly manner, but came across to Chandni as terrifying. 'So don't tarry, Honoured Vessel, they will be as keen to eat as I am.'

And with that, Yadavendra left the chamber, allowing Chandni to worry about new things, like how to switch Pik for Satyendra without the hunters noticing.

CHAPTER SEVEN

As Arkav slept and the carriages rumbled along the Godroad, Pari considered the best way to achieve her secret meeting.

The problem with secrets, thought Pari, *is that they have a way of getting out.*

Overhead, the suns spun brightly while the forest rushed by on either side, a vibrant blur of green, brown and yellow. Their carriages were making good time, the earlier encounter at the tower almost forgotten now it was behind them. Almost. It seemed that once the Sapphire border had been breached, it was easy to travel their lands unmolested. While they had got a few odd looks from the road-born, most treated them with courtesy, their lives and manners untouched by the strangeness going on above.

In fact, the fleeting glances she had seen of Sapphire settlements suggested a prosperous people. Though the Wild remained a constant threat, the worst of its ire was directed elsewhere, at Ruby and Spinel. No doubt the Sapphire High

Lord would put it down to his inspiring leadership. Pari, meanwhile, suspected something more sinister.

Soon, she would need to make a detour, which was problematic as she didn't want anyone else to know her movements. Arkav wouldn't betray her and their servants would be discreet, that went without saying, but if the Sapphire turned against them, no amount of discretion was proof against torture.

Better that they do not know.

'What is it?' asked Arkav, his eyes still closed, his head resting against the cushioned wall of the carriage.

'I thought you were asleep.'

'I was. Your worrying woke me up.'

She wondered what he was referring to. *Do I grind my teeth? Mutter to myself? Or does he just feel it, the way I do? The way he used to.* 'I need to get out.'

Without moving his head, he gestured to the door. 'Don't let me stop you.'

'I wouldn't, believe me.' He chuckled sleepily and she realized how much she'd missed the sound. 'I need to get out without being seen.'

'And you want me to make a distraction?'

'Yes.' He sighed, and it was Pari's turn to chuckle. 'But you're so good at it, at people, I mean. You always have been.'

'Used to be.'

'No,' she replied warmly, firmly, and rested her hand on his. 'Are. You just need to remember. Treat this as a warm up before we have to deal with the Sapphire.

He opened his eyes so that he could give her a disbelieving look. 'So you're doing me a favour?'

'Yes, I suppose I am.'

'Thank you.'

'You are most welcome, dear brother. Now, tell me what you have in mind.'

He closed his eyes again. 'Something brilliant.'

'There it is again,' called Arkav to the servants, as he leant out of the carriage window. 'A Whispercage, I'm sure of it.'

Pari sat crouched by the opposite door. She had changed out of her regalia and into clothes more fit for travel. Truth be told, she didn't entirely approve of the plan. It seemed too likely to result in pain, hers, which was by far her least favourite.

'No,' said Arkav, sounding impatient. 'Look lower, just on the edge of the sunlight, it's there, keeping pace with us. Do you see it?'

As the servants tried to assess the threat, Pari opened the door, marvelling at how much faster they seemed to be going than before. *No doubt another side effect of this 'brilliant' plan.*

She didn't think too hard about what she was going to do. This wasn't the first time she'd thrown herself into the air without wings, and it certainly wasn't the worst. A memory of being ejected from Lord Rochant's castle came to her, of a great expanse of nothing between her and the cracked earth, and then another, of unknown depths into the chasm itself. In comparison the few feet between her and the ground seemed laughable.

However, Pari wasn't laughing.

With a last look to her brother, she kicked out, sailing wingless through the air, clearing the Godroad and angling

111

towards the dead stalks that lined its edge. Though contact with the Godroad was sure to kill anything of the Wild, the senseless hunger of the forest drove it towards the crystal again and again. Each time the vegetation would burn, the tips turning to ash on contact, the trunks and stems reduced to dry husks that formed a yellow-brown band between the road and the forest.

With a soft crumping sound, Pari hit the bed of dead plants, rolling with the momentum several times to come up standing by the nearest tree. She kept close to it, taking advantage of the cover as she dusted herself down. Neither carriage was slowing, suggesting that her absence had gone unnoticed.

She waited until they were out of sight and then made her way along the edge of the tree line, trying to find the sweet spot that would keep her obscured from passing travellers on the Godroad, yet still be close enough to minimize the chances of meeting any of the Wild's denizens.

While the suns blazed above her, Pari felt safe. Sometimes the ear-shaped leaves would tilt in her direction, but only for a moment, her presence not enough to wake the forest from its slumber. The smaller inhabitants gave her a wide berth, and aside from the occasional Birdkin, shouting at her from the highest branches, she felt alone.

It took her a while to find the path – the trees had shifted many times since she was last here – but when she did, she was pleased to find it had been used recently. A short walk later and Pari came within sight of a familiar wagon. Time and travel had caressed it a little too eagerly, making it as rough and battered as its driver. The wheels had been repaired more than once, and the roof was mostly patches and thread, but it still looked robust, and Pari found herself smiling at the sight of it.

As a Deathless, she took profound comfort in the familiar, each thing from her last lifecycle that endured was like an anchor, linking her to the present. A large Dogkin lazed in front of the wagon, a fat teardrop of white fur, five legs and just the one tail. Her name was Glider, and she looked up as Pari approached, barking in recognition.

Pari stopped when she saw the Dogkin's face. The last time she had seen the animal, it was injured, and had struggled to do its duty. Only Varg's insistence had kept her from killing it. Old puncture scars were visible on Glider's face, one on the left side of her jaw, the other directly above, on the temple, running down towards her left eye.

To her surprise she saw that Glider's human eye was open, glaring every bit as effectively as her canine one.

'It's only me, you stupid animal.'

Varg's shaggy head appeared at the front of the wagon. The first streaks of grey had appeared in his beard, which was trimmed shorter than she remembered it. Perhaps that was why he looked a little slimmer, a little sadder, but he seemed otherwise unchanged. He stared at her for a few moments, bushy brows coming together in a monstrous frown.

'Oh', she muttered, 'not you as well.'

His lips moved and she noted they were not forming the shape of her name. *He wants to say 'Priti', the vessel who lived in this body before me.*

'Pari?' He eventually asked.

'Who else would it be?'

He gave her a nod and then jumped down, resting one hand on Glider's flank. 'You look . . . uh . . . '

'Thank you, my dear. I see you haven't lost any of your usual eloquence.'

'Shit. Sorry. It's just you look like her until you talk. I didn't think . . . '

'Didn't think what?'

'That it would be this hard.' He stared at her, then realized he was staring, then looked away. 'She's really gone, hasn't she?'

Pari pursed her lips. 'Yes.'

'Right. I knew she had. It's just seeing you now makes it real, you know?'

'Can we talk about this on the move? I have places to go and people to see, and I need to rendezvous with my carriages before they reach Lord Rochant's castle.'

'Where are we off to? Ami didn't tell me much beyond passing on your message to come here.'

'Sorn. And I'd add that we're running late.'

Varg took the hint and started to attach Glider's harness, but when Pari went to climb onto the wagon, the Dogkin started to growl.

'Calm down,' snapped Pari, but Glider's growl only deepened. 'Varg, will you tell her that it's me.'

'I think she knows,' muttered Varg under his breath. 'That's the problem.'

'What did you say?'

'Nothing. Come on Glider, calm it down, there's a good girl.' The growling continued and Varg took a deep breath. 'Shut it, I said!'

Glider's growl settled into a grumble.

'Honestly,' said Pari as she settled into the back of the wagon, 'I don't know why you put up with her. We could get another Dogkin.'

'Not like her we couldn't. She saved my life, and not just mine either.' Varg's face took on a faraway expression, causing Pari to roll her eyes.

'I wondered how long it would be before you started mooning over her again.'

'Fuck off.'

'I think the words you're searching for are "fuck off, my lady."'

'Fuck off.'

'You're still determined to go back to little—'

'Don't say her—'

'—Chandni then?'

Glider threw back her head and howled.

'What is it now?'

'You said her name. Glider always does this when she hears her name. She misses Chand same as I do.'

Pari held up her hands. 'Unbelievable. Can we go now?'

They both shouted at Glider until she settled, and then they set off, following paths that wove roughly parallel to the Godroad. Though few were brave or foolish enough to use the other paths, there were always some who preferred to travel unnoticed, enough that the way was mostly clear and easy to follow.

'I trust,' said Pari, 'that Lord Taraka didn't suspect you when you were in his lands?'

'Nah.'

'You're sure?'

'He wasn't even there most of the time, and when he was, I kept out of the way.'

'Let us hope that was enough.'

'Mhn. So, once we get this business with Sorn over with, I'm coming with you to the castle?'

'Yes, what of it?'

'Then you're going to get me a place there. Like you promised.'

'Yes, Varg. Then I'm going to negotiate you a place there . . . ' She paused for effect. 'On one condition.'

'I thought training Priti for you was the condition!'

She waved away his protest. 'It was, but you must also stop calling the Honoured Mother "Chand", at least in my presence.'

A blush began to spread beneath his beard. 'What's wrong with that?'

'Honestly? It makes her sound like some common object to be haggled over at a market stall. For example: I'll take three bottles of honeywine and a bag of chand. You see?'

'Piss off.'

She chuckled. 'I'll take that as a yes. Now, let's hurry, I want to be in and out of Sorn long before the suns go down.'

Chandni stepped out of the Chrysalis Chamber into the courtyard, steeling herself against the sudden drop in temperature. Yadavendra's hunters seemed more relaxed now that their High Lord was elsewhere, but no less dangerous.

'Where is the Honoured Vessel?' asked one, a man she had seen before but never been introduced to. He looked strong but in a way that intimidated rather than reassured. His hair was long, braided, and thrice-clipped to his back to prevent it moving during flight.

'He is with our Gardener-smith, having his armour removed.'

'And where are you going?'

Such impertinence! She narrowed her eyes just a fraction,

to indicate displeasure without making a scene. 'I am going to ensure that the Honoured Vessel is able to join our High Lord in suitable attire as swiftly as possible.'

'Alright,' said the hunter, gesturing for her to continue.

Chandni's teeth ground with the force of her smile. 'I will be back presently.'

How dare he! She thought, sweeping past them and across the courtyard. She did not need his permission and she certainly did not need his approval!

However the truth was more complicated. Chandni ran the castle and spoke for Lord Rochant in his absence. This meant that she was host and they were guests who should defer to her. However she was not Deathless, and the hunters served Yadavendra, who stood above all, including Lord Rochant. While acting under his authority, the hunters would feel free to speak and do as they pleased.

As they have just demonstrated, most likely for my benefit.

She did not think about what would happen if the hunters decided to enter the Chrysalis Chamber. Nor did she think about what would happen if Pik lost his nerve, or her Gardener-smith. These things were beyond her control. Instead she concentrated on maintaining a mask of calm and moving as fast as she could without appearing to hurry.

Somehow she would have to get Satyendra from his room and into the Chrysalis Chamber without Yadavendra's hunters or anyone else recognizing him. And she would have to do it quickly.

So while she imagined everything going wrong and the sense of dread rose and rose within her like a tide, she nodded to those she passed as she would on any other day.

It is fine. Everything is fine. Convince yourself and they will believe it too.

The familiar distance to the bedrooms seemed to have doubled, and were it not for the guards at the end of the corridor, she would have burst through Satyendra's door, rather than pausing to sing for entry.

He didn't immediately reply and it enraged her. *On top of everything else I have to endure his petty protests!* Very aware that the guards were watching her, she gave them a polite smile and they saluted.

It is fine. Everything is fine.

From where they were standing it was possible for someone in the room to reply and the noise not to reach them, so she nodded, as if she had heard Satyendra give her permission to enter, and strode inside.

The room appeared empty at first glance. Of course it did! Satyendra was still hiding in the wardrobe. He wouldn't come out until he'd heard the knock. They'd agreed long ago that unless he heard the knock he should assume it unsafe.

He's only doing what I told him to. She felt bad about her earlier frustration. No wonder the guards were looking at her strangely, to them it would appear as if she was asking for permission to enter from an empty room!

It is fine. She thought as she moved over to the frosted glass. *Everything is still fine.*

She gave the knock, a rapid succession of beats with very brief pauses, three, two, three, five. Considering what a hateful thing it was part of, she'd been surprised how much she'd enjoyed setting it up. There was a pleasure in taking on a challenge, and Satyendra had worked with her, one of the rare times when they'd both pulled in the same direction.

He didn't come out straight away, so she gave the knock again, sharper, her barely repressed anxiety coming out in the notes her knuckles made on the glass.

When there was no response a second time she pulled open the door and it was all she could do not to scream.

Satyendra was not there.

Do something, Chandni! She urged herself, and yet she remained rooted to the spot, repressing the uncharacteristic urge to break something.

If she could work out where Satyendra was, she might have a chance. She knew his favourite haunts, and his secret ones. Even the courtyard he went to when he thought she was distracted. But if he'd left the room, surely the guards would have seen and recognized him?

I'm doomed. My Satyendra is doomed. We are all going to die a horrible and painful death. There will be a trial that will last for ever as they strip the flesh from our bones and the dignity from our souls, and then we will be cast into the Wild.

No. Everything is fine. It is fine. I have to make a plan. Stay with the plan and it will all work out.

After selecting and folding a few of Satyendra's best clothes, she left the room, making her way swiftly – but calmly! – back towards the Chrysalis Chamber. Without the armour, Pik would be discovered as a fake within moments, provided the person looking knew him. Yadavendra did, but as far as she knew his hunters did not, and from what she had seen, they were hardly conversationalists.

She would get them to escort Pik back to Satyendra's

room and then she would make up an excuse, say that he was feeling too ill to eat. She could even use Pik's instability on the Sky-legs to her advantage; claim it as the first signs of sickness.

Then, she would have time to scour the castle, find her son, vent her anger, and prepare him for the High Lord. It was a good plan. She could already feel the tension starting to ease.

As she reached the courtyard however, she heard jeering.

The hunters had not moved from their position, though they watched the other inhabitants of the castle openly, aggressively, staking their claim to the courtyard. The poor souls that had to pass them did so at a scurry. Unfortunately the apprentices had no choice but to practise in the court-yard, and it seemed Yadavendra's hunters were not impressed by what they saw.

Alongside the need to carry out her plan, Chandni felt an urge to put the hunters in their place. Until Lord Rochant's return, the people here were under her protection, whether that threat came from within or without.

They made way for her as she approached, but only just. The space between them was slight, forcing her to duck if she wished to pass beneath their crystal wings.

Instead of going through she came to a stop in front of them. 'I don't know your names,' she said.

The one who she had spoken to her before smirked at his fellows before replying. 'I'm Zax, leader of the High Lord's hunters.'

'You misunderstand, I was not asking for your name, hunter. I was making a statement.'

His smirk disappeared and he inhaled deeply, making his chest expand. 'I don't follow.'

'I'm saying that if you were worthy of introduction, the High Lord would have made one. He did not. He simply said that you were here to help protect my son. To help me. Do you understand? You are here to help me.'

Zax understood now. He nodded but she saw his fingers tighten on his spear. Clearly the man had poor self control. Though that saddened her, it also hardened her resolve.

'So there is no misunderstanding, I will make myself crystal clear: you will do what I say, when I say it, and nothing more. If you shame yourselves in my house again, I will pass that shame to the High Lord. Do you understand?'

They all straightened at that, speaking in unison: 'Yes, Honoured Mother Chandni.'

She noted that the gap between them had suddenly got wider and passed through it, head held high. She also noted that they all knew who she was, which proved her point rather nicely.

The Gardener-smith had been busy while she'd been away. Each sapphire piece of armour had been lovingly removed, polished and returned to its stand, leaving a diminished Pik shivering in a corner, despite the heat. Though he was wearing Satyendra's clothes, he had never looked less like her son.

'Put the cloak on,' said Chandni.

'But it's so hot in here, Honoured Mother.'

She didn't bother answering that, glaring at Pik until he'd put on the cloak, and then pulling the hood as far forward as she could. 'Are you ready to go?'

Pik shook his head. 'I can't. The hunters are out there!'

'Yes. They're going to escort us back to Satyendra's room.'

'But they'll see me, they'll know I'm not him.'

'Not if you keep your head down and your mouth shut.'

'But they'll know!' repeated Pik, the last word stretching out into a whine.

Before she could reply, a familiar voice came from behind her, making all three of them jump. 'For once, I'm afraid I have to agree with Pik.'

She span round to find Satyendra standing there in a servant's cloak, a sly smile on his face. For a moment she couldn't decide whether to hug him or hit him. 'What are you doing here?'

'Isn't it obvious, Mother? I'm saving us.' He began to shrug out of his clothes and she got Pik to do the same, facilitating the swap.

'That was brave of you,' she said, 'but foolish. The hunters must have seen you. How are we going to explain that?'

'The hunters see what they want to see,' scoffed Satyendra, 'a servant, nothing more. Besides, they were too busy recovering from the dressing-down you gave them.'

'You saw that?'

'I did,' his smile broadened, flashing in the bright light of the chamber, 'and I loved it. I think one of them was trying not to cry.'

'It was my duty. I took no pleasure in it.' He raised his eyebrows and she couldn't help but smile. 'Well, perhaps just a little.'

'You were magnificent,' he said.

'Thank you. Now, the High Lord is waiting. Are you ready to be magnificent?'

'I suppose so.'

'I said: Are you ready to be magnificent?'

He sighed. 'Yes, Mother. I am ready, willing and able. Delighted, in fact.' He offered his hand. 'Shall we?'

Nobody else was quite as rude as Lord Lakshin Opal but all made it clear he was tolerated rather than welcome in their own ways. Lady Anuja Ruby kept to her rooms, no doubt conserving her energy, and the other Deathless actively avoided him, though he was sure his name was often on their lips.

He constantly worried about his affairs back home. Had High Lord Yadavendra noticed his absence yet? Did his mother need him? What if there was an attack on one of his settlements? Though things had been eerily quiet in the Sapphire lands of late, he couldn't help but fear that now his back was turned, the creatures of the Wild would stir once more.

But he could not leave the Ruby High Lord's castle.

To do so would be to confirm the worst suspicions of the other houses. If he was going to win their trust, he had to stay until he had proven himself. He needed to triumph. And so he felt a guilty kind of relief when he was urgently summoned by Lady Anuja.

As before, she sat in the Ruby High Lord's throne. Now that he knew about her injury, it was easy to see that she still suffered from it. 'Lord Vasin, please be welcome and attentive. I have news.'

He grasped her wrist, and she his. 'I stand ready.'

She smiled, though it barely reached her tired eyes. 'Good. Fourboards is requesting a hunt and I need you to go in my stead.'

'Fourboards? Again?'

'Yes.'

'But it's only been . . . this is unbelievable!' The idea of a third hunt in the same place in less than a year was so absurd it was all he could do not to laugh. 'It makes no sense. Where will they find more tributes? How will they sustain the losses?'

'Fourboards has called for aid. It has offered a sacrifice and we must answer, except . . . ' she gestured at herself, 'for me to hunt would mean the end of this body. If things were different I might risk it, but my house needs one of its Deathless in the living world, and so I turn to you, Ruby-friend. Will you lead a hunt in my name?'

'You honour me.' This was an understatement, and more than he'd dared to hope for – she was giving him a chance to show that, in the right hands, House Sapphire could be trusted again. However, in the current climate, putting him in charge was controversial. The Opal and Peridot Deathless had been here longer, and had hunted around Fourboards before. They would not be happy. That too was an understatement.

'Is that a yes?'

'Of course,' he replied. 'I'll leave at once.'

She nodded in relief. 'Good,' she said, and then a second time, to herself. 'That's good.'

Vasin spoke his thoughts aloud. 'This is all connected somehow, I'm sure of it. The repeated attacks, the way the demons went after you, even what Quiverhive was up to on the Godroad.'

'I agree. But I don't know how or why. This is beyond me, Vasin. I need to bring my mother back now or there won't be a House Ruby left when she returns.'

He paused to look at her. This was a Ruby matter, and

not his place, but he had grave misgivings about a rushed rebirth. Subtlety had never been his strength, and Anuja sighed when she saw the expression on his face.

'An urgent summons for the Bringers of Endless Order is already on its way.'

'You know they won't like this either.'

'I do, but it is my decision to make and my burden to bear.'

'Forgive me,' he said, bowing.

'Of course. I have neither time nor energy for pettiness. Now go, prepare yourself, and take care with my hunters.' She lowered her voice. 'They are brave but their wings are fresh, and their spear-tips clean.'

'I will look after them as if they were my own.'

She inclined her head, dismissing him. 'Hunt well and thorough, my friend.'

Sa-at hid in his favourite tree, trying not to think about food. He should have found something hours ago but he'd been too miserable. Now it was dark and he had no choice but to wait until morning.

At least the tree was comfortable, the branches wide and curving, forming perfect resting places for his back and bottom. It hadn't always been this shape, but it had taken pity on him when he was small, and in return he had fed it, given it gifts, and the two had grown together.

He liked to sleep squished between the branches in a ball, feet propped up, knees tight against his chest. It gave him the sense of being held, the pressure of his own legs reimagined as the pressure of another.

Crowflies had settled on his feet, warming them. Despite

the comfort its closeness brought, Sa-at still sniffled from time to time, punctuating the night with comments like:

'It isn't fair.'

And:

'Why are Gatherers so horrible?'

And:

'I hate them. Stupid Tal. Stupid Rin.'

And:

'Next time I'll let the Spiders eat them all.'

The Birdkin regarded him but didn't answer, the tilt of its head communicating a most profound boredom.

'Next time I'll . . . ' Sa-at trailed off, then sighed. 'I hope Tal is alright. If I see him again, I'll tell him how I saved him and—'

Crowflies cawed derisively.

'—How *we* saved him and then he'll be our friend. I wish I could see him again.'

Sa-at sighed and his stomach grumbled.

Crowflies yawned.

Eyes, normal and faceted, closed, and the two slept.

When Sa-at woke again, it was still dark, Crowflies still sat on his feet, and a second Birdkin had arrived. It too had black feathers though its beak was grey rather than white.

'Hello. I'm Sa-at. Are you a friend of Crowflies?' It shrieked at him in reply, and he nodded. 'Thought so. I don't have any food, but you can shelter here if you want.'

A third Birdkin arrived, pushing through the leaves to stand next to the second one. Then three more came, all of the same stock.

Crowflies got off Sa-at's feet and hopped onto a nearby branch.

He had the feeling that something was about to happen, there was a sense of familiarity about it, the way the nerves and excitement jangled together in his tummy. A seventh Birdkin settled inches from his head, an eighth, next to Crowflies; who he noticed was standing differently from normal.

There was a uniformity about the Birdkin, and the more of them that arrived, the more alike they became in demeanour. The soft dark of the tree began to change, began to breathe, becoming a thing of its own. And within that feathered dark, a head emerged. Not a human head, but a thing much like it in shape. Its eyes were large, multifaceted orbs, it's nose a sharp triangle, the other features lost to the shadows. It pressed itself gently upon Sa-at so that their foreheads touched. There was a gentleness in the gesture, quieting but not quite dispelling his fear.

It spoke, and its voice issued soft from the assembled beaks, making the branch hum against his back.

'So the seed has become a stripling.'

At the sound of its voice, Sa-at remembered:

It is Murderkind.

Its name is Murderkind.

'Still quick. Good, this is good. I have need of quickness.'

'I know you. Are you my friend?'

'A blood-bound friend am I, and a greater friend you'll never have.'

Sa-at smiled at that, he liked the idea of having a great friend, it made him feel special. 'Did you come because I was lonely?'

'I came to grant your wish, and you came to grant mine.'

Sa-at wanted to help but he was no fool. Though he knew

Murderkind meant him no harm, knew it deep in his bones, he had grown up in the Wild and had learned not to agree to anything hastily. 'What do you want me to do?'

'There is a changing of the tides, a shifting of the powers. I wish to know what it means. Many demons flock to the Scuttling Corpseman's banner, many dance to its tune. This, I know. It is not right. This, I know. How the tune plays out, I know not.'

'You want me to talk to it?'

'No. Beware the Corpseman. Its kind were wiped out long before your seed spilled into the world. It should be, not. It should breathe, not. But it does, scuttling between life and not life, beyond my understanding.'

Sa-at felt relief, but also confusion. If it was beyond Murderkind then surely it was beyond him too.

'You are small, ungoverned by the laws of greater things. You may go where I cannot. Do, what I cannot. Strike, where I cannot. The Corpseman has allies. They will know things, they will tell you.'

'Why would they listen to me?'

'Because among these allies are the Red Brothers.'

I know them!

I've met them.

Broken memories flashed through his mind. Impressions, incoherent, and feelings. Sweat broke out on his skin and the knuckle of his missing finger began to tingle in an old echo of remembered pain.

I am afraid, he thought.

'Yes. Be afraid, this is good.'

'Why?'

'They owe you, for your flesh, for your suffering. Let the

hurt swell inside, and let the debt be all the greater. Go to them, demand retribution, demand their knowledge. Bring their understanding to me.'

'I don't want to.'

'If you do this, I will grant your wish for an unbound friend.'

Sa-at bit his lip. 'What kind of friend?'

'A sapling, like you. The one you want.'

'Tal?'

'Yes.'

'How do you know him?'

'I have tasted his ears. He is here, in the Wild, and he is in danger.'

'Is it bad?'

'He will not live to see the sunrise.'

'Where is he?'

'He weeps within my sight, close to the Red Brothers. Find one and you will find the other.'

'Tell me!'

'You agree, then? A wish for a wish?'

'Yes. Tell me, please.'

'Crowflies will show you.' Murderkind's head pulled up into the shadows, his last words carried in the fluttering of many wings. 'Be quick, be sharp, be triumphant.'

Birdkin scattered in all directions, their screeches caught in the leaves and recast on the wind. When they were gone, only Crowflies remained, settled again, its usual self. 'Sa-aat!' it said, and hopped from the branch, spreading its wings and taking flight.

Sa-at gave chase without a second thought.

CHAPTER EIGHT

There were rules to living in the Wild. Sa-at knew them, and he abided by them. He looked after the trees and they looked after him. Crowflies looked after him too, and Murderkind claimed to be his friend. He did not know why and he did not question it, things had always been that way.

However, Tal did not know the rules, he had proved that when he and the other Gatherers from Sagan nearly got eaten by the Spiderkin. The trees would not look after Tal, quite the opposite, and he would have no Birdkin on his shoulder to guide him.

Sa-at was painfully aware of this as he ran, chasing Crowflies through the nighttime. No starlight found its way this deep into the forest, and he navigated by touch and sound as much as sight. By day, the Wild was dangerous, by night, it was deadly, but not so for him. The leaves rustled appreciatively of his efforts, and the sound of the Birdkin's wings came from only one direction, the true one. His feet did not get tangled in the roots nor caught on the hanging vines. When he took a wrong turn, they waved out, brushing roughly, correcting, nudging him onwards.

Soon, just audible beneath the sound of wings, was the sound of crying, human crying. This spurred Sa-at on even more, for he knew that this sound would be like a siren's call to the demons that lurked just beyond his perception.

The flapping of wings slowed, stopped, and a familiar call sounded close by. He leapt between two trees, ducked under some branches, twisted through a tight space – brambles pulling at his coat of feathers – and then he was clear, standing in a place given faint illumination by the stars, Crowflies perched not far from his head.

Tal was stumbling in the dark less than six feet away, a miserable shadow, lost in all senses.

Sa-at's throat grew tight again but he forced himself to be brave. He took a deep breath and said: 'Hello.'

'Aargh!' replied Tal. The young man jumped into the air, then turned and ran headfirst into the nearest tree. There was a crack and another cry of pain, and Tal collapsed on the floor.

'Ssh,' Sa-at urged. 'You need to be like a Mousekin.'

Tal sprang up again. This time he backed away slowly, feeling his way. 'I'm not looking at you. I'm not looking.'

'You can't. It's too dark here.'

'I won't be tricked, I won't look!'

'Ssh! Don't shout or they'll get you.'

'What about you?'

Sa-at smiled, though the gesture was lost in the dark. 'I've already found you.'

Tal whimpered and continued to edge away.

'Don't be scared, Tal, I'm not here to eat you.'

'How do you know my name?'

'I saved you from the Spiderkin, remember?'

'Oh,' Tal stopped. 'I remember. Rin said you tried to kill me outside Sagan.'

'Not kill, save. You were sick. That's why you fell down. I saved you and took you home. You should have stayed there.'

He had the sense of Tal slumping. 'They threw me out.'

Sa-at felt bad and good about this at the same time. Tal was upset, and that was bad, but if he had nowhere else to go, he was more likely to need a new friend. 'Why?'

'My ears! They're all different now.' Crowflies cackle-cawed softly above them as he continued. 'Rin noticed and there was this big meeting and then they said I had to leave! I begged them, I did. Said I'd do anything, even asked to be the next tribute. It didn't work.'

I did this, thought Sa-at. *It is my fault. But if I hadn't got Crowflies to help, he'd have died. Him being alive is my fault too.* He wanted to say something to Tal, but the words escaped him. Somehow it was much more difficult talking to people than it was to demons or trees.

'Now I'm dead,' said Tal.

Sa-at forced the words out before his nerves could stop him. 'I could help.'

'What?'

'I could help you not be dead.' He reached out and touched the young man's arm.

'I knew it!' said Tal, brushing him off. 'You're a demon! I'm not agreeing to anything and I'm not looking at you! Get away from me!'

'I'm not,' Sa-at protested but it was no use, Tal was trying to run again. He didn't get far, tripping over the first thing he went past and crying out as something sharp cut into the thick leather of his gloves.

The scar on Sa-at's little finger began to itch and he absently scratched at it. He couldn't think of any way to make things better and Murderkind's words were sharp in his mind: '*He will not live to see the sunrise.*'

If only Tal would calm down and listen. Then he could explain and they could start being friends.

'Oh no,' said Tal, sounding anything but calm.

Sa-at squinted but couldn't see that anything had changed.

'Sa-aat!' said Crowflies with a note of warning. Then he understood. In the fall, a bramble must have got past the protection on the young man's hands, grazing them. There would be blood, just a tiny trivial amount, more a smear than a drop. But that was all it took.

A strange hush fell amid the trees, as if the creatures of the Wild had all paused in their dealings to sniff the air and listen. Every leaf swivelled on its branch to point at Tal.

'Oh no,' the young man said again. 'Oh no.'

This time, Sa-at didn't bother telling him to be quiet.

'Oh ho!' replied a voice. It was much deeper than Tal's, and rougher, and uglier. The sound of it made his scar itch like fire. In his guts, he knew that this was Crunch, one of the Red Brothers, and where there was one, the other two would not be far behind. Instinctively, he swung up into the tree next to Crowflies just as Crunch lumbered into view.

Tal was taller than Sa-at, and Crunch was much taller again. He was broader too, and in one meaty hand he held a bunch of burning leaves tied to a stick. He wore no clothes, though thick ropes of skin grew from his head, covering everything save for the red skin of his arms and toes. Big ears guided him, for Crunch had no eyes, his face dominated by a vertical mouth, half-open like a pair of sodden curtains. 'What's this? What's this? An unclaimed morsel?'

Eyesore, the second of the brothers, emerged on the other side of Tal. Physically, he was near identical, save that instead of a mouth, he had three eyes. He too carried a burning stick, and Sa-at realized that its purpose was not to guide, but to obscure. As Eyesore waved it behind him, plumes of grey smoke hung in the air, masking the odour of human blood.

'Is it plump?' asked Crunch.

Several clicks and pops could be heard as Eyesore worked his knuckles. Sa-at could only assume that he was communicating assent as Crunch's mouth began to water.

'Is it ripe?'

The third brother, Pits, came out behind Tal. Unlike them, he did not carry a torch. His hands unerringly found their way to Tal's shoulders, lifting the young man off the ground as if he were a babe. There were no features at all on Pits' face, just a single hole, a nostril, that he pressed against Tal's forehead.

For a horrible moment, Sa-at thought that Pits was going to inhale the gibbering young man's head completely, but then he dropped Tal between them and clicked his own knuckles.

'Good, good,' said Crunch, patting his belly. 'I was wasting away, so I was.'

If he did not do something quickly, Tal would be eaten, and Sa-at couldn't bear that. An idea, half grown, began to form. Murderkind had said that the Red Brothers owed him.

134

Perhaps he could use that favour to free his friend? But, if he used his only currency on Tal, he would not be able to find out what the Scuttling Corpseman was planning, and he would not be able to grant Murderkind's wish. Murderkind was his friend too, and he'd made it a promise.

Tal scrambled to his feet and tried to get away, but Eyesore caught his arm and swung him towards Crunch.

'Right,' said Crunch, catching Tal and pushing him towards Pits. 'Who gets first chunk?'

Sa-at bit his lip. He was afraid of the Brothers. He was afraid of speaking and giving himself away. He was afraid of doing nothing. He was afraid of failing his friends.

The Brothers closed in, their bodies three walls of meat, their arms, six bars of a fleshy cage. They challenged each other to be the first to sample Tal's flesh by striking each other's fists. There was a crack as the Brother's knuckles rapped together, hard enough to hurt, once, twice, and Pits withdrew his hands, three times, four, and Crunch raised his. 'Eyesore it is! Then me, then Pits, then we split what's left.'

Eyesore clapped, delighted. He took one of Tal's arms and began to slowly twist.

Safe on his branch, Sa-at began to shake.

'That's it!' said Crunch. 'Pop a bit out and give me a taste, I'll soften the bones and meat to paste.'

Pits clapped.

Tal screamed.

Eyesore continued to twist.

'W-Wait!' shouted Sa-at.

The twisting and the clapping and the screaming stopped. Three eyes, one nostril, and six ears all attended to him.

'What's this? What's this?'

Sa-at jumped down and took a step towards them. He didn't dare take a second, any closer and he'd be in reach of their long arms. 'You can't have him.'

Crunch laughed. 'We do have him. We have him first. Find your own morsel, Birdspawn.'

'No. Look again. I marked him.'

Pits began to sniff, Eyesore began to glare. First one eye narrowed, then the other, then the third. He guided his brother's hands to the edges of Tal's ears.

'See?' asked Sa-at.

'He's been nibbled!'

'Yes. I did that. He's mine.'

Crunch shrugged, making his ropey head-skin sway. 'Was yours. Ours now. Nibblings is over.'

The Brothers turned away, dismissing him.

'Wait!' They turned back and he had to swallow a few times to get his throat working. 'You . . . ' his voice trailed off to a whisper.

'What? We what?'

'Owe me. You owe me.'

The three brothers shook their heads. 'No.'

'Yes.' He held up his hand so that Eyesore could see his missing finger. 'You took a bite from me and you have to pay for it. I want . . . '

This was the moment. He already knew what he was going to do, the decision made in his heart some time ago, he just needed his courage to catch up. 'I want you to release my friend.'

Pits sniffed at him, suspicious, then the brothers reached out to each other, fingers dancing in one another's palms, conferring. 'We remember you now,' said Crunch when they had finished. 'You used to be much better. Much more tender.' He sighed. 'Shame. Anyway, I only had a taste and Pits only had a scrap. It was nothing.' The Brothers hands moved together again, and Crunch made an unhappy grumble. 'But fair is fair. We'll give you a toe, if you want.'

'I don't want his toe!'

'You can have his toe or you can have nothing.'

'I choose nothing.' And as he said those words, a terrible idea blossomed in his mind. The kind that once there, could not be ignored.

'Done!' said Crunch, 'The deal is done,' and the three of them turned back to Tal who began to wail.

'Give it to me then!' demanded Sa-at.

Crunch slapped a hand over Tal's mouth to silence him. 'Go away, or I might forget we're not supposed to eat you.'

'Pay my price and I'll go.'

The three brothers quickly conferred, then shook their heads as one, confused. 'We agreed we owe you nothing.'

'Yes,' replied Sa-at, and pointed. 'That's the nothing I want.' As Eyesore followed his finger he felt the fear inside up its tempo, transforming into a kind of manic energy.

Three eyes widened in shock as they realized what it was Sa-at was pointing at: the hole in the middle of Pits' face.

Crunch tried to protest, Eyesore gave him a pleading look, and Pits clasped his hands together, begging, but it was no use. The forest was watching, the deal was done, and all knew the rules. There was no going back.

With a strange solemnity, Eyesore and Crunch planted their burning sticks in the ground and walked slowly towards Pits, who, realizing what was about to happen, began to back away. He made two steps before being snared in the undergrowth. He twisted and turned, but his great strength did nothing against that of the forest, and soon he was obscured by the bodies of his brothers.

Sa-at knew that he should be moving but neither he nor Tal did, both captivated by the spectacle. Despite their bulk, there was a gentle grace about the way the Brothers moved. They worked in silence, the only sounds were those of Pits thrashing against them, of his breath coming fast and hot, misting the air above their heads. The sound of that breathing became strained, and the clouds of mist became plumes, then threads, then nothing. Something had happened. Something permanent. Somehow, the hole in his face, the one that he sensed with, that he breathed with, had gone.

Pits began to convulse in a different way but his brothers continued to hold him, firmly, tenderly, until the movements calmed, slowed, stopped, dead.

Sa-at would have stood there longer had the spell not been broken by an impatient beak tapping his shoulder. Moving as quietly as he could, he pulled one of the burning sticks from the ground and glanced at the Brothers to find them laying Pits out, heads bowed. He crept over to where Tal sat and took his arm. This time, there was no protest, and Sa-at was able to get him on his feet.

Using the weak light from the glowing leaves, Sa-at guided Tal, getting him to place each footstep so as not to disturb the forest floor.

They were just putting a few trees between them and the Brothers, when Crunch spoke. 'Don't leave without your price.'

Sa-at froze.

Tal tried to pull at his arm. 'Run for it!'

But Sa-at did not move, could not move. He was bound by the rules as surely as the Brothers were. There was no point trying to escape, it would only make things worse. The weight of that knowledge fell heavy on his heart and feet. 'Here,' he said, and gave Tal the stick. The light wouldn't last for long, but the scent would linger, keeping other predators at bay.

'Don't go,' said Tal.

'I'll find you, if I can.'

'Please don't go.'

There was nothing else to say, so Sa-at turned and walked back to the Brothers. Pits was still at their feet, his face a smooth triangle of red, flat and featureless.

Sa-at held out his hands and Eyesore slapped away his left while grabbing his right. He felt a pain as Eyesore pressed something into his palm, a pain so exquisite and so immediate that he did not even have time to call out.

The next thing he knew he was on his knees, clutching his hand to his chest, the pain like a living thing writhing in his palm. He felt his skin opening as the aperture that had been in Pits' face burrowed inside, settling into its new home.

'We will get you,' said Crunch. 'We will grind your feet and eat them. We will vomit you and make you eat it. We will grind your hands and eat them. We will vomit you and make you eat it. We will grind your shins and eat them . . . '

Somehow, Sa-at managed to get up. He was aware that tears were running in rivers down Eyesore's face and that Crunch was moaning as he talked. Crowflies was shrieking, plucking at his sleeve. Somehow, he managed to stagger away, while Crunch shouted after him.

'. . . We will grind your hips and eat them. We will vomit you and make you eat it. We will grind your wrists . . . '

Sa-at kept going and the words followed, carried in whispers by the trees.

The drum beats were like those of his own castle during a hunt, but they were not his drums. The drummers were different too, as was the size and construction of the castle, not to mention that the rubies in the walls had a different resonance to the sapphire he was used to, and they clustered in strange ways. All of these things combined to make a sharp but subtle dissonance in Vasin's heart. He knew the rituals, but felt as if he was a pace behind, each beat and change seeming to come too fast.

Worries nibbled at his thoughts, about his ability to lead the hunt, about the changing Wild, about the state of his house and the fate of his mother, following him as he entered the Chrysalis Chamber. It was only when the crystal plates of his armour were against his skin that they began to fade. As he rose up on his Sky-legs, he also rose beyond all other concerns.

I can do this. I will do this.

In his own castle, the glass that formed three of the walls would open onto a balcony where he could address his people. Here, he was forced to ascend wing-width stairs painted to resemble a cloud-touched sky. As he took them three at a time, he began to have a new sense of unease. Usually, a hunt began with an address, something to set the tone and bond the crowd, such that their shouts and song would empower the hunters' wings when they took flight. But he did not know these people well, nor had he hunted with Lakshin or Quasim before. A good speech came from the heart, but his was full of misgivings.

How can I speak truth here?

The stairs brought him out into a long and narrow court-yard. The suns were only just clearing the walls, the gold light of Fortune's Eye splayed through the crenellations, making finger-beams overhead. He was used to standing above the crowd but in the Ruby castle, the crowd were lining battlements, packing stairways and standing on boxes, all looking down on him.

In the middle of the space stood another Deathless, garbed in glittering green. Elaborate flutes of peridot twisted away from his elbows, shoulders, and the sides of his helmet, making it look as if jets of water had been frozen mid-motion. His wings were smaller than any Vasin had seen before, providing extra manoeuvrability at the cost of power. It would take great skill to use such wings well.

Let us hope Lord Quasim Peridot possesses such skill.

Quasim had obviously been enjoying the sole attention of the crowd. As Vasin emerged into the light, the Peridot Deathless was bantering with the hunters in a loud voice. ' . . . Perhaps so, but mine is bigger, and a more interesting shape!'

The laugh of the crowd was raucous, the kind of thing he'd expect at a feast, not a hunt. It was disrespectful, wrong, and worse than that, dangerous. *What is Quasim thinking!*

He was so outraged that for a while he couldn't find the words to speak. Perhaps something of his feeling communicated itself however, for laughter faded and died, and all eyes gradually turned to him. It was time for the speech, but traditionally, all had to be present before he started, and they were missing a Deathless. *Where is Lakshin?*

In two bounding steps, Quasim crossed from the hunters to stand in front of him. 'Greetings, Vasin, lone hunter of the Sapphire Everlasting. Greetings, Vasin, Bane of the Scuttling Corpseman. And thrice greetings.'

Quasim offered an arm and they clasped wrists. Lone hunter was a not very subtle barb but he didn't dare rise to it. 'Greetings to you Quasim, child of the Peridot Everlasting, your stout heart and strong arm are always welcome in my company.'

They raised their hands together and the crowd cheered, though not as loudly as they might. *They feel Anuja's absence keenly, as do we all.*

He took a moment to appraise the three groups of hunters that would fly with them. Quasim's were a seasoned block, hard of face and muscular, while Lakshin's were a mix of old and new, some barely more than apprentices, others veterans of the sky. The ones that Anuja had provided for him to lead were all young, their faces flitting from pride to terror. He could see the training written in their bodies however, and was heartened to see that despite being rushed, their wings appeared sturdy. He wouldn't know their worth for sure until they were in the sky.

When it will be too late.

'Aha!' boomed Quasim. 'Here is our beloved Opal.'

Lakshin came out to greet them more stiffly, speaking quietly rather than to the crowd. The warmth he and Quasim shared made the cold regard Vasin received even more pointed. Like them, Lakshin was fully armoured. His Gardener-smiths had carved feathers onto the chest, back and legs, giving Lakshin the appearance of some giant bird. The work was exquisite but made the armour and its wearer

seem more vulnerable somehow. Lakshin's spear was shorter
and lighter than Vasin's, designed more for throwing than
thrusting. A short crystal blade was fastened at his belt,
curved like the wings they wore. Vasin found himself wishing
for one of his own.

It was time to begin his speech but as he was taking
breath, Quasim cut across him, almost as if he believed
himself to be in charge.

'Are you ready?' he asked the hunters.

'Aye!' they replied together.

'And are you ready?' he asked the crowd.

'Aye!' they shouted.

Quasim clicked his gauntleted fingers and a servant struggled over under the weight of a giant sword cut from a
single chunk of peridot. It was almost as big as her, and at
one point obscured her entirely, giving Vasin the impression
it was floating across the courtyard in accordance with
Quasim's will. He took it from her as if it weighed nothing
and pointed it towards the sky. 'I too am ready!'

Clearly, the blade was lighter than it appeared, but it still
looked unwieldy, as unwelcome an addition as Quasim's
impromptu address, which had further ruined the rhythm
of his preparations.

Vasin lifted his own spear to get their attention. There
was a brief flip of nerves in his stomach as he drew breath
to speak, and then they were gone, and the words, as always,
were there.

'The Wild has been especially cruel to House Ruby of late.
So many hunts, so close together. In all my lifecycles I have
never seen the like. We often talk of bravery and courage,'
he glanced towards Quasim as he said this, 'but we rarely

talk of fear or pain or loss. House Ruby has suffered and it has bled. It has suffered and bled to hold back the Wild. It has suffered and bled so that our lives might be that bit safer. It has suffered and bled for Opal, Peridot, Sapphire, Spinel, Tanzanite, and Jet.

'Once when I came here, and I was in danger, Lady Anuja answered my call. When my wings failed, she was there to catch me, and you,' he swept his spear across the crowd, 'you were there to catch her.

'House Ruby has never failed its friends, and I promise you that we will not fail you today. It is our turn to suffer and bleed for you.' He paused for a moment to feel the thudding of the drums. All were playing now, the energy building, thrumming through the castle floor, making the crystal in their wings hum softly. 'Now, tell me, in the name of Lady Anuja, she who speaks with House Ruby's voice: who leads this hunt?'

'Vasin, of the Sapphire Everlasting, leads this hunt,' came the chorused reply.

'And who hunts with him?'

'I, Quasim, of the Peridot Everlasting.'

'I, Lakshin, of the Opal Everlasting.'

'And who hunts with us?'

'We do!' called the amassed hunters.

'And who sings us on our way?'

The crowd roared at them, and he felt the pressure of their combined voice pressing on his wings, threatening to lift him off his Sky-legs. He took a deep breath, and shouted back at them, inviting Quasim and Lakshin and the hunters to join in. 'I said who sings us on our way? Who sings us? Who?'

'Who?' chanted the hunters.

And then they began to run, the bellow of the crowd chasing behind.

The courtyard was long and narrow, funnelling them towards the main gates. Unlike his own castle there was no bridge here, and the arch opened out into empty air.

Drum beats kept them all in step, their Sky-legs bending with each stride before flinging them forward, the chorus at their backs flinging them forward, the very air pulsing with the power of it.

In his own hunts he would drop down and the strength of his people would hold him. Here, they were propelled, getting faster and faster, until the running became flying, through the archway, over the edge, hurled from the castle like a flight of winged arrows.

Each one of them fought to control the currents at their backs, and to stay on course. Quasim was one of the first, darting ahead on his back so he could wave at everyone.

Show off, thought Vasin. In his first lifecycle he'd have been tempted to match the Peridot, but not this one. Though he was sure he could outperform Quasim in the sky, today was not about him as Vasin the hunter. It was about him as Vasin, High Lord in waiting, and it was about House Ruby. It was a day for being careful and sure.

As Quasim's hunters scrambled to follow their lord, Vasin signalled Anuja's flight, then banked slowly, giving them plenty of time to read and follow his actions. It was not the most efficient way to do things, but it was the most likely way to keep them in formation.

Satisfied that they were on course, he glanced back to see that Lakshin was following, but was further back than he'd expected. The Opal was struggling. It struck him that there was a similarity between Lakshin and his brother, Gada. Both were officious, and both used their stern front to hide their inadequacies. It was possible Lakshin had suffered an injury on the last hunt and not mentioned it, and like Vasin, he might be holding back to support an inexperienced hunter. It was also possible he was terrible in the air.

He was glad Anuja had played it safe with this hunt's timing. Most began just before dawn, the tributes starting their run while it was dark to lure as many demons as possible. By the time the hunters arrived, the suns would be peeking over the horizon, dissuading other demons from joining in, and allowing everyone to travel home in the light.

Given how strange things had been, Anuja had opted to delay, allowing the suns to rise and maximize their chances of coming back alive.

The swamp spread out below them, peppered with islands and clumps of trees. Thick clouds of insects swirled above the dirty water, gathering to greet the first tribute as she burst into view. From this distance she was little more than a stick-figure with a firefly torch.

Quasim signalled that he had seen the tribute, then began to turn over, preparing to dive.

'Wait!' shouted Vasin, displaying his palm to emphasize the point, but Quasim ignored him, plunging down at a steep angle. His hunters took longer to follow, unable to match their lord's agility in the sky. Even when they arrived, there would be few places to land, and many for demons to rise from the water . . .

Vasin looked back again. His own hunters were still

catching up to his position, Lakshin's were even further back. Unable to join the rash charge of the Peridot Deathless without abandoning Anuja's people, he watched, frustrated, as the swamp began to stir.

CHAPTER NINE

Satyendra was frustrated. He'd been ready to face the High Lord, and then, at the last minute, Yadavendra had changed his mind and postponed their lunch. He and his mother had spent a fretful day preparing themselves for a summons at any moment.

None had come.

They'd all slept badly and felt worse as a result.

As for Yadavendra himself, he hadn't left his rooms. According to the servants' gossip, he'd neither eaten nor slept, but they'd heard constant movement.

Satyendra wondered if the waiting was one of Yadavendra's constant tests or whether the High Lord was as mad as he sometimes appeared.

And then, out of nowhere, a summons had arrived, brought by a hunter, still in her wings despite being grounded.

Come on then, High Lord, I'm ready for you and your tests.

It was a delicate balance he had to strike – to seem able

enough a match for Lord Rochant to keep Yadavendra happy, yet not be too perfect. To have made enough progress since the last visit to avoid reprimand, but to leave room for more work to be done. The chaotic subjectivity of his judge made this almost impossible, but Satyendra was a living, walking impossibility.

I should not be here, but I am. Every day is a scramble that I manage to survive. Today will be no different.

Yadavendra's hunters marched behind them. They too were afraid, his mother had seen to that. Most of the time she irritated him. She worked too much, and when she wasn't doing her duty she was prattling on about its importance. But sometimes, when she showed her steel, he saw a kindred spirit. And though he rarely admitted it to himself, he knew deep down that without her, he would not have survived his first year, let alone his seventeenth.

Most of the castle's staff had made themselves scarce, so it was mainly guards and a few unfortunates that he encountered on his way to the feast hall. More rigid salutes, more unease to soak up as he passed by.

It annoyed him that his mother sang for entry when she clearly didn't need to. *Doesn't she see that it makes her appear weak?* It also annoyed him when she was cut off partway through by the High Lord waving them in with an irritated hand.

Inside, the tables were empty, their food conspicuous by its absence. Yadavendra stood by the window, massive on his Sky-legs, sunslight flaming on the edges of his wings. *How small we must seem to him. How puny.*

'Ah, the young Satyendra arrives at last. Come forward so that I can greet you properly.'

A ripple of revulsion passed through him but he made sure it did not get near his face. Though he wanted to glance at his mother for one last bit of support, he did not.

There is nothing she can do anyway.

He crossed the space with faux eagerness, as if his love for the High Lord made him forget the proper decorum. Most thought the best way to please was to be perfect in all things but Satyendra knew that was too simplistic. People wanted perfection, but they also wanted to be the one to break that perfection. It was a subtle art, and one that he'd spent a lifetime honing.

A smile burst onto his face, all teeth and joy, and he bowed low.

Yadavendra put a hand on Satyendra's shoulder. 'I am pleased to see you have recovered yourself.'

Recovered myself? What is he talking about? What has Pik done?

The weight of the gauntlet on his shoulder was heavier than it should be, and through the fabric of his cloak, he could feel the skin that was being pressed down on beginning to prickle.

'Forgive me, my High Lord, I knew you were coming yesterday, and Mother had told me to prepare myself but when I saw you in the Chrysalis Chamber I . . . ' He trailed off to try and show that he was struggling to put his joy of seeing the High Lord into words but instead of pleasing Yadavendra, it had the opposite effect, and he felt the grip on his shoulder tighten.

'Don't falter, Rochant is always clear in his intent.'

'I meant to say that my memories were a poor substitute for seeing you in person. Forgive me.'

'Of course.' Satyendra was pulled into an embrace, his right cheek crushed into the armour of Yadavendra's belly. 'None who love the house as you do need ever fear. It is not my forgiveness you should seek, but to do better. To be better.'

'I will.'

Now well inside Yadavendra's aura, he was paralysed by it, and where his bare flesh was touching the glowing crystal, it quickly began to burn. And with it came the terror of discovery. It wasn't the first time he'd endured being close to the High Lord but this was worse than normal for some reason. Perhaps it was the sunslight charging the armour, or perhaps it was the High Lord's sterner than usual demeanour, or perhaps it was because Satyendra was changing, getting older. In that moment he didn't really care for the why. He could feel his facial muscles moving strangely, contracting, drawing back into his skull. *It's as if they're trying to get away.* Though it sounded absurd, he knew it was true, his body was literally trying to turn itself inside out in an effort to break contact.

Terror coursed through him, however he dared not pull away, to do so would be to reject his High Lord, all he could do was endure, gritting his teeth and holding his breath. Whatever strength he had so recently gathered into himself was quickly burned through, so that when he was finally released, he was left gasping.

'Sit,' said Yadavendra. 'Let us eat.'

Satyendra turned carefully to keep the right side of his face pointing towards the wall. The area around his cheek felt wrong somehow, and he was worried it would show. Though his mother's lectures about his allergic reaction were well known to him, to the rest of the castle they were a well-kept secret.

A couple of the hunters filed in, taking up posts around the room while the others sat down on the cushions around the table. It was strange watching them all delicately try to get in position without bumping into each other, for they too still wore their wings, breaking tradition to show solidarity with their master. It was wildly impractical and in other circumstances, highly amusing.

While that was going on, Satyendra risked bringing a hand to his cheek. It was hot, and he could feel the flesh settling under his palm, strange ridges smoothing out, like the spines of a fish slipping beneath the waves.

'Come and join us,' said his mother.

Their eyes met and he saw such pity there it made the hate boil up inside. *What did she see? What is happening to me?* But he took the hint and went to sit at the right side of Rochant's throne.

'No,' said Yadavendra, who had remained by the window. 'Take Rochant's place.' At Chandni's obvious surprise, he added. 'Not for the whole meal of course. I wish to see how he sits.'

Like his mother, Satyendra was not the tallest of people, but he had inherited her posture as well as her height. He tried to sit as he imagined Rochant would. Straight, but not rigid, open but not aggressive, thoughtful but not passive. The scrutiny was unpleasant, but nothing he wasn't used to. Though his cheek was starting to feel better, he tilted his head down and to the right, just in case.

'He has his manner, does he not, Honoured Mother?'

'Yes,' she replied, and she looked as if she believed it too, the pride evident in her face.

'Yes,' said Yadavendra, holding up a hand in front of his eye as if to frame the image between thumb and index finger. 'His aspect is just so. Uncanny. It is as if he were among us again already. You may return to your seat now, Satyendra.'

A group of servants began setting down a variety of dishes. Most of it was finger food, save for a small bowl of soup set at the head of the table. Satyendra made a play of waiting for them to finish their work to give the right side of his face as long as possible to settle before taking his usual place.

The High Lord perched uncomfortably on the edge of Rochant's throne and signalled for everyone to begin, though he himself made no move to pick up his spoon, nor even remove his sapphire helm. With evident relief, the hunters started to eat, making short work of what was put out. His mother seemed prepared for this however, new dishes appearing as quickly as the empty bowls were whisked away.

For Satyendra, it was a tortuous affair. He knew that everything he did was being scrutinized and evaluated, measured against a figure he had never met. Yadavendra made no secret of his fascination, watching with birdlike intensity. 'What do you think of the lizard wings, young Satyendra?'

'Soft in all the right places, my High Lord.'

'Are you going to have more?'

He reached towards the bowl but then noticed his mother's slight frown and changed direction, instead picking up a small cube of cheese. 'Perhaps later, I want to enjoy the other dishes first.'

Yadavendra nodded. 'And why is that?'

'Because I want to know what my guests are experiencing.'

A look, meaningful, passed between Chandni and the High Lord. 'Does that mean you will try the soup?'

There was something in the manner of the question that gave him pause. A quick glance down the table confirmed that there were no other bowls like it. He looked back to Yadavendra, the man was clearly enjoying the exchange, the part of his mouth visible through the helmet twitching towards a smile.

'I am curious . . . but no. It is a gift, prepared especially for you.'

'And if I insisted?'

'Then I would obey.'

He was rewarded with a full smile. Up close, he could see how gaunt Yadavendra's face had become. *Even thinner than I remember, and yet he seems as strong as ever.*

The meal continued, the hunters talking amongst themselves in low voices while Chandni and the High Lord exchanged polite conversation about the state of the castle, the weather, mixed in with shared reminiscence about Satyendra's early years, and veiled references to the time before that, which, if they were to be believed was much better than this one. *It's as if all three suns shine from Rochant's arse, the way they go on.*

After a third course had been devoured by the hunters, Yadavendra signalled that he was finished, asking that the soup (which was now cold) be left for him to enjoy at his convenience. 'Thank you, Honoured Mother. You may leave us now.' He gestured to his hunters. 'You also.'

Chandni stood and bowed, catching Satyendra's eye as she did so. It was hard to read her look, not least because she gave so little away, but Satyendra knew her well enough to guess: she desired to show concern, that she was thinking of him, and remind him to stay wary. All obvious and unnecessary.

Besides, he thought bitterly, *her encouragement only urges me faster towards my death.*

Two by two, the hunters stood, saluted and left the chamber, following Chandni out until they were alone.

'You have his manner, yes, that is beyond doubt, but I wonder, do you have his mind?'

Satyendra hoped this was a rhetorical question.

'As you know,' Yadavendra continued, 'Lord Rochant is known for his wisdom, and I have come to trust his advice above all others.' He pointed his jewel-bladed staff at Satyendra. 'Let us pretend that he stands before me now, ready to offer guidance.

'As you know, my sister, Nidra Un-Sapphire, betrayed us to the Wild, the second Deathless to do so in our history. It is our shame to be the only house to have failed so, and it is my duty to ensure it never happens again. So my question to you is this: how can I test the loyalty of my Deathless? How can I truly know that they will not follow my sister's path?'

He blinked. This was an impossible question! Rochant would at least know all of the other Deathless personally. Satyendra had met Lord Vasin a handful of times and the others once or twice that he could remember. It seemed like he'd impressed Yadavendra on the visit so far, perhaps it would be okay to fail on this one task – if he was to put off the rebirth ceremony, it may even be advisable.

'You can't.'

Yadavendra's eyes narrowed. 'That is your answer?'

'You won't ever know for sure if they are tempted or not, and any test can be cheated.' He could feel Yadavendra's regard cooling with every word and it struck him that perhaps this was more than just a test. The High Lord really did want advice on how to manage the other Deathless. 'I'm sorry but that's the truth.'

The staff made a contemptuous flick towards the door. 'Leave me.'

He gave a deep bow and turned to go. A part of him was pleased to have failed, but another was worried, and yet another annoyed not to have a better answer. *How pathetic am I to want to please my executioner?*

And yet he did want that. Some part of his mother's hated need to be right had seeped into him over the years, and it tugged at him until he stopped and turned round. 'The answer, my High Lord is not to test them at all.'

Yadavendra's gaze snapped up to meet his own. 'What did you say?'

'I said that you should not test them.'

'Go on.'

'You should motivate them.'

'What kind of motivation did you have in mind?'

The truth was he didn't, but Satyendra was used to making things up, his quick mind weighing his words in the breath he took to speak them. 'You have the power to make and unmake Deathless. Find another traitor, make an example of them.'

'I have already done this with the punishment of Nidra Un-Sapphire.'

'Do it again, my High Lord, and there will be no doubt.'

'And if there is no obvious traitor?'

'Unmake the one that pleases you least and put another in their place that you have chosen. Find someone that you trust as well as Lord Rochant and raise them.'

There was a long pause, but he knew his answer had pleased Yadavendra. 'Are you suggesting I act without proper cause?'

'No, my High Lord. I am saying that there is no cause more proper than yours. Fear will keep your Deathless in line. Make them fear you more than they fear the Wild and they'll never be tempted.'

'Very well.' Yadavendra surged to his feet, forcing Satyendra to crane his neck to look up at him. 'Which Deathless should I make an example of?'

He wasn't sure if they were pretending any more. How could the High Lord even voice such a question? How could he possibly answer it? It certainly wasn't his place. Was Yadavendra leading him into some kind of verbal trap or was he serious? He certainly seemed serious.

And another thought, a darker one, was emerging in Satyendra's mind. *How can I turn this to my advantage?*

He began to talk, paying close attention to Yadavendra's reactions as he spoke. The crystal armour made his face harder to see, and its aura made him harder to read, in fact it was mildly unpleasant for Satyendra to look at directly. 'Lord Rochant and Lady Yadva were both elevated by you, so they are beyond question.' *He nods in agreement, but with less enthusiasm for his daughter than I expected. Interesting.* 'Lord Umed,' he paused for just a moment, seeing a flicker of concern cross the High Lord's features, 'has served the house well for a long time and always supported you, leaving Lord Gada and Lord Vasin.'

'This is all well and good but you have not made a decision. If you were advising me as Lord Rochant does, which would you choose?'

He'd been unable to glean much by the mention of their names. Assuming that this wasn't all a terrible mistake, he'd narrowed it down to the two likeliest candidates. 'I assume both of your nephews are coming here for the rebirth?'

'They are.'

'Then they can work to keep your favour. Let them learn quietly that you suspect a traitor. Test them, one against the other, and see which one shines the most.'

Yadavendra banged his staff upon the ground in appreciation. 'Yes! Yes. This could work. You are a devious one, young Satyendra. We could not hope for a finer Honoured Vessel.'

'You have always honoured me, my High Lord. Might I ask for one more honour?'

'Honour is given, not asked for.'

'Then, might I give one more piece of advice, in Lord Rochant's voice?'

'Very well.'

'When you make your example, there will be space for a new Deathless. I ask that you consider me.'

Yadavendra laughed. 'If things had been different, perhaps I would have. I have no doubt that Rochant's grandchild would serve me well. But you are the last of his line, and there is no other.'

'But if another could be found?'

'Enough. There is no other. There is only you. Another reason why you are so dear to me.'

Satyendra bowed deep, a picture of humility, but his thoughts were anything but.

Here is my chance to cheat death. I have to find another

of Rochant's blood to take my place. And if they really don't exist, I'll fake one.

Sa-at's hand was curled into his chest, which was curled into his body, which was curled tight into a ball. It still hurt, but pressing it tight eased the pain slightly. The best thing to do was to have his thumb touching the knuckle of his missing finger, to keep his palm squeezed shut. He did not want to open his hand as he was sure that if he did so, something else would open inside it: the little nothing he had stolen from Pits.

Just the thought of that was enough to make him feel ill.

He'd stumbled through the trees for as long as he could, letting Crowflies guide him through the dark until they'd come to a hollow tucked within a hill. There, he'd collapsed, falling straight into restless sleep.

Several times through the night he'd woken, sweaty, sure that the remaining Red Brothers were standing over him. But they were merely phantoms, quickly blinked away.

The throbbing in his hand was real, however, as were the threats of vengeance. Sa-at knew that Crunch and Eyesore would come for him now, no matter the consequences. Either he would kill them or they would kill him. That was clear and undeniable. One night ago, his life had been simple. Now he had true enemies, and he had failed to keep his promise to Murderkind.

He wasn't sure which of those things worried him more.

It was only when sunslight began to light up the canopy overhead that Sa-at realized Crowflies had gone. This in itself wasn't unusual, the Birdkin often went off to pursue its own matters, but when he was hurt, it tended to stay close.

'Crowflies?'

He sat up, propping himself with his left arm, keeping his right close to his body, and looked around.

There was no sign of it, but in a small divot next to him were several berries and a dead Wormkin. Sa-at ate them greedily, even though cold Wormkin was one of his least favourite things.

He wasn't sure if they'd been left for him by Crowflies, some other creature of the Wild, or by the hill itself, so to be on the safe side he spoke a general thanks and then kissed his middle and index fingers, letting a little saliva catch on the tips before smearing it on the inside of the hollow.

Just as he was wondering what to do next, he heard clumsy feet scrambling up the hill. By the time they were passing overhead, he'd identified their owner, and smiled for the first time that day. 'Hello, Tal.'

There was a squeal of surprise, and then: 'Is that you?'

'Yes.'

'Where are you? I can't see you? Suns! Are you dead?'

'No, I'm down here.'

The footsteps came closer, then Tal's thick boots appeared, dangling over the edge of the hollow in front of Sa-at. He prodded the back of Tal's leather-clad ankle. 'Down here.'

'Aargh! Don't do that.'

'Sorry.'

With a plop, Tal slipped down and landed. He was still clutching the stick Sa-at had given him, though the leaves tied to the top had long since gone out, leaving a bumpy black smudge behind. He stared at Sa-at and Sa-at stared back, both suddenly shy. Tal looked cold, the edges of his ears bright red, his nose pinched and sore. He cleared his throat. 'Can I . . . can I sit with you?'

'Yes.'

There wasn't much room, but Tal managed to jam himself in. 'Ah, that's better. It's so good to sit down.' He rested his head against the earth behind them and closed his eyes. 'And out of the breeze too. I thought I was going to . . . going to . . .'

Sa-at waited for Tal to finish his sentence but he didn't. After a couple of minutes the other boy's breathing became deeper, heavier, each exhalation ending in a sigh. Then, very slowly, his head began to loll sideways until it came to rest against Sa-at's.

Somehow, things didn't seem quite as bad as they were before. He was still scared. All of his problems remained, and yet his heart refused to stay heavy.

The other boy woke up with a start, lifting the stick as if to ward off attack. When it was clear there was no immediate threat, he lowered it again. 'Did I go to sleep?' Sa-at nodded and Tal looked appalled. 'I'm so rubbish!'

'Why?'

'Because we're in the Wild! You're never supposed to sleep in the Wild.'

'I do.'

Tal's eyes widened and his mouth made a small pale circle. 'Are you a demon?'

'No.'

'Really?'

'Yes.'

161

He thought about that for a while and then seemed to slump. 'I believe you. I probably shouldn't but, well, I don't have much choice do I? I, er, I wanted to thank you.'

'Why?'

'For saving me from those demons. They were the Red Brothers weren't they?'

Sa-at shivered, the mention of their name making the threat real again. 'Yes.'

Tal looked into his eyes. 'Thank you for saving me from them. I've never been so scared in all my life. Except maybe that time when the Spiderkin got me. No, actually, this was worse because it went on for much longer. Anyway, thank you. I owe you my life.'

Some of the horror gripping Sa-at's heart melted a little. It felt nice being thanked.

'Is it okay if I stay with you?' asked Tal. 'Only I don't know where else to go.'

I'd like that, thought Sa-at. He was trying to work up the courage to say so but ended up nodding instead.

'Good. So, we should get to know each other. You're not supposed to travel with folk you don't know. It's bad luck.' When Sa-at didn't reply, he added. 'What's your name?'

'Sa-at.'

Tal pulled a face. 'That's weird.'

It felt as if he'd been slapped in the face, though he could not articulate why. Was his name weird? He'd never thought so. It was simply who he was. Just like Crowflies was Crowflies and rocks were rocks.

'Is it a Wildborn name?'

Sa-at shrugged, which was awkward in the confined space. Although Tal's shoulder was pinning him against the side of the hollow, it was pleasingly warm, comforting, like his favourite tree but much, much better.

'What does it mean,' asked Tal, 'your name?'

He shrugged again.

'It must mean something. All Wildborn names do.'

'Do they?'

Tal nodded, though Sa-at wasn't sure he believed him. 'Course they do, everyone knows that. Hey, have you got anything to eat?'

'No.' He checked the divot which was now mostly under Tal's leg, just in case some food had miraculously appeared. It had not.

'Do you know where to find some? I'm hungry, and I don't know this part of the forest. I'm not sure what's good to eat and what's not.'

'Yes.'

'Great! Can we go now?'

Sa-at looked down at his hand and frowned. It was still sore and he felt exhausted from the events of the previous night.

'You should wear gloves, like me,' said Tal. 'Don't you worry about getting cut?'

He shook his head. Gatherers must be very clumsy to keep getting cut all the time. If they were more careful, like him, they wouldn't need to wear so much.

'Is it hurt bad? It's not bleeding, is it?'

It was a good question. He hadn't noticed any blood, but then, he hadn't dared to look. He gave a miserable shrug.

'Can I see? If it is there's this sap Rin was talking about that could plug it. Course, I'm not sure which tree it comes from, but I'd know the sap if I saw it again. It's more orangey than most, and really thick too. Do you know it?'

'No.'

'Hmm. Show it anyway? We can't let it go bad, can we?'

Sa-at hesitantly offered his closed fist to Tal, who gently turned it over.

'I don't see any blood. That's a good sign. Can you open it?'

He closed his eyes and took a deep breath and held it, uncurling the fingers one by one. As he did so, he felt the skin of his palm move in a way he'd never known before, opening. It felt tender and the air tickled it differently, feeling especially cold, fresh and alive with information. He got a sudden waft of Tal's scent. The musk of his sweat, the different tones of hair, skin and clothing, all so distinct, and then bile, also Tal's, sharp, tingling in his nostrils. No, not his nostrils, his *palm*.

'I think I'm going to be sick,' said Tal, getting up and hurrying away.

Sa-at forced himself to open his eyes. He saw bruising that corresponded with the stiff pain, but it wasn't as bad as he feared. However, that wasn't what had disturbed Tal. For in the centre of his palm was an oval hole, or, more precisely, as it did not penetrate through to the back of his hand, a pit. Despite its shallowness, however, the hole was dark, unfathomable, the sunlight unable to illuminate it fully.

When he looked up, he was surprised to see Tal's stick pointing at his throat.

'Tell me again that you're not a demon.'

'I'm not.'

Am I?

I know Crowflies is a demon.

I know Tal is a human.

But what am I? Why do I not have a human name? Why did Crunch call me Birdspawn? Was it just a name or is it what I am?

The stick wavered. 'That was the price, wasn't it? When you saved me.'

'Yes.'

Tal sat down again, but further away this time, his back to the cold. 'Does it hurt?'

'Yes.'

'Badly?'

'No.'

He wanted to cry and he wanted to be held, the way the wings used to hold him, or the arms that he barely remembered. He wanted it so badly. But he couldn't bring himself to ask Tal, nor could he allow himself to cry. If he started, he might never stop.

'Are you okay?' asked Tal.

'No.'

'You can tell me about it, if you want.'

'I wasn't supposed to bargain with the Brothers for you,' he held up his palm, 'or for this. I was supposed to learn about the Scuttling Corpseman.'

'Why? The only thing you need to know about the—about that demon is to stay away from it, and to never say its name!'

'I don't know but it's important. And, I made a promise.'

'Can you break it?'

Sa-at's face began to crumple. 'No.'

'What would happen if you did?'

'I promised Murderkind I'd learn what the Corpseman—'

Tal flinched at the word '—is doing and in return it helped me to find you and save you.'

'So you're saying that if you don't learn the stuff you need to, something would happen to me?'

'Yes.'

'Something bad?'

'Yes.'

Tal touched his lobeless ears. 'Worse than has already happened?'

Sa-at bit his lip. 'Oh yes.'

'Then we have to keep the promise. Together, yes?'

Sa-at nodded.

'Okay then.' Tal paused, frowned. 'How are we going to do that?'

'I don't know.'

'We could go to Sorn. Everyone says to keep away from it because the Corpseman is there. But if I needed to find it, that's where I'd go.'

Yes, his friend was right. He should have thought of that himself. He made to stand up, and noticed Tal hadn't moved. 'Will you come?'

'To Sorn? I . . . I'm not sure I can. The truth is I'm afraid. I mean, I'm afraid of the Wild, and I'm afraid of being alone but I think I'm even more afraid of the Scuttling Corpseman. How many times have I said its name now? You're not supposed to say it more than three, or it appears. At least, I think it was three.' He looked over his shoulder, just in case.

'I'm afraid too,' said Sa-at. 'But . . . ' he trailed off.

'But what?'

'I'd be less afraid if you came with me.'

'Well, I can't go home, and I probably won't last the day on my own, so . . . Okay, but only if you promise that we can forage on the way. I'm starving!'

'I promise.' Sa-at offered to help Tal up.

Tal lifted his hand but then seemed to notice Sa-at's injury again and quickly lowered it, using his spear to lever himself upright. 'Then it's agreed. We'll go to Sorn. Together.'

Vasin circled above Lord Quasim's position, thoughts whirling. It had all gone wrong and the hunt had barely started. Yes, the Peridot Lord had found the first of the tributes, and yes, he had rushed to their side with impressive speed. But the tribute was dashing across a narrow strip of land surrounded by swamp. Any hunters that landed there would have a hard time taking flight again. Shapes moved within the swamp's waters, most likely Murkers, but the mud-stirred surface was so dark that a variety of monsters could be concealed there.

If he brought the other two flights down to support Quasim, they'd be fighting for spaces to land, getting in each other's way as much as helping. But if he didn't, and the Wild was out in force, he'd be abandoning the Peridot at a time of need.

Vasin ground his teeth in frustration – he'd only know if he was right or wrong when it was too late.

High in the sky behind him, Lord Lakshin Opal and his hunters were still trying to keep up, a gleaming band of white, magnificent and useless. *This could all be over by the time they arrive.*

Not confident in his own flight of hunters, provided by Lady Anuja Ruby, he signalled for them to circle, knowing that they wouldn't be able to maintain height for long, and dived down after Quasim.

The Peridot's battle cry was rapturous, the kind made by a man without fear, totally given to the joy of the moment, and Vasin could not help but be impressed by the sight of the great crystal sword flashing down into the water again and again. Where the blade struck, miniature waves sprayed up either side and the hiding shapes beneath the surface ruptured and split, a mix of steam and blood spouting into the air.

Quasim's hunters dropped down around him, two of them moving to protect the tribute, the others stretched out single file, their Sky-legs cutting too deep into the soft mud.

Quasim was laughing again, raising his sword in salute to Vasin. 'Do you see me?' he called. 'Do you see how they fall?'

Vasin saw. He saw the bubbling water at Quasim's feet testifying to the death throes of the things that lingered there, but he also saw other disturbances in the water moving to Quasim's back, and still more rising up around the other hunters. They had a vaguely human shape, but with blubbery pale skin and white filmy eyes, and flesh spanning the gap between fingers and toes.

Murkers, lots of them. They usually like to hunt alone or in threes, but I count six at least.

'Behind you!' he yelled as the first set of webbed hands broke the surface, reaching for Quasim's ankles. Another quickly followed. Both Murkers endured the aura radiating from Quasim's armour; suffering, their pallid skin blistering, a sacrifice of flesh given to get close.

Another oddity. Murkers never seek out pain this way. Is

this another change? Is something else forcing them? Vasin glanced about, but there was no sign of any greater demonic presence. Whatever had put the Murkers up to this was either far away or still in hiding.

The Peridot Deathless started to turn, but his Sky-legs were held fast in the mud. He wobbled, regathered his balance, and tried to lash out with his sword, but he could not turn far enough, and they were too close for him to bring the huge weapon to bear. One Murker wrapped a rubbery arm about his neck, while the other grabbed an ankle and began to try and drag Quasim back into the swamp.

'Protect your lord!' urged Vasin, but the Peridot hunters were suffering similar problems, some forced to fight, others reduced to a creep, stopping to haul their Sky-legs free every few paces.

Pulling up at the last minute, Vasin lined up the point of his spear with the lower of the two Murkers swarming over Quasim and pressed the trigger on the shaft. With an eager hiss, the sapphire head of the spear shot forward, burying itself between the Murker's shoulder blades.

As it let out a high-pitched scream, Vasin passed by overhead, tilting back, heading skywards, raising the spear in front of him, two-handed. The slender cable running between shaft and head went taut. There was a jolt, a moment of resistance followed by a sudden decrease in momentum, and then Vasin was moving again, the Murker dangling below him like a fish on a hook.

The essence currents were thin here, and Vasin could feel the power in his wings fading fast with the additional weight. Even so, he rose thirty feet straight up, higher than the tops of the scattered trees, before coming to a stop in the air.

Above, he could see the Ruby hunters circling, watching him. He could almost taste their eagerness to join in. 'Wait!' he shouted, hoping that they would understand. He couldn't signal them, needing both hands to hold the spear. Tearing his gaze away, Vasin dived again, briefly passing the flailing Murker in the sky. It hovered there for a moment, skin wobbling on its bones like agitated jelly, before the cable went taut again, dragging it after him.

Vasin flew as low as he dared before pulling up, making the most of the weak currents to climb once more; the Murker swung below him on the end of the cable, describing a perfect curve as it arced towards its fellow Murkers engaging the Peridot hunters. Nodding to himself, Vasin twisted the shaft to free the spear head, and banked away, leaving the Murker to fly on, like a living stone cast from a catapult.

He wasn't able to see the results of his labour, but there were a series of crunches followed by a very satisfying splash. When he was able to look again, Quasim was repeatedly punching the face of a Murker that was grappling him. Creatures of the Wild could not bear close proximity to their crystal armour and this Murker was no exception. It seemed to melt as much as fall away from the attacks of the Peridot Deathless. Meanwhile, his hunters were pinning down the Murkers that Vasin had floored in a cage of crisscrossing spears.

'We have this tribute!' shouted Quasim. 'Find the other.'

You have this because of my intervention, thought Vasin bitterly. *And I am the one leading the hunt, not you.* But he did not voice these thoughts, instead nodding and flying on.

He soon spotted another torch nearby, which was good as Vasin would struggle to stay aloft much longer. He signalled for his hunters to follow and set off after the flickering light.

There was something alarming about the way the torch waved back and forth, as if the bearer was desperate, and the light seemed too low down. As Vasin sped closer he began to make out details: a young man waist deep in the swamp, face obscured by remnants of morning mist. In a moment of horror, he realized that the tribute had been caught and was being dragged under.

I'm too late.

But he swept down regardless, giving up the safety of the air in a last bid to reach them in time. He came down heavily, cutting two new channels through the wet mud as he skidded to a halt next to the young man.

One-handed, he plucked them from the earth. There was a moment of fierce resistance, then sudden movement. He half expected a monster to come with them, teeth locked around the tribute's legs. He half expected only a torso to emerge, but no, with a wet kissing sound, the tribute came free, legs and all. Vasin raised them above his head, watching for signs of attack from below.

At his feet, the spines of something broke the surface, but not in aggression. The creature of the Wild that had captured the tribute was making for deeper water. Vasin kicked at it, but it was too fast, slipping away into the swamp.

'Thank you!' said the tribute breathlessly. 'Oh thank you, I thought it was never going to let go.'

Vasin held him out at arms length, studying for injury. They were filthy, but aside from the long ritual cut on one cheek, he could see no red amid the filth, no broken skin. 'Are you hurt?'

'I . . . ' The tribute seemed to consider this as the first of Vasin's Ruby hunters came in to land alongside them. 'I don't think so.'

Using his Sky-legs like stilts, Vasin made his ponderous way back towards solid ground, the hunter following behind, spear ready. He set the tribute down on a slimy piece of rock and looked around. The swamp appeared quiet but his instincts told him otherwise. 'Did you see what it was that grabbed you?'

'No, my lord. I felt it though, wrapped around my legs. Kept squeezing, it did, every time I stopped moving.'

Vasin jerked his attention back to the tribute. 'What? Explain yourself.'

'It held me there. I tried pulling free but I wasn't strong enough. Wondered about using my torch to burn it off me but I was scared it'd go out. I got tired, but when I stopped fighting it squeezed me so hard I thought my knees were going to pop. I fought then, and that's the truth. I never fought so hard in all my life!'

More and more of the Ruby hunters were joining him, forming a protective circle around their position.

'I don't understand,' said Vasin. 'It grabbed you and then forced you to struggle?'

The tribute nodded hurriedly.

'And it didn't cut you or bite you or try and drag you under?'

'No, my lord.'

Was it holding the tribute in place for something else? He knew that things of the Wild sometimes made deals with each other as well as humans. Perhaps this creature 'owed' another and was simply trying to repay a debt. But Vasin didn't believe that. With everything that he'd seen since arriving on House Ruby lands – Quiverhive's experiment on the Godroad, the escalating number of attacks on Ruby settlements, the strange focus and grouping of the Murkers – he felt sure there was more to this.

And at that moment, there was a change in the air, confirming his fears.

The water began to thrum, softly at first, but he felt the dissonance run up his Sky-legs and across his armour. The sensation was as familiar as it was unpleasant. And it was directly below him.

'Weeper!' he shouted.

The hunters began scrambling in their pouches for earplugs but Vasin already knew from the way the water began to boil about them that it was too late.

The first thing to break the surface was the noise, a sharp wailing sound that knifed the ears of all that heard it. Vasin's sapphire helm mitigated it somewhat, pulling the teeth of the sound such that it was merely unpleasant. His hunters had no such protection, however. They began to add their cries to the Weeper's, making a chorus of misery, unrehearsed, yet horribly, organically in time.

The second thing to break the surface was the Weeper's crest. A hexagonal web of skin that stood proud from its neck on long, thin lines of bone. On the tip of each line was the head of a human child, wrinkled, hairless, and each head was stretched open in a scream, and each wept blood. The

Weeper's true head was only just emerging from the protective folds of its neck, like that of a tortoise, only without eyes, and a moist tube where the mouth should be.

Third came the Murkers. Where the cry of a Weeper caused people pain, it seemed to stir the Murkers into an ecstatic frenzy, emboldening them.

Vasin had one moment to take in the scene – his hunters, helpless. The tribute under his care, helpless. Murkers, too many to count, rushing in from all sides – and then he was moving.

Shifting his grip to the bottom of his spear, he swatted the first Murker away from his people, sending it spinning back the way it came. He took a step, swung again, dispatching another, then grabbed one that was trying to climb the rock to get to the tribute. The touch of his gauntlet immediately set its flesh to hissing as he hurled it at the Weeper.

The great demon turned its back, protecting its delicate crest and the Murker bounced off, falling into the swamp, only to rise again moments later.

All the while, the Weeper continued its dirge, rooting his hunters to the spot. Blood was beginning to leak from their ears now, calling to anything of the Wild not already aware of their presence. Soon, they would begin to cry blood like the heads on the Weeper's crest, and then he would have only moments before the pressure would build inside, and the blood would start to leak from their skin.

Vasin moved as fast as he could, but there were too many Murkers to handle alone, and too many targets to protect. He fought desperately as first one, then another hunter vanished from sight, dragged under by the Murkers.

Despite his efforts, he was losing. He could not fight them all at once. Out of the corner of his eye he saw red tears on the cheeks of a nearby hunter and knew he was almost out of time.

As he lifted another Murker over his head, it occurred to him that he alone was fighting, and if the demons pooled their strength he would be swiftly overcome. But they didn't. They were so busy attacking the Ruby hunters that he was left free to do as he wished.

This makes no sense.

A cry from above made him look up. Lord Lakshin Opal had finally arrived, sending his hunters down to aid them.

'No!' shouted Vasin. 'No, you fool! Call them back!'

But it was too late. None of them had taken proper preparations, and as soon as the Opal hunters came within range, the Weeper's power took them, and they fell from the sky, one after another. More targets for him to protect.

Furious, Vasin smashed the Murker he was holding against a nearby rock, and started wading through the swamp towards the Weeper. It had partially raised itself from the water, revealing a thick serpentine body, encrusted with milky boils.

Unlike his hunters, Lakshin was cautious, hovering above the Weeper on huge pearlescent wings. With meticulous care, he took aim, but didn't throw, adjusting several times as Vasin advanced.

He should have thrown already. He's too hesitant.

By now the element of surprise was gone, the Weeper well aware of the Opal's presence. *Perhaps that's his plan, get the Weeper to look up and expose its face.*

As if reading his mind, Lakshin took that moment to

throw. He and the Weeper watched the elegant weapon arc through the sky, the crystal tip singing with purpose. It came down fast but too low, sinking alongside Vasin's hopes. A good shot would silence the Weeper, turning the tide of battle in their favour. Lakshin's throw was only adequate however, striking the belly rather than the head.

In answer the Weeper directed its shout towards Lakshin. Though the Opal Deathless was protected from the malice in its cry, the sound disrupted the already weak essence currents, sending him tumbling from the sky. He hit the swamp face first, broad wings slapping the water with a loud splash.

Vasin grabbed the nearest Murker and jumped onto it, using its body as a platform to kick off from. It didn't give him much height, but it was enough to glide the last twenty feet to where the Weeper was. He punched his spear through the first of the five heads, leaving it there as the Weeper tried to ram him with its thick skull.

Something made it hesitate, however, as if it had second thoughts at the last moment. Taking advantage, he kicked out sideways to avoid the attack, and twisted his body so that the sharp edge of his wing sliced through another of the smaller heads, taking off the jaw completely. Suddenly afraid, the Weeper lurched away from him, but Vasin was faster, grabbing the edge of the crest and tearing, using the Weeper's own momentum against it. Thin bones snapped and skin shredded, leaving him with a handful of crest and another head, now silent, and the Weeper rolling with pain at his feet.

Vasin didn't dare take the time to finish it off, instead reaching into the water to wrap his fingers around Lakshin's shoulder plate and heave him upright.

Behind the visor, Lakshin's eyes were wild with fear.

'You are Deathless!' shouted Vasin, shaking him. 'Your hunters need you. Now!'

Lakshin coughed up water several times, and managed to give a ragged nod.

'Are you ready?' Vasin didn't wait for an answer.

To his credit, the Opal drew his curved dagger even as he spat the last of the filth from his mouth. Together, they began to fight back, knocking back the Murkers, and helping the stunned hunters regather their wits.

There came a moment, before the battle had fully turned, when Vasin paused amid the chaos, some instinct telling him that for once he should think instead of do.

He looked around and realized there were yet more demons tucked between two fallen trees. A thick cluster of them, at least as many again as they were fighting, and within them, a familiar many-eyed shape. *Quiverhive.*

It struck him that they were not engaging nor were they fleeing. *They're watching us. But why? What is it they're looking for?*

He turned his attention to the fight, trying to see it as the demons might. Lakshin and his hunters were making a real impact now, but at least in part because the Murkers were targeting the Ruby hunters, only engaging the Opal when they were forced to. *It is just as Anuja said. They're singling out the Rubies? Why do that? And why spare me? Nothing has even tried to attack me. And when I confronted the Weeper, it pulled away rather than take advantage.*

A second look at the demons confirmed his suspicions. *If they committed to the fight, they could inflict terrible damage upon us, but they're holding back. It's not that they're afraid. It's like . . . they're observing. Studying us.*

Lakshin was fighting with his hunters now, but still there was a lack of conviction that could be exploited. Quasim was the opposite, reckless to a fault. Quiverhive would know this now. *What else would it have learned?*

A small-winged Lizardkin, no longer than Vasin's hand, alighted on Quiverhive's back. Its long tongue shot out and adhered to one of the demon's rippling eyes. After a few seconds the Lizardkin shivered and straightened, it's red and green scales glimmering in the sunslight. Suddenly purposeful, it flew away, swiftly vanishing from sight.

Another movement caught Vasin's attention, a glint of silver moving in the swamp that he recognized. *My spear!* It was still attached to the Weeper, which was trying to slink away. Three splashing bounds caught him up to it. Grasping the shaft in both hands he pulled it free before plunging it back into the Weeper's body, letting the crystal spear head burn it from the inside. Four times he repeated this. Three to kill it and one more to be sure.

When it was truly, finally dead, he turned back towards Quiverhive, struck by a compulsion to impress it, to show that they weren't all flailing amateurs. But it and its demonic entourage had already left.

Only when the last of the Murkers had been dispatched, and the three flights of hunters reunited to join the tributes on a slow trudge back to Fourboards, did realization strike. He'd heard about this strange behaviour from the Wild before. Once, a demon had spared his mother. The same demon had also spared Lady Pari Tanzanite, because of a deal made by the traitor, Lord Rochant Sapphire. And Quiverhive's surveillance of them felt like the sort of thing Rochant would do. Wait, observe, then strike when it would have most impact.

He'd always assumed that Rochant had traded the people of Sorn in exchange for power, but what if the deal had been for more than that? What if he had given the Scuttling Corpseman wisdom as well? Tactical knowledge? What if the attacks on the Ruby were not an anomaly but rather the next step in the Wild's evolution?

With a sudden, sickening certainty, he knew that he had to get back to his mother, and to the one man with the answers they needed.

CHAPTER TEN

The suns were at their zenith when Varg pulled the wagon to a stop. Pari swung herself out to land lightly on the ground. 'Such a joy to be mobile again!' she said aloud. Though it had been a much bumpier journey than the one from Tanzanite to Sapphire lands, she had rather enjoyed her time with Varg. It had been like putting on an old slipper, easy and comfortable.

'Wait here,' she said as she looked up at his frowning face. 'I shan't be long.'

He grunted acknowledgement. 'You got your gloves on?'

She held up her hands to display the thick leather. 'Yes. And my cloak and my boots. And I've tucked my trousers into them. I have done this before you know, many times.'

Many times more than you, she added silently.

'Yeah, I know,' Varg muttered. 'It's just that you're normally in the back of the wagon or in your armour when you're out here.'

'Am I now? And what do you know about what I normally do?'

He waved her away. 'Forget it. I'll be here.'

She turned towards the Wild and walked into the trees with a final offended shake of her head. Varg was many things but he was rarely overprotective. *This is because of my new body. He's still thinking of me as the young girl he needs to teach and watch over.* Clearly, he'd become attached to Priti. It was inevitable really, beneath his grizzled exterior, Varg was disgustingly soft. *Too soft for this world.*

A part of her mind was already considering that he'd need to be replaced by the end of this lifecycle, and it made her sad. That was one of the hardest parts of being Deathless, saying goodbye to so many good people. And, with lamentably few exceptions, having to endure eternity with so many irritating ones.

Ideally, she'd acquire a very young child and have Varg raise them in the right way to take over his duties when the time came, but to do that, he needed to travel and teach the routes, not be cooped up in some Sapphire castle, mooning after Honoured Mother Chandni. Perhaps once he'd had a year or two of the realities of living as a spy in a Sapphire castle, he'd be begging her for his old life back.

Yes, she thought to herself. *Better always to be patient. Let Varg think it was all his decision. As much as he wants to be with Chandni, I know he wants to be a father too.*

Things had changed sufficiently in the forest that she began to worry that she'd got lost. It seemed like nobody had used the paths to Sorn during her time between lives, the vegetation of the Wild having swiftly and completely erased all evidence of human footsteps. However, this was not her first jaunt in such places, and she kept her attention on the canopy above her and the position of the suns in the sky, using their light to guide her. Some of the more ancient of the trees were familiar too, their gnarled shapes like giants, miserable, with crooked spines and clawed hands. Of course she wouldn't put it past them to have moved since she'd last been this way, the better to confuse travellers. Only a fool placed their trust in the Wild.

It took Pari longer than she'd expected to reach Sorn. Not a lot longer, but enough for it to feel significant. The effect was enhanced by the fact that the forest had started to encroach upon the ghost town, obscuring its borders, and providing an unasked-for camouflage for the outer buildings, blending them in with the greens and browns of the trees. But Pari couldn't help feel it was more than that. As if the Wild itself had somehow reached out with its vines and branches and brambles, and dragged Sorn deeper into its embrace.

Despite her best efforts to dismiss it as nonsense, she couldn't shake the notion. The distant glow of the Godroad seemed too far away, vanishing entirely by the time she arrived on Sorn's streets.

Though for her, it had only been a year since her last visit, it was apparent that time had very much passed here. She thought of Nidra, exiled and alone in this forsaken place, and began to worry. Though the once Sapphire Deathless had lived many lives, and was one of the more competent of their kind, the settlement seemed awfully quiet.

Spongy moss has spilled out across the main street, covering it in asymmetrical patches, and numerous saplings had elbowed their way into the light. *Another few years,* thought Pari, *and it will be as if Sorn never was.*

She tried not to think about the last time she'd come here but it was impossible. The beating she'd received at the hands of the Scuttling Corpseman, the casual way it had killed Lan. Even in his last moments he had looked to her for protection, only to be let down. *How many others have I let down over the years?*

She paused to have another look at her surroundings, staring hard at the shadows for hidden predators.

There was no sign of the Corpseman now though, no sign of any trouble. Standing out in the sunslight, everything seemed bright and quiet and oddly beautiful. A few animal sounds could be heard but even they sounded small and far away.

It did not take her long to reach the ruined house. A door, not the original one, had been forced into the frame. Large parts of the house were covered in great tangles of ivy, but she noted the doorway and front step were clear. She also noted a thin wire had been stretched across the gap.

With a nod of approval, Pari stepped over it.

Her first impulse had been to walk in and make a quip about what Nidra had done with the place, but an instinct told her not to. Instead she stopped in front of the door and sang for entrance, as she might if Nidra were still a lady of the Sapphire, and this was her audience chamber. It was the first time Pari had really sung in this lifecycle, and the sound of her own voice made her jolt in surprise. *A little too girlish for my liking. Ah well, at least there are things I can smoke for that.*

The last echoes of her song were picked up by the nearby

trees, setting their ear-shaped leaves trembling. Pari did her best to ignore that and stared at the door. She was just beginning to wonder if Nidra was out, or worse, in no state to answer, when she felt something sharp press itself into her back.

'Who are you?' said a stern and scratchy voice.

'Ah, my dear Nidra,' replied Pari. 'No need to draw blood, especially not here. It's me. I'm sorry I didn't come sooner but circumstances with my house—' a prod to her back cut her short.

'Prove it.'

'Do you mind if I take off a glove?'

'So long as you do it slowly.'

Pari did so, then lifted her hand so that her palm faced over her shoulder. She wiggled her fingertips, drawing attention to the golden tattoos.

The sharp object withdrew from her back. 'Turn around. Slowly.'

Pari did this too, smiling so as to make the gold on her lips sparkle in the sunlight.

'Pari?' asked Nidra, disbelieving. The years had not been kind to her, as if this space in the Wild operated at different speeds to the rest of the world. Sixteen summers seemed to weigh double on Nidra's frame. Her skin was prematurely creased with toil and hardship, her spine taking on the curve of one beyond her six decades. Pari was uncomfortably reminded of the trees she'd just passed. For all of that, Nidra still seemed quick, her eyes as hard as the crystal blade in her hand. Once, that blade had sat atop a spear but now it was held more like a knife, as diminished as its bearer. Somewhere within the bundle of fabric that Nidra wore would be the remnants of her legend, white where they had been gold, burnt where they had been inked, turning marks of pride into brands of shame.

'None other,' replied Pari.

The two clasped wrists, Nidra gripping Pari so tightly it hurt, a woman clinging to life. A story of suffering was communicated in that gesture, in the catch of her breath and the haunted look in her eye.

'It's not much by way of apology but I've brought some food with me,' said Pari, pausing before adding with a smile, 'and some wine.'

For a moment, she thought the other woman was going to cry but that moment swiftly passed, replaced by steel and quiet anger. Nidra gave a curt nod. 'Let's go inside.'

The inside of the house hadn't changed since Pari had last visited. A spartan space, the hangings were faded and functional, used to cover the broken windows rather than to decorate. There was a small fire pit in the centre of the room, a token gesture towards comfort, and that was it. Nidra had left no mark of herself on the place. *This is no home for her, merely a place to wait out the storm.*

Without ceremony, they opened the bottle and began passing it between them.

'I expected you before now. What happened?' asked Nidra.

'A delay with my rebirth. Beyond my control.'

'High Lords!' From Nidra's lips, the title sound like an insult.

'High Lords!' agreed Pari.

'To Yadavendra, temporary High Lord of the Sapphire.' Nidra raised the bottle. 'May his end be slow and miserable!'

They both took long swigs of the bottle.

'To Primyamvada, temporary High Lord of the Tanzanite,' said Pari. 'May all her vessels be afflicted with piles!'

The bottle was shared once more, along with a smile, wicked in Pari's case, slight in Nidra's.

'Well,' said Pari, 'I'm afraid to say that not much has happened in my absence. House Tanzanite are sending my brother, Arkav, to investigate House Sapphire. They say it is to bring Yadavendra in for trial, but I think it is to provoke him into killing Arkav. If Tanzanite blood is spilt, then the other houses will be forced to act.'

'Good.'

'No, not good. If Arkav fails in his mission, the High Lord will not sanction his rebirth. I imagine she'll blame it on Yadavendra, but the result will be the same. And she's made it abundantly clear that my fate is tied to my brother's.'

Nidra offered the bottle again. 'There isn't much I can do from here. You must help Vasin move against Yadavendra, that way we'll all live to see another lifecycle.'

'May they be many and glorious,' replied Pari, accepting the bottle and drinking from it. 'How is your son doing?'

'Too slowly, I'm still here.'

'No progress at all?'

'Oh, he's doing a fine job at ingratiating himself with others, I don't doubt that most of the houses would be delighted if he took over, but few of them will stand with him until it's clear he'll win. And he can't move until Lord Rochant's rebirth fails. But for some reason it keeps being put off.'

'Odd. I'd have thought Yadavendra would be desperate to have Rochant back.'

'He is, but he's also terrified of the rebirth failing and so he's taking pains to make sure Satyendra is the perfect vessel before authorizing the ceremony.'

Pari smirked. 'If he only knew.'

'It's not funny,' Nidra snapped. 'His caution could undo our plans. Time is no longer on our side.'

'Is something wrong with your body?'

'Not mine. Rochant's.' Nidra's gaze went to the door of the room where the man they once both loved was kept. There was little love in her eyes now.

'Please tell me you haven't been overzealous in your care.'

'I've barely touched him since . . . ' The slight pause spoke volumes. 'Since you were last here. Vasin saw to that. Once we'd found out the nature of Rochant's deal with the Corpseman, I let him be. Not because he deserved mercy, but because Vasin needed me to stop. My son is still young in his soul. He doesn't understand like we do.'

Pari decided this wasn't the time to question what it was she was supposed to understand. 'What did you learn?'

'What we expected. Rochant sold out to the Scuttling Corpseman, gaining Yadavendra the position of High Lord, and himself elevation to the ranks of the Sapphire Deathless. In return, he gave the Corpseman the old High Lord, Samarku, and the people of Sorn.'

An image of Samarku, his body merged with that of a slender tree, rooted and suffering, came to mind. She shuddered. 'Did you find him? Was he still . . . '

Nidra nodded. 'I've done what you should have. The Corpseman can't hurt him any more.'

'That's a very quaint way of putting it.'

'I know how you Tanzanite prefer the truth to be dressed up a little.'

Pari sighed. 'What about the people of Sorn? Are they still buried in the hill?'

'Yes. But they're not as they were.'

'What do you mean?'

'Better that you see for yourself. I'll take you there after we've eaten.'

'Alright. You still haven't told me what's wrong with Rochant.'

It was Nidra's turn to sigh. 'He soon realized that the best way to stop us was for him to end his current lifecycle. If he dies, then Yadavendra really can bring him back. First, he tried to cut himself to summon something of the Wild. Then he tried battering himself to death on the wall. After these attempts failed, he simply refused to eat. I've managed to force a certain amount of sustenance on him, but his body is weak now. Vulnerable. It's been all I can do to keep him alive. I'm not sure he'll last much longer.'

'I want to see him.'

Nidra looked away. 'Better that you don't.'

'Now I have to see him.'

Pari expected there to be a fight but the other woman seemed to sag within her clothes. 'It's your choice. Don't say I didn't warn you.'

Pari closed the door behind her and waited for her eyes to adjust to the gloom. One corner of the room had been invaded by a grey-stemmed plant with leaves that tapered to elegant points, and where it had forced the beams apart, a few of Vexation's slender rays managed to creep through.

Though Rochant's current body was younger than Nidra's, it too had aged badly. When she compared the wasted thing in front of her to the fine specimen she had left behind, it was enough to make her weep. But she didn't. *No more tears will be shed over you, my love. That is an oath I intend to keep.*

He was propped up in a corner, a thick wad of fabric jammed between his teeth, presumably to stop him calling out or biting himself. His hair had been left to grow into a neglected tangle reaching halfway down his back, dirty and dark. Most of his face was covered by a thick growth of beard but what she could see of it appeared sunken, and the little of his limbs that were exposed were painfully thin. A strap of leather secured his head to the wall but she noted that his arms were no longer bound and wondered if he simply lacked the strength to use them, or whether Nidra had seen through her threat, and numbed sections of the man's soul with her poison.

Pari wasn't sure how long she stood there – trying to decide if she was still angry with this man, trying not to feel such crushing sorrow at the sight of him – but at some point he become aware of her attention.

Their eyes met.

'Hello Rochant.'

She saw nothing of his usual spark, that subtle and sometimes mischievous intelligence. *He's broken,* she thought sadly. It would have been much easier if he had been angry or defiant or smug. Pari shook her head. *What a waste.*

'Would you like to talk?'

He raised his eyebrows, which Pari took for agreement and pulled the fabric from his mouth. She waited as he worked his jaw, running his tongue over cracked lips. 'Pari,' he rasped. Not a question, a statement.

189

He knows me. Of course he does. He knows me better than anyone.

'Yes. I thought I'd come and see you. For old times' sake.'

'Do you have any . . . drink?'

'Not to share with you, my dear. Those days are behind us. I'm not here to play, I'm here to talk.' He didn't say anything and she continued. 'When I was last here, you said you could explain it all if I gave you the chance. You made it sound as if there might be some reasoning behind your madness. I don't believe it for a second, but I'm nothing if not open minded, as you well know.'

'You don't sound open minded.'

'If anyone could persuade me, it's you.'

He looked disbelieving, but a little spark had returned, his features slightly more animated. *Is that why I'm doing this?* She wondered. *Some desperate need to see that the man I admired is still in there, buried within the husk.*

'Will it make a difference?' he asked.

'If you're asking me if I'll release you or change my plans, the answer is no. You made this bed, my dear, thorns and all.'

'Then why bother?'

Yes, what are you doing, Pari? 'Oh you know me,' she said, keeping her voice light, 'I hate not knowing something.'

'Perhaps that will be my revenge.' *Was that a little of the old sparkle in his eye?*

'You monster!'

'Yes. But I was your monster, Pari, and I could be again.' *Suns scorch me, but I still want this man.*

'Though to be honest, your body is a bit young for my tastes. Maybe come back in a few years?'

She laughed.

'Best be careful Nidra doesn't hear you. She hates joy, especially in other people.'

The laugh died on her lips, his mention of Nidra's name bringing back all of his misdeeds in brutal clarity. 'If you want to explain, this is your last chance. I'm not coming back.'

'I'm not sure you'll understand.'

She folded her arms. 'Now I know you're trying to bait me.'

'I'm not doubting your intelligence, I'm doubting your life experience.'

'I have several lifecycles over you, Rochant.'

'Yes, but all of them the same. You were sky-born from the start, bred to enjoy eternity. It is what you are. I was road-born. I've seen what life is like down there. Not from the air, nor looking down from a pair of Sky-legs. In the dirt, in the cold, a stone's throw from death. When you come down here, you come as a visitor, protected by title or armour. It's not like that for the rest of us. We have to live with the threat of the Wild every single day. Can you imagine what it's like?'

'Not really, no.'

His neck flexed as if he was trying to nod, but the strap across his forehead prohibited the movement. 'Exactly. I did what I did to escape that.'

She looked into his eyes and nodded to herself. 'Thank you, Rochant. A bit of me has always wondered if I had made the right decision. Despite your betrayal, I couldn't help but cling to the memories of our time together. And now you've shown that beneath your bravado and brilliance, you are actually quite a shallow, desperate little creature. Had I not such a weakness for wit and perfectly shaped bottoms, I suspect I would have seen through you long ago.

'You see, while I may find it hard to see life as a Road-born does, and while I have always been Deathless, I still hold life sacred. A true Deathless sacrifices their vessel again and again for road-born and sky-born alike, because unlike them, we can return. My immortality is given gladly in service to my people, precisely because their one life is so precious. Whereas you, for all your supposed empathy, were quite happy to sacrifice this entire settlement for personal gain.

'The thing that really cuts deep, my dear, is not that you are capable of such horror, but that you display no remorse, nor even guilt for your actions. You make out that I don't understand you or the road-born. But the problem, your problem, is that I see all too clearly.'

He opened his mouth to reply and she stuffed it full of fabric. 'Actually, I think that's enough from you. Goodbye, Rochant.'

And with that, she turned, leaving the room, and her past behind.

It was late afternoon as Sa-at peered around a tree and caught sight of Sorn. After a glance about its silent streets, he waved for Tal to join him, wincing at the sound of the Gatherer's heavy boots crunching, crunching, crunching.

The more Sa-at looked, the more confused he became. Very little of the outer fence remained, allowing him a clear view into what remained of the settlement. The buildings were so buried by greenery that it was hard to guess their true shapes. 'Is this Sorn?'

'I think so. Looks weird though.'

'Where are all the people?'

'With the Corpse—' Tal slapped a hand over his mouth, then added, '—with that demon. Must be it's eaten them all by now. If they're lucky.'

Both boys shivered.

'But where is it?' asked Sa-at. The place looked deserted, aside from a few animals that had made nests in rooftops or within the abandoned houses. More than that, it felt . . . *unclaimed*. As if Sorn didn't really belong to the Corpseman after all, like it didn't really belong to anyone.

'I dunno,' mused Tal. 'Hiding maybe? Demons have to sleep in the day.'

Crowflies took this moment to land in the tree above them, throwing back its feathered head to give a screeching laugh. Tal jumped.

'Crowflies,' said Sa-at quietly, smiling. He always felt a little safer when Crowflies was around.

'Sa-aat!'

Tal glared at it. 'Horrible thing! Get away!'

'Don't be like that.'

'Why not?'

'Crowflies is my friend.'

'Really?' When Sa-at nodded, he muttered, 'It looks funny to me, even for a Birdkin.'

'It's a demon but it's a nice one.'

'There are no nice demons!'

'Well, it saved your life once.'

'When?'

'When the spiders tried to put a baby inside you. Crowflies sucked it out so you wouldn't die.' He nodded towards the branches. 'You should be grateful.'

Tal's face paled but he faced the Birdkin. 'Uh, thank you, Crowflies.' He lowered his voice and turned back to Sa-at. 'I still don't see why it had to scream like that.'

'It wasn't screaming. It was laughing.'

'What's funny?'

You talking about demons like you know them, when you don't, Sa-at thought but didn't say. 'Nothing.'

Crowflies laughed again, which made him feel conflicted, because now he wasn't sure if the Birdkin was laughing with him or at him.

'Come on,' he said to Tal. 'Let's go and see if we can find any signs of the Scut—,' he paused at the look of horror on his friends face, '—of the demon.'

'Okay.'

They'd not gone far when Crowflies gave a warning screech, the kind Sa-at knew all too well. *Danger.*

He glanced up at the Birdkin to see which way its beak was pointing and then pushed Tal in the opposite way.

'Wha?'

'Sssh!'

Sa-at could see an empty kennel in front of them. Its lower door was shut but the upper one was open. He started to push faster, until Tal stumbled backwards, his legs smacking against the wood and flipping up, over, and out of sight on the other side. Sa-at dived in after him, coming to a rolling stop by the far wall. The action had forced him to open his hands. The bruises on his palm complained, and then a flurry of scents sailed from his right palm to his brain, intoxicating in their intensity. The rags here bore the barest scent of Dogkin overlaid with a tang of Mousekin droppings. There were a family of them here, he suddenly knew, two adults and at least as many children. Tal's breath was a strong presence in the air, as was his sweat. He clenched his fist, muting but not entirely blocking the new sensory input. As he processed all of this, he heard tiny legs scurrying away, most likely the Mousekin. Sa-at didn't bother to check, crawling low past Tal to peer through a crack in the kennel's lower door.

His friend had the presence of mind to stay quiet, and though they couldn't see anything at first, they soon became aware of voices. Two women, one older, one younger, engaged in lively conversation. It was hard to make out the words and a flame of curiosity lit within him. That flame only intensified as they came into view.

The first was wrapped in layers of thick fabric, appearing in many ways like a Gatherer, save for the fact that she moved differently. She wasn't clumsy like the ones he'd seen before. She was purposeful, and something sharp glittered in her hand, like a slice of the sky.

The second was shorter, and unlike anyone Sa-at had ever seen. It took a while for him to identify what it was, at least in part because when he caught a glimpse of her dark face he found it hard to think anything at all. But as they continued on, heading deeper into the Wild, he realized what it was: she seemed at ease. He'd never seen another human look like that before and it was mesmerizing.

He was just starting to follow when Tal's hand landed on one shoulder, and Crowflies landed on the other. The Birdkin made itself uncharacteristically small and buried itself into the crook of his neck.

'What are you doing?' Hissed Tal.

'I . . . ' he crouched back down again. 'Did you see her?'

'Which one?'

'The one that had lips like Fortune's Eye.'

'Yeah.'

'She was . . . '

Tal nodded, blushing. 'Yeah.'

'We could talk to them.'

Tal gripped his shoulder more tightly. 'No!'

'Sa-aat!' croaked Crowflies in agreement.

'But I . . . why not?'

'Gold faces? Sapphire weapons? At least one of them is Deathless. It don't do to get in their way.'

'Deathless? I thought they were bigger and made of sunlight?'

'Not always. Sometimes they go small like us. Thing is, this is House Sapphire land and I don't know any Sapphire Deathless that have golden lips. And that other one might be a Hunter but she didn't have no wings. We should keep hidden, there's probably more of them about.'

'They seemed nice,' he murmured.

'Not to us they wouldn't. One look at my ears and your hand and we'd be goners. Don't think they'd take too kindly to your demon either.'

Sa-at flopped down, cradling Crowflies in his arms. He'd never seen the Birdkin behave that way before. It was scared, and that scared him.

They waited until the women were long gone before leaving the kennel. Crowflies seemed to have recovered itself, and took up a perch high up in the trees, scanning the streets with its compound eyes before announcing it was safe. Sa-at moved to the place where he'd seen the women and crouched down. The ground was hard here so there wasn't much in the way of tracks, but he was able to discern which way they'd gone and from that which direction they'd come from.

He looked longingly for them but there was no sign of either woman now, their shapes already lost to the dark beneath the trees.

'We should go before they come back,' said Tal.

He sighed, hearing the wisdom in his head but nowhere else as he turned back towards Sorn. 'Come on then.'

They kept to the buildings, ever-watchful, but saw no sign of other hunters or Deathless. Sa-at was relieved and disappointed in equal measure.

'Where are we going?' Asked Tal.

'To see where they came from.'

'I didn't see any travel bags. Might be they've got a carriage or something nearby.'

Sa-at's eyes widened in delight. 'What kind of things will they have?'

'Don't know but— No! You can't go taking a Deathless's things.'

'Why?'

'You just can't!'

Sa-at nodded. 'We won't just steal. I know the ways.'

'No. You give to Deathless, you don't take. That's the way it works.'

He nodded but didn't say any more, because he was determined to have a look and suspected Tal would be against that too.

One of the houses caught his eye. Like the others, it was run down and under siege from the Wild, but the door was clear of vegetation. He stopped and told Tal to wait while he had a closer look.

Tal put a hand on his arm. 'Be careful, yeah?'

The gesture set a little tremble in Sa-at's heart. *He cares for me. He is my friend.* 'I will.'

He approached the house from the side. Someone had set a trap there but Sa-at had grown up in the Wild, and so he always attended to where he placed his feet. The door was not locked and it was easy for him to slip though. There wasn't much to see inside, but there were some interesting smells in the air. Despite some slight misgivings, he opened his right hand.

The air was musty, and smelled of damp wood mixed with unwashed clothes. Under all of this was a subtle aroma of fruit-laced drink, that he was able to connect to an empty bottle that had been set in a corner. People had eaten here, but the food smelled odd, almost fiery in a way that made his palm tingle and his mouth water. Most exciting of all was a subtle fragrance of apples and spices that he knew, just knew, had to belong to the mysterious young women with the golden lips.

Sa-at crept across the room to another door. He could hear very soft breathing from the other side and when he placed his palm by the gap beneath, he detected another person smell, different to the ones in the room: male, sickly.

Very slowly, he inched the door open, waiting after each one for a change in the breathing. It was so regular, he became convinced the occupant was asleep, and risked putting his head through.

A man was inside. He too had dark skin – *like my own!* – and he could see an elaborate gold tattoo, a spiderwebbing zigzag of lines on the right side of the man's face. For reasons

Sa-at could not understand, the man's head was strapped to the wall. And something was wrong with him, deeply wrong, like an animal that had something broken inside and was waiting for death.

He was so still that it took a while for Sa-at to realize that his eyes were open just a crack, and staring right at him. He froze, then began to slide back out of the room.

The man tried to speak but his mouth was stuffed with fabric. On a sudden impulse, Sa-at dashed forward and pulled it out before dashing back to the door again.

'Please,' said the man, 'don't go.'

Generally, in the Wild, one either kept away from dying creatures or fed on them. He suspected he should run. The man's apparent helplessness did little to put him at ease, and there was something about him that seemed dangerous. Keeping a hold of the door should he need to close it in a hurry, Sa-at tried to find his words.

'It isn't often I get visitors.' The man's voice was so raw, it sounded like it hurt him to talk. 'Come a little closer so I might see you properly.'

Sa-at shook his head.

'Fair enough.' He closed his eyes.

Now that Sa-at had been here for a little longer, his palm was telling him other things too. Something terrible had happened in this place, it reeked of pain. Sa-at couldn't follow the translation from scent to emotion clearly, but he knew that someone, most likely the man, had suffered here. He was still afraid to enter the room properly, but he found he didn't want to leave either. Caught between pity and wariness, he remained where he was until his heart, unable to maintain its tension indefinitely, began to settle.

'Hello,' he said softly.

The man's right eye cracked open. 'He speaks!'

'Yes.'

'Does he have a name?'

'Yes.' Sa-at pointed a finger. 'You first.'

'Ah, interesting. So you are not with my captors then?'

'Is that a demon?'

The man made a barking sound and Sa-at wondered if he was getting ready to die. 'Of a kind, I suppose. But no, not a demon as you would think of one. A captor is one that holds another prisoner. Did you know I was a prisoner?'

Sa-at shook his head.

'Now you do.'

He ducked out of the room back into the main part of the house and picked through the things there until he found some bottles of water. Then he went back to the man and offered one to him. When it became apparent the man couldn't take it, Sa-at put it to his lips.

'Thank you. I still don't know your name.'

He was just about to answer, then frowned. 'You first.'

'Very good! I think you and I are going to get on. My name is Lord Rochant, child of the Sapphire Everlasting.'

'Does that mean you're a Deathless?'

'It does.'

'Why are you here?'

'That is a long story. The simple answer is that my enemies caught me and brought me here.'

Sa-at thought for a moment. 'I could help you.'

'I hope so. I could certainly use some help though between us, I wish you'd come here fifteen years earlier.'

'Sorry.'

'No need to apologize.' His other eye opened and he peered at Sa-at. 'I doubt you were much more than a babe then.'

'Do you know about the Scuttling Corpseman?'

There was a pause, then: 'Yes. Oh yes, I know more about the Corpseman than any living thing.'

Sa-at smiled. 'Good. Tell me.'

'And what will I get in return?'

'What do you want?'

'I was going to say death but you can't very well kill me and then expect me to answer your questions, can you?'

Sa-at frowned. It sounded like Rochant was asking a question and yet at the same time like he wasn't.

'How about this,' he continued. 'You get me away from here and then I will answer your questions about the Corpseman.'

'Swear.'

'And do you swear to get me to safety and keep me safe from my enemies?'

This seemed oddly familiar to him, like making deals in the Wild. 'If you swear to answer my questions truthfully.'

'On my blood, I swear it.'

'What about your bones?'

Rochant's eyebrows raised slightly. 'What are you?' he said softly, then, louder: 'I swear it, on my blood, bones and Deathless soul.'

'I hear it and swear it on my blood and bones.'

Outside, the trees rustled, and he knew the oath had been heard.

'Good,' said Rochant. 'Now you best help me up, we need to be gone before my enemies return.'

'Is the Corpseman here?'

'There isn't time to get into that now.'

'You swore!'

Rochant sighed. 'Not here in Sorn, no, but close by. Can we go now?'

'Yes.'

He undid the straps around Rochant's head and waist, and was alarmed when his head flopped forward, too heavy for his weak neck to support. 'I'm afraid I can't move my arms or legs,' said Rochant. 'You're going to have to carry me.'

'Okay.'

Though Rochant was much taller, there was little weight to him, the man seeming to be made more of rags and bone than flesh. Sa-at slung one of his limp arms over his shoulder and dragged him towards the door.

They were met there by Tal, who was running over, stick at the ready. 'You're back! Thank the thrice blessed suns!'

'Who is that?' asked Rochant by his ear.

'Who is that?' asked Tal, clumping to a stop in front of them.

Before Sa-at had time to answer either of them, he heard a sharp twang from Tal's feet, and then a bell began to ring inside the house. The noise was high and resonant, making all three of them jump.

A beat later, the nearby leaves rippled as if disturbed by the wind, and the chimes of the bell echoed in their rustling, passed from one tree to another like a wave.

'Oh no!' said Tal.

'Run!' said Rochant.

'Sa-aat!' called Crowflies three times, and Sa-at knew what it meant: *Run. Run. Run.*

CHAPTER ELEVEN

Vasin forced a hard march along the Godroad back to the Ruby High Lord's castle, desperate to discharge his duty and return to his mother. As soon as they'd dropped off the tributes at Fourboards, he'd moved them on again, allowing only the briefest time for the elders to offer thanks. Quasim made his disappointment about this clear, but Vasin ignored him, too wrapped up in his own thoughts to indulge egos.

We've been plotting all this time focusing on Rochant and never once thought that the Corpseman might be acting outside of Sapphire lands. It's had sixteen years to prepare! Perhaps longer. Perhaps it's been working on this for generations. I have to get back to mother and face Rochant again. Together, we can get the truth out of him.

'Lord Vasin!' called Quasim. 'Slow down, my courageous friend.'

'No, we keep this pace.'

The Peridot Deathless gestured to the bedraggled line behind them. 'I'm not sure all of us can.'

One look at the hunters showed Quasim was right. Many of them were caked in mud from head to toe, moving awkwardly from injuries sustained during the fight in the swamp. Lord Lakshin trailed at the back, though Vasin suspected that was partly to avoid his gaze. The Opal Deathless had said little since the battle but there had been a marked change in attitude. Gone was his sneer and air of superiority, replaced with a frosty politeness which did little to hide his shame.

I've seen him now and he knows it.

With a sigh, Vasin stopped. 'I'm going on ahead and ask that you take my flight of hunters under your care.'

'But why? Why the rush? We should walk together, sing together, enjoy the shared glow of our victory.'

'You call this victory?'

Quasim laughed. 'Of course! Have you ever seen so many Murkers in one place? I haven't.' He slapped Vasin on the arm, the peridot gauntlet chiming merrily against the sapphire bracer. 'Yet we dispatched them, in style, saved both of the tributes, and took down a Weeper. A great day indeed. And here was me worried that a late morning hunt would scare off the prey!'

'It's true, but we were careless in our duty. We outnumbered them but lost four Ruby hunters.' *Hunters Anuja entrusted to me,* he added silently. 'And how many of your own are fit to fly again tomorrow? How many of Lord Lakshin's? I look down that line and see tired faces, bruised bodies and chipped wings. What if another hunt is called for? What numbers could we field then?'

'You underestimate the Peridot spirit, Lord Vasin. My hunters will fly whenever they are needed.'

'And Lord Lakshin's? They fell from the sky with the grace of hailstones. It's a wonder they're alive.'

'Hmm, well, I can't speak for them,' he added hastily.

'I say again: today, we outnumbered them. But look around you, think of your time in the sky. The Wild is vast. Our people live in tiny stretches along the Godroad. All of them together, even if you include every road-born and sky-born across the seven houses, are nothing compared to what lurks out there.'

'Hah, one of us is worth ten of them.'

'What if a hundred came for every one of us? Or a thousand?'

'Yes, if the whole Wild was to rise up together, that might be a problem.' He paused, then grinned. 'A glorious problem we would crush!' Vasin shook his head in anger and Quasim held up a hand. 'I see this troubles you but fear not, my noble friend. The demons of the Wild are terrifying, but most are little better than animals, and the clever ones stay well away in the deep places.'

'And if that changed?'

Quasim scowled for a moment, then said, in an unnecessarily loud voice: 'Then we would hunt them as we have ever done. There aren't enough demons in the world to blunt my sword.'

Vasin sighed. 'I have to go.'

'Stay, please. Even with your determined stride, you won't get back much faster than us. I haven't had a chance to hear how you stopped the Weeper yet.'

'I'm not planning to walk.'

'What? Even you can't fly back from a standing start.'

For the first time that day, Vasin found himself smiling, a bit of his old self resurfacing. 'Watch me.'

He started to run, every step made longer and higher by

his Sky-legs. The energies of the Godroad pulsed beneath him, giving each bound even more lift than usual. Behind him he could hear Quasim laughing, but it sounded good natured, even excited.

Unlike in the Wild, the essence currents around the Godroad were strong and constant. If one knew the right way to cut into them, it was possible to generate tremendous power quickly, enough to turn fall into flight. The problem was that if the approach wasn't perfect, he would plant his face into the Godroad in front of his peers, and a new song of Vasin would be sung, one he'd never live down. But he wasn't worried. Wrapped in his armour, working in his element, Vasin feared nothing.

When he had as much height as he could manage, he dived hard, catching the essence beneath his wings and compressing it under them so that it was trapped between him and the Godroad. In the space between them, the essence became so concentrated it began to fizz.

Skimming only inches from the surface of the Godroad, Vasin's vision was a blur of dancing sparks, red and blue. Then there was a flash, and Vasin was driven into the air, accompanied by roars of delight from Quasim and the hunters. He gave them a quick salute and set his course for the castle, floating high above.

An hour later, he was striding through the corridors of the castle, wishing they were wider. Even twisting his body, he worried that his wings would chip on the stone. It was bad form not to go direct to the Gardener-smiths to have them removed, even worse form to barge in on another Deathless armoured, armed and caked in swamp muck. But he told himself there was no time to lose.

Despite his haste, he could not help but think of his own High Lord, and the uncomfortable feeling that from the outside his behaviour would seem like a mirror to Yadavendra's. But by then he was committed.

Anuja received him without comment in the main throne room, though her expression made it clear he'd better have something important to say.

'The hunt was a success,' he began, and though she nodded, none of the tension left her. 'Both tributes survived. We faced unprecedented numbers of Murkers and a Weeper.'

'How many did we lose?'

'Four hunters were lost, my lady.' He forced himself to hold her gaze. 'All from my flight.'

The gold around her eye flashed as she nodded. 'And the other flights?'

'Alive, though the Opals have a lot of injuries. Can we speak freely here?'

'Yes.'

'Why didn't you warn me about the others? I've never hunted with such a . . . ' he forced himself to think, to try and remember the close ties between the three minor houses and be polite. He failed. 'Lord Quasim has skill but all the restraint of a hungry Dogkin at dinnertime, and Lord Lakshin is possibly even worse in the sky than my brother!'

'The Opal and Peridot lands have always been peaceful. There has never been need for them to hunt as hard as we do.'

'It was like last time, Anuja. The demons waited for your people to land and then went for them exclusively. If they hadn't, I suspect the losses would have been much higher in the other flights.'

'There can be no doubt now.' Her fists clenched in frustration. 'But why us? What has brought such rage upon my house?'

'I don't know, but I intend to find out.' He started to turn and then remembered his manners. 'My apologies, Lady Anuja. I said I would stay to hunt for you as long as you needed me, however I must return to my own lands.'

She half rose out of the throne, then sat back heavily with a wince as her injuries complained. 'But you can't! By your own admission, you are the only one here that can manage a hunt. It will be a long time before I can fly again. House Ruby needs you.'

'That is why I have to go. I fear we haven't seen the worst of this yet, and the key to understanding it isn't here. I will return, I promise.'

'As you promised to fight with us?'

He bowed his head in apology. 'I know what this must look like. All I can say is that it's clear we're not hunting mindless demons any more. They've changed, and if we're to survive, we have to change too.' He'd been edging towards the door as he spoke but a thought made his stop. 'Actually, I have an idea about that. Now we know that they target your people, you can use Ruby hunters as bait to draw the demons into traps of your devising. You can plan ways to keep them safe at the same time as turning the Wild's new obsession to your advantage.'

'Yes, I like the sound of this.' Anuja looked at him, allowing a little of her fatigue and worry to slip free from her painted mask. 'I ask you a second time, as my friend: stay. At least long enough to eat. We can talk more of these plans and what you experienced out there.'

'I dearly wish I could, but as your friend I have to go.'

He got one last glimpse of her face as he left, and it was as hard and impenetrable as the walls. 'So be it.'

Pari kept a wary eye on the suns as they travelled, mindful of the need to get back to Varg, and then Arkav, before her absence was noticed. Despite many lifecycles of dire warnings from the Story-singers and her own personal experience, the forest seemed peaceful, almost pleasant. As far as she could tell, Nidra was the only dangerous thing moving between the trees.

'Have you had any trouble with demons?' she asked.

'No.'

'None at all?'

'No.'

'Perhaps you might elaborate a bit?'

'There's not much to say. The demons don't come to Sorn. Maybe it's because the Corpseman marked it, maybe it's because they don't think I'm worth eating.' She shrugged. 'All I know is that it's been forgotten by them just as easily as it has by the Sapphire.'

'I haven't forgotten.'

Nidra's face cracked for a moment, like a dam threatening to burst, and while Pari thought a good cry would do her the world of good, she also knew that the Sapphire were rather funny about such things, so she added: 'It really is impressive how you've managed to live out here all this time. Even accepting Sorn is safe you still had to find food for two. However did you manage it, my dear?'

'Vasin arranges food drops, and when that isn't enough, I venture into the Wild and take what I need.'

She makes it sound so simple but the new lines in her face say otherwise.

Nidra's vulnerability was shocking to Pari. Last they'd met, the woman had been unshakable, a force of nature. Now she seemed to be barely clinging on.

They arrived at a large grassy hill, with steep sides and a crown of silver birch. When she was here before Samarku Un-Sapphire had been growing out of one of those trees, as if somehow the tree had infected him, become a part of him. The thought of his tortured form made her shiver.

Almost guiltily, her gaze turned upwards. The angle was too sharp to see what, if anything, Nidra had left of the man, but she knew that before they left, she would have to see for herself. Perhaps that way she could banish the image of him from her thoughts and dreams.

Nidra picked her way up the hillside with an almost painful amount of care, and Pari had a sudden insight into what her life must have been like. *She's alone out here and on constant guard against the Wild and herself.* Seeing the hill with new eyes, Pari was suddenly aware of all the places one could trip or slip, her imagination conjuring up a hundred different ways to sprain an ankle or break a bone, or open a cut.

That insight gave her a great deal of patience, even though she could feel time slipping away. It made her think of her brother and how fragile he was. *Please let his mood hold until I get back. Please.*

'Here,' said Nidra, drawing Pari's attention to a small mound about halfway up the hillside. She began digging at it, scraping back the mud until a curve of smooth amber was revealed. Preserved within was the shadowy shape of a body.

'They're still here,' said Pari sadly. 'I wonder why the Corpseman did this. Do you think it's a burial rite?'

'No. Look closer.'

Pari did so. The shadow within the amber slowly resolved itself, only becoming clear when her face was an inch away. Something had eaten the flesh from the body and dissolved the clothes. Hard bony plates had grown to replace them, bulky and angular around the chest and shoulders, and stick thin where the lower spine met the hips. In places the original skeleton could be seen, a nodule of collarbone peeking from the black, finger bones and their yellowing tendons, oddly preserved. The top half of the skull remained, held within a carapace hood, the teeth jutting out like a ledge.

'Delightful,' said Pari.

Nidra gestured to the hill with her sapphire dagger. 'They're all like this, more or less.'

'More or less?'

'Some are more . . . covered than others.'

'I think House Sapphire needs to come here and purge this place.'

'Good luck convincing Yadavendra of that.'

'Surely even he would want to do something about this?'

'He might, but my brother never does anything suggested by anyone other than Rochant, and especially not someone from another house.'

'I'll just have to convince him it was his idea then.'

Nidra snorted and began to move further up the hill. 'Easier to be rid of him and have another take charge. Quicker too.'

They made the rest of the climb in silence. At the top, she

saw the forked tree where Samarku had once been but there was no sign of him now. Though one of the branches bore an unsettling resemblance to a human arm. With Samarku gone, the trees were no longer the strangest thing at the top of the hill. A ridged oval of amber now stood in the middle of it. As she approached, she realized that the lower half of the structure was buried beneath the ground. It was thicker than the one she'd just seen and it was harder to discern what lay within. Her instincts more than made up for her eyes however.

'The Corpseman is in there, isn't it?'

Nidra nodded.

'You seem awfully calm about that, my dear.'

'Better it be in there than out here. I've thought about trying to kill it, but it's awake. It's probably aware of us.'

Pari saw the truth of this and stopped. She didn't feel under threat but she did feel . . . unwelcome. She considered trying to attack the Coprseman while it was in this state but dismissed the idea. Somehow she didn't think that it was helpless, and with just the two of them, without armour, she didn't fancy their chances.

'I think we should go.'

Nidra didn't need telling twice and immediately began the climb down. Pari was about to follow when she caught a flash of red and green in the air, of something flying towards them. She took cover behind the forked tree and waited. The creature was small, a Lizardkin of some sort. Its wings beat heavily, and it fell as much as flew the final few feet to land on the amber containing the Corpseman. It sat there for a while, panting, then there was a subtle movement within and the Lizardkin shifted to match it, poking out its tongue to touch the surface, like two people pressing their hands on either side of a window.

Pari had spent many years honing her intuitions, trying to find ways to read the faces and bodies of her enemies. She was much better at it with humans than monsters, but she knew something was being passed between the two. *That Lizardkin is talking to the Corpseman. I'm sure of it.*

The moment only lasted for a few seconds, at which point the Lizardkin jerked straight, blinking at its surroundings in surprise.

Perplexed, Pari went after Nidra, catching up the other woman partway down the hill. Neither of them spoke. They'd nearly reached the bottom when she heard the trees begin to whisper as if stirred by a distant wind. A sound was carried from one leaf to another, a sharp unnatural sound. 'If I didn't know better,' said Pari, 'I'd say that was a bell.'

'No!' hissed Nidra.

'No?'

But the other woman didn't deign to explain, setting off in the direction of Sorn at speed, leaving Pari with little choice but to follow.

Over the course of his life, Sa-at had been given cause to flee many times. He was adept at navigating the Wild at speed, at knowing when to run and when to hide, and knew the shifting movements of the safe places, and where the nearest one would be.

Alone, it would be a simple matter for him to vanish, trackless. He looked across at Tal, his heavy-footed friend, and at Lord Rochant slung between them, and despaired.

He did not know the trees around Sorn, and the price for

their protection would be high. Everything here hated the Deathless and it occurred to him that if he were to give Rochant to one of the greater demons, like Murderkind, he could ask for anything he wanted, he could even ask it to kill the Red Brothers for him.

Then I will be safe again.

As fast as he'd thought that, his heart replied: *But I promised to keep him safe and safe from his enemies. Deathless are enemies of the Wild. Deathless are enemies of Murderkind. Does that mean they are my enemies too?*

Either way, he knew he could not betray Rochant. He would have to find another way to deal with the Red Brothers. At least Rochant could help him learn about the Corpseman. *He will tell me and then I will tell Murderkind and then I will have kept my promise.*

Murderkind will be pleased and I will get to keep Tal as my friend.

This thought gave Sa-at comfort as they struggled their way down Sorn's main street.

Rochant's breath was laboured by his ear. 'What is your plan?'

He exchanged a glance with Tal. 'I don't have one.'

'My lord,' Tal added, with no small amount of fear.

'You,' gasped Rochant, 'are going to need one. My enemies will come for me.'

'How many?' asked Sa-at.

'One, maybe two.'

'Women?'

'You saw them?'

'Yes.'

Sa-at could still picture them in his mind now. So unlike

214

anyone he'd seen before that he hungered to see them again. Tal had said that one of them was Deathless too. Did the Deathless fight each other then, like the princes of the Wild? Sa-at would have to ask. Somewhere beneath his fear, a little excitement bubbled at the idea of all the new knowledge he could get. *New things are the best things.*

They were reaching the edge of Sorn now and the time was coming to make a decision about what to do.

'When you saw them,' continued Rochant, 'which way were they going?'

Sa-at pointed.

'Then we have a head start. They'll be coming faster than us though, and they are skilled hunters. We can't outrun them, our only chance is to outthink them.'

'Out . . . think them, my lord?' asked Tal. 'But how?'

'That is the question. Our enemy is quick, experienced and thorough. They will know the immediate surroundings well, and they know me and the kind of tricks I am likely to try.'

Sa-at frowned. Even though the man was describing a terrible situation, his face had become more animated, his eyes lively. *He is backwards. He says good things like they're bad things, and bad things like they're good things.*

'They might expect me to try for the Godroad,' Rochant mused. 'It isn't far from here and offers protection from the Wild. However, it would be easy for them to spot me and catch me on it.

'They might expect me to use the cover of the forest near the Godroad. Following it home but keeping out of sight. That's actually not a bad plan. If a traveller came by, I could get a ride with them to the nearest settlement and then get an escort back to my castle. However, it would still be a gamble. There's always a chance that my enemies have their own people on the Godroad. If we met one of them, it would not go well for us.'

He used so many words so quickly, it was hard for Sa-at to keep up. 'But you said there were two.'

'In the forest, yes,' said Rochant, 'but my enemies have many, many servants.'

'Do you have servants, too?'

A strange expression crossed Rochant's face, one Sa-at couldn't name. It wasn't really one thing nor the other, like a movement just beneath the water, a hint of an action rather than the action itself. 'Yes,' he said. 'Some of the greatest women and men of the land are loyal to me. Perhaps one day, you will meet them.'

'I'd like that.'

'I'm sure they would too.'

The conviction with which Rochant spoke lifted his heart. He had been so lonely for so long that the thought of meeting the greatest people in the land – and them liking him! – made him feel warm inside. Filled with new purpose, he started turning left, guiding the others with his arm so that they all faced the same direction. 'This way.'

'Listen,' said Rochant. 'If they catch us, then, if you are to keep your promise, you need to do something for me.'

'What?'

'Kill me. Preferably swiftly.'

Sa-at frowned. 'Why?'

'Because that will keep me safe from them. Do you understand?'

'No.'

Rochant gave a little smile. 'Will you do it anyway?'
'Yes.'

He closed his eyes, though Sa-at couldn't tell if it was from relief or fatigue. 'Good.'

They completed the turn and left Sorn, crossing the unkempt grasses and moving into the trees, heading away from the Godroad.

Travelling quickly with the extra weight between them was hard work. Conversation soon became impossible, the two young men reduced to gasps and puffs. Crowflies kept its distance, flying above them or waiting in the higher branches. Sa-at could feel its eyes on him though, and knew it was troubled.

At last they came to an old oak tree. Despite the fact he'd been keeping an eye out for one like this, he had the odd sense that it had put itself in their path, finding them rather than being found. It towered over them like some moss bearded giant. Parts of its root network were exposed, as if it had recently moved, disturbing the surrounding earth. After lowering Rochant to the ground, Sa-at approached the tree. He took an instant dislike to the arrogant lean of its trunk but he knew they were running out of time and so tried his best to look friendly.

'Hello,' he said.

The tree gave no indication that it had heard but he was sure it was listening. 'I ask that you shelter my two friends. In return, I will give you two locks of my hair.' He took a handful of its sleek, black length and pressed it against the bark. 'I will hang them from your mighty branches.'

The tree did not move.

'And . . . three feathers from my coat.' He drew his sleeve

across the side of the tree, letting the feathers brush against it.

There was an indifferent rustle.

'And I will touch your roots with my own blood . . . ' He glanced up at the tree for a sign. When it gave none, he sighed. 'And when I return I will do so thrice more, to show my gratitude.'

There was another rustle, not exactly happy, but when Sa-at looked at the roots again, he saw they had parted slightly to reveal a small hollow. 'Thank you,' he said. He had to call Crowflies down to help cut his hair.

'Sa-aat,' it said, looking at the tree and then back at him, disapproving. The tree was getting far too good a deal and the Birdkin was not happy about it.

'I know,' he murmured, 'but we're in a hurry.'

Despite those words, he did not rush tying the hair, choosing the branches where they could be displayed to greatest effect. He examined his coat, and when his eyes alighted on a feather he didn't want to lose, he swallowed the sadness down and plucked it, repeating the process three times. These he tucked into the branches of the tree. Lastly, he pricked his finger on his Birdkin's beak, and touched it to the roots, before holding it out to Crowflies again.

He felt the nip, painful, as it resealed the wound, and gave a nod of thanks.

That done, he turned back to his friends and pointed at the hollow. 'In you get.'

Tal regarded him with an expression of horror. 'In there?'

'Yes.'

'No.'

Sa-at nodded encouragingly. 'Yes. You first.'

As he approached it, the Gatherer got slower and slower. 'We'll never all get in there.'

'Just you and Rochant.'

'Lord Rochant,' amended Tal.

'Yes.'

'But what about you?'

'I have a –' he looked at Rochant '– plan.'

Rochant's eyes were shut but it didn't surprise Sa-at that he was still awake and listening to them. 'Tell me.'

He tore a strip from the rags Rochant was wearing and held it up. 'I'll make a new trail for your enemies and lead them far away.'

'It might work. You'll need his boots.'

Tal had crouched down by the tree but still hadn't managed to climb into the hollow. 'What?'

'If they find our trail they'll know I'm not alone. The new trail needs two sets of boots if it's to match the old one.'

Sa-at nodded, smiling in appreciation. 'Yes.'

'Take your time coming back. If they see you, they might use you to find us.'

'Yes.'

It took some cajoling to get Tal to trust the tree but eventually, he was stuffed into the hollow and Sa-at bent down to pull off his heavy boots. 'I'll bring them back.'

'Do you promise?'

He exchanged a glance with Crowflies, knowing that it would disapprove of him making any more promises. 'No,' he replied, tucking the left boot under his arm.

Tal grabbed at the right one. 'But I'm dead without them!'

'Alright then—'

'Sa-aat!'

'I promise I'll bring back your boots.'

Crowflies squawked again, not angry. Disappointed. Sa-at sighed as he took the second boot. He hadn't realized how hard it would be keeping friends happy. It seemed that to please Tal he had to upset Crowflies, and it seemed that Tal's discomfort brought the Birdkin pleasure.

Between them, they began the tricky business of inserting Rochant into the hollow. Unlike Tal, who wore the expression of a man trapped in a nightmare, Rochant was alert, his eyes studying the roots from the inside, flicking from detail to detail. Not from fear, but curiosity. *He's excited!* Thought Sa-at, suddenly excited himself. *He's excited because he's learning something new. He's just like me!*

Rochant's attention turned back to Sa-at, one set of sparkling eyes mirroring the other, and for a moment he felt that he saw past the man's guarded mask, truly saw him, and that he too was being seen, and it felt good.

He had the urge to say something, but the words got lost somewhere between his thoughts and his tongue, burrowing themselves deep into the back of his throat like shy animals. By the time he had collected himself enough to speak the tree was shifting, squatting down like a Birdkin over its eggs.

'Aargh!' he heard Tal say, before the sound muffled and then abruptly cut off, but it was the sound of fear rather than the sound of someone being crushed to death. The tree may not be the best of its kind, but it would honour their agreement. *My friend is safe. No, my friends are safe. I have two friends now.*

'Sa-aat!'

Three friends now. And Murderkind makes four.

After pressing his hand against the its trunk in farewell,

Sa-at sped away, skipping from root to stone, swinging from low branches, anything to keep his feet from marking the soft mud. Crowflies flew ahead of him as he ran back towards Sorn, giving the occasional cry to let him know it was safe. He did not know how quickly the two women would come for them, but when he conjured them in his mind again, confident and capable, he felt sure it would not be long.

When he got closer, he began looking for the places where their boots had imprinted. When he found one, he obscured it, breaking the link between them leaving and when they headed for the oak tree. Then he made a new trail with his feet and the thread he'd taken from Rochant's clothing, moving in the direction of the Godroad and then turning parallel to it. Sa-at had never dared go to the Godroad before. The one time he'd talked to Crowflies about it, the Birdkin had got so upset he'd never mentioned it again. He knew from the forest that the Godroad was poison but if that was the case, why would Rochant think of using it? He had so many questions to ask, he worried that he might not be able to remember them all.

Aware that Crowflies was getting agitated, he turned towards the Godroad, making sure the trail was heading towards it, and then stopped. In the distance he could just make out a faint glow in the air. It didn't look like poison to him. It looked pretty, but he remained wary. Everyone knew that the most dangerous things in the Wild were the pretty ones.

He leaned against a nearby tree as he pulled Tal's boots on, and it touched a branch to his back for support. 'You're so much friendlier than the oak,' he said, and the words were caught in its leaves and whispered back, pleased. Once this was done he walked backwards alongside the trail he had just made, so it would seem like two people had come this way instead of one. However, the prints didn't seem right and so he began to stomp more heavily.

'Better.'

He decided it was quite fun walking backwards whilst pretending to be Tal. The only problem was that the boots were far too big for him and he had to stop every few paces to keep his feet from slipping out.

By the time he'd got back to where his new trail started, Crowflies was calling his name.

They're here.

He slipped off Tal's boots, tucked them under his arm, and scurried away, heading deeper into the Wild. He travelled quickly but did not run, focusing on making as little impression as possible. Instincts led him back towards parts of the forest that he knew, until he found one of his friendly trees and climbed into it, letting the branches close around him. Crowflies came to join him, settling into the crook of his arm.

They stayed there like that for a time, bird and boy, hearts beating quickly together, until they calmed and calmed some more, and slept.

CHAPTER TWELVE

When they got back to Nidra's dwelling in Sorn, the trip-wire by the front step was broken. Pari knew Rochant was no longer there, she could just feel it. She followed Nidra inside anyway, in part to see how the other woman would react and because there might be clues as to what had happened.

The little side room seemed bigger without Rochant to fill it, but just as sad looking. There was no sign of a struggle.

Nidra ran her hand over the leather strap that had been attaching Rochant's head to the wall. 'He had help.'

'Perhaps not. He could have planned an escape and saved what little of his strength remained, waiting for us to lower our guard.'

'No. He couldn't have rescued himself.'

'You sound very certain, my dear.'

'I am certain,' Nidra retorted, pushing past Pari and walking out the front door. Pari had one last look at the room. There were no obvious clues to indicate who had come or what had happened, but her instincts agreed with Nidra's assessment. Someone else had been here.

When she stepped outside, she saw Nidra inspecting the ground. 'Rochant wouldn't be able to travel far in his condition,' Pari said.

'He wouldn't be able to travel at all.' She kept her attention fixed on the ground as she added, 'I took the use of his limbs from him.'

That explains why his hands weren't tied. 'I thought you said you stopped the torture for Vasin's sake.'

'I did, but I'm not a fool. My situation was too uncertain to leave him whole. Besides,' her voice dropped, 'he deserved to suffer.' Before Pari could say anything to that, and she did have quite a bit to say on the subject, Nidra held up a hand. 'Look, drag marks.'

Pari gestured the way they'd gone. 'After you.'

The two moved quickly towards Sorn's edge. The trail was easier to follow when it hit the long grass. She could see where the escapees had ploughed their way through, trampling down stalks.

'Two of them,' said Nidra.

'Agreed. The question is, who are they?'

'No, the question is, how did they find us?'

Pari didn't like the way Nidra glanced back as she said this. Ignoring it, she took what she could from the trail. There were two sets of prints, close together and mostly in step. One set belonged to an adult wearing the kind of heavy duty boots favoured by road-born that had to travel the Wild. The other was lighter, made by smaller feet. *A young woman's or large child's perhaps?*

'At the risk of being pedantic,' said Pari, 'I think there

might be a third question: Did they take Rochant against his will?'

'There's no point speculating. We find him. We find the answers.'

They followed the tracks out of Sorn, moving towards the Godroad. It was all as Pari suspected but something didn't seem right, though she couldn't put her finger on what.

'Here!' said Nidra, running ahead to a particularly thorny bush. Amid the spikes were some strands of grey, threads torn from human clothing. 'That's his.'

They upped the pace, moving parallel to the Godroad, and Pari wondered if Varg might have seen anything. *Knowing Varg, he may even have caught them by now.* She chuckled to herself, making Nidra turn and glare.

'What?'

'Oh, just laughing at my own naive optimism.'

A few more threads were found, then the tracks turned towards the Godroad. Nidra ran to the side of it and leapt, scrambling up the sheer crystal side to stand on top. Her face was lit blue from beneath as she stared first one way, then the other. 'Nothing. We're too late.'

Pari didn't follow, staying amid the mud and dead plants that bordered the Godroad. Her intuition was trying to tell her something if she could just be quiet enough to let it. She took a deep breath and released it slowly, then looked from the road to the trees and back again. She allowed her eyes to rest on details as she did so, trying to be open to anything. She even looked up at the sky, her eyes drawn across the swirling mass of cloud.

'If they had a carriage waiting for him,' said Nidra, 'they could be halfway to Sagan by now.'

'Mmm.' Pari's attention came back to the tracks. She was vaguely aware of Nidra jumping down, curses spilling from her lips.

'Damn that bastard! I should have killed him when . . . no, I should have done more to break him. Then this wouldn't matter. All that time. He's been in my grasp all that time and I could have . . . I should have . . . '

'Does this look odd to you?' said Pari, pointing at the tracks.

Nidra came to join her. 'What do you see?'

'It's not easy to climb onto the Godroad here. You had to jump and pull yourself up.' She pointed to where Nidra had just been. 'And that's where you disturbed the ground to do it. If we assume they walked fairly directly from the trees to the Godroad, we should be able to see some sign of their climb but there's nothing. When we first tracked them, there were signs of dragging, but they've gone. It may be that they found a better way to carry Rochant between them but if so, I'd expect the tracks to get heavier, and yet this set, the bigger footprints, seem lighter here than they did before.'

Nidra stared at them. 'Maybe the other one carried Rochant.'

'You may be right, my dear, but I'm not sure they actually took the Godroad at all, and even if they did, there's no evidence that they still had Rochant at this point.'

'You think they hid him somewhere?'

'Yes, or gave him to another party. Either way, I think we've lost him.' She received another of Nidra's suspicious looks and decided to ignore it. *She's like dry wood waiting for a spark.* 'We don't know where he is but we can make an educated guess that he'll be going home. If I can get there ahead of him, I'll be able to watch the roads at least.'

'To what end?'

'I don't know. Perhaps an opportunity will present itself, perhaps it won't, but better to try something than do nothing, I always say.' The truth was, Pari didn't always say that. She actually felt that doing nothing was often far better than making things needlessly worse. However, she was gripped by a powerful urge to keep talking, saying whatever popped into her mouth in an effort to keep things upbeat. There was a growing sense of darkness around her companion, one that threatened to suck them both in if she didn't fight it.

'One thing we do know,' said Nidra, her eyes narrowed. 'This isn't the work of my brother. If it was, there would be hunters everywhere and we'd both be facing our last lifecycles.'

'Some good news at least.'

'Which means,' Nidra continued, 'that it's Rochant's people, or a force from the Wild, or random travellers.'

'As you say, speculation doesn't help us now. The best thing is for me to get moving.' She turned to go but Nidra hadn't finished.

'Those tracks look human, and things of the Wild go deeper with their victims, they wouldn't come here. We can rule them out. Travellers avoid Sorn, have ever since the Corpseman came. No reason for that to change.' Her body was rigid with tension, gloves creaking around the hilt of her sapphire dagger. 'Which leaves Rochant's allies. But why now, after all this time? Why not take him ten years ago, or just after it happened?'

She glanced up at Pari, the unsaid words hanging between them. *Because I was between lives. She thinks I did this! Don't laugh, Pari. Whatever you do, don't laugh. She might burst an eyeball.*

'I honestly don't know, my dear, but I intend to find out.'

But Nidra wasn't having it that they had lost Rochant. 'You retrace these tracks to Sorn, see if you can find anything new. I'm going back. If only two found him, they may have hidden Rochant somewhere nearby while they went to get backup.'

'I agree, and I think it's a good idea . . . ' She was just building up to explaining why she couldn't stay when her instincts caught the words before they left her mouth. *She suspects me. If I leave now, I'll appear even more guilty in her eyes, and neither of us can afford this fragile alliance to break.* 'But I can't stay long. If I don't get back to Arkav by morning difficult questions will be asked.'

'Difficult questions?' Nidra almost choked on the words. 'I have suffered in ways you cannot imagine, and face my final death, and you're worried about being given a hard time by your brother?'

Not my brother, she thought but did not say. *Now is no time for pedantry.* 'My apologies. Let me go now and do as you suggested. I'll come back and report my findings either way.'

She hurried off, not wanting to give space for things to sour further.

On a second viewing the tracks remained suspicious. Apart from the early stages near Sorn, there was no sign of dragging nor any indication that they'd set Rochant down to rest. *Am I to believe they just marched the whole way with him on their shoulders like a sack?*

And then she found it, a mostly covered footprint leading in a different direction. Now that she knew what to look for, she saw several signs of obfuscation that made it difficult to see the original footprints, but nonetheless created a followable trail of their own. Soon after, she found the tracks again. *This is it!*

However, the path led deeper into the Wild, deeper than she wanted to go without armour and company. If she went on, she would be putting herself at risk, and if anything happened to her, it would leave Arkav alone in Sapphire territory. *He might break again, or worse, he might break someone else.* She imagined him turning his back on his mission to come and find her, and all of the terrible consequences that would follow.

But I'm close to something here. If I leave, Rochant will get away and all of our plans will be for nothing. Nidra will die, Vasin will likely follow, and Rochant will be back at High Lord Yadavendra's side.

The weight of responsibility was crushing on her shoulders. She felt the various factions wheeling about in her imagination, forces that she could influence but not control. Nidra needed her. Arkav needed her. And beyond them, the very balance between the Crystal Dynasties and the Wild was being threatened. House Sapphire had to be purged if the rot was to be kept from spreading elsewhere.

She looked up at the suns and was troubled to see them halfway towards the horizon. There were only a few hours until sunsdown, and only a fool stayed in the Wild after dark.

If I find nothing soon, I'll have to turn back.

The trail continued before her, the footsteps closer together now. In a few places a print was smeared, as if the person making it had slipped but not fallen. She could imagine the ones carrying Rochant getting tired. They too would need a place to hide at night. They were heading away from any known Sapphire settlements, suggesting that the pair had a camp or fortified location nearby.

Or that they're as desperate as I am.

At some point she lost the trail. It took her a while to retrace her steps, and she had enough time to worry that the forest had played a trick on her before she found the end of it again. A few different prints merged here, suggesting they'd stopped a while. A little more investigation revealed some grey threads tramped into the mud. She crouched down to sift more closely and found leaves pressed down too, not by boots but by a body.

They put him down here. They rested for a time. Where did they go afterwards? Did the Wild take them? There'd be a strange irony in that.

Here, the canopy was thick, oppressive, the sunlight able to make it glow overhead but not penetrate deeply. It was already getting hard to discern fine details on the ground. She made one last search, vowing to go back if no new clues presented themselves. When that failed, she made one more, vowing that this really would be the last one.

That was when she saw the tree.

In and of itself, there wasn't much to tell it apart. The Wild was full of large imposing trees that seemed to loom over her as she travelled. This one was old and many things, from moss, to mushrooms, to tiny Lizardkin, seemed to have made a home there. Again, hardly remarkable. However, hanging from its branches like slender banners were two lengths of hair, of a colour that seemed tantalizingly familiar. Pari cursed the lack of light and moved closer, stepping up on a lower branch for a better look.

I know you, she thought. *Or someone very like you.*

A name was on the tip of her tongue, so close she could almost speak it, when she heard a footstep from somewhere behind her. It was heavy, too heavy for the smaller of the two carrying Rochant, too heavy even for the larger one. It was followed by a second footstep, just as heavy.

The hairs on the back of her neck prickled, as the two things – her senses, cultivated over lifecycles, screamed at her: *things, not people!* – got louder.

It was clear that they would find her at any moment and it was just as clear that she could not allow that to happen.

Quickly but quietly, oh so quietly, Pari slipped around the wide trunk of the tree, just as the first of the lumbering figures arrived.

The suns were going down by the time Honoured Mother Chandni had a chance to speak to her son alone. They'd kept up their pretence of assured confidence through the afternoon, nodding to staff as they wandered the corridors, and in Chandni's case, giving quiet words of encouragement. With High Lord Yadavendra in residence, everyone was tense, and working twice as hard as usual.

It was only when they were safely inside Satyendra's chambers that they allowed themselves to relax. Chandni found herself dizzy with stress and reached out to the wall to steady herself, while Satyendra threw himself onto his bed face first and lay there, splayed, like a dead Squidkin.

She helped herself to some water and went to the window, taking comfort at the sight of the solid walls, and the sense of being high above the world, safe.

'What happened?' she asked.

His reply was muffled by the bedding.

'Satyendra, what happened?'

He turned his head enough to give her a sullen look. 'I said, don't ask. I don't want to talk about it.'

'At least tell me if you did well.'

'I didn't embarrass you, if that's what you're asking.'

'Was High Lord Yadavendra very difficult?'

'Awful.'

She went and sat by the side of his bed, and began stroking his long hair. 'From what I could see, you were excellent at lunch.'

She watched him try not to perk up at her compliment. 'I was?'

'Yes. The High Lord is clearly very impressed with you. Can you tell me why he wanted to see you afterwards?'

'No.'

'Should I be worried?'

'That depends,' his despondent expression returned, 'on whether you love me more than Lord Rochant.'

Chandni didn't answer. She loved her son, of course she did, but she also loved her Deathless Lord. It was her sacred duty to groom a vessel for Rochant's soul. In her mind, those loves coexisted. If it hadn't been for the assassins killing the other potential vessels, Satyendra would never have been called, and it wouldn't have been an issue. Now though, there was no one else. She looked at her son and asked herself if she was strong enough to see this through.

When it became clear she wasn't going to take the bait, his face became pleading. 'Tell him I'm not ready. Tell him we have to wait a little longer.'

'We've already been through this. I will offer my thoughts but in the end it is his decision.'

'Tell him!' hissed Satyendra, turning over and grabbing her arm. Tears glimmered at the corners of his eyes. 'I need more time.'

She knew what he really meant by that. Knew that he was plotting to escape his duty. A part of her was appalled by it, while another understood all too well. She waited, wondering whether to say anything or stroke him, or to simply sit. *Maybe I should go.* It was so hard knowing how to handle him when he was like this. *Whatever I do will get twisted. If I am tender he will get angry, if I give him space he will accuse me of neglect.*

'How can I best serve you, my son?'

He tilted his head, curious despite himself. 'I don't understand.'

'It is your duty to serve House Sapphire and it is mine to make sure you are ready. How may I serve you? How can I help you through this?'

'You really want to help me?'

'You know I do. Talk to me.'

'Then tell me, Mother, what do you really feel?'

Tired. Sad. Terribly sad. Afraid that the Wild has made you unsuitable to house Lord Rochant's soul and all of this suffering will have been for nothing. 'I feel proud that you are giving so much to us, and relief that our house will soon have Lord Rochant back again.'

His face twisted with distaste. 'I don't believe you.'

'Then I feel sorry for you. I have a lot of feelings right now, Satyendra, too many for me to put into words. But I am proud of you, please believe that.'

'What will you do when I am dead?'

The words struck her like a blow but she did not flinch from them. *Whatever I am suffering it is a thousand times worse for him. I must be a role model. I must show him how to bear that suffering.* 'When Lord Rochant returns I will continue to serve him and House Sapphire in any way I can.'

'You don't think they'll get rid of you, then? After all, you won't be needed to look after me or the castle when Lord Rochant is back. You'll be,' he gave an impish shrug, 'irrelevant.'

Instead of needling her, the suggestion stirred her fantasy. If House Sapphire didn't need her, she'd be free. 'That will be for my lord to decide.'

The facade of calm that he was wearing crumbled away and his voice rose in anger. 'You're always so bloody fucking dutiful!' He paused, no doubt to see if she'd react, but in this as in so many things, she disappointed him. Normally such language would upset her but today it had the opposite effect, and it was all she could do not to laugh. *After all, I've heard far worse in my lifetime.* It made her think of Varg. Too many things made her think of Varg lately. She missed him. She missed the feel of his arms around her, her head on his chest, the bass of his voice resonating against her ear. But most of all, she missed having someone to talk to openly and honestly.

I am so alone.

'Are you even listening to me?' yelled Satyendra.

'When you calm down and speak to me in a respectful, civilized way, I will listen to anything you wish to say. Until then,' she turned to the door, 'you do what you must, alone.'

To her surprise, she made it out of his room, and away down the corridor, without a retort. For once, she had had the last word and it gave her a guilty thrill of victory.

She had not got far when she saw Zax walking towards her with intent. Yadavendra's lead hunter still wore his wings, which forced him to move timidly to avoid catching the walls and ornaments. Seeing the brute so uncertain was gratifying, though it pained her to see any Sapphire less than perfectly composed. He showed such relief to have found her that she almost felt sorry for him, however an odious man in trouble was still an odious man, and she kept her sympathy in check.

'Honoured Mother Chandni!' he said and did his best to bow.

Better, she thought, but did not let any of her approval show. *Some animals are best treated with cruelty rather than kindness.* 'What is it?'

'High Lord Yadavendra requests that you join him on a most urgent matter.'

'Then we had best not keep him waiting.'

And with that she moved off purposefully, leaving the hunter to struggle in her wake.

To Chandni's surprise, Yadavendra had asked her to visit his personal chamber rather than Rochant's audience room. She sang for entrance, and when permission was given, she put aside the feeling of terror that always assailed her when in

235

the High Lord's presence, and went inside, stately, like a true Sapphire.

Zax floundered some way behind. She could just make out the sound of his Sky-legs tapping on the floor, a series of tottering tiny steps, toddler-like. By arriving before him, she had made his presence unnecessary, and because he would not dare interrupt his High Lord, he would be forced to wait at their pleasure. *As it should be. A lesson or two in humility is just what that hunter needs.*

As she expected, Yadavendra remained in his armour, which made the normally spacious room seem cramped and the furniture undersized. A bottle of wine had been set next to a bowl of soup, and she wondered if it was the same one from lunch. Both appeared untouched.

'Honoured Mother,' he said, beaming.

'High Lord,' she replied with a deep bow. 'How may I serve?'

'Rest assured, we will come to that. But first, I wished to express my satisfaction with your son.' He pointed at her. 'And with you. Any fears I had at the fitting were banished during our lunch together. He really has our beloved Rochant's aspect, don't you think?'

'It pleases me to hear you say so, High Lord.'

'Uncanny. But what impresses me most is the way he thinks. He has Rochant's way of coming at a problem and cutting through it. If my old friend is the sword of the house, then your Satyendra is the knife.'

He paused long enough for her to consider saying something.

'Would that I could have both weapons at my disposal. Alas, it cannot be. Did you know, Satyendra suggested that

I make him a new Deathless instead of using him as a vessel?'

'I did not.' She felt the heat of shame on her throat and cheeks as she bowed again. 'I can only apologize, my High Lord.'

As she straightened, she saw that his smile remained bright and broad. Perhaps a little too broad to be entirely comforting. He leaned forward, the intensity of his presence magnified in the intimate space, and she found herself wanting to back away, to put distance between herself and the room, between herself and her High Lord. But she didn't. Her posture remained straight, her face free of any misgivings.

'Apologize? For showing initiative?' Yadavendra laughed. 'Would that the rest of my family follow his example.' He put a hand on her right shoulder and she could feel, not heat exactly, but the weight of his personality radiating from the gauntlet, pressing down on her. 'Today has shown me beyond all doubt that Satyendra is ready to fulfil his duty to the house. The Bringers of Endless Order are on their way and will arrive this very night. In the morning, I will have them conduct the rebirth ceremony.'

Unable to bow with his hand still on her shoulder, Chandni nodded her acceptance of his words. She was unable to speak, stunned by the suddenness of it all. *I've known this was coming and yet I didn't think it would be now.* She knew she should be honoured, but all she could think about was Satyendra's crumpled face, desperate, teary. He would be devastated when she told him, and she determined that it had to be her that brought the news.

'You're quiet,' said Yadavendra, leaning down to peer at her.

'Forgive me, High Lord. I had assumed the ceremony would not be quite so soon. It is just a . . . surprise, that's all.'

'I understand, you know. It is lonely being in power. You have to make decisions for the house, not yourself. Like you, I have no wish to see Satyendra go. He will be honoured to serve as a vessel for Rochant's soul, yes, but he will also be missed.' His other hand rose to cover her left shoulder, and squeezed gently. 'By us both.

'But my house needs your lord . . . I need him.' As his face twisted with emotion he let go of her abruptly and turned to the window. 'More than you know.'

Chandni had no idea how she should respond. A small part of her felt sorry for Yadavendra, and honoured to be included in his confidence. A larger part disgusted that he display such weakness. But most of all, she wanted to get away. The instability of the man was palpable and she had the irrational thought that if she stayed too close to him, she would catch it, like a sickness – a sickness of the soul. She took a step back and bowed. 'I will be there to greet the Bringers of Endless Order myself, and I will have my people make the necessary preparations here. Invitations will be sent to the Deathless Lords of the Sapphire.'

'No need,' said Yadavendra. 'They've were sent long ago. And I gave the order for the ceremony to be prepared for at the same time as I summoned you.'

'Then, with your leave, I will go directly to my son.'

He nodded. 'Of course.'

With great relief, Chandni left the chamber. She wondered how she would break the news to Satyendra, and how she would find it in herself to say goodbye. *No doubt he already senses the changes in the castle.* She sighed, a shuddering potent thing, so heartfelt that she had to stop and cover her mouth lest it become a sob. *He will not make this easy on me nor do I want him to.* She realized then that she wanted Satyendra to be angry with her, to argue and fight for his right to live. And more than that, deep down, she wanted him to win.

CHAPTER THIRTEEN

Satyendra waited for Chandni to finish, nodded solemnly, and then took her hand. 'I understand, Mother.'

She was braced, no doubt expecting him to lash out verbally or otherwise, and did not react instantly. When she did it was with a gasp of disbelief, and a strange mix of relief and sadness. The emotion was strong, but not the kind that he found nourishing. 'You do?'

'Yes.'

A tear ran down her cheek as she spoke. 'I did not expect you . . . that is I was worried that . . . ' She collected herself and squeezed his hand. 'I am proud of you, my son.'

He smiled at her, keeping his thoughts locked within a cage of teeth. *Enjoy the feeling while you can.* 'It's funny, I've been terrified of this moment all these years but now it's here I feel . . . ' *Furious? Betrayed? Trapped?* ' . . . calm. I suppose there's nothing to fear any more.'

'Oh Satyendra,' she whispered, stepping forward to embrace him.

'Might I ask one thing before I go to present myself to the Bringers?'

'Of course.'

'I'd like to say goodbye to some of my friends amongst the hunters, and say thank you to Story-singer Ban for being so patient with me over the years.'

'Yes.' She gave him a sad smile. 'He would appreciate that.'

'And then, afterwards, might we have some private time together, before . . . '

Her tears were flowing freely now. 'Yes. Yes, I promise. It's the least I can do.'

'Be brave, Mother. It isn't for much longer now.' He hugged her again, suddenly aware that he was taller than her. *Perhaps I have grown, or perhaps she is shrivelling up.* With her defences down it was tempting to plant a barb, something to make her suffer. One well-crafted sentence was all it would take. The idea stirred his hunger. But no, he had to keep her in this state, off balance and unfocused, if he was to succeed. 'When it is time, I may need help.' He looked down as if hiding shame, when in truth he wanted to avoid his mother's scrutiny. 'Can I count on you?'

'Yes, always.'

'It's just, if the fear comes back, I might need a little push and it would make it easier if I knew you were here to help me make my last preparations. I mean, instead of the servants.'

He could see her weighing it up in her mind. She would have many things to oversee in the castle tonight, things that could take her all over. But he needed her out of the way, and to know exactly where she was.

'Yes,' she said at last. 'It will take a bit of arranging, but I will be here when you get back.'

'Thank you. I think I can do this, Mother, if you're with me.'

He could see her trying not to cry again. Tears of joy were collecting in the corners of her eyes, and tears of pride. Useless tears. 'Please don't,' he said, the slightest tinge of irritation betrayed in his tone – *oh, so you want me to go quietly and to feel sorry for you as well!* – 'or you'll set me off too.'

They hugged one more time and Satyendra left his chambers. Let them all think he had come to terms with his fate. Then, when his mother was ensconced in his room and the rest of the castle was busy dealing with the Bringers of Endless Order, he would make his escape.

Chandni watched her son go, blurred through her tears, his form shimmering, fluid. *He's not coming back.*

She swayed under the weight of emotion. Duty dictated that she go after him and drag him back, but she couldn't move. Satyendra was making a bid to live. In his typical way he was being selfish and thoughtless, thinking nothing of the house or any greater concerns.

And yet she could not move.

Bad enough that she had denied her own heart for so long. Would she now deny his as well?

I remember when everything was so clear. It was the Wild that did this to me. Being with the road-born. And with Varg. Seeing the exile, Fiya, and learning that things are not quite as the Story-singers tell them.

I love my lord and I want him back. But is that enough

to justify Satyendra's murder? He is not the child I wished to raise, but how can I blame him, given the burden he has always been under?

The Wild didn't just get to me, they got to him too. Neither of us quite fit any more. Perhaps Lord Rochant's soul will purge my son, or perhaps it will find Satyendra's flesh unworthy.

She steadied her breathing, dried her eyes, and summoned Pik. The boy arrived shortly afterwards, a worried expression on his face. He bowed to her.

'Report.'

'Satyendra is on the move, Honoured Mother.'

'I know.'

'What should I do?'

An excellent question. 'Go to him and . . . '

There was an awkward pause.

'Yes, Honoured Mother?'

'And help him.'

Pik gasped.

'Do this and I'll see that your place here is assured. No more difficult tasks. No more deception. You and your descendants will have a place here, forever. I swear it on the Blood of the Sapphire Everlasting.'

'But . . . '

She could see him wrestling with his conscience.

'This is for the good of the house. Lord Rochant cannot come into a vessel that isn't ready.'

'But the High Lord says—'

'When Satyendra is ready, I'm sure he'll do what is right. Remember, Lord Rochant came from the road-born. Perhaps my son needs to spend time with them in order to do as his

243

High Lord asks. But you don't need to worry about that. Satyendra is my burden to bear.

'Now, go to his side. Give him whatever he needs to leave, and I will see you richy rewarded.'

Pik saluted. 'Yes, Honoured Mother Chandni.'

'Make sure he isn't seen. And please, make sure he has food and something warm to fend off the night.'

'Yes, Honoured Mother. I won't fail you.'

There. It is done. Let Satyendra follow his heart, and let it lead him to a happier place.

Sa-at woke with a start. He was in a tree, a safe tree, and Crowflies was with him. *I am among friends.*

But his heart was pumping hard in his chest and the old scar on the knuckle where his little finger had once been was itching. He wondered if the Red Brothers had come into his dreams again. It happened sometimes, especially when he was feeling small.

He parted the branches above him to get a look at the sky. It was still dark but the night was coming to an end, that quiet time of transition when the predators of the Wild returned to the deep places. Normally he would stay in the tree for a few more hours before venturing out, just to be on the safe side, but he felt unsettled, burdened with the sense that things were not as they should be.

Crowflies regarded him as he began the climb down, head tilted in surprise.

'Something isn't right. I think we should go back to the others now.' This made the Birdkin cackle derisively. 'It's that oak. I don't trust it, and . . . I'm worried about my friends.'

'Sa-aat,' cawed Crowflies, a mixture of warning and pity in the sound.

'I'm sorry. I have to go.'

He thanked the tree and slipped from its embrace and down the trunk. It was hard travelling before dawn. The night seemed to cling on underneath the thick canopy, and he was painfully aware that the only thing that seemed to be moving, at least the only thing making any noise at all, was him.

The journey back to the oak was slower than he would have liked too, but despite a rising sense of desperation, Sa-at knew better than to rush at this time. Yes, the sunrise was near, but any decent prey could tempt the demons of the Wild out of the shadows.

After a while, he heard the familiar sound of wings flapping in the dark and smiled to himself. *Crowflies.* Now it was clear that he wasn't going to change his mind, the Birdkin had come to join him. *It always comes,* he thought. *It thinks we should wait but it came to help me anyway. It is my friend. I think we should wait too but I am going to help Tal and Rochant anyway because they need me. Because they are my friends.*

It was strange, thinking about other people, and what they needed or desired. Tal and Rochant were very different from him, both complicated in their own way. He liked that. They were new and strange, and made his thoughts fizz in a pleasant way. He did not want anything bad to happen to them.

By the time he reached the oak, the night was paling, allowing rocks and trees to take shape before his eyes, grey and hazy. He slowed as he got closer, that sense of foreboding rising again in his chest. Without thinking about it, he began to scratch the scar on his knuckle.

Crowflies settled on a nearby branch but kept its distance from the oak.

Sa-at nodded to himself. *Crowflies feels it too.*

At first glance, things appeared as they had before. The tree remained aloof, and he could see a length of his hair hanging from one of the branches. The feathers were there, just as he'd placed them. But something wasn't right.

He exchanged a look with Crowflies before edging forward. If he wanted the tree to release his friends he was going to have to give it three more daubs of his blood.

As he got closer, he realized what was wrong.

I gave the oak two locks of my hair but I can only see one.

However, there was something else where he'd tied the second lock of hair, but it was wrapped around the branch and partly obscured by the leaves. Sa-at frowned, not liking the sense that the oak was deliberately hiding something from him.

He pretended not to have noticed and walked over to the trunk, keeping his eyes on the roots as if intending to fulfil his bargain. Then, when he was close enough, he leapt up, parting the lower branches so that he could see what was being hidden.

The oak rustled indignantly, but was too late to stop him getting a good look at its new decoration.

A thick string of crimson flesh had been wound along the length of the branch, as if a snake had coiled there before shedding its skin. He had seen flesh like that before, sprouting like hair from the heads of the Red Brothers.

Heart sinking, he spun round, to find two of the trees had moved in behind him. *No,* he thought as their shapes wavered, *not trees, demons.* And as he blinked, they resolved themselves into the hated forms of Eyesore and Crunch.

Sa-at experienced a moment of terror so pure that he didn't even notice Tal's boots slipping from his grasp and dropping to the ground.

'Well,' said Crunch, his voice rumbling with satisfaction. 'Is that the trembling of a Birdspawn I hear?'

Eyesore rubbed his hands together.

Sa-at backed away until the oak bumped roughly against his shoulder. Its branches formed a funnel either side of him, the only way out blocked by the Red Brothers.

The tree had betrayed him! Such an act wasn't just under-handed, it was wrong. Sa-at had acted in accordance with the ways, and their deal had not concluded. He still owed blood to its roots. But then, if the Red Brothers got their hands on him, he had no doubt there would be bloodshed, enough to slake its thirst many times over. And his deal had been to protect his friends, not him. In a way, the tree had done nothing wrong.

It occurred to him that if he bled on the roots, their deal would be complete, and the oak would release his friends directly into the hands of the Red Brothers.

I should have listened to Crowflies and waited. Why didn't I listen?

Eyesore took a step forward, guiding Crunch to do the same. There was no way he could fight them, no way to evade them. He couldn't even climb the tree. It had made its allegiance quite clear.

The only thing he had left was his wits. If he could think

of something clever to say, he might be able to stall them or slow them down. Could he threaten them with something? Offer them something? He took a breath, knowing he was done for but that his friends might still be saved. He just needed to think of some way to tempt them away from the tree. But no ideas came and one look at the hate in Eyesore's glare was enough to crush any words in his throat.

The two brothers took another step forward. One more and they would be able to grab him and then it would all be over. He held up his hands, his mouth opening but no words coming out.

'You've gone quiet,' said Crunch. 'We'll change that, won't we, Eyesore?'

The other brother nodded and clapped his hands, making the thick ropes of flesh-hair swing back and forth.

'We'll make a scream from every bit of you. No need to fight over who gets first chunk this time.' He gave Sa-at a vertical smile. 'We've already agreed to split you down the middle.'

Though there was nowhere for him to go, Sa-at couldn't help but try and back away, the bark pressing painfully into his spine.

'Does he look scared?'

Eyesore clapped his hands again.

'He should be. We'll grind his feet to paste and eat them slow, and then vomit them up and make him eat them. We'll grind his legs to paste and eat them slow, then vomit them up and make him eat them. We'll grind his hips to paste and eat them slow, then vomit then up and—'

'Yes, yes,' interrupted a voice from behind them. 'I think we get the idea.'

Sa-at didn't recognize it but was struck by how calm it was, as if she were talking to someone she knew.

'What's this? What's this?' roared Crunch, turning one ear towards the newcomer. 'Sounds like a human has come to join the feast.'

'Sounds can be deceiving, I'm afraid,' replied the woman. 'To be honest, I was planning on slipping away, but having just heard your . . . speech? Yes, I'll be generous and call it that, I feel compelled to stay and stop you.'

Crunch laughed at that. 'You are too small to stop us.'

'I've come to make a deal.'

Eyesore slapped Crunch on the bicep. 'No more deals. No more chains. No more tricks. We will take the flesh and pain that's owed us. If you're still here after, we will take you as well.'

The woman sighed. 'No, not with you, you great shambling oaf. I'm talking to the one behind you.'

Sa-at gasped at the audacity. She had just killed herself as surely as if she'd opened up her veins and run screaming into a Spiderkin nest. Eyesore turned, cracked his knuckles and took a step towards the woman, allowing Sa-at a glimpse of her. She stood, dressed as an ordinary traveller, like those he'd seen from Sagan, but standing with extraordinary ease. He recognized her instantly, the woman with the golden lips!

'If I save you,' she called, 'do you promise to help me?'

For the Wild, the offer was vague, but given his situation, not unreasonable.

'Yes!' he said, his voice high and fearful.

'Good.' She turned her attention to Eyesore. 'This is your last chance, you disgusting insult to the human form. Stand aside or be destroyed.'

'You shut her up,' said Crunch, 'and I'll get the Birdspawn.'

Sa-at flinched away, uselessly, as Crunch took the final step, his bulk more than enough to block off any chance of escape. The woman did not flinch however, standing stock still as Eyesore charged towards her.

Though his attention was mostly on Crunch's hands as they groped their way towards him, Sa-at saw something rising behind Crunch's back, a strand of his thick hair, knotted to a strand of Eyesore's. He realized the woman must have tied them together before she revealed herself. The conjoined strands rose as one to form a taut line, straight as a bowstring, and then Eyesore's and Crunch's heads were jerking backwards to the crack of vertebrae, and Crunch was stepping away, stumbling, struggling to keep his balance.

Eyesore wasn't faring any better, appearing like some shaggy tree about to fall.

While Sa-at stared and the brothers flailed, the woman began to move. The twilight was suddenly pierced with shining violet as she pulled out a small piece of crystal and weaved after Eyesore, ducking a thick arm as it swung for her, stepping lightly on one of his ruddy knees to spring upwards, until their gazes were level. In his attempt to hit her, Eyesore had lost any hope of staying upright. He fell, and she fell after him thrusting down with the shard of crystal, her strength and weight burying it deep into his middle eyesocket.

There was a popping, followed by the sound of wild thumping as Eyesore began to thrash on the floor. The woman wasn't finished however. She sat on his chest, knees either side of the demon's neck, and drove a hand into his face, into the injury, pushing the crystal still deeper.

In an animalistic state, Eyesore lashed out wildly, and managed to catch the woman a mighty blow that launched her into the air. She landed, stunned, a few feet away. It would have been easy for Eyesore to finish her off but the pain had driven all sense from him. Light now shone from his face, a beam of violet that made his skull glow red from the inside. Steam was swirling from the wound, and Sa-at could suddenly smell burning.

Though the demon could not scream, it began to buck violently, clawing at itself in an attempt to remove the tanzanite. But the shard was buried deep, and burned to the touch. Soon Eyesore's fingers were smoking too, their tips seared black.

Meanwhile, Crunch had managed to steady himself. 'Brother?' he called. 'Brother?' Though Eyesore was in no state to reply, it was clear where he was, and Crunch felt his way over, until he was kneeling by his brother's head. Both of them tried to get the tanzanite out of Eyesore's skull with little success. Hands bashed into one another, and the actions of both brothers became increasingly desperate and aggressive.

By contrast to the noisy spectacle, the woman had recovered quietly, rising in a crouch. A fresh bruise was blooming across the side of her face, a purple flower, planted by Eyesore's fist. She beckoned to Sa-at to come to her but he stayed where he was. He wanted to go, he dearly did, but to reach her would mean walking past Crunch, and he could not bring himself to do that.

She beckoned a second time, nodding to him as if to say: *You can do this.*

He tried to make his feet move but they remained stubbornly planted. Crunch's words were ringing in his mind. There was no way the demon would miss his footsteps. It would grab him and then it would do all of the things it had promised, grinding and eating and making him eat. His bottom lip trembled. Tears began to well in his eyes.

With the softest of sighs, the woman started moving again, circling round behind Crunch, who was still clawing at his brother's face. Eyesore's movements were sporadic now, wild but less frequent, as if his body briefly forgot it was in agony, then remembered in a rush.

He's going to die. The woman with the golden lips has already killed him. The thought didn't give him any relief, for he knew this would make Crunch even angrier than before, and his suffering would be all the worse for it.

The woman stepped up to Crunch's back. Even kneeling down, the demon wasn't much shorter than her, yet she remained as calm as ever. She swept up a couple of strands of his fleshy hair and looped them round his neck. Then she began to pull.

Crunch's roar of anger was muted, choked off, and for a moment, Sa-at thought she was going to kill him as well. But then he saw Crunch's weighty hands lifting from Eyesore's face and reaching up for the woman. One grabbed for her clothes, trying to get purchase to pull her off, while the other felt its way towards her head.

It was all too easy to imagine him crushing her skull in his grip.

I should do something, he thought, whilst also thinking: *I'm scared!*

The woman continued to pull, wrapping her legs around Crunch's body and clinging on like a spider. Crunch grunted and pulled, pulled and grunted, but he could not prise her off.

Fears rose in Sa-at's chest, of failing to help the woman with the golden lips, of being captured by Crunch. They raced each other merging together into a feeling of utter panic. Unable to bear it, he rushed forward, certain that he must do something but with no idea what.

Both the woman and the demon were wheezing, the last shreds of breath rattling as they strained against each other. He could see the veins standing proud on the woman's temple. It was clear she wasn't going to last much longer. Crunch's face was too alien to read, the curtain-like lips curled back in a snarl. Perhaps he was close to collapse, perhaps he could endure being strangled for hours.

Sa-at tried to grab the demon's fingers and prise them off the woman, but he couldn't budge them. He tried hitting his arms, kicking them, even biting them, but Crunch didn't seem to even notice, let alone react.

He looked around, desperate for something he could use as a weapon, but nothing presented itself, and then a sly thought came. *I could run now. Crunch would never catch me. I could come back in the day for my friends.*

The dark of the forest looked inviting, offering places to hide, places where he could feel safe again. But he had promised to help the woman with the golden lips. *Why do I keep promising things? Stupid. Stupid.*

At his feet, Eyesore had stopped moving, his two remaining eyes staring up at the sky. He was dead. Sa-at crouched down, took a deep breath, and slipped his hand into the middle eyesocket. The gem still glowed within, its light splaying between his fingers. The skin inside was crisped and rough and too hot, but the sides of the tanzanite were smooth and cool. With effort, he started to wriggle it free.

As the woman weakened, Crunch was able to wriggle her free too. Pulling her left, then right, gradually loosening her grip on him, until, with a mighty heave, he lifted her over his head, one hand still clamped on her arm, the other wrapped around her thigh.

Though her eyes were half closed, she managed to croak: 'I'm too busy to die.'

'No dying for you. Not yet,' replied Crunch. 'We kill you slow and painful, won't we brother?' The demon stopped to listen and his mouth quivered with concern. 'Brother?' Letting go of the woman's leg, Crunch squatted down to touch Eyesore's face, his fingers only inches from Sa-at's.

The tanzanite was coming loose now but he had to slide it slowly or risk losing purchase.

'Brother?'

Crunch's hand came to rest over Eyesore's upper eye. It brushed against the unmoving lashes for a moment, then began to shake. In his other hand, the woman began to shake too, her breath coming out in a stuttering gurgle.

The top of the Tanzanite was visible now as it slid free.

'What's this?' rasped Crunch as the light from the gem hissed on his skin. He turned his head towards Sa-at who kept very still, not even daring to breathe, though the air was starting to burn in his lungs.

The demon's tongue flapped in front of him, tasting and probing, spattering Sa-at's cheeks with flecks of heavy phlegm. Then, Crunch's hand moved swiftly, unerringly, to find Sa-at's throat. 'Got you!'

The demon stood again, taking Sa-at with him. The

tanzanite shard was still in his hand, still glowing. He pulled back his arm and then swung the shard towards Crunch's face.

The gemstone struck the demon square in the teeth and shattered, the larger chunks spraying in all directions, the smaller ones expanding out in a shimmering cloud.

Crunch coughed and then pulled Sa-at close. 'Now for the grinding and the hurting and the chewing and the savouring.' Where the fragments of tanzanite had embedded themselves in Crunch's gums and lips, thin plumes of smoke began to appear. 'Ahh! What's this? Ahhhhh!'

A fire was starting in Crunch's mouth. He dropped his prey and screamed, pressing his hands against his face, before letting go and screaming again. Sa-at watched, horrified, hypnotized, as the demon jumped up and down batting at the flames.

'Ahhh! Ahhhh!' he screamed, and again, 'Aaahhhgh!'

The next moment Crunch was fleeing into the forest, his howls of pain captured by the leaves and spread from one tree to another, making it sound as if a screeching army were fleeing in all directions.

And then, all of a sudden, it was quiet again, the howls shutting off abruptly, as if swallowed by some great beast.

Sa-at wrapped his arms around himself and shivered.

Eyesore's body remained nearby, as did the woman's. He knew the first was dead but he wasn't so sure about the second. A quick check revealed she was still breathing, although her neck and face were swollen. He was about to try and wake her when he stopped.

The woman with the golden lips is Rochant's enemy, and he is my friend, so that means she is my enemy too. But the woman with the golden lips saved me and I promised to help her in return. But, I saved her from Crunch so maybe I've already helped her.

He shook his head, not sure what to do. He wanted to help Rochant and he certainly didn't want the woman to get him, but he also wanted to help her, she had been so brave and strong, and without her he would be dead.

'This is too hard!' he said to Crowflies. 'What do you think I should do?'

The Birdkin looked at him as if to say he shouldn't even be here.

'I know. I should have listened to you before, but I'm here now. Help me!'

Crowflies flew down to land in front of him, and Sa-at squatted next to it and held out his hand.

'Sa-aat,' it cawed softly, taking his hand in its beak, its proboscis pricking at the knuckle where his little finger used to be.

He felt the contact, and the connection between them, vibrant, strong, as a sudden wave of emotions and thoughts – not his own – juddered against the edge of his mind. Crowflies had a lot to say, and this time, Sa-at gave the Birdkin his full attention.

CHAPTER FOURTEEN

Satyendra didn't seek out anyone else to say goodbye to as he'd told his mother, instead he began the last preparations for escape. He hadn't stockpiled food, the old cook was too sharp for such things, but he had planned the best ways to obtain it in a hurry. For years he'd watched the guards, getting to know which ones were diligent, which were not, and the routes through the castle that were least used.

A side benefit of this was that he'd discovered the guards had their own stash of food in their supply room and, unlike the kitchens, there were times when it was left unobserved.

Times like tonight.

It was simple for him to swoop in and fill a sack with dried meat and fruit. He sucked on a crispy Lizardkin wing as he walked towards the abandoned courtyard, feeling an unusual sense of purpose. All of his life had been leading to this night, and now it was here, that planning was paying off.

He'd almost arrived at the courtyard when he realized someone was following him. Another boy. He recognized the feel of them before his eyes had matched the silhouette: Pik.

'What do you want?'

The other boy shrugged, but didn't look as deferent as Satyendra would have liked. 'What are you doing?'

'Things that are well beyond you.'

'Like what? Maybe I could help.'

Satyendra wondered if he might be able to satisfy his hunger after all. It would make him stronger, able to get much further from the castle in one night. He checked over his shoulder to make sure nobody else was around. 'It's a secret.'

'It is?' The boy was clearly desperate to know but also a little cautious, having been fooled by Satyendra a few too many times in the past.

'Yes. Would you like to see?' Pik nodded and Satyendra beckoned him closer. 'It's not far from here. Follow me and I'll show you, but you have to promise to keep this between us.'

'I promise.'

Satyendra started walking again, he wasn't sure exactly what he was going to do to Pik yet, but the excitement was building nonetheless. They went into the courtyard, weaving their way through the vines towards the far corner, probably the most intimate space in the whole castle, cocooned in a weave of plants, held in a box of stone, tucked away, forgotten.

His stash of clothes and tools was here. Waiting for him to collect. He just needed to deal with Pik and he could be away. He had to be careful though. If he made too much noise, it could raise the alarm.

A brief flicker of doubt passed through him. *This is too risky. I should just make an excuse to get rid of him and go hungry.*

But even as he thought that, he knew he wasn't going to do it.

'Is the secret here?' asked Pik, and to Satyendra's irritation, his gaze moved naturally to his hidden hiding place.

'Yes,' he replied. 'Let me show you.'

He moved a few old bricks and unwrapped his treasures. Pik came to crouch next to him. 'These look like road-born things.'

'They are.'

Pik looked from the collection of tools and supplies to Satyendra. 'Are you going to run away?'

His fingers twitched at his sides. 'What if I was?' Whatever he was going to do to satisfy the hunger, it would be soon. The risk mattered less to him with each passing second.

'I . . . ' Pik hesitated, as if he didn't know himself. 'I'd help you.'

'What? You'd help me run away on the eve of Lord Rochant's rebirth ceremony? I find that hard to believe. Isn't it your duty to stop me?'

'No. An Honoured Vessel has to sacrifice themselves willingly. That's what they say.'

'They say a lot of things.'

'I don't want to die,' came the quiet reply. 'I don't see why you would.'

He looked into Pik's eyes. Could the other boy be telling the truth? Had he misjudged him all this time? He'd assumed

Pik's scrutiny was born of jealousy or the desire to catch him out. What if he'd been turning away from the one person who might have been a friend?

'If I wanted to,' Pik added, 'I could call the guard on you. It would only take a shout.' He shrugged. 'But I haven't.'

Satyendra shook his head, trying to understand this new situation. 'Are you saying you want to come with me?'

Pik actually laughed. 'Suns, no! I like it here in the castle. I don't want to go out there where the Wild is. But then, I'm not you. Nobody wants to sacrifice me.'

It made sense, but Satyendra felt sad. *It would have been so much easier to have an ally, even one as stupid as Nose.* He watched the boy's eyes move eagerly to the more unusual items of his stash and an idea came to him, a horrible one. 'Before I go, do you want to try on my Gatherer's coat?'

'Yes, please.'

He helped Pik into it. It was too big for him, almost comically so, and with dismay he realized the same would be true of himself. It would have to be left behind.

'It's so heavy!' Pik exclaimed.

'Yes, it has to be to protect me from the weather and the Wild . . . ' If he was going to do it, it had to be now. The need for Pik's companionship faded, drowned out by the rising need to feed that other, inhuman part of himself. 'I have a hood here too. Let me put it on you.'

He pulled the hood over Pik's head backwards, causing the other boy to make a muffled complaint.

'Oops,' said Satyendra, reaching down for one of the bricks, his heart beginning to beat faster, 'let's try that again.'

Pik was struggling with the hood himself, but before he could twist it round, Satyendra hit him. The boy's groan was caught in the thick leather as he fell to the floor. His pain and surprise surged into Satyendra, and with them came energy. He leapt onto Pik, straddling his chest and pressing down on his throat.

'Sssh. No more talking. I've never liked you, Nose. Did you know that?' He was more than strong enough to hold the other boy down now. But this was only the beginning. There was a rich seam of treasure here for Satyendra to mine. He applied just enough pressure to obstruct the air flow, but not enough to cut it off completely. The key was to make Pik's suffering last, and to give him time to panic properly. With his free hand he poked and prodded his victim, aiming for the soft places, and mixing his rhythm, so that each one was an unpredictable shock.

He leaned down to whisper in Pik's ear. 'The funny thing is, they'll barely notice your absence, Nose. Everyone in the castle will be far too busy worrying about me. By the time they do find your remains, most of you will have been nibbled away by one thing or another.' He poked at Pik's face through the leather. 'The body they find will have no eyes or tongue. If they find it at all, that is. Perhaps they'll assume that you did come with me, and never search here. Wouldn't that be ironic?'

The rush was coming slowly, gloriously slowly, and he revelled in it, letting it fill his senses.

He didn't hear the footsteps behind him, barely even registered Pik's struggles.

Then, two sets of strong hands twisted his arms behind his back and lifted him into the air.

In a belated rush of awareness he noticed that others had entered the courtyard, two guards who now held him fast, aloft, and behind them, watching with eyes of stone: his mother.

How did she know I was here? She should be waiting for me in my room!

His quick mind came to a conclusion even before his feet were once more on the ground: she had played him. All this time he thought he was tricking her, and all this time, his mother had known. Unable to meet her eye, unable to face what was going to happen, he focused on the boy in front of him. Like an animal, he kicked out, catching Pik on the shin. There was a satisfying crack, a last gasp of fear, and then he was dragged away.

Unable to hurt anyone physically, Satyendra fell back on the only tool left to him: words. 'Mother, how could you do this to me?'

She helped Pik to stand and dismissed the boy before turning to him. 'I promised I'd be here for you, right up to the end.'

'Here for me? You've killed me!'

'No. I'm just giving you the push you asked for.'

'I won't do it!' he hissed. 'I'll fight you. I'll kill myself if I have to rather than let Rochant take my body.'

She looked sad to him, but it was the wrong kind of sadness to feed from, for it was wrapped around a core of steel, resolute and unyielding. 'I'm sorry, Satyendra, but your life belongs to House Sapphire. What happens to your body is not your decision to make, it never was.

'I would like it very much if you did your duty with honour and dignity, but we can drag you to the rebirth chamber, unconscious if need be. Would you prefer that? If it will make this easier for you, I can give you something to drink.'

'Is that supposed to be mercy, Mother? Should I be grateful?' He shook his head. To accept her offer of oblivion would remove any chance of escape. *But how can I escape this? They've already caught me in their trap.* He let his head hang down, defeated, and for once it was not a ploy. 'Let's get this over with.'

They took him from the courtyard, back towards his own chambers, and he allowed himself to be led, meek, lifeless, as if some part of his soul had already left his body. There was no hope within Satyendra, he knew he could not put off the ceremony any longer, and so he clung to something else, a last spark of hate. If this was truly to be his end, he would use his dying breath to ensure that he didn't go alone.

The Godroad shone silver-blue below Vasin, a lone light in a nighttime sea. To either side of it was the Wild, an undulating, endless blackness. Occasionally, it would be broken by the circle of torches made by one of the Sapphire settlements clinging to the side of the Godroad. He flew past them, one after another. There would be no torches where he was going.

However, he knew these lands well, and memory told him when it was time to bank right and begin his descent. In some ways it was a blessing to be arriving in Sorn at night. It was easier to ignore the ruined overgrown buildings. Easier to pretend that perhaps people still inhabited them. Even so, he felt a great shame every time he came here. For Sorn was a ghost village. A monument to his house's betrayal of its people.

He skimmed over the top of the encroaching trees, and

263

dropped fast, bouncing twice before coming to a skidding stop in the middle of the village.

The door to his mother's house was already open, Nidra's body silhouetted black in the doorway, her blade a glowing slash of blue at her side.

He started forward to embrace her but something in her manner gave him pause. His bounding stride faltered a few paces from her. 'Mother?'

'Now you come. Too late as usual. Why are you always too late, Vasin?' He was close enough now to see her in the light of his armour. Each time he came she seemed so much older. Not just in her body but in her soul. Like the spark of Nidra Un-Sapphire was dimming inside.

'I need to speak to Lord Rochant. He's been holding out on us.' She made a sound. He wasn't sure if it was a snort of laughter or a suppressed sob. 'Mother, what's happened?'

'He's gone.'

'Dead?' He remembered her treatment of him in the early days and shuddered. 'Did you?'

'No. You should know better than that. I wouldn't give him the mercy of death, especially not this close to the rebirth ceremony. He's escaped.'

Vasin thought of Rochant. Crippled and bound, with barely the strength to eat. 'How?'

'Lady Pari came to visit. She spoke to Rochant and then I showed her the hill where the Corpseman sleeps. When we came back, he'd gone. He'd been carried out. We don't know numbers.'

'What do we know?'

'Nothing!' Her eyes narrowed. 'But I have my suspicions. We had no trouble while that Tanzanite bitch was between lives. Then, she comes back to me on the very eve of our plan coming to fruition . . . and he just happens to disappear.'

'No. I can't believe that. Lady Pari is our friend and ally.'

'She loves him still! I see it in her face. You can't trust a Tanzanite. You can't trust anyone. If you're to be a High Lord you must hold that truth close and never forget it.'

He pushed aside the feelings of despair stirred by his mother's words. 'Where is Lady Pari now?'

'Out hunting for Rochant. She hasn't come back so perhaps she found him.'

'I should go after her.'

'Yes. Find her. Find him. Before it's too late. If he goes between lives all is lost.'

He turned to go, then stopped. 'Don't give up hope in Lady Pari yet.'

'They are out there right now laughing at us, Vasin! Don't you see? Pari tricked me into looking after Rochant all these years. She made me think of her as a fellow victim, but she is Rochant's lover still. And now, it's too late to touch her. Rochant will return with Wrath's Tear's ascencion, and he will destroy us both!' She sagged against the door frame, displaying a fragility he had never seen before. 'And there is nothing I can do. We spent everything on this gamble. I've nothing left.'

He went to her and scooped her into an embrace. 'You have me.'

'You? What use are you?' She pushed him away. He could easily resist her in his armour, but he moved back, one hop on his Sky-legs putting her on the edge of his aura. 'What use is an embrace to me? Look at me. Look. I am dying. I am dead.' Her eyes bored into his. 'Did you even bring me any food? Any drink? I am sick of foraged mush and stolen leavings.'

'I'm sorry. I rushed here from the Ruby lands. Things are dire there, and it all comes back to Rochant. I have to find him for all our sakes.'

'Maybe if you'd spent more time in the Sapphire lands, where you belong, this wouldn't have happened.'

'I had to go. They needed me.'

She turned away. 'I needed you.'

'I'm sorry.'

'Your apology is worthless. Find Rochant. That is my only hope now.'

'I will. I promise.'

But she had already shut the door.

Vasin sighed and began to jog back towards the Godroad. Finding someone in the Wild was a fool's errand, but he had no other option but try his luck. Grim thoughts about his mother followed after him.

Have I left it too late? Have I lost her already? He tried to remember her as she was, the strong leader, the quick mind, the absolute certainty. But those memories increasingly felt like a kind of dreamy nostalgia.

The smallest of the suns, Wrath's Tear, was just starting to rise as he launched himself into the sky. The weak red light did little more than tint the horizon, and Vasin scanned the tree tops, hoping for a glint of tanzanite in the dark.

However, the forest gave nothing away, presenting him with miles of canopy, a vast green that would make an army impossible to find, let alone one individual.

The Godroad was a different matter, and he spotted the

black silhouette marring its silvery blue perfection immediately, not on top of the Godroad itself, but propped against
its side. A few minutes later he was coming into land,
bounding the last steps to come skidding to a stop by the
prone form of Lady Pari Tanzanite.

The last time he'd seen her, her body had been at the end
of its years, whereas this one was in its prime. Though dressed
simply, the sky-born skin and golden tattoos on her lips and
fingertips marked her as Deathless.

She did not look well. Her face was puffy, one side of it
discoloured by bruising, her clothes scuffed, dirty, as if she'd
been rolled in the mud. Other than that however, she seemed
fine. With the way her cloak was neatly arranged around
her, it was almost as if she'd decided to take a nap.

Perhaps she has. With Pari, anything's possible.

Gently, he set about waking her. She groaned and squinted
up at him.

'Lord Vasin?'

He nodded.

She put up a hand to shade her face from his armour's
aura. 'You're too bright, you know.'

'I think you're the first person to ever say that to me.'

She laughed. 'I was talking literally. My last memory was
of being in the forest. Did you bring me out here?'

'No, I found you on the Godroad.'

She sat up and looked around. As she did so, a black
feather fell from her cloak. Pari picked it up and twirled it
between her fingers.

'Why is it,' asked Vasin, 'that every time I see you, you
look to have come fresh from a brawl?'

'Life just has a way of happening to me, my dear. Though

267

in my defence, I only see violence when travelling through House Sapphire's land.'

'Then I take it you haven't been to visit House Ruby lately.' Before she could respond to that he offered her his hand. 'Can you stand?'

'One way to find out,' she replied, taking it. Once upright she examined herself critically. 'Well, I seem to be in one slightly battered piece.'

'Good. I'm sorry to rush things, Lady Pari, but we need to talk.'

'Can we do it while we walk? I should have been in Sagan hours ago, and my brother won't be happy. I have a man waiting for me with a wagon.' She glanced up and down the Godroad. 'Not too far from here, I think.'

He nodded, and the two of them started to walk together, Pari forced to a near jog in order to match the bounding gait given by his Sky-legs. 'Though I wish the circumstances were better, Lady Pari, I'm very glad to see you again.'

'Thank you, though I'm not sure the sentiment is shared by your mother.'

'I'm sorry about that. It's been . . . hard for her in the Wild, and I haven't been able to see her as often as I'd like.'

'You don't share her concerns?'

'What? That you were involved in Rochant's escape?' He shook his head. 'No. No, not at all. It makes no sense for you to do this now and I'm sure my mother will realize that when she's had some time to reflect.'

Pari was quiet long enough for him to look down at her. She was frowning at the road ahead. 'Are you? I'm not. Truth be told, Lord Vasin, I'm worried about her.'

He sighed. 'I'm worried too.'

'Tell me.'

'What I just said, about her reflecting and having time to calm down, that's the sort of thing Mother used to say about me. This isn't like her. Turning on allies, being unreasonable, and . . . ' he forced himself to say the words, 'torturing other Deathless, even enjoying it . . . it's like I don't know her.'

'Desperation drives people to terrible things.'

'I feel like I'm fighting so hard to keep a sense of myself in all this.' He looked at Pari. 'Everything we've done, with Rochant, with the other houses, has all been to bring my mother back. But what if it's too late? What if her soul has changed so much that we can't put things back the way they were?' He choked back a sob. 'I thought she'd come back from the dead but sometimes . . . I don't know.'

Pari stopped walking and put a hand on his bracer, turning him to face her. She pulled on his arm until he looked down into her eyes, which were unusually serious. 'Nidra may have forgotten who she is, but so long as you haven't, there's hope. You have to be the anchor, and the more lost she gets, the stronger you have to be. Do you understand? She is not gone until you let her go.'

'You really believe that don't you?'

'With every fibre of my being.'

There was such intensity in her face, and such sadness, that he didn't know what to say. She held his gaze for another moment, then let go, her manner becoming light again. 'Now, let's get back to the rest of this mess we find ourselves in.'

'Mother said that Rochant had accomplices.'

'Yes, at least two of them. They carried him.' A slight frown creased her brow. 'He wasn't in a state to move himself.

They'd left a false trail to mislead us and by the time I caught up with them there was . . . ' she trailed off.

'It's not like you to be stuck for words.'

'Well I'm not sure what I stumbled onto exactly, some kind of fracas between the Red Brothers and a young man. Not much more than a boy, really. I think he's the one that left me here.'

'You hunted demons without armour?'

'Yes.'

'Without weapons?'

She rolled her eyes. 'Yes.'

'Alone?'

'You're missing the point. This boy, he was dressed oddly, like a Wild-born, but his features were familiar. Sky-born features.' She tapped Vasin's chest plate with her fingernail. 'Sapphire features.'

'Which family?'

'No prizes for guessing.'

Vasin tried to keep his mouth from hanging open. 'He's had another vessel hidden away all this time?'

'Yes. We shouldn't be surprised really. It's a very Rochant thing to do.'

'But this ruins everything! With Satyendra at the castle, and this other vessel, his line is more than secure. Suns! He doesn't even need to leave the forest, all he has to do is kill himself and wait for the rebirthing ceremony to happen. That's it. We've lost!'

'That seems a little premature, my dear.'

'Are you making a joke?'

'No. There's still a chance to turn this around. Lord Arkav and I are here on official business, to bring High Lord

Yadavendra Sapphire to the council of high lords to face judgement for his desecration of Nidra's Godpiece.'

Vasin scoffed. 'He'll never go with you.'

'I'm rather counting on it. If he refuses us, he'll be in breach of another sacred tradition. It will be a perfect time for you to step in and remove him. Replace Yadavendra as High Lord, and you can cancel Rochant's rebirth ceremony before it happens, and you can use his Godpiece to restore your mother.' Pari tapped his chest plate again. 'What is it? What aren't you telling me? I was expecting you to cheer up, or look relieved, but you look as if someone just smoked your last bit of Tack.'

'That isn't funny.'

'Don't avoid the question.'

Vasin looked up to the sky for guidance. *Even when I'm sober, she's two steps ahead of me.* 'Lady Yadva knows our people murdered Lord Rochant's descendants and kidnapped him. When we take down Yadavendra, she wants me to support her as the new high lord. If I don't, she'll expose me to the others and see me destroyed.'

To his surprise, Pari chuckled. 'Oh really? And how does she know what you did?'

'She tortured the information out of Rochant's guard captain, the one mother turned.'

'Ah yes, Captain Dil. I knew him when he was boy. Such a shame. And this was, how long ago?'

'Around the time I last saw you. Does it matter?'

'Think about it. If she exposes you now, she also exposes the fact that she knew about this for sixteen years and did nothing. It's hardly the behaviour of a loyal servant of House Sapphire.'

Was it that easy? He couldn't believe it. It also occurred to him that this could be a warning. He knew things about Pari that would damn her, and yet he had sat on the information for just as long. Perhaps that was her point. 'Are you saying that it doesn't matter that she knows?'

'No, but I am saying that she can't use it in a public move. She could use it privately to discredit you, I suppose, but again, she risks making herself look bad if she does so. Lady Yadva is many things, but cunning she is not, which is why you cannot let her succeed her father as High Lord.'

'I'm not exactly cunning either.'

She gave him a knowing smile. 'No, but you can listen, and that means you can learn.'

Somehow, when Pari talked about things, they made sense. *She makes it sound so simple!* He knew from bitter experience that it would not be simple when his family next convened. 'There's another problem.'

'Another one?' She tutted. 'Honestly, I slip between lives for a decade and a half and the whole world falls apart.'

'I'd like the chance to listen to more of your wisdom, if I may.'

'Flattery will get you everywhere. Go on.'

He told her about the strange behaviour of the demons in House Ruby's lands, and his suspicion that it was somehow connected to Rochant selling out to the Wild. 'There was something in their manner that reminded me of him. Quiverhive and the others were watchful, measured. And they were sharing that knowledge with others. He knows what's going on, I'm sure of it.'

Pari nodded. 'I agree that Rochant knows more than he let on. What's this about them sharing knowledge?'

'During the battle, a small Lizardkin came to Quiverhive, communed with it, and flew off, like a messenger.'

'Was it red and green?'

'Yes. How did you know?'

'I saw the same creature, or one very much like it in the hills around Sorn. The Scuttling Corpseman is there, and that Lizardkin was communicating with it.'

'But it can't be the same one, they're miles apart.'

'Would you like to take a bet on that one, Lord Vasin?'

'I knew they were coordinating, but not on this scale.'

'None of us did.' She gave him a stern look. 'You need to call a hunt with every Deathless you can muster, and destroy the Corpseman while you still can.'

'I will. I think Yadavendra is in on this. He turned his back on Sorn and forbade us to intervene. It seems too much of a coincidence now.'

'Perhaps. I'll know more after I've seen him.'

'So, what now?'

'Now we go to your High Lord. We'll have to travel past Lord Rochant's castle on the way. There, we can find out if he's returned or if he's still hiding in the Wild somewhere.'

They walked on. Though Pari hadn't solved his problems, Vasin did feel better. It had all seemed too big before, too complex, and she had a way of putting things in perspective. At least now, he could see a way forward.

Not long after, they came across a wagon tucked away on the edge of the tree line.

'There he is,' said Pari.

'Thank you,' Vasin blurted. 'I want to say something before we reach your man.' It felt awkward trying to put feelings into words, especially under Pari's scrutiny. 'I've felt so alone this lifecycle, and unsure of who to trust. And, well, I know these are strange times but I wanted to say that I'm glad you're back. It is good to have someone to talk to about all of this.'

'We've come a long way since you threatened to punch me in the face, Lord Vasin, and for whatever it's worth, I'm glad that I didn't have to beat you to a pulp.'

'I would have won that fight. You were barely able to stand.'

'That's just what I wanted you to think.'

'You only had one wing!'

'At least I wasn't drunk.'

The banter continued back and forth and, by the time they reached the wagon, both of them were laughing.

Chandni couldn't decide whether Satyendra's sullen silence was better or worse than his crazed behaviour in the court-yard. He no longer fought them or argued, but she didn't dare let her guard down.

After she'd sent Pik to help Satyendra escape, she'd found herself following. Not to interfere, but to see her son one last time. To see him happy. To capture a last memory to cling to in the aftermath and confirm in her mind that she was doing the right thing.

And I have confirmation: he was happy, he was ecstatic . . . torturing Pik! My son is a monster. Either his body is fit to serve the house or it will be destroyed along with his rancid soul.

And now she knew what he was she wished with all her heart that she didn't.

True to her word, she had taken on the duty of preparing

him herself. No servants, no support, just two guards by the door in case he became violent again.

Normally, an Honoured Mother would not be expected to be present for the preparatory part of the rebirth ceremony. It was deemed cruel. Normally, this would be the point where she would say goodbye to her son and hand over responsibility to others, who would get him ready to meet the Bringers of Endless Order.

But to Chandni it seemed right that she suffer alongside him. After all, his failure to accept his duty was her failing, and deep down she knew his early contact with the Wild was to blame.

If I had not cut myself that day, the Whispercage would not have come, and he would never have been twisted like this. Or maybe it was when I sacrificed Fiya. Maybe my deal to protect him also cursed him. Either way, the fault is mine.

She thought about his allergic reaction to Lord Rochant's armour, his moods, and the day she'd brought him home and his face had become a transparent mask.

After today, it will all be over. I can only hope that my lord's soul will purge his body.

He didn't stop her as she removed his top, allowing her to guide him to a chair. His expression was blank, his eyes downcast. He appeared pitiful, but she didn't allow herself to feel any pity. *This could just be another ploy to hurt me. How sad that I have to think that about my own son.*

She took out a pair of scissors and began to cut Satyendra's hair. With the first snip, her eyes began to water. *He has such beautiful hair. But it has to go, Lord Rochant keeps his short.* Her numbed hand was clumsy, and she had to work slowly to make sure she didn't cut him by accident.

The silence between them was almost unbearable but she didn't dare say anything, fearing that the wrong word from her would set him off. Afterwards, she removed the rest of his clothing and scrubbed him from head to toe, using water infused with Lord Rochant's favourite flowers. When he was towelled dry, she wrapped him in a robe, ready for his walk of transition.

With the kind of timing Chandni cherished, a servant arrived to inform her that the Bringers of Endless Order were ready for them. They walked the corridors in silence. She kept close to Satyendra, alert for any trouble, and four of Yadavendra's hunters joined their escort, to create a moving cage around them. She wondered if she would see the Bringers herself when they got to the rebirth chamber and hoped not. Mystery and rumour surrounded them. It was said that they could see into a person's soul. It was said that even the Deathless feared them, and that they could curse with a word, kill with a look, and that any who died that way would be born again in the Wild as something monstrous.

She thought about the hidden feather sprouting from the back of her head and wondered what the Bringers would make of it, and shivered. Though the day may come when she would have to face justice for her crimes, she was determined it would be Lord Rochant that dealt it, not them. Anyone but them.

Satyendra was watching her from the corner of his eye, though he was quick to look away when she turned her head in his direction. *He noticed me shiver, perhaps even read something in my face. Of course he did. He doesn't miss a thing.*

A last set of stairs, a turn, then another, and she could hear High Lord Yadavendra's voice, a constant stream of words, like a brook, babbling endlessly. She forced herself to admit that she didn't really like the man, worse, she didn't respect him. All these years later, it was hard to forget the image of him lying prone on the floor, the broken pieces of Nidra Un-Sapphire's Godpiece at his feet. How could a house built on discipline and dignity have such a man at its head?

Yes, she was afraid of him, disturbed by him, but it was love of Lord Rochant and the house that kept her loyalty. To save House Sapphire, restore it, that was worth sacrificing herself and her son for. With a start, she admitted to herself that one of the things it needed saving from was Yadavendra and the kind of people he had surrounded himself with.

But what if Lord Rochant was unable to help? He had failed to save Nidra Un-Sapphire's people from Yadavendra's wrath, and Chandni was sure many of them were innocent. He had failed to save her Godpiece too, failed to save their High Lord from his own madness. In the end, would Satyendra's sacrifice actually count for anything?

She forced herself to calm down. It was natural to have doubts at the point of no return. She would crush those doubts and be sure to let none of her inner conflict show. *I must be strong for Satyendra,* she reminded herself.

One more turn would bring them to the Rebirthing Chamber, where the Bringers and the High Lord were waiting. Chandni had the absurd impulse to stop and run in the opposite direction and she wondered if Satyendra was feeling the same.

This is my last chance to speak to my son. She turned to look at him but he did not meet her eye, his attention fixed on the opposite wall. It occurred to her that she should take the opportunity, that she would look back on this time with regret if she kept her silence, but could not think of anything to say. Normally, one would praise the Honoured Vessel, citing their courage and how they were honouring the house. To listen to the Story-singers speak of it, it was as much a celebration as a goodbye. But even Ban would struggle to make Satyendra's recent antics sound heroic. She could hardly praise his attempts to escape his duty, nor his outbursts of rage.

Anything I say would be a lie and we'd both know it.

They turned the corner to come face to face with Yadavendra and his lead hunter, Zax. Behind them, garbed in black and white robes, were the Bringers of Endless Order. As always, seven of them were present.

Yadavendra was still in his armour. This probably shouldn't have surprised Chandni, but it did. She'd assumed he'd have dressed traditionally for the ceremony and wondered what the Bringers thought of it. The High Lords stood above all, but even they had good reason to fear those that presided over the soul's journey and ultimately decided which were suitable to return to the world and which were not.

'He is here,' declared Yadavendra, somewhat needlessly, Chandni thought. He stepped towards them and lowered his voice to add, 'I trust there was no trouble?'

The hunters escorting them shook their heads, and Chandni did the same.

'This pleases me.' He beckoned for Satyendra to approach. 'Let me see you.'

Satyendra did not say anything and there was an awkward pause.

'I see he is already focused on the task ahead,' added Yadavendra. 'Good.' He reached out a hand towards her son's shoulder and Chandni was uncomfortably reminded of the last time the High Lord had been close to her. 'This will be a great day for you, your family, and our house.'

'Don't touch me,' said Satyendra.

The hunters' eyes widened, their hands tightening on their weapons.

Yadavendra's hand paused mid-air.

Even the Bringers broke off their private deliberations to look over.

Outwardly, Chandni maintained an appearance of calm. *Pretend everything is fine. Don't give him a reason to be angry. Think, Chandni! Say something before someone else does.*

'Don't,' said Satyendra a second time, glaring up at the High Lord with barely concealed malice.

The moment stretched out, Yadavendra's gauntleted hand hovering in the air above Satyendra. To touch her son now would appear wrong, and yet to lower his hand, to not follow the gesture through to completion, would seem like weakness.

'Please, my High Lord,' said Chandni, finding her words at last. 'Satyendra is filling his mind with thoughts of Lord Rochant. He must stay focused. I fear his love for you is such that your presence is overwhelming him.'

Yadavendra's fingers curled into a fist, which shook, as if he was considering bringing it down on her son's head. 'I see. Then I will leave you to your task. Know that I have faith in you, young Satyendra. You will succeed.' He looked at Chandni, making it feel as if he had delivered a threat rather than an endorsement.

She bowed quickly, pressing herself against the wall as his crystal wings cut the air in front of her nose.

Two of Yadavendra's hunters went with him, while the other two assumed positions in the corridor, positions that should have been taken by her guards. She could see the potential clash of egos, adding it to the list of things to resolve.

The clump of Bringers opened out into a semicircle, like a great rustling hand preparing to wrap itself around Satyendra.

'Does the Honoured Vessel have any last words?' asked one.

Satyendra glanced back at Chandni, his eyes cold and dark. 'No.'

She watched as the Bringers closed the circle around him, trying to form a memory before he was snatched from view. The great door opened, a heavy disc of stone that swung ponderously, silently. It was dark inside, and the Bringers entered that darkness, the black half of their robes vanishing quickly, the white half shortly after. And then they were gone, and the door closed behind them. Her guards moved forward and sealed it shut. There was no way to open it from the inside. Either the Bringers would give the signal that all was well or it would remain locked, a tomb for an abomination.

Chandni had imagined this moment many times, and had expected to feel grief, pride, perhaps sadness. In her darker moments she wondered if she'd be relieved. But there were none of those emotions. None at all. She was as numb as her arm.

CHAPTER FIFTEEN

When Sa-at returned to the oak, Eyesore's body had vanished. Whatever was responsible had left no sign of its passing. This did not surprise Sa-at. He wondered if Crunch had come back for his brother and then wondered if Crunch would come back for him.

His right hand still felt itchy. Ever since he had taken the woman with the golden lips to the Godroad, it had started to complain. In the end it had got so bad he'd just dumped her against the crystal wall, pausing only to tuck her cloak around her with his left hand, leave a feather, and run away. It was easing now, slowly, but it niggled him that he hadn't had the chance to talk to her.

He went and crouched by the oak's exposed roots, rubbing three more daubs of his blood into them, before getting Crowflies to seal the cut. Grudgingly, the roots began to move, parting just enough to allow Tal and Rochant to climb out, but not enough to make it easy.

He glared up at the tree, which seemed to do its best to

281

ignore him, and then began the difficult business of dragging Rochant out of the hollow. They were all out of breath by the time it was done.

Tal followed on his hands and knees. 'I thought we were going to die in there! What took you so long? Are you okay?'

Sa-at thought about the Red Brothers, and the woman with the golden lips, and the fight. He was very aware that Rochant was watching him. 'Yes.'

'Did something happen?'

He was wary of answering the question. If he did, they would want to know details, and if Rochant found out he had helped an enemy, it could make him angry. Sa-at did not want to upset his new friend. 'We should go.'

'Okay,' said Tal. 'Where are my boots?'

'Oh,' with a rush of guilt, he realized he'd forgotten all about them. 'I don't know.'

'But I need those boots! You promised you'd bring them back! You promised! Where are they?'

'Calm down,' said Rochant. 'I'm sure that . . . ' he paused ' . . . You never did tell me your name.'

'My name is Sa-at.'

'Interesting. I've not heard a name like that before in all my lifecycles. Who gave it to you?'

'Crowflies did.'

'Who's Crowflies?'

'My friend.' He was about to point it out, but caught himself just in time. Rochant was a Deathless and Crowflies was a demon. They were enemies so he probably shouldn't tell one about the other. Had he already said too much? Whatever he did, he always seemed to be letting one of his friends down. He bit his lip. This was all so hard!

'What's this got to do with my boots?'

Rochant coughed politely, cutting off Tal before he could work himself up again. 'I'm sure that Sa-at knows where they are. He just needs a moment. Think back, when was the last time you had them?'

A memory came to him, of standing by the oak with the boots under his arm, the Red Brothers looming, trapping him against the tree. 'There,' he pointed to the spot.

Tal crawled over to look. Buried beneath a knot of roots was the toe of a boot. 'The tree's got them! You have to make it give them back.'

It will want to trade, thought Sa-at miserably.

The oak's leaves rustled in a rather smug fashion.

'Please, Sa-at, make it give them back.'

'We should go sooner rather than later,' said Rochant. 'My enemies will still be hunting me.'

In a small voice, Sa-at replied, 'I don't know what to do.'

'Can Tal manage in the Wild without his boots?'

'No, my lord,' said Tal.

'No,' murmured Sa-at.

'Then the only question is how you get them back. Do you have something the tree wants that you are willing to give?'

'It will want more bits of me.'

'Are you happy about that?'

Sa-at gave a grumpy shrug and muttered under his breath.

'What?' asked Rochant. 'I couldn't hear you.'

'It's not fair.'

'Life isn't fair. If you want justice, you have to make it yourself. Would you like my advice?' Sa-at nodded. 'It's easy to be trapped by a situation when you accept things as they are presented to you. Ordinary people react to what they're given. They're passive in the way they solve problems, not active. But we are not ordinary people, are we?'

'I'm ordinary, my lord,' said Tal.

Rochant chuckled. 'There is nothing ordinary about a Gatherer making his own way in the Wild.' And though Tal sat up a bit straighter, a grin splitting his face, Sa-at suspected Rochant was saying and meaning different things again.

He isn't talking about Tal. He's talking about me.

'Tal has only recently started this life, but you haven't, have you?'

'No.'

'You grew up here?'

'Yes.'

'And how did you survive?'

'My friend helped me.'

'You mean this Crowflies?'

'Yes.'

'That's it there, isn't it? The Birdkin with the white beak.' Sa-at nodded, wondering how Rochant knew. 'Can you talk to it?'

'Yes.'

'And it can understand you, I'm sure, better than anyone ever has. It knows what you like and what you desire. I'll bet that when Crowflies wants something from you, it knows exactly how to get you to do it.'

Sa-at frowned. He wasn't sure what Rochant was saying, and something about it was making him uncomfortable.

'Do you know what Crowflies likes?'

He smiled. *Wormkin. Laughing at people. Being listened to.* 'Yes.'

'And do you know what the tree likes?'

'No.'

'You need to find out. It knows we need the boots, so it has the advantage.'

'But how?'

'If you had time you could investigate. As you don't, you have to fall back on what you can see and what you know.'

'I know it isn't very nice.'

Rochant eyes sparkled. 'And?'

'It isn't nice to deal with.'

'Good. And what do you think it wants?'

Sa-at tried to think. 'Blood? To make us cry? I don't know.'

'All living things, whether human, demon or animal, want to live and to go on living. Demons have ways of prolonging the lifespan of their bodies, Deathless move from one body to another. Everything else lives on through offspring.

'Look around you, how many oaks can you see?'

He and Tal both did. 'One.'

'Exactly, and the trees are packed in close, there's no room for new saplings to grow here. I know the trees of the Wild move, but I also know that they do not roam far. Offer to take a seed from it and have Crowflies take it to plant somewhere new. Give it what it wants, and you can keep your blood in your veins and the hair on your head.'

Sa-at noticed the tree had gone very quiet. *It's listening!* He turned to Crowflies who was perched above them. 'Would you plant a seed for me, to get Tal's boots back?'

The Birdkin twitched its head one way, then the other, then gave a reluctant shrug of its wings.

'Thank you.'

Something had changed about the oak. When Sa-at looked

closer, he saw one of the branches was angled lower than before, and that an acorn was hanging from it. He held out his hand underneath. 'We will plant your seed in return for my friend's boots. I swear it on my blood and bones.'

A cold wind rustled though the trees, making the branches shake.

With a soft sigh, the acorn fell onto his palm, and when he looked down at the roots, he saw they had retracted into the earth, exposing the boots.

While Tal dug them out, Sa-at handed the acorn up to Crowflies.

'Sa-aat,' it crowed with concern.

'Come back quickly,' he whispered, and the Birdkin bobbed its head before taking the acorn in its beak and flying off.

Sa-at was glad to leave the oak behind. There was little conversation as they travelled, both of them focused on moving Rochant as quietly as possible. Sa-at thought about what had happened. Rochant's advice had worked and he had learned something important, a new way to think. He had changed in some way he did not fully understand, and in doing so, the world had changed too. Sa-at found this very exciting.

Wrath's Tear was well into the sky now, the other two suns not far behind, and the forest was quiet. However, it was not just demons that were hunting them. There was the woman with the golden lips and her knife-wielding companion. The rising suns would do nothing to slow them down.

When they'd put as much distance between them and Sorn as they possibly could, the trio stopped to rest in a spot where the earth had sagged, leaving a grassy nook for them to shelter in. They propped Rochant against the side of the nook, flopping down either side of him so that he wouldn't topple over. At first all that could be heard was their panting for breath, then came the rumbling of bellies not fed in far too long.

'Give me a bit,' said Tal, 'and I'll go and find us some food.'

'Where are we?' asked Rochant.

'Safe,' replied Sa-at.

He closed his eyes. 'Go on.'

'Go on where?'

'You said you'd get me away from my enemies and keep me safe, and you have. That means it's your turn. Ask your questions.'

'I want to know about the Corpseman.'

'You need to be more specific.'

He tried to think about what Murderkind had told him. The demon had wanted understanding about the Corpseman and something about its relationship with the other demons. 'Why are the other demons flocking on its banner.'

'To its banner.'

Sa-at frowned at him. 'I said that.'

'You didn't. You said "flocking on". They don't land on its banner. The Corpseman doesn't even have a banner.' He opened his eyes again. 'Do you know what a banner is?'

'No.'

'Then why are you smiling?'

'Because I'm going to learn new words.'

Rochant didn't exactly smile back, but the skin around his eyes crinkled like he was happy with that answer. 'A banner is a flag, a piece of cloth that bears the sign of a group or a person.'

'Do you have one?'

'Yes, every Deathless has their own.'

'Can you tell me about it?'

'I'd like to show you one day.'

Sa-at nodded. *I'd like that too.* 'What does flocking to a banner mean?'

'It's a way of saying that other demons have joined the Corpseman and are fighting with it.'

'Ah. I want to understand it.'

'The Corpseman?'

Tal put up a hand. 'Can we stop saying its name, my lord. If we say it three times, it will come and get us.'

Rochant chuckled, as if he'd been amused by something Tal had said, but Sa-at couldn't see the joke. 'We've already said its name five times. If it was going to come it would have by now.' He looked at Sa-at. 'I can tell you the Corpseman's story if you want.' Tal covered his face at the sixth mention of its name, making Rochant chuckle again. 'It is a story that nobody else has ever heard before, the details known only to me.'

'Yes,' said Sa-at. 'Yes, yes!'

Rochant looked at Tal. 'You may want to get that food now as I'll be saying the demon's name quite a lot.'

Tal seemed torn between wanting to do just that and wanting to stay and listen, but he stood up quickly and bowed. 'Yes, my lord.'

When he had gone, Sa-at asked: 'Why did you make him go?'

'Because you traded for this, not him.'

'I don't mind if he hears it.'

'How can you say that? You don't even know what I'm going to tell you yet.'

Sa-at stopped to think. Talking with Rochant was making him think a lot. It was great! 'You don't want Tal to hear the story. You want to keep it a secret from him.'

'I want you to make your decisions actively, not passively. Don't take an action because it's easy or because your friends want it, take the right action, the one that serves you best.'

'Why?'

He raised an eyebrow. 'Why?'

'Why do you want me to be like this?'

'Because I think you have potential.'

'Potential?'

'I think you could be more than you are. Much more.'

'You do?'

'Yes. You have a spark, something that reminds me of myself when I was young. If you let me, I could help you grow into something amazing.'

Sa-at couldn't help but grin. 'You can tell the story now.'

'Get me some water, and I'll begin.'

Varg grumbled all the way to Sagan, Glider growling along with him. *They sound like an old couple,* thought Pari. If she hadn't been so worried about her brother, she might have found it amusing.

'Not sure about that Sapphire knowing about me either,' Varg continued.

She looked at Lord Vasin moving effortlessly ahead of them in great bounding glides. *How is he getting so much height so easily?* 'He doesn't care about you, Varg. And besides, we have nothing to fear from that quarter.'

'That makes one of them.'

'Quite. Now do stop talking, I'm trying to think.'

With the unexpected excitements in the Wild, Pari was hours later than she'd planned. She worried about what Arkav had done in that time. Had he managed to maintain the ruse that she was still in the carriage or had the servants found out? Had he stayed in Sagan or continued on their mission to bring the Sapphire High Lord to justice, or had he abandoned the mission entirely to search for her?

Just so long as he hasn't had another another episode. Anything but that.

They met a patrol of guards who were much more polite than the last ones she'd encountered, even offering to provide escort. An unexpected side benefit of travelling with a Sapphire Deathless. Pari noted their faces with distaste. Something in them spoke of meanness, and a delight in petty power. She felt a moment's pity for the other traders that would have to come this way and almost asked Vasin to bring the guards along, if only to get them out of other people's business for a time. However, the risk of being identified was too great and so she remained in the back of the wagon, hidden.

Not long after, they arrived outside Sagan. Things appeared quiet, enough to give her hope, and she saw that the Tanzanite carriage was parked on the Godroad. The Dogkin had been untethered and had taken off, and only one servant remained, suggesting that Arkav and the others had gone into Sagan itself.

She came to sit next to Varg. 'It looks like I won't be needing you for a while. Check the house here is still intact and then get back on the road.'

'You said you were going to go past Lord Rochant's castle.'

Here we go. 'I did.'

'Does that mean I can go up and see her?'

'Hmm,' she said, drawing it out a little. 'I suppose so. But don't get too distracted. I want you on hand when we confront Yadavendra, just in case things don't go to plan.'

'Things never go to plan.'

She admonished him with a finger. 'You're starting to sound like Sho.'

'Reckon that's a good thing.'

'Ha! Perhaps it is.' An image of the old seneschal came to mind. She'd seen a lot of different servants in her life-cycles. Most were lost to the grind of time but some managed to haunt her long after they were gone. Sho would be one of those. She knew it.

'Lord Vasin,' she called, and the Deathless landed by the wagon instantly. 'Might I ask you to honour Sagan with a visit?'

'I could,' he replied, 'but it will seem strange. The elders of Sagan will be unsettled.'

'All the better to allow me to slip back within my entourage unnoticed.'

'Very well, but I need a reason to be here.'

'Tell them you're watching out for their wellbeing during Lord Rochant's absence. Or tell them you're here to see Lord Arkav Tanzanite. Or tell them nothing. After all, the Sapphire are known for keeping their own counsel.'

He turned away from her. 'Were we always like this, Lady Pari? I'm sure things used to be better. Less . . . broken.'

'Please,' she said, holding up a hand. 'I would usually relish a discussion on the flaws of House Sapphire, but now really isn't the time.'

He gave one nod, abrupt, and strode off into Sagan.

Varg and Glider watched him go, one pulling at his beard, the other whining softly.

'What?' snapped Pari.

'Nothing.' At her glare he added: 'Glider doesn't like it when people are sad.'

'We're all sad, Varg. Some of us are just better at hiding it. Now, if you want to have some quality time with a certain Honoured Mother, you'd better get moving.'

The way his face lit up was sickening. 'Right. Good luck with your . . . with everything.'

She pulled her hood further forward and jumped off the wagon. 'Go on, before I change my mind.'

Was it her imagination or did Glider move off with much greater speed than before? If she didn't know better she'd say that the Dogkin was as excited as Varg. *Nonsense. The beast is probably just picking up on Varg's energy.* It wasn't that she didn't want Varg to be happy, but she had a gut feeling that his infatuation was only going to lead to trouble further down the road.

Since her last visit, sixteen years ago, Sagan had grown considerably. Stretching out long and thin on either side of the Godroad in order to enjoy some measure of protection. The refugees from Sorn had been fully absorbed into the settlement, swelling the population towards five figures. In order to accommodate this, the forest had been pushed back, and new buildings jammed into the space. Given the risks inherent in cutting down trees, she wasn't surprised to see how cramped everything had become. Some of Sorn's aesthetic had crept in as well; much higher fences now surrounded the settlement, forming a half circle each side of the Godroad. There were gates leading out to the Wild, which were shut, funnelling all travellers to one of the natural gaps. It occurred to her that this would also make it easier for the Sapphire to control the human traffic . . .

Another gloomy thought to add to my collection.

A large crowd had gathered to greet Lord Vasin. He stood in the middle of them, a softly glowing giant of blue crystal. The mood was jubilant. A Deathless rarely came unless there was a hunt. This visit would add to Sagan's legend, drawing Story-singers, traders and profit for some time to come.

It was easy for Pari to move past them, and as easy to spot the Tanzanite livery in Sagan as it was to spot the suns in the sky. She recognized the Dogkin that had pulled her carriage lazing in a messy clump at the front of one of the larger buildings. Its door was open and one of her servants was leaning out of it, her attention fixed on Lord Vasin. She looked worried.

Pari tried not to think why that might be and moved quickly to the back of the building. The windows on the lower floor were too small to climb through, but she could see larger ones on the upper floor, and during the day, they kept the shutters open. Prepared for just this situation, Pari fixed her climbing claws into place, prepared her silk rope, and quickly scaled the wall.

It still felt fresh and fun to do things physically, and she continued to revel in her new body's agility. A part of her wished that she'd had the chance to spar with Lord Vasin, as she was confident she'd win this time. *And in style.*

The window was shut but not locked. Pari worked it open and peered inside. She was in luck. No servants were in the room, but she could see her brother curled up on one of the beds, his bare feet peeking from under the covers.

She gripped the windowsill tight, struck with savage relief. *He's alive!* This was a pleasant surprise. Some part of her had been quietly preparing for the worst. And yet she didn't fully relax. Her brother was here, breathing, and that was good. But not that good. *It's the middle of the day and he's in bed.*

She pushed the worry from her voice and moved softly over to his side. 'Arkav?'

'Pari?'

'Yes, it's me. I'm back.'

'Who hurt you?'

'Oh, that.' She silently cursed herself for not hiding the bruising. 'I just, overreached myself that's all.'

The next thing she knew he was in her arms, hugging her tightly. 'You lied to me.' She heard reproach, and the threat of anger, like storm clouds on the horizon.

'I'm sorry,' she said, pushing him back gently so she could see his face, but keeping hold of his upper arms to stay in physical contact. 'I honestly thought I'd be here sooner. Things were more complicated than I anticipated. It was a poor estimate rather than a lie.'

'No. Not that. Not the time. I don't care about time.'

'What then?'

'Other things.'

'You'll need to be more specific, my dear.'

'I . . . I don't know.' The hardness left his eyes and he looked away. 'But I feel it. There's more going on and you're keeping it from me.'

She sighed. 'I thought you had enough to worry about without my problems.'

'I should be helping you, not the other way around. I'm the eldest.'

'Not by much.'

'And I've lived more years than you.'

This was especially true after the extended time between lives she'd just been forced to endure. 'It's not about how many years you live, but how you live them. Besides, we don't need to fight over this. We can agree to help each other.'

'So you'll tell me what you're hiding?'

'If you want me to. But first I want to know if my absence has been noted.'

'They suspect something's off, but I set the servants tasks so they wouldn't realize you weren't here. They think you're in the room next door.'

Pari thought about what she'd seen of Sagan. 'We have two rooms?'

'We have the whole of this floor.'

She let go of her brother and walked round the room, peering closely at the walls and floor, noting the little marks where the wood was darker, unbleached by the sunlight. 'There's normally another two beds in here.'

'Yes,' agreed Arkav. 'They've cleared them out to make room for my things.'

'Along with the people who live here.'

'That's right.'

For some reason, she found herself thinking of Lord Vasin. *He wouldn't be happy about this. Am I happy about this?* It was all too easy to imagine the usual occupants stuffed into another room, already full, like trying to get both feet into the same boot.

While she knew the importance of keeping Nidra and their plans secret, it pained her to know that someone had been ejected from their home to give her a room she hadn't even used.

'What a mess. Let's be on our way so these people can have their lives back.'

She was just about to go next door when she noticed Arkav scratching at his chest. The silk was already pulled loose there, suggesting it wasn't the first time he'd worried it. 'Are you alright?'

'I'm fine.'

'Now you're lying.'

At his offended look, she crouched in front of him and gently pulled the silk away. The skin underneath was raised and raw, old and new scabs crisscrossing each other. 'Arkav, this is not fine.'

He looked down, and seemed to be as surprised as she was. 'I . . . '

'You have to stop.' She took his hands in her own and made sure he was looking at her. 'This is important. You could have drawn blood.'

'I wouldn't go that far.'

'By the look of this, you have before.'

He sagged, nodded. 'I'm sorry. I was just trying to . . . ' He trailed off.

'Trying to what?'

'Nothing.'

'No, tell me.'

'Only if you promise not to judge.'

'I won't. You know I won't.'

He managed a partial smile at that. 'I know. I was trying to find the hole.'

A shiver ran down her spine. 'Go on.'

'There's a hole, in here.' He touched his chest. 'I can't think of another word to describe it. It moves sometimes and I . . . I need to find it. I can't explain how I know that, but I do.'

Words hovered on the tip of Pari's tongue but she couldn't quite find them. *I feel like I've been here before. Like I know what he's talking about.* 'When you cut your arm, the first time. Was that to find the hole?'

'Yes.'

'And what happens if you find it?'

'I'd . . . ' he looked up at her, stricken. 'I don't know.'

'Perhaps you should figure that out first before you do any more digging.'

'You're right. It's so much easier when you're here Pari. My thoughts jump less, and they're quieter.'

She smiled at him. 'I don't have any more side trips planned. From now on I'll be at your side for as long as you need me.'

'Good.'

'What was it like when you were with our High Lord?'

'Awful.' Then he started talking so fast it was hard for Pari to keep up. 'She likes me but she's so loud I can't find myself and I get this pressure in my head to do something to be someone and I don't know who-what that is and it makes me scared and I try so hard not to embarrass her and in the end I don't do anything and I don't say anything and I'm not anyone.' He took a breath. 'And I get so tired, Pari.'

'It's alright. I'm here now. We'll find a way through this.' *I feel like I'm missing a piece of the puzzle. Yes! That's almost it.* She allowed her thoughts to unfurl naturally, letting intuition guide them. *Arkav is looking for a hole. He cuts*

297

himself. The hole is inside him. The hole is inside him because . . . something is missing! A part of him is missing. And with a sudden jerk she knew what it was: a part of his soul.

She had seen it when she was between lives. *His face in the void calling my name. I remember!* A piece of Arkav's very essence, trapped in that other place, unable to return to Arkav's body with the rest of him.

She allowed herself a moment of despair – if her brother's soul was torn, there was little hope for him – and then she rallied. *I saw it. It remains out there, beyond this world, intact. That means I can find it.* Doubts about this being true were brushed aside, questions about how she would do this were left to address later. *I will seek it out, and I will bring it back, and I will find a way to make my brother whole again.*

'I didn't always look this way,' began Rochant. 'In my first lifecycle, I was road-born, in a place called Veren and I was as pale as Tal.'

'What has this got to do with the Corpseman?' asked Sa-at.

'You'll see. Now, where was I?'

'You were in Veren.'

'Ah yes. I was not like the other children. You see, in my first life, I was smaller than the others, weaker.'

Like me, thought Sa-at.

'This meant I was slower to complete my tasks. And when I had ideas of how to tackle a job differently, I was told to stop being lazy and get on with it. I soon learned to keep my thoughts to myself.

'At that time, Veren was overseen by a Deathless called Lord Yadavendra Sapphire, and we were generous in our gifts to him. Because of this, he often sent his hunters to visit. I knew from the first time I saw them that I wanted to be one. You can't imagine the excitement every time they came. They were so big on their Sky-legs, bigger than the adults of our village in every way. There was a directness in their manner, a crispness, a . . . purpose. Yes, it was their purposefulness that I loved most, even more than seeing them fly.

'I wasn't the only child of Veren who wanted to be lifted to the sky. It was well known that a Deathless could elevate someone if they were deemed worthy. However, none of us could name a single road-born who had become a hunter in our lifetimes. We asked our parents but they couldn't either. So we asked our grandparents, and when they couldn't, most gave up on the dream.'

'But you didn't.'

'No.'

'Why?'

'That's a good question. In part because I wasn't as happy as the others, and that motivated me to want to change things.'

'What's "motivated"?'

'Encouraged, inspired . . . Ah, I have it! When you're comfortable and warm after a sleep, it's hard to get up, yes?'

'Yes, but then you get hungry or you need to pee and you have to.'

'That isn't quite where I was going but it will do. The other children of Veren were comfortable and warm, but it was like I needed to pee.'

'All the time?'

'Yes, all the time.' Sa-at sniggered. 'But even that wasn't enough on its own. Without the Corpseman things would have been very different.'

'When is it coming into the story?'

'Soon. One night, the whole settlement was kept awake by strange noises coming from the forest. There was buzzing and shrieking and cracking, and it sounded like the trees themselves were fighting. It got so bad that in the end our elders roused the whole of Veren and led us to the Godroad. We stayed there till dawn and returned to find our homes untouched, and the forest looking much like it had the day before. Most were happy to accept this apparent good fortune and return to their beds, but I wasn't.

'I crept out of Veren and into the trees. It was much quieter than I'd ever known it before. The strangeness of it scared me.'

Sa-at nodded. The Wild was only quiet for blood and bad things.

'There was one tree that had a knot like a frowning eye. We called it the Stern Tree. I noticed that the Stern Tree had a new scar on its trunk, four feet long and jagged. It wasn't autumn but there were leaves everywhere, enough that I could kick flurries of them in the air when I walked. Several trees had fallen in the night, leaving patches in the canopy above. After a while, I began to smell death.'

'Did you run away?'

'No, I went deeper. Where the forest had been silent I started to hear sounds of activity. While I was trying to listen, my foot came down on a pile of leaves that crunched like an eggshell. When I cleared the leaves away, I saw the carapace of a giant Flykin. I cleared more leaves and found another, then another, all broken up. Black legs with single-toed feet that jutted into the air. Bodies with the heads bitten off, shreds of glittering wings impaled on branches. Too many to count. And not just Flykin corpses. There were Dogkin too, and other creatures I didn't recognize.

'All these bodies had brought scavengers. An army of them, big and small: Roachkin, Ratkin, Birdkin. Hundreds of them, crawling over the corpses and each other. As I watched, severed limbs began to disintegrate, eyes were sucked out of sockets, tongues nibbled out of slack mouths.'

'Was that when you ran away?'

'No. Maybe I should have, but I ventured further. Carefully at first, then more confidently. I realized the scavengers were too busy with dead meat to worry about the living. As I walked, I could see how the fighting had moved through the forest, getting more intense as it went.

'I'd never before seen Flykin like these corpses. Parts of their carapace were covered in pale skin. Human skin, like Tal's. At first I thought they were wearing the patches like trophies but as I probed the bodies with my hands—' he paused to look at Sa-at, who had gasped. 'What is it?'

'Don't you know that you should never touch dead Flykin?'

'Oh yes, I knew. After the weather, the favourite topic of conversation in Veren was "things you should not do". In my defence, at first I did just look, then I tried prodding the corpses with the toe of my boot, but that didn't tell me enough. I needed to know what had happened, to understand what these things were. Maybe that's why the Wild is so good at tricking people, we aren't very good at following instructions.' His expression didn't change much but Sa-at felt he was hiding a smile. *He is so strange. He sees the same things as me, hears the same things, but they are different to him.*

'Could I trouble you for some more water?'

Sa-at provided some and helped him to drink. 'You said you touched the dead Flykin with your hands.'

'Yes. The patches of skin were fused with the carapace, as much a part of them as their wings.

'I knew little of hunts back then, but I knew that a handful of dead demons was the normal result. Half a dozen was considered unusual, more than that and it would be a story for the ages. Here there were countless bodies. Hundreds, thousands. It was conflict on a scale I'd never imagined.

'There was a circular mound of dead Flykin where the fighting had been at its worst, as tall as you are. I had to climb the corpses to see what was inside it. The smell was . . . ' Rochant shook his head. 'I can still taste it on my tongue.'

'And,' said Sa-at, unable to contain his excitement any longer, 'what was inside?'

'More Flykin. Three of them, maybe four. They'd been so badly savaged it was hard to tell. The sight of it, the stench . . . it was too much and I was just turning to go when I saw it.'

Sa-at was leaning forward now. 'Saw what?'

'The Flykin had been protecting their young. I hadn't noticed because they were beneath the bigger ones, but there were tiny bodies too, mashed into the ground. One of the young was moving. It wasn't making any noise, but I could hear it. Not in my ears like you're hearing me now, but in my head. And not words either, just pain. I could hear its pain.'

302

'Was it dying?'

'Yes. The front of its head was missing. Its antennae were high enough to survive, but its eyes were gone and the meat of its brain was exposed. The rest wasn't much better, its legs were broken and its carapace cracked all over, like an egg that had been rolled too hard on a stone.

'But worst of all was its grief. The closer I got the more I could feel this . . . loneliness.' He shrugged. 'I don't have the words for it.'

'What did you do with it?'

'I picked it up and we . . . ' his eyes took on a faraway look ' . . . connected. Despite its grievous injuries. It was the last of its kind, an exile, and I was a misfit in Veren, too clever for my own good. We found something in each other that our own people couldn't give us. True friendship.'

I want that too! thought Sa-at.

'In those few hours I broke nearly every rule of the road-born. I'd gone into the Wild alone. I'd approached a demon. Listened to it. Touched it. And I'd offered to help it. Much like your Crowflies, it didn't need words to tell me what it wanted: blood. It asked for my blood and I gave without question. Actually the problem wasn't one of inhibition but practicality.'

'What's a "bishion"?'

'I mean I didn't care about the risk to my soul or the judgement of my elders. The only thing I was scared of was being discovered, or not being clever enough to keep my new friend alive.

'Even though the forest was quiet, I bled myself on the Godroad just to be safe, using skins I'd stolen from our Cutter-crafter. I still needed to get the blood inside it, and

303

my new friend had no mouth. To feed it, I had to rub blood over its body and into the cracks by hand, dripping what was left into its neck. Inspired by what I'd seen of the Flykin in the forest, I used my own skin to cover the hole in its face.' His mouth twitched then became blank, the expression banished before Sa-at could identify it. 'Have you ever tried to cut away a slice of your own skin?'

Sa-at shook his head. The idea made his stomach churn.

'It's hard. Much harder than drawing off some blood. Even a small scrap leaves a wound. And it hurts. It hurts so much I still remember it to this day. The hardest part was having to do it alone, in secret. The others wouldn't understand. If they'd found out, I'd have been killed and my friend destroyed.' He glanced up, making eye contact. 'But you understand, don't you?'

Sa-at swallowed, his throat suddenly dry. He did understand. He would give of himself to help Crowflies, just as he had to help Tal and Rochant with the oak. And yet he had to force himself to answer, because it also felt as if there were things he did not understand, and if he agreed with Rochant, he was saying yes to those things too.

Rochant seemed relaxed, patient, but the pressure to speak grew nonetheless.

'Yes,' he said at last. 'You are friends with demons and humans. I am friends with demons and humans. We can be friends with both.'

A crinkle appeared around the man's eyes again. *He likes my words.* Sa-at smiled. *I like that he likes my words.*

'Yes,' replied Rochant. 'But they can only understand half of us. That is why you are the first to hear this story. Like me, you are on the edge of things. That means you can see them for what they are, and perhaps, change them for the better.'

Sa-at found himself nodding. *Tal would not understand as I do. Rochant was clever to send him away.* Though he felt sad for his friend, a part of him delighted in being special enough to hear a secret. 'Did it work?'

'Using my skin as a patch? Yes. I had to use glue to hold it in place at first, but over time it drew the edges of the patch into itself, integrating my skin into a new carapace that was forming beneath the old one. Even though it healed well, it couldn't repair the holes. They ran through the old shell to the new one, and appeared in every one after that. The worst damage was to its face, but there were other wounds, places where the original chitin had fallen away entirely. I replaced these with parts of my skin over time, but it troubled me that my friend had weak spots, for I knew that one day its enemies would find it again, and it would need to be strong to survive.'

Sa-at couldn't contain himself any longer. 'The Flykin is the Scuttling Corpseman!'

'Obviously.'

'Then why don't you call it that in the story?'

'Because at that point I hadn't named it.'

Sa-at's mouth fell open. 'You named the Corpseman!'

'Yes.'

His thoughts were whirling. Before he could order them, or ask to hear more, he heard the sound of Tal's boots stamping back towards them.

'Here,' he said, offering his open bag. Inside there were sweetberries and some nuts. 'It's not much, but I didn't want to go too far on my own.'

305

'Well done,' said Rochant.

'Thank you, my lord'.

Sa-at was less impressed but didn't say anything. *Hopefully Crowflies will come back soon. It always brings good things to eat.* He wanted Rochant to carry on his story but knew he couldn't with Tal around. *I like secrets,* he thought. *I'm learning lots about the Corpseman. Murderkind will be pleased.* But when he imagined telling Murderkind, of sharing his secret knowledge, it made him feel sad. When he'd told Murderkind, it wouldn't be special any more.

CHAPTER SIXTEEN

Satyendra flinched as the door closed behind him. Though it was dark in the Rebirthing Chamber as he entered, the light shining from the diamonds on the Bringers' wands was bright, the nature of it painful to his eye. He suspected they would burn to the touch as surely as Yadavendra's crystal armour.

And so it was a relief when six of them pivoted on the spot, putting their robed bodies between him and the light. The seventh lowered their wand and held out a hand towards him. In it, Satyendra could see a small chunk of sapphire. It did not glow, but he sensed it was important.

'For you, Vessel,' said the Bringer. 'Take it.'

'Take it,' echoed the others.

Satyendra did as he was told and the bringer tapped it with the tip of his wand. There was a brief flash of discomfort as the sapphire and the diamond chimed together, and he could feel the beginnings of a headache.

'Listen to the past, Vessel, and listen well.'

The seventh Bringer of Endless Order turned and they all walked away from him in different directions, a slowly expanding circle of murmurs and rustling robes. Satyendra wondered if they were performing part of the ritual or whether the murmurs had another purpose.

In his hand the crystal shook softly, and words began to spill from it. He heard a man's voice and knew with a sick certainty that it was Lord Rochant Sapphire, speaking to him from some other time. *And some other poor fool's body.*

'Honoured Vessel. You are about to make the ultimate sacrifice for me and for House Sapphire. I have no doubt that you have spent long hours preparing for this moment, and that my deeds and decrees are well known to you. However, to truly understand me, there is something that I must share with you. What I am about to say is never given voice by the Story-singers, and is not recorded in our histories. It is something that I share with you, and you alone, to bring us further into alignment.'

Satyendra's lip curled into a sneer.

'When I was a hunter, I had the honour of serving Yadavendra, now High Lord of House Sapphire. This is well known. Less well known is that I also served his sister, Nidra, and that I was her lover. When Yadavendra elevated me into the ranks of the Deathless, he changed me in many ways, but my love for Nidra remained.

'However it is forbidden for Deathless to lie together, as such an act endangers the cycle of rebirth. I knew this, but I was weak. Nidra knew this too. When I invited her to my castle, she refused. When I asked to see her, she ignored me. When I sent gifts, she returned them.

'Then one day, when my second body was old, I received

a letter from her. In it, she made clear that what we had enjoyed was over, and that for the good of the house, I had to move on. My behaviour, such as it was, would not be tolerated any more.

'That was the message that broke my heart and ended my second lifecycle.'

Oh yes, thought Satyendra. *I have heard the story of Lord Rochant dying of a broken heart. What a charming way to dress up a death. Did you take your own life I wonder, or were the circumstances so embarrassing that you made up this nonsense to cover it?*

'There are many stories about my loyalty, and I am famed for the counsel I have given House Sapphire, but there are few stories about my heart. I tell you this because I want you to know that I am not perfect, nor am I without passion. Do not be ashamed of your feelings. However dark your thoughts may be, they do not need to come between us.'

A bark of laughter escaped Satyendra's lips. He couldn't help it. It echoed around the chamber, and by the time the sound was fading away, he could see the Bringers of Endless Order walking towards him again, like some diamond-toothed mouth closing on its prey. He didn't like the way they looked at him, nor the glint of bright green eyes within the masks. *They see too clearly for my taste.*

The lead Bringer held out their hand for the message crystal and Satyendra was happy to be relieved of it. Then they escorted him deeper into the chamber. Slowly they spiralled towards the centre. Occasionally the light from their wands would catch the side of a wide, dull pillar, or the edge of a curving wall, but otherwise there was nothing but black all around him, pillars disappearing into an illusion of vastness, his imagination conjuring a space far larger than the castle could contain.

Though it felt like they would walk forever, they soon came to the chamber's centre. Seven triangular bricks formed a circle in the floor, with a slab of stone laid on top of it, long enough for him to stretch out on. He saw thick straps and thicker buckles set at intervals along the slab, and froze mid-step.

This was it. It was real and it was happening to him right now. *I am going to die here.* Uselessly, his brain thought of all the times he could have run away, the opportunities he'd squandered. But now he was sealed in by heavy stone. There was nowhere else to go, his options funnelling down until all that was left was to choose the manner of his death.

'I don't want to,' he said.

The Bringers said nothing, just watched him from beneath their hoods.

'Let me out.' He knew it was futile but a part of him didn't care. He wanted more time! He wanted to taste his favourite foods again, to run free across the courtyard, to compete with his friends. He'd even enjoy sitting with Ban for more stories, or spending time with his mother. There was so much he'd never told her.

'Let me out!' he repeated, louder this time.

Again they said nothing. They said nothing as he turned and ran for the door. Said nothing as he stumbled into the dark. Said nothing as he scraped his knuckles on one of the pillars.

He could hear them behind him, following in their slow, measured way, and he pressed on, making sad desperate noises, not caring how he looked or who heard.

He saw his own shadow thrown against the wall, and looming over it, too large, the shadow of a Bringer. He had time to notice its strangeness and be afraid. *The shape isn't right. There are too many limbs.*

And then it was on him, tearing the clothes from his body, hands clamping on his wrists, forearms, thighs and ankles; and he was lifted off the floor. He felt movement, swift and oddly smooth, then more hands, and then he was on the slab and bound faster than he could scream. When he did scream, they caught his jaw and held it open. With his head, body, arms and legs strapped down, the only thing he could choose to move was his eyes.

Satyendra couldn't decide whether it was better to keep them open or closed.

He caught a glimpse of a wire mesh being held by one of the Bringers and knew they were going to do something to him with it.

He closed his eyes.

The taste of metal on his tongue made him open them again. He was surrounded by the Bringers, who were gesturing, going through some kind of ritual. With the mesh in his mouth, his jaws were wedged open. Bile began to stir and he willed himself not to throw up. The lead Bringer took out a needle and gestured with it in each of the seven directions: up, down, left, right, across each shoulder, and once at a diagonal past the right leg. There was a strange humming sound coming from the Bringer's midriff, and he could see something pumping there, like an extra heart beneath the robes.

He closed his eyes.

The humming became more pronounced, and as it got

311

closer, he opened them again, just in time to see the needle, tipped with golden ink, descending towards his face.

It burned. Not terribly, but incessantly. His hands clenched by his sides as the tip danced in and out of his skin. He wanted to scratch his face or pour water on it. He wanted to call out.

It did not matter what he wanted.

The Bringer's face was close to his but they gave no sign of noticing his discomfort. The black and white mask was intent only on the work, as if he were nothing more than an inconvenient canvas. *They are so calm! How are they so calm?* And then he realized why. *They've seen vessels struggle before. It's nothing new to them. And it's never talked about in the songs nor taught in my lessons. How convenient that our sufferings are lost to history.*

He knew that Lord Rochant had an elaborate patchwork of gold on the side of his head, and he also knew there was a mark on his heart. Satyendra was prepared for these. Somehow knowing what was going to happen made it easier to bear. When they were done, he lay there, panting through the mesh, hoping that this part at least, was over.

The lead Bringer made some adjustments to the needle and then the humming began again, this time a silver liquid appearing at the tip. The Bringer moved along the slab to stand by his hips and lowered the needle towards his cock.

Satyendra closed his eyes.

Afterwards, he felt sweaty and hot, but cold too, the stone unforgiving on his naked skin. Fresh ink tingled on his head, his chest and between his legs, and still the Bringers continued to work. He did not really attend to what they were doing, his brain too shocked to make sense of the strange words and movements. Time blurred for a while until one of them produced a box, and from that box a sphere of platinum.

There was something about it that repelled him, even more than the Bringers did.

The lead Bringer took the sphere and carefully, reverently, placed it into Satyendra's mouth. It clicked into place within the mesh. Not long after, he became aware of his heart pounding in his chest, the brief respite of shock wearing off to be replaced with utter horror.

In his mouth, the ball tasted of metal and death. He bucked within his bonds like a desperate animal, trying to get it out. The presence of the ball terrified him, but when he had spent the last of his energy, he realized it wasn't as bad as he expected. The ball had no resonance, as if he were touching the ashes of a fire rather than the fire itself.

The Bringers chanted and moved, slowly circling him, their wands moving in unison, their shadows dancing on the ceiling above. In motion, their robes did less to conceal their bodies, and while he could not determine what was wrong with them, he knew that something was wrong. For one, a hump on the side of their ribs, for another, the suggestion of an additional limb hidden away. *Are the masks to hide their deformities?*

He could feel the ritual building to its conclusion and braced himself. One final sliver of hope remained. An Honoured Vessel usually invited the Deathless soul inside. On some level, for reasons unfathomable to Satyendra, they wanted to be sacrificed. Perhaps he could fend off Lord Rochant's soul by force of will, though he had no idea how. He tried thinking of how unlike Rochant he was, how unsuitable a match he would be. He thought about how much he

313

wanted to live, and how much he hated everything. Underneath his internal ranting lingered a seed of doubt. For in many ways he *was* like Rochant: clever, devious, secretive. Would he be willing to take another's life to prolong his own? *Without hesitation.*

All the while, the Bringers' chanting got louder, their movements faster, the energy in the room more charged. At the peak of their working, the Bringers brought their wands together above Satyendra.

There was a clink, and the expected unpleasant sensation as the chime passed through him, and then . . .

Nothing.

How will his soul take mine? he wondered. *Will it be as sudden as fingers clicking? Or will it be so slow that I'll not even realize he's in here until it's too late?*

The Bringers were bending over him again. The sphere was reverently placed back into its box, and the mesh removed from his mouth. The straps stayed in place however.

One of the Bringers made a gesture and the portal beneath the slab groaned open, not enough to drop him and the stone into oblivion, but enough for him to understand the threat.

'One man is welcome here,' said the lead Bringer.

'Are you that man?' asked another.

Satyendra blinked at them. The ritual had ended. *If Rochant was going to come, he would have already. It didn't work!* He tried not to smile but he wanted to. He wanted to grin like someone who had taken too much sweet wine, or like the lovers in the stories, or the Wolfkin catching its prey. Looking at the Bringers anew, he saw something behind the masks and the theatrics. *They are uncertain of me.* It was subtle but it was there, a tiny hint of fear that confirmed his suspicions. *They do not know if the ritual worked. They have no idea that it failed!*

He let his own fear fall away. After all, they would expect him to be different now. Lord Rochant was calm, measured. He must be those things too. Having just heard the man's voice made it easier to mimic his cadence. 'I am.'

'Name yourself.'

'I am Lord Rochant Sapphire.'

'Lord Rochant Sapphire is welcome, if you are he.'

'If,' hissed the others.

'If you are he,' said another, 'you will prove your humanity. Look at yourself and tell us what you are.'

He could see the new tattoos describing Rochant's Legend – significant deaths that High Lord Sapphire wished remembered. He'd heard the stories connected to them, and had no doubt the Bringers were waiting to hear a recital. But there was a tattoo on his cock, silver where the others were gold, that made no sense to him. *Why is it in a different colour? And why does nobody talk about it?* It struck him that perhaps this was a measure of security, a single thing not shared with a vessel, to ensure that only the true Rochant could pass the test.

Aware that the Bringers were watching him and that to hesitate would raise their suspicions, Satyendra reeled off what he did know whilst trying to think of a clever answer for the bit that he didn't.

'I feel the mark on my skull. It shows that I fought and died for my house. I see the mark on my heart. It shows that I fought and died for love.' His eyes fell on the last tattoo. 'I see the silver mark . . . ' He paused. Without

315

knowing any context, it was hard to guess what to say. Did it depict victory? Honour? Shame? He noted the Bringers' mood seem to lift slightly, as if they were less concerned about the silver mark than the others or perhaps they found his answers reassuring. He stared into their masked faces, struggling to read anything there.

'What does the silver mark tell you?' said one of the Bringers.

He'd never heard of a silver tattoo on any Deathless before. *This is something private, it must be. But is it marking Rochant's mistake or a prized secret?* Satyendra cleared his throat. 'It tells me that some stories are best not shared.'

'And what should High Lord Yadavendra fear, if Lord Rochant has returned?'

'There are many things a High Lord should fear. Betrayal, failure, the price of a bad decision. But he no longer need fear being alone.'

'A bad decision?' said one.

'A bad decision,' echoed the others.

'Tell us,' said the first, 'of a bad decision the High Lord has made.'

There was a slight change in the air, any sense that the Bringers were more relaxed had vanished. Their green eyes fixed on him like a circle of scavengers waiting for an animal to finish dying.

Though nobody spoke of it openly, the destruction of Nidra Un-Sapphire's Godpiece was considered a mistake. Indeed, he knew from bits of overheard gossip that beyond House Sapphire, it was seen very poorly indeed. He also knew that Yadavendra living inside his crystal armour went against tradition and was viewed as a sign of instability, but to criticize either of these things felt too dangerous somehow.

'His only mistake has been to be too generous. Threats to our way of life come from more than just the demons in the Wild. He needs to be harder on those above, be they servant, soldier, Cutter-crafter, yes, even Deathless. Two betrayals cannot be allowed to become three.'

Even as he spoke, he felt his words falling flat. *The Bringers are not pleased.* One of them looked past him, at someone outside the circle, and then nodded slowly, though Satyendra thought that this gesture also communicated displeasure.

'Lord Rochant Sapphire is welcome.'

'Welcome,' agreed the others, stepping forward and undoing the straps.

As the Bringers filed out, someone began to clap. It sounded like two glasses being rung together repeatedly, immediately setting his teeth on edge.

'Well said, my friend.' Yadavendra's voice came from the far side of the chamber. 'Well said.'

Now that the immediate threat of death had passed, he became even more aware of how cold he was. He started to sit up. 'High Lord—'

'No,' Yadavendra cut him off, crossing the space between them in three great strides. In the dark his armour glowed like a star in the night sky, his Sky-legs turning him into a giant. Satyendra hissed as a gauntleted hand pushed him back onto the slab. 'You must rest, my friend. There will be a great feast tonight, to celebrate your return. And then, we must talk, you and I.'

Yadavendra seemed jubilant, but there was a brittleness there too, a need in his bloodshot eyes.

'Yes,' agreed Satyendra, thinking about his mother, and Nose, and all of the little grudges he'd nurtured over the years. 'There is a lot to do.'

With so many Deathless in attendance, Chandni would normally be rushed off her feet seeing to their needs. However, today was the day of the rebirth ceremony, and tradition dictated that an Honoured Mother be spared any other duties so she could make peace with the vessel's soul leaving the world. This put Chandni in an impossible position. On the one hand, she loved tradition. It gave a sense of stability and connection to something larger than oneself. On the other, she hated the thought of relinquishing control. Her staff were well trained, but she knew their foibles better than anyone, how best to motivate them. In short, this was a very important time for House Sapphire, and it galled her to have to sit back and be idle when there was so much that needed doing.

By tradition, she was supposed to take this time to reflect. The minutes stretched before her, the sound of her water clock tapping out the minutes drip after drip, while a stranger stared back at her from the mirror. *Why aren't you crying? Why don't you feel anything?*

With Satyendra gone, her own time of judgement was coming. While he was alive, her crimes had to be hidden for the good of the house, but from today there would be no more excuses to hide behind. It was time to confess. She had been touched by the Wild, tainted, and soon everyone would know.

Deep down, there were feelings, a great flood of them that she neither understood nor wanted to experience. *Being alone is torture! Without distraction I am left with my thoughts.*

I am tired of them. They only bring misery and are of no practical use.

It was time to do something. Though she would not be so crass as to get involved with proceedings, she could at least go for a walk around the castle to reassure herself that things were in hand. *And then,* she reasoned, *should someone wish to quietly ask my advice, I could give it in a non-official capacity.*

She got up and immediately felt better. Checking that the feather was still hidden within the rest of her hair was automatic now, the shame reduced to a dull twinge, mostly forgotten, mostly bearable. Satisfied, she left her chambers, being careful not to seem too purposeful. *I'm just going for a walk to help clear my head. A mourning mother hoping to see a friendly face.*

The staff that she passed inclined their heads to her. Some showed respect for her sacrifice, a few showed happiness for her great honour, but most of them didn't know what to show, and just seemed awkward.

Perhaps the tradition isn't for me at all. It's for everyone else.

She began to suspect that she shouldn't have come out. It was selfish, and the castle seemed to be running perfectly well without her.

Soon, the Bringers of Endless Order would emerge from the Rebirthing Chamber and she would know one way or another if it had succeeded. Yadavendra seemed confident because on the surface Satyendra was an excellent match for Lord Rochant. Only she knew about his allergy to the very crystals that gave the Deathless their power. Only she knew about his other face.

A barking drew her from her reverie. At some point she had wandered into the main courtyard, which was full of strangers and their tents. The various entourages of the visiting Deathless, and those that had come from the settlements to welcome their returned lord, too many to accommodate within the castle itself. Old friends were catching up, gossip and goods were being exchanged, and the air was full with happy noise.

There were many Dogkin tethered here, and their barking was to be expected, but something about this one Dogkin made her stop in her tracks. It sounded excited. It sounded familiar.

'Glider?'

A joyous howl answered her and she rushed towards it, pushing her way through the crowds. Though her status should have got them to part at her approach, her size counted against her, most of the adults not even noticing someone was there until she had gone past.

She was almost to the outer gate when she finally slipped free of them and walked straight into a wall of white fur. Chandni let herself sink into its softness and wrapped her arms as far around the Dogkin's body as she could. Glider's great head came to rest on her chin.

'I've missed you,' she said, and was rewarded with a nuzzle. 'I've been worrying ever since we parted ways. You were in such a state! Now, let me look at you.'

Glider sat back and Chandni scrutinized her. If anything, the Dogkin was even bigger than she remembered. A bite scar under her chin, with a matching one above Glider's left eye. The eye itself, the human one, seemed undamaged. In fact better than before: the film had gone from it, and she noticed for the first time that it was blue.

'The Wild changed us all,' she whispered.

They stared at each other for a while.

'I am so delighted to see you, Glider. You look magnificent.' Glider raised her chin proudly. 'Is Varg here?'

The Dogkin barked affirmatively, and then raised a paw to point.

She spun round to see Varg standing just a few feet away. His beard was trimmed shorter than she remembered, making him look less feral. A decade and a half had added lines to his face, weathered his pale skin still further, but otherwise he was unchanged. His hands flexed at his sides but he stayed where he was. Locked in place as the flush rose in his cheeks.

He wanted to come to her, that was clear, and she wanted to go to him too, but it would not do, not here in the courtyard with everyone watching. 'Welcome to Lord Rochant's castle,' she said politely, as she would to any stranger. 'When did you arrive?'

'Just got here. I was trying to puzzle out the best way to get a message to you and then Glider started barking. I, uh . . . ' his hands twitched again, and she saw he was holding a small painted stone – the last piece of mosaic. 'Pari kept me busy, more than usual, so it took longer to come see you than I'd like. But I wanted to come, and now . . . I still . . . shit . . . ' She winced and his blush darkened. 'Sorry, Chand. Old habits. I stand by what I said, before, you know? About being with you.'

'Oh Varg.'

'An' Pari thinks you'll have changed your mind, which I don't want to believe but,' he shrugged, 'it got me worried.' The hope in his eyes was enough to make her want to cry.

'So can you give me a sign, of how you feel? Only it's killing me standing here like a fucking post.'

She stared at him, wondering why she wasn't saying anything. *After all these years, why did he have to come now, when it's too late?* The truth was, there had been no good time for Varg to arrive. They might have stolen a few nights together, but her time had never been her own.

It would be so easy for her to go with him. To leave the castle behind and never come back. She wanted that. She wanted to make the fantasy real, but . . .

Glider barked expectantly and she looked at the floor, unable to meet Varg's gaze. She could feel it on her though, nakedly hopeful. It was not in her to kill that hope, nor was it in her to lie to him.

She felt Glider's nose press against her back, and when she didn't move, the Dogkin butted her gently, sending her stumbling forward, straight into Varg's arms.

He had the same smell, and it brought back memories of earlier days, of them struggling to survive in the Wild, of them huddling together, out of fear at first, and then because they wanted to. Her left hand began to move on his back, betraying the feelings she wanted to bury. After a moment's hesitation, Varg's hands began to move too, gently, guiding her close.

I must not encourage him any further, she thought as she watched herself cup her fingers around the back of his neck.

After that, she didn't think too much at all. His lips brushed hers, shy at first, but becoming more confident as she leaned into him, going on tiptoes to stop him from breaking contact. She did not want to stop kissing him. It occurred to her that

in the past, Satyendra had always disturbed their brief dalli-
ances with his crying. The thought of him sobered her, forced
her to face reality again. Reluctantly, she pushed back from
Varg. *Even now, he finds a way to come between us.*

Varg grinned at her, the expression taking years from his
face. 'I liked that sign. Can I have another one?'

She shook her head.

'What's up?'

'It's complicated. The rebirth ceremony is today.'

'Course it is. I'm sorry, Chand. Really. Do you want me
to come back later?'

'No. I don't want you to go at all . . . He's gone. My son
has really gone. I failed him, right at the end, I . . . '

Chandni began to cry, the tears coming like an assassin
from the shadows, springing up before she even knew they
were there.

Varg's arms were slower, more comforting, as they drew
her into an embrace. She let herself lean into him, let his
strong frame take her weight, let the tears and the grief take
its course.

When she was done, she leaned back, wanting to see his
face properly but unwilling to break contact. He smiled at
her, and placed the last bit of stone into her hand.

'I'm sorry I didn't get to see him full grown. I don't know
what happened, but I do know you'd have done your best
for him, Chand. You never do anything less.' He looked into
her eyes. 'I'm here now. I ain't going anywhere.'

'I've thought about you often over the years, too often.
It was wrong of me to want this. It wasn't fair on you and
I should have said so at the time. I was selfish and I am
sorry.'

The frown appeared as the smile left, as if one was pushing the other off his face. 'What are you saying?'

'I can't be with you Varg. I want to, but I can't, not yet.'

'I don't understand.'

'If Lord Rochant returns to us, it is up to him to decide what happens to me. If the ceremony fails,' *please let it not fail,* 'then my fate will be decided by High Lord Yadavendra.'

'Yeah, but that don't matter for us. I don't care what job they give you, it won't stop me and Glider being here.'

Glider barked agreement and Chandni couldn't help but stroke her head in appreciation.

'I love you both, and if things were different I would be with you without hesitation.' She lowered her voice. 'But you know what I did to keep Satyendra alive. For years I have kept my crimes secret in order to protect my son. Now he is gone, that duty is discharged. I must face the judgement of my lord.'

'Bollocks. Like you said, it was years ago and no harm has come of it. Why risk exile now?'

'Because life is nothing without dignity. How can I expect Lord Rochant to restore the house if I am not willing to restore myself? How can we have a new life together, a good life, if I come to it corrupted by my past deeds?' She shook her head. 'If I stay silent, I am no better than Samarku Un-Sapphire, no better than Nidra Un-Sapphire. Unlike them, I put my house first.'

'Just once, I wish you'd put yourself first.'

Her hand began to creep towards him and it took all of her will to put it back by her side. 'I can't change who I am, Varg, not even for you. But if my lord is merciful, we might still be together.'

'Then I really bloody hope Lord Rochant makes it, because that's the only chance we've got.'

He has to, she thought, *for all our sakes.*

'Alright then,' Varg said, 'I'll wait here for you so long as you promise me that whatever happens, you'll come out and see me one more time.'

If her lord was angry, there would be no room for final requests, but she couldn't tell Varg that. *He won't understand.* 'You have my word.'

'Right. Good. That's something. Be careful.'

'I will.'

'I mean, pick your time. Make sure he's in a good mood. I always forget that when I'm asking Pari for stuff but you're more patient than me.'

'Lord Rochant trained me himself. I know how best to approach him.'

'Right.' He pulled her close again. 'Sorry. I don't want to let you go.'

'But you must. I should be in mourning, not –' she paused as Varg blushed again '– celebrating. I've already lingered too long. If word gets back it would count against me.'

Very slowly, she removed his hands and gave Glider a last fuss before stepping away. It was hard to turn her back on them, harder still to walk away. *Lord Rochant's wisdom will guide me on the right path. Please let him have returned in his full glory. I would rather face his righteous anger than High Lord Yadavendra's mercy.*

Glider's howls followed her all the way into the keep.

Vasin let the energies of the Godroad carry him. Lady Pari had offered to squeeze him into their carriage but he'd refused. While it was tempting to catch up with Lord Arkav Tanzanite, and solidify their strategy, the idea of sitting still was impossible. They were on their way to face Yadavendra and remove him from power. It had always been the plan, but for so long it had been a distant necessity, below the horizon. Easy to ignore. Now it was here, right in front of him, and he was terrified. And when Vasin got like this, he had to act, to spend the fear in movement, or it would coil up inside like a burrowing Wormkin, and devour his convictions.

Lord Rochant could not have got loose at a worse time. If he managed to escape the forest – which seemed likely given that he'd allied himself with the Wild – then Yadavendra would have his closest ally back. Vasin fancied that he could stand up to his High Lord, but Rochant had a way of twisting things. A few words from him and Vasin would become the enemy. It would be far better to wait if that was the case, but Lady Pari had made it clear that the Tanzanite would not wait. And the Rubies were already out of time.

Gradually, Lord Rochant's floating castle became visible amongst the clouds, the hazy outline gathering more and more solidity until it was a great weight, suspended in the sky. His eyes tracked up the structure, from the tapered point of rock at the bottom, rock threaded with veins of sapphire, to the solid walls and slender towers rising above them. He pushed ahead of Pari's carriage, trying to see if Rochant's flag was flying and was so disheartened by what he saw he came down to land with none of his usual flair.

The carriage pulled up alongside him, and Pari opened a window. Mounted on his Sky-legs, Vasin was still slightly taller than her. He could see Lord Arkav sat opposite, head down as if in deep contemplation.

'What is it?' asked Pari.

'Lord Rochant's flag is flying.'

'Damn, it's as we feared.'

'No,' replied Vasin, 'it's worse. Yadavendra's flag is flying too, as is Gada's, Yadva's and Umed's. I knew the High Lord was keen for Rochant's rebirth to happen but it's been postponed for so long, I'd assumed it would be again.' A horrible thought occurred to him. 'Do you think Rochant planned this?'

'Possibly.'

'I could face Yadavendra, maybe even Yadva, but the whole of House Sapphire?' He shook his head, despair threatening to claim him. 'It's over.'

'Now let's not embrace our true deaths just yet. All we know for sure is that House Sapphire is gathering at Rochant's castle, and that he has returned there.'

Vasin had the sudden urge to smoke some Tack. He could flee to his own castle right now and open up his stash and smoke it all in one glorious session. Oblivion called to him, appealing. But if he lost, Yadavendra wouldn't just destroy him. Mia, his children, Old Sen, all of those who served him loyally would be cast into the Wild as well. *And what will happen to Mother?*

'Please, Lady Pari. Explain to me why this isn't a disaster.'

'Your High Lord still has to answer to the other houses.'

'But Rochant—'

She cut him off, 'Still loves me. I don't believe he'll turn on me directly, not yet. Not if I make him think that I still love him.'

Arkav looked up, concerned, but said nothing.

'That's good for you,' said Vasin bitterly.

'For you as well. House Sapphire won't want to air its private business with us around, so you'll be safe for at least as long as we're there. And if we succeed, Yadavendra will come with us. We can remove him before he can hurt you.'

'I suppose so,' he said whilst knowing it would not be nearly as straightforward as she was making out.

'We're not beaten yet, Lord Vasin. Trust me.'

CHAPTER SEVENTEEN

A drop of rain plopped onto the end of Sa-at's nose, waking him up. It had been quite comfortable in the nook, nestled deep in the soft earth, and tucked away from the winds. They had all taken turns to sleep.

He looked up at the clouds and frowned. They hung low in the sky, overlapping one another, dark and darker. There was a malevolence to rain clouds that troubled him, and these seemed particularly vicious.

Tal was already gathering their things. It didn't take long but by the time he was done, little spots were dampening their clothes. 'May we carry you, my lord?'

'Yes,' replied Rochant.

Between them, they hefted him off the ground and set off. With Sa-at being smaller than Tal, and both of them smaller than Rochant, they made awkward progress. It bothered Sa-at that Rochant's feet dragged behind them. *It will leave a trail for his enemies to follow.*

They sought shelter under the nearest trees, all three of

them panting by the time they got there. Moments later, the spots turned to a shower, which then became a deluge. They'd had to put Rochant down, and his feet stuck out past the edge of their cover. Sa-at tried drawing up his knees, but they wouldn't stay up. He was about to try crossing Rochant's legs when Tal slapped his arm.

'Ow!'

'What are you doing?' Tal whispered. For some reason it felt as if he was being told off.

'Getting his feet out of the rain,' Sa-at whispered back.

'Ask first.'

Sa-at looked at him blankly.

'They're his feet, not yours. Ask him for permission.'

A grumpiness settled on Sa-at's shoulders. While Tal was talking, Rochant's feet were getting soaked. He was being nice and Tal had slapped him for it! It didn't make any sense. 'Can I move your feet out of the rain?'

'My lord,' added Tal in a whisper. Sa-at had the impression he was supposed to add those words. He slapped Tal's arm instead.

'Yes,' replied Rochant.

It was boring waiting for the rain to stop. He desperately wanted to hear the next part of the Corpseman's story and spent most of the time trying to think of an excuse to get Tal to go somewhere else. Then he felt bad for thinking that way about his friend, but it didn't do anything to lessen his curiosity.

'Do you both have plans for the future?' asked Rochant.

Sa-at and Tal looked at each other, and then Tal shrugged.

'I have to find out about the Corpseman,' said Sa-at.

'And after that?'

'No.'

'It's time you started making them.'

'Why?' asked Sa-at.

'Because that is the best way to get what you want. Nobody is just going to hand you the things you desire.'

'Crowflies does.'

'Interesting. Have you ever wondered why that is?'

'No.'

'There will be a reason. You know the Wild perhaps even better than I do. You know how it works. Everything has a cost.'

'Even Crowflies?'

'Especially Crowflies.'

Tal gave Sa-at a pointed look.

Crowflies has always looked after me. That's how it is. Why does there have to be a reason? Why are these thoughts making me feel horrible?

Rochant turned his attention to Tal. 'Will you go back to Sagan?'

'I can't, my lord. They exiled me.'

'What was your crime?'

Tal hung his head. 'My ears. They used to be normal but then we went deeper in than we should have and got caught by Spiderkin. When we came back, my ears looked like this. The elders said I couldn't be trusted but it wasn't my fault, my lord, I didn't make any deals, I swear.'

Sa-at took his hand. 'He's with me now. We're friends.'

Rochant nodded. 'If you have no plans, why don't you both come with me?'

They looked at each other.

'Where are you going?' asked Sa-at.

'Home.' Rochant looked up into the sky, then back to them. 'Don't answer yet. Think about it.' He smiled oddly, a gesture to communicate something other than happiness. 'I'm not going anywhere.'

Not long after that, he fell asleep.

Tal settled in next to Sa-at, who was grateful for the warmth. 'This is brilliant. I've always dreamed of seeing a sky castle. It's never dark there, and nothing of the Wild can get you. It's safe. I mean all the time! Can you imagine it? We have to go. I'm going to go.' He assumed a hopeful expression. 'Will you come with me?'

Sa-at didn't think about it for long. 'Yes.'

They were both so excited that they hugged to celebrate.

When Rochant finally woke up, the two of them were sat watching him.

'Yes!' said Sa-at.

'We'd be honoured to come with you, my lord,' added Tal.

'Good,' Rochant replied. 'But I should warn you, it won't be easy. My enemies will be watching. To get past them will take cunning and courage. Tal, I need you to get us new clothes. I will die of exposure if I don't get something better soon, and Sa-at's clothing is too conspicuous. Can you do that?'

'I don't know, my lord. I don't have much to trade with, and if they see my ears . . . '

'Cunning and courage, Tal. Keep your hood secured and forward, nobody expects a Gatherer to do otherwise. As for the goods, if you can't trade for them, take them.'

Tal gasped. 'Steal?'

'Yes. In desperate times, a servant of the Sapphire does whatever is required to save the house.'

'But stealing is wrong, my lord.'

He doesn't understand, thought Sa-at. *This is bigger than clothes.*

'Make note of the person you take from, and I will see them compensated when I am returned to power. Does that satisfy you?'

'Can't we just say that you need it, my lord? Any good person would be happy to help you.'

'My enemies will be listening for my name. It is too dangerous. Can you do this for me, Tal? Can you rise above your own concerns to serve your house in its time of need?'

'I— I can, my lord.'

'Good, then go. And go carefully.'

Tal is a good friend but he is clumsy. He shouldn't have to go alone. 'I'll come with you,' said Sa-at.

'No,' replied Rochant. 'I need one of you to stay with me.'

'I'll be alright,' said Tal.

He does not sound alright.

He sounds all sad.

He sounds all scared.

But Sa-at did not say these things. He sensed that to do so would make it worse for his friend, not better. *I must be like Rochant and make my face and feelings say different things.* So instead of showing his worry, he said: 'Yes, you will.'

Tal nodded to him and bowed to Rochant, and then plunged into the rain. Sa-at watched his hunched form get smaller and smaller, and he wondered if he would ever see him again. To his shame, it only took a minute for him to realize that now he could hear the rest of the story.

Rochant seemed able to read his thoughts. And when he

asked: 'Shall I continue?' Sa-at could not help but smile and nod.

A scene of happy chaos greeted Vasin as he crossed the Bridge of Friends and Fools, and walked through the gates of Lord Rochant's floating castle. He was late. High Lord Yadavendra would notice. The others would notice too, a mark against him at the worst possible time. There was no sign of judgement in the courtyard however, quite the opposite. It was usual for there to be an air of celebration when a rebirth was successful, but this was something else, jubilation bordering on mania. His arrival, armoured, and with two Deathless from another house, only added to the mix.

There is such love for Rochant among the people, he thought, not without a little envy.

He did his best to smooth the way for Lady Pari and Lord Arkav with the guards, and started towards the keep. The crowd parted for him and his appearance did prompt cheering, which lifted his spirits somewhat.

By the time he reached the Chrysalis Chamber the Gardener-smiths were waiting for him. Each piece of armour was carefully removed and he saw how they had put up temporary dividers to split the room into sections, to give each set of armour its own space.

As he stepped down from his Sky-legs and into a robe, his knees buckled and only the quick reactions of the staff saved him from a fall. They put him back on his feet without a word while he silently berated himself. *This will get back to Yadavendra. Damn it! I cannot afford to show weakness now.*

It was understandable though. Without the support of his sapphire armour, he felt keenly aware of his unbroken flight from House Ruby to Sorn, and then from there to the castle. *And that journey came off the back of the hunt! When did I last sleep?*

He allowed himself to be guided to his usual room, grateful for the practised hands that moved him up stairs, down corridors, and into bed.

The next he knew, a servant was singing for entry.

He blinked sleepily, then sat up as the smell of smoking Nightweed and cooked meats tickled his nose. Not for the first time, it struck him that Rochant's staff really were excellent.

After he'd inhaled a little too much of the Nightweed and devoured most of the food, he noticed the servant had remained in the room. 'Yes?'

'Are you up to receiving visitors, my lord?'

'Not really.'

'Ah.' The servant's face fell.

Vasin's quickly mirrored it. 'Let me guess. My brother, Lord Gada, is already on his way here to speak to me.'

'Just so, my lord.'

I feel as if I have lived through this moment a thousand times and it never gets any less tedious. 'As you can see, I am hardly in a state to receive anyone. Tell my beloved brother I will send for him when I am ready, and recommend that he try some of the yellow Birdkin flesh while he waits, it really is excellent.'

The servant's face fell yet further. 'At once, my lord.'

Yes, he thought, *I've fallen for Gada's tricks in the past, but no longer. I will not allow myself to be rushed and caught off guard again, nor will I dance to his beat when I can make him dance to mine. He may be my elder brother, but I have to stop thinking of him that way if I am to be a credible candidate for High Lord.*

Despite this sentiment, he found it hard to be relaxed as servants prepared him for the day. They brushed his long hair, scented his body and then wrapped it in silk. Though his own people would have been better, they also did a credible job of painting his face, and daubing it in gold.

When he signalled for them to fetch Gada, he felt a flurry of nerves in his stomach. *This is worse than the morning of a hunt.*

As expected, Gada was in full regalia, his long-limbed body swathed in flowing blue that further emphasized its length. No matter the lifecycle, his brother's eyes always communicated a slight disapproval. His smile, only a vague hint of affection.

Vasin waved him inside and the two clasped arms. Despite their differences, blood and a mutual love of their mother bound them. Each gripped the other firmly, as they had through the ages.

However, when Gada spoke, his voice was peevish. 'It is good to see you, at last.'

'I would have been here sooner, had I been aware anything was happening.'

A bit of genuine surprise crossed Gada's face before quickly vanishing. 'Messengers went to every castle, travelling with the High Lord's seal and a great deal of urgency. Where have you been?'

'With House Ruby.'

'For your sake, I'm going to pretend that you are joking.'

'The situation there is no joke, brother. We need to send aid.'

Gada put a hesitant hand on Vasin's arm. 'But please, not today. Promise me you won't speak of this until we've had a chance to enjoy Lord Rochant's return. It might even be wise to speak to him first.'

In another lifecycle, this would be good advice, but Rochant was anything but an ally now. 'This is too important to wait. The Rubies have no Deathless able to fly, and they're down to their last hunters.' He thought of Lord Quasim Peridot's recklessness and Lord Lakshin Opal's fear. 'They need us. This challenge is beyond the minor houses.'

'There are several major houses. Why us?'

'We are closer than House Tanzanite, and they have sent aid.'

Gada's eyes narrowed. 'Is this why you arrived with Tanzanites in tow? If you think the High Lord is going to change his mind because you've brought them, you're sorely mistaken.'

'No, I don't think that.'

Gada continued as if he hadn't spoken. 'If his own daughter can't persuade him, you have no hope. The High Lord will see this as a challenge to his authority. He'll dig in even deeper.'

'I know that,' Vasin muttered.

'My advice would be to take things slowly. Get Lord Rochant's support. Better yet, get him to suggest it.'

Don't lose your temper, Vasin counselled himself. *How would Mother handle this?* But when he tried to remember Nidra in court, the only images he could bring to mind was of her in Sorn, broken and incoherent. He gritted his teeth

337

and then held up a hand until Gada stopped talking. 'They aren't here for the Rubies. They are here to bring High Lord Sapphire to trial for destroying Mother's Godpiece, and I intend to support them.'

Gada's mouth opened. No words came out. He closed it again.

'Will you stand with me?'

'Oh, Vasin. Mother is gone. Attacking Yadavendra won't bring her back. He won't go with the Tanzanites. In fact, they'll be lucky not to be put between lives. If you stand with them, you'll die with them too, only you won't get to come back.'

This was the moment of crisis. *Do I tell him about Mother?* She had always said that when the time came, Gada would support them. He was not so sure. If he told his brother about her, he would soon have to tell him about Rochant, which would mean confessing his own crimes against the house. Did he trust his brother with their lives?

I don't know.

His instincts told him to wait. His mother had told him to act. He hesitated, unable to commit to either path.

I don't know what to do!

But when Gada started to speak again, Vasin grabbed him, so sudden and fierce that he saw genuine fear on his brother's face. 'Mother is not gone,' he hissed. 'She lives. I have seen her and talked with her. Do you understand? She lives! And she deserves justice, not Yadavendra's madness. We can get rid of Yadavendra, restore the house, and restore her. We can bring her back!'

For once, Gada had nothing to say.

'Don't you see?' continued Vasin, unable to stop now he'd

started. 'We have a chance to put things right. We have to take it, together. Yadva will stand with us, maybe Umed too. It's going to happen. When the celebrations are over, the Tanzanites will make their decree on behalf of the Council of High Lords. We have to be ready.'

There was a long pause, and then Gada nodded to himself. He removed Vasin's left hand from his arm, then his right. 'We did not have this conversation. Whatever you saw was not our mother. She has been exiled by official decree and is dead to us. Our first loyalty is to our High Lord, not the political games of the other houses. We live and die by his decree, not theirs. We follow his lead in all things, not theirs. We did not have this conversation.'

Gada nodded to himself again, and walked out, leaving Vasin confused. *Did he mean those things or was he saying them in case we were overheard? Was that nod a signal that he did support me?*

He pressed his knuckles against his temples, trying to ease the pressure there. His brother may have just pledged himself to restoring their mother or washed his hands of her. The only thing Vasin knew for certain was that either way, all of the risk would be his and his alone.

Pari watched the crowd from her window as the staff parked the carriage. Though they were happy to see their lord returned, that happiness was directed away from her, another kind of barrier between the Sapphire and outsiders. Since their arrival, she had seen many such barriers, from physical ones like the bridge, the guards, and the walls themselves, to more subtle ones; the abundance of blue flags, the smiles kept for locals only, the way traders from other houses had been partitioned into a separate area. All were weapons to dishearten non-Sapphire visitors.

Well, we have weapons of our own.

'I'm not sure I can do this,' said Arkav.

'I am.' She took his hand. 'I'll be with you all the way.'

'High Lord Tanzanite is using us.'

'Of course she is.'

'She says she wants me to succeed, and I believe her. But in her heart, she expects me to fail. She's planned for it.' He looked away. 'If our words don't bring High Lord Sapphire to justice, then our blood will . . . I don't think we're coming back from this, Pari.'

'Nonsense! We will see this through, save House Sapphire from itself and annoy Priyamvada in the process, and look fabulous while doing it.' She frowned. 'How is my face looking? Be honest?'

'They've covered the bruises and I can only see the swelling up close.'

'That will have to do. Shall we?'

The door was opened, and the two of them climbed out, her dress and his jacket so long that servants carried the ends of them to keep them from the dirt. At her nod, they unfurled a banner of seven colours – purple, black, blue, violet, red, white, green – and marched behind them with it. It made clear that they came as representatives of all the houses joined together rather than just Tanzanite.

People hushed as they passed, and Pari approved of this. She did not look at them, keeping her eyes forward and her mind on the future. A servant, rather than Rochant himself, came to welcome them, and led them into the keep. A rather unnecessary number of guards were in evidence inside, and she wondered if they were for her benefit. In fact they were so ubiquitous that when she passed a corridor without any, it invited comment.

'What's wrong with that hallway?'

'I beg your pardon, Lady Pari?'

She stopped. Arkav and his staff stopped, and, a step later, their escort stopped. When she was sure she had their attention, she gestured lazily towards it. 'That hallway there. Does it not deserve protection too?'

'Ah, that has been cleared for the Bringers of Endless Order to use, as is tradition.'

'Marvellous,' she replied, and started down it. When she began to walk, so too did Lord Arkav and his staff.

'Lady Pari, I'm afraid I cannot allow you to go that way. Lady Pari, I must insist . . . Lady Pari! Lord Arkav! Please! Come back!'

She smiled as his protests grew fainter. 'It's good to know,' she said to Arkav, 'that people are still more afraid of the Bringers than they are of their Sapphire masters.'

When they had left their escort far behind them she came to a stop and dismissed the staff. 'Go back to the main corridor and wait for word that the Bringers have left, then return to us here.'

To her surprise, she found that Arkav was smiling. 'Are you doing this just to upset the Sapphire or are you planning something?'

She smiled back. 'Yes.'

'Did you see their faces when you brought out the banner?'

'I did.'

'They're scared, Pari.'

'So they should be.'

He thought about this for a while. 'No. They shouldn't. This isn't right. Don't you see? The people out there aren't scared *of* us. They're scared *for* us, and what we might make Yadavendra do.'

'We're not going to make Yadavendra do anything.'

Arkav raised an eyebrow. 'You're lying again.'

Pari wasn't sure what to say to that.

They hadn't been waiting long when the Bringers of Endless Order came round the corner. As always, there were seven of them, all identically garbed in black and white robes, all masked, all carrying golden wands. They came to a stop before her and looked at the two of them, their green eyes expectant.

'They don't look happy,' whispered Arkav.

'Tell me something I don't know.'

'I don't think it's anything to do with us.'

She wondered how he knew, but didn't question it. In his better days Arkav had a knack for seeing the truth in people. It was one of things that made him such a good ambassador for the house.

'Lord Arkav—' said the lead Bringer.

'And Lady Pari—' said another.

'Tanzanite,' echoed the others.

'How unexpected,' finished the first.

How do they talk in time like that? she wondered. *Is it a trick? A power? Do they practise in their rooms all the time?* There was too much about the Bringers she did not know, which made what she was about to attempt all the more a gamble.

She and Arkav bowed.

'I apologize for ambushing you like this, but given that you're here, I was hoping we could talk.'

The lead Bringer gave a slight nod.

'Thank you. My brother and I have been tasked to bring Yadavendra, High Lord of the Sapphire before the Council of High Lords. He has ignored all summonses so far.'

'This, we know,' replied the Bringers.

'Twice now, he has broken tradition, and I fear he will break with it again when we see him. But if you were to invite him to the Hall of Seven Doors, he could not ignore it.'

There was a pause.

'You have slept long, child of the Tanzanite. You have missed much. We made invitation to Yadavendra six years ago.'

'And he didn't come?'

A look was shared among the Bringers. 'He has not yet graced us with either reply or his presence.'

'Then why haven't you taken action?'

'It is not our place to interfere in the business of the living. But when the time comes we will do . . . nothing.'

'Nothing?' Her first instinct was to be angry, but then she noticed the way they were staring at her and thought about it. *They mean that literally.* She exchanged a look with Arkav, and he nodded in understanding. *They're saying that when Yadavendra dies, they won't bring him back! That's how they will deal with this.* She thought about it some more and quickly got angry again. 'But that will be too late! I've heard about the situation at House Ruby. They cannot wait for Yadavendra to die, nor for House Sapphire to pull itself together.'

'We cannot interfere. To do so would be to upset the balance.'

'The balance is long past upset. It's furious! It's running around and setting things on fire!'

'Pari,' warned Arkav.

She went on, determined to make her point. 'As we speak, people are dying. And I'm no seer, but I am confident that it's going to get a lot worse if we don't stop Yadavendra immediately.'

'Then stop him,' they replied. 'That is your task, not ours.'

They seemed unmoved, her words unable to touch their strange hearts. She bowed again and said as politely as she could, 'I am sorry for wasting your time.'

The lead Bringer waved away her apology. 'We are all rich in time here, but we are wondering when you will raise the real reason for this meeting.'

'I don't understand.'

They all looked from her, to Arkav and back again, their eyes flashing unnaturally. 'You understand.'

Pari conceded the point with a tilt of her head. 'When we are between lives, our souls drift in another place. Is it possible to go there without dying?'

The Bringers were now giving her their full attention. 'It is.'

'Then I wish to make that journey. How do I get there?'

'Below this castle, below every castle, are the fountains of essence that the Deathless ride. If you were to dive into the fountain, and fly against the currents, you would pass beneath the rock of this world and into another place. That is where the soul goes between lives.'

'And if I wanted to find a particular soul, would it matter which place I went in?'

The Bringers did not answer.

'They have no idea,' said Arkav.

'That is a simplistic answer,' replied the lead Bringer, 'and as with any simplification, it distorts truth.'

'Will you enlighten us?' asked Pari.

'In that place, up is no longer up. Distance is irrelevant. Maps are meaningless. Would it matter where you entered it? Perhaps. Perhaps not.'

'I'm going to go there. Will you help me?'

'That depends on why you wish to go.'

Pari hesitated. She had feared they would ask this. To tell them the truth would place Arkav at risk of being branded an abomination. But to lie to the Bringers was a crime. To lie to their faces was insanity.

'My reasons are my own. But perhaps we could come to some arrangement? What can I do in exchange for your help?'

The Bringers said nothing. It soon became clear this was not a pause, but a reply in and of itself. *They're not interested*, thought Pari, and began to despair.

'She wants to go for my sake,' said Arkav.

Pari turned sharply towards him. 'Don't. We know where to start, we can work out the rest on our own.'

One of the Bringers at the back of the group snorted.

'Imagine if our situations were reversed, Pari. Would you let me do this without help? Without even knowing the risks?'

She pouted. 'No.'

'Would you let me die for you?'

She felt the urge to cry but pushed it down. 'No.'

'Then I have to tell them. It's our best chance.' He broke eye contact with her to address the Bringers directly. 'When

I am reborn, a part of me doesn't come back. Pari saw it when she was between lives. She wants to go and get it. To make me whole again.'

Pari felt their attention move swiftly to her. 'You remember your time between lives?'

'Not all of it. Snatches. And, I think I've seen Arkav there more than once. The memories are hard to hold onto though. It's like trying to recall a dream.'

The Bringers formed a circle that excluded them and began to whisper amongst themselves. Pari didn't need to be able to make out the words to know they were having an argument.

At one point, two of the Bringers came over to stare at Arkav. They moved their wands up and down his body, studying the way the light played on his skin, then they returned to the others and the whispers continued.

'You seem very calm about this,' Pari murmured to her brother. 'I'm jealous.'

'For the longest time, I've been lost, and I haven't even been able to say why. At least now, thanks to you, I know that something will happen.'

'Even if it means the end of your life?'

'Look at me, Pari. This isn't living, it's suffering. I'd rather die than go on this way. I'm sick of letting House Tanzanite down, and I'm sick of being a thing that you or the High Lord have to look after. I've had enough of pity.' He gave a short, sharp shake of his head. 'I don't want to be a burden any more.'

She took his hands. 'You know I've never seen you that way.'

'I know, and I love you for it. But it isn't enough.'

He kept hold of her hands while they waited. When they

broke their circle, a different Bringer stepped forward to speak with them. Despite the identical dress, Pari could see that this one was of stouter build and, she was fairly sure, female, where the last had been male.

'Do you have your armour with you?'

'We both do,' Pari replied.

'Good. When you have discharged your duty with the Sapphire, meet me on the edge of the chasm beneath Lord Rochant's castle. Come after sunset.'

Pari nodded. 'You're going to help us?'

'Yes.'

'Thank you.'

The Bringer's eyes widened. 'You may not wish to thank me when this is over.'

'Why are you helping us?' asked Arkav. She saw he was looking at the other Bringers, some of whom had turned away. For the first time they appeared like separate clumps of people, rather than one mass. *They are not all in agreement. Someone's pride has been hurt in all this. Suns, they are no better than we are!*

'It is our role to shepherd the soul from one body to the next. In this, Lord Arkav, we have failed you. And,' she added, a little excitement creeping into her voice, 'such a thing has not been attempted in over a thousand years.'

Pari decided not to ask why. 'We'll be there.'

'Before you come to us, you will pay your respects to the recently returned Lord Rochant, yes?'

Pari fought to keep the frown from her face. She wasn't sure where this was going but Rochant was the last person she wanted to see. 'Of course,' she said. 'It would be rude not to.'

The Bringer was already walking past her, the others following. It seemed the conversation was over. Stunned, Arkav and Pari watched them go.

'Well,' she remarked when they were well out of earshot, 'I suppose that explains why nobody ever invites the Bringers to dinner.'

'They are unhappy about Lord Rochant's rebirth.'

'Aren't we all?'

Arkav ignored her sarcasm. 'Their mood was off when they first arrived and it darkened again when his name was mentioned.'

Pari frowned. 'They want us to go and see him. No, they want us to see something about him. But what?'

'There's only one way to find out.'

She gave his hand a squeeze. 'I might need your help this time. Are you up for it?'

He squeezed back. 'Always.'

CHAPTER EIGHTEEN

There was so much on his mind that Satyendra was almost back to his own chambers before he realized his mistake. *This room isn't mine any more and Rochant has no reason to go this way. Idiot! I might as well have the word 'imposter' tattooed on my forehead.* Luckily, he knew where Lord Rochant's rooms were, as he'd been taken there in the past as part of the alignment process. None of his entourage questioned the sudden change in direction. After all, a little disorientation was to be expected after a rebirth.

It struck him that, in a way, his life would not change that much. He'd still be pretending most of the time, and if people found out the truth about him, he'd still be destroyed. However, in one very big way, things had changed: for as long as he could convince people that he was Lord Rochant, he had all the powers of a Deathless Lord at his disposal. And he intended to make swift use of them. So, instead of resting, he turned to the most senior member of staff present. 'What is you name?'

'Win, my lord. Do you not remember me? I was still coming into my beard when we last met.'

Satyendra peered at him, and then feigned fondness. 'Win? Ah yes, you were bright as I recall, full of promise.'

The man beamed. 'You said so to my father.'

'Indeed I did. It is pleasing to see I was right. Now, Win, I need you to summon all of my hunters, their apprentices, and the senior staff, but quietly. I don't wish the other guests to know what we're up to.'

'All of them, my lord? In secret? It will be difficult. Very difficult.'

'But not beyond your abilities.'

Win swallowed. 'No, my lord.'

He felt like he needed time alone, but that didn't seem a very Deathless thing to ask for, so he said: 'I will be bathed, changed and prepared by the time you've gathered them.'

'Yes, my lord.'

Win's nerves began to stir the hunger, but were not enough to satisfy it. 'One more thing. I wish to keep with tradition. Honoured Mother Chandni should not be disturbed today.'

He would have to face the challenge of his mother's scrutiny at some point, but the longer he could put that off, the better.

The next hour passed pleasantly enough, as he was scrubbed, massaged, scented, combed, and painted. Then they wrapped his body in soft silks. He was careful to pick out things that matched what he'd heard of Rochant. Simple cuts, with fewer layers than the other Deathless favoured. *Ahh, to never clean or dress myself again! It is no wonder the Deathless have so much energy.*

He was just enjoying a moment's peace before the meeting

when a servant entered, brazen, as if they were welcome despite not having sung for permission. To his surprise it was the old hag, Roh, from the kitchens. She'd never been particularly nice to him, and he'd never liked her as a result. It didn't help that his mother was strangely deferent to the old cook, allowing her to rule the lower castle without interference. *Well, that will have to change.*

He turned an imperious look in the cook's direction. She was carrying a tray of cold meats but the portions looked far too small, mainly tails and innards, hardly appropriate for such an occasion. 'What's this?'

'Food, my good lord,' she said with a hearty cackle. 'A snack for the ages.' He had the feeling she was waiting for him to say something, but by the time he'd realized it was too late. 'And may I say how good it is to see you returned to us once more. You've been sorely missed.'

'I'm not hungry.'

'Not hungry, he says? Just come back from the dead and he's not hungry. Go on, my lord, just have one thing for old Roh. Just one.'

She held out the tray and before he could think to dismiss her, he found himself considering the options.

'How about a nice bit of bird liver?' she said, tilting the tray to one side. 'Or I've got fried tongue here, Lizardkin and Dogkin, thin and thick. Nothing better than a crispy bit of tongue, is there, my lord?'

'Yes, alright. I'll take a tongue.' *Anything to get her out.*

'Oh yes, you get your teeth around that, get the blood flowing in that new body of yours.' She gave another laugh as she trotted out. Satyendra frowned. He of all people knew a fake laugh when he heard one. He tried a nibble of the tongue anyway. It tasted of fat and little else. *And on top of it all she can't even cook! The sooner I get rid of her, the better.*

Win returned shortly afterwards to declare all was ready, and the two of them went to the main receiving room. Servants were busy preparing it for the celebratory feast. Three additional tables had been added, long and low, with chairs around the top end, and thick cushions towards the bottom.

Upon his entrance, everyone bowed deeply. He let them stay like that as he crossed the room, and took his place on the throne. *My throne.*

He gestured for them to stand and they moved together, as surely as if he had pulled their strings. A childish urge to make them do it again – to sit or stand on his command, to dance – rose and was put aside. 'It is good to be with you again, my people.' He saw them straighten. 'As you know, our enemies have tried to come between us. What you may not know is that they have done so again.'

Shock passed around the room, then anger, then fear. He took a moment to drink it in. 'There is a spy amongst us, profiting from our trust.' He let his gaze rest over Pik, long enough to make him squirm. *Oh, I am going to enjoy this.*

'Hiding in plain sight, right under our noses.'

Gradually, the rest of the staff began to take the hint, and their fear turned back to anger, their looks likes spears directed at Pik's head.

'This one,' continued Satyendra, 'has been creeping about at night, passing messages in secret, stalking my vessel on the very night of the ceremony. He is a traitor to me and to House Sapphire.' The room erupted into shocked mutterings.

'Take him into the depths of the castle and confine him there. Bind his mouth, and leave him in the dark.'

As the guards complied and began dragging Pik from the room, he called desperately over his shoulder, his voice a terrified squeak over the roar of the room.

'Wait, my lord. I beg you! I can explain.'

Satyendra raised a hand for silence. Instantly, the floor was his. The people's rapt attention was pleasant, but it was nothing to Pik's terror; that was like a burst of adrenaline running through his body, wonderful, invigorating. He surged from the throne to get closer to it, until he could whisper in Pik's ear, 'There is no justification for treachery.'

'B-but,' replied Pik in a whisper, 'I was serving Honoured Mother Chandni, my lord. In secret. Ask her! She can explain everything.'

'Have no fear, traitor.' Satyendra gestured for the guards to take him away. 'I will deal with her too, soon enough.'

Vasin paced in his room. One floor away, people would be gathering for the feast. People like his brother, who was painfully punctual for everything, and his uncle, Lord Umed, who seemed to genuinely enjoy these occasions. Vasin paced some more, just to be sure that he wouldn't bump into them, and then stepped out into the corridor and went a few doors down to where Lady Yadva would be getting ready.

He sang for entrance, and she admitted him immediately.

No matter how many times he saw his cousin, he never got over how big she was. Raw physical power radiated from every inch of her. She wore a sleeveless robe to show off the muscles in her arms, with the silk bound tight around her waist. It made her trunk seem thicker, not thinner, which was no doubt her intention. The servants painting her nails seemed like children next to her.

'Welcome, little cousin,' she said.

'Thank you. I was hoping we might speak before the festivities.'

She dismissed the servants with a flick of her eyes. When they had gone, she moved to the window, gesturing for him to join her. 'When will you do it?'

'Tomorrow,' said Vasin. 'After the Tanzanite have declared their intentions. After he has refused them.'

She grunted. 'That works.'

'Do you think Yadavendra will go quietly?'

'Ha! That is the one thing he will not do. He might fight, he might scream, but it will be loud, count on that. It is well past time though, even House Jet have taken notice.'

'What happened?'

'I got an anonymous message from one of their Deathless. It just said: "Deal with him or we will."' She laughed. 'I've always liked House Jet, they're slow to start, but when they do, they don't mess about.'

'When was this?'

'About six months ago. Any chance my father had of making amends is long gone.'

'Will you wear your armour tomorrow?'

She shook her head. 'No. Will you?'

'I've thought about it. I don't like the idea of your father being ascended, armed, and angry, and us without protection . . .'

'We can take him, armour or not. You keep him focused on you, and I'll deal with his glaive. The rest will fall as it does. And then,' she put a hand on his shoulder, 'you will

354

declare me the new High Lord.' Her hand squeezed. 'Or I will expose your dirty secret to the rest of the house.'

He gritted his teeth. 'You don't think it would make you look bad too?'

'No.'

'Well, you've known and said nothing for all these years. If you admit that, you admit your part in hiding the betrayal.'

'What?' The pressure eased slightly as she thought this through.

'Yes,' he said, trying to remember the phrase Lady Pari had used. *I'm sure it sounded better when she said it.* 'They won't accept a High Lord who has broken the rules. If you take me down that way, you go down too.'

Her face was blank with thought and then she gave a nasty little laugh. 'It's simple, little cousin. You back me, and you live. You stand against me,' she started to squeeze again, 'and you know what's coming. Remember, all I've done is stay quiet. I'll just say I was waiting for Rochant to come back before I spoke out. Or I'll say something else. It doesn't matter. Nobody's going to care about me because they'll be too busy looking at you. You kidnapped Rochant, you ordered the death of his line, and you're the traitorous son of Nidra Un-Sapphire.

'So,' she added, squeezing his shoulder with renewed vigour, 'do we understand each other?'

He could feel her fingers boring into the bones of his shoulder. The instinct to shrug her off or push her away was strong. He did neither of these things. The old Vasin acted on instinct and lashed out whenever his pride was threatened. Those luxuries were denied him now.

I cannot fight Yadavendra without Yadva's help. I must

make her think she has won, get her to underestimate me.

He lowered his head and forced himself to say: 'Yes.'

'There.' She released her grip. 'That wasn't so hard was it? Now, let's go join the others. I'm starving.'

She left, assuming that he would follow. He hated her for that, and hated himself for falling into step behind her.

Whatever happens to me tomorrow, I have to make sure the house is restored and the Rubies send aid. And I have to find a way to help Mother.

But, noble as those thoughts were, they did not satisfy him. In that moment, he realized that over the years something in him truly had changed. He was no longer content to hunt and play. He wanted to be High Lord. He wanted to win.

'Why aren't you talking?' asked Sa-at.

Rochant closed his eyes. 'It all happened a long time ago. To remember, I have to send my mind back there, like taking a walk through the years.'

'You said you named it. That's the last thing you said.'

'I did. Names are important, especially in the Wild.'

'Why did you call it the Scuttling Corpseman?'

'That is probably the most important question to ask.'

'It is?' Sa-at felt quite pleased with himself.

'Yes. I told you that the Corpseman had weak spots. Holes in the hard shell that I covered with my skin.' Sa-at nodded. 'And I told you that I wasn't happy about it as a solution.' Sa-at nodded again. 'Well, there was this little boy, called Nant, who thought he was something special. He liked to show off by taking risks. If I stayed out later than I should, he'd have to stay out one minute later. If I found a half dozen twigs to use for the fire, he'd have to find a dozen. He didn't really care about doing these things, just so long as he did them slightly better than the other children in Veren.

'One day, one of the apprentice Gatherers had found a nice ripe Fleshfruit, about as big as my fist. Of course Nant, who was also an apprentice Gatherer, had to find one bigger. We all knew it was impossible but Nant wouldn't hear it. He went tearing about the forest, turning over stones and poking in holes and coming up with nothing. Anyway, the suns go down and they make the call for everyone to come in, but when the elders are counting heads at the end of the day, guess who isn't there?'

'Nant,' said Sa-at without hesitation. 'It was Nant!'

'Correct. I found his body the next morning hanging from the Stern Tree. What was left of it. The funny thing was it looked like it had been there much longer than a night. Whatever had killed him had stripped all the skin from his bones and sucked away every last drop of blood, leaving a remarkably clean skeleton with its insides completely dried out.

'After I'd stared at it for a while, I had an idea. When I was sure nobody was about, I pulled Nant's body off the tree and I took the skull and some other bones, like the shoulder-blades, that I thought might be useful. And I took these parts to my friend.'

'What about the Stern Tree?'

Rochant opened his eyes. 'What about it?'

'You took something. What did you give it in return?'

'Nothing. I didn't know how things worked back then.'

Sa-at looked appalled as Rochant continued.

'My plan was to make armour out of the bones for my friend. This proved difficult. I'd managed to borrow some of our Cutter-crafter's tools, but I lacked the skill to use them. Even for a master, bones are hard to work. They chip and break easily. It didn't take me long to waste half of what I'd recovered. When it came time to use the skull, I abandoned all subtlety.

'After a bit of pondering, I ditched the jawbone. There was no way to attach it, and my friend had no mouth anyway. The skull was perfect though. I guided the antennae through the eye holes and they held it in place like a helmet. The other pieces I bound in place, hoping that they would eventually be absorbed like my skin had been.'

'Were they?'

'No, and when my friend moved, they slipped out of place.'

'How did you make it better?'

'I became an apprentice Cutter-crafter.' Rochant glanced at the water-skin. 'Could you?'

After a drink, he continued.

'A few years went by. My friend grew rapidly, to the point where I had to hide it outside of Veren. Each time it shed an old carapace, I provided it with fresh skin and new armour. It soon outgrew Nant's skull but, as you know, there are always bones to be found in the Wild. I cultivated friendships with the Gatherers and listened to their stories, always waiting for news of a fresh corpse. I rarely had to wait long.

'Despite this, the forest was quiet, and we enjoyed a time of relative peace. It wasn't long before my friend became able to fend for itself. Sometimes, it would scurry, sometimes it would rise up on its back legs and walk. I know it wanted to move like I did, but its gait was . . . ' he gave another of those almost smiles. 'It used to get so angry when I laughed.'

'When did you name it?'

'The trouble with any small settlement is that everyone knows you. I thought I'd been careful to cover my tracks but one day, when I slipped out to see my friend, I was followed by a young girl. Her name was . . . ' he frowned. 'Funny, I can picture her face, it was sour, one of those faces that looks middle aged from the cot to the grave. But I can't recall her name. It's been such a long time . . . She watched us together, long enough to see the extent of my crimes against Veren. She saw me giving blood, and she saw me fixing some of the armour. Now I think about it, it must have taken a lot of courage for her to see my friend and not call out. Jes! I remember now. Her name was Jes.

'Of course, it didn't matter in the end. My friend doesn't hear the sounds you make with your mouth, it hears the sounds you make with your soul, and hers was making a terrible racket. It waited until I'd finished my repair work, and then it jumped. Jes was dead after one scream.

'That was when I named it the Scuttling Corpseman. When the defenders of Veren came running, they saw her body, me standing next to her, and the shape of my friend as it fled. I had to explain how she had died and why I was there. I made up a story that I was courting Jes and we'd sneaked away from our duties to have some time alone together. The elders believed me, but they were most unhappy. They called for a hunt, and I was put forward to be one of the tributes. But that's a different story.'

'You called it the Scuttling Corpseman because it has bits of dead body on it?'

'Yes.'

'And because it walks in a funny way?'

'Yes.'

Sa-at was quiet for a while. He couldn't help but feel disappointed. Also, the suns were going down and Tal hadn't returned. *I should have gone with him. I should not have left him alone. If bad things happen to my friend, I will feel it forever in my stomach.*

The feeling of foreboding would not go away. Sa-at wanted to go and look for Tal, but knew he could not. To do so would be to abandon Rochant, and he was helpless. Whenever they heard a noise, he sat up, peering into the gloom. He became aware that Rochant was watching, bemused, and his mood soured further.

'I didn't like your story.'

'It wasn't for you to like or dislike. It was to provide you with information about the Corpseman.'

'And you lied.'

'I promise you, it was all truth, told for the very first time.'

'You said that its name was important and it wasn't.'

Instead of looking offended, Rochant looked – Sa-at struggled to identify the emotion from his placid expression – *pleased?* 'Are you sure? Its name is connected to its weakness. I'd say that was important.'

'You told me about the holes in its body before the name.'

'What does that suggest to you?'

Sa-at shrugged. 'That you lied?'

'Or?'

'That it's important that the Corpseman has a funny walk.'

'Or?'

'Those are the reasons. You said those are the reasons. You said so!'

'You suggested those were the reasons, not me. I agreed that they contributed to the name.'

'There's another reason?'

'Yes.'

Sa-at wanted to shake the man in the way a Dogkin shakes its prey. 'Why didn't you say? You should have said!'

'Because if you work it out yourself, it will mean more to you.'

'You tried to trick me!'

'Perhaps a little.'

'We made a pact. You swore!'

'Please, calm yourself. I swore to tell you everything about the Corpseman and answer your questions about it. This is my way of doing that. It may be frustrating now, but in the long term, it will help you to understand. I'm trying to do more than just give information, I'm trying to ignite the spark within you.' He looked at Sa-at's face and added. 'Not literally. I mean I want to help you become more than you are. That's what friends do for each other.'

Sa-at tucked his arms behind his back and thought hard, the way Crowflies did when it was pondering a problem. He liked the sound of Rochant's words but he still felt like he'd been tricked. 'What is the other reason you named it the Scuttling Corpseman?'

'There are two. It's an unusual name and I'd hoped it wouldn't be associated with the strange Flykin my friend was related to. Something had gone to a great deal of effort to wipe them out and I didn't want it coming back for my friend. This name was new. I hoped this meant the Wild

361

would take it as a new creature, rather than the spawn of an old one.

'The second reason is that I suggested it was male. It's not. It's asexual. I wanted to suggest it was a lone wanderer, a freakish anomaly. Something unique and singular rather than the progenitor of a new line.'

'Why is that important?'

'Because of the agreement my friend and I had made. One just as binding as the one between us, but without words. I would help it grow to its full strength, and then I would find a way for it to breed and restore its kind to power. And that's exactly what I did.'

'Won't the thing that killed them before be angry?'

'Yes.'

'Will they fight?'

'Yes. But I have a feeling it will go differently this time.'

'Why?'

'Because the Corpseman is not what it was before. Its injuries made it weaker in some ways, stronger in others. It doesn't think like a thing of the Wild any more, nor does it think like we do. It's something new, and is evolving in ways even I can't predict.'

Sa-at was quiet for a long time. He believed Rochant and this made him nervous. *If there is a fight and all the demons are with the Corpseman, is Murderkind on the other side? Murderkind said the Red Brothers are with the Corpseman and the Red Brothers are my enemy. Does that mean the Corpesman is my enemy? Murderkind is my friend and Rochant is my friend. The Corpseman is my enemy and Rochant is the Corpseman's friend. So is Rochant my enemy or my friend?* The thoughts swirled round inside, confusing and sad. He did not want any more fighting. He did not want to have to pick between one friend and another, any more than he wanted his friends to fight over him.

And Tal has still not come back!

'Rochant?'

'Yes?'

'What did the Corpseman agree to do for you in return?'

'That is an excellent question. However it is one not covered in our deal.'

'But it was a deal with the Corpseman, and –' Sa-at tried to put the shape he had in his head into words '– it will help me to understand it better, so it is part of our deal.'

'Admirable logic. I will reward you with this much: it agreed to help me realize my dream, and become more than I was. It also agreed not to harm me or those I love. There is more, but I won't be pushed into revealing it. Perhaps, if you come with me, I'll tell you one day over a glass of good wine.'

'I'd like that.'

'Yes,' replied Rochant. 'I rather think you would.'

CHAPTER NINETEEN

Satyendra remained aloof through the celebrations, nodding his way through course after course. Tender meat that fell from the bone, vegetable sticks with just a hint of firmness, sliced fruits on baked biscuits; none of it registered on his tongue. He only sipped at his drink, not daring to let his guard down. Every moment he expected the Deathless to catch on to him. After all, they had lifetimes of shared experience he knew nothing about. It would only take one question or one mishandled reference, and then they would know. There was no precedent for a crime such as his, which meant the punishment would likely be long, painful and involved. Perfect for a Story-singer to dramatize.

It made him wonder though. What if there *was* precedent? What if others had tricked the Bringers before him? What if the whole thing was a sham, and all of the Deathless were just terrified vessels, pretending to be immortal. He snorted at the thought and then discarded it. The others weren't like him. Their armour accepted them. They fitted in. They belonged.

I never will.

But as the evening went on, he dared to hope he might make it. While Yadavendra was in his armour – a fact studiously ignored by all present – and the close proximity was making Satyendra's face itch so much he kept his hands full to stave off the desire to scratch, it also kept the other Deathless at a distance. In fact, he suspected they were up to something. There seemed to be a social gap left between them and their High Lord. *And me.*

He spent most of his time wondering whether he should mention this to Yadavendra or slip over to their side and ask if he could join.

The other thing in his favour was Rochant's reputation of being economical with his speech. While this meant he was occasionally bored senseless by the drunken gabbling of others, it minimized the need to reply and risk giving himself away.

Several songs were sung in Rochant's honour, and the courses were broken up with entertainments: jugglers, dancers and Story-singers. While these went on, he took the opportunity to study the other Deathless in attendance, hoping for insights.

The easiest to watch was Lord Umed Sapphire, the High Lord's elder brother. He'd settled into his seat early, and not moved from it since. The gold tattoo curling around his neck attested to one of his brutal deaths in the Wild, and his now cautious nature. Though Umed's current body was well-worn and comfortably into its seventh decade, he delighted them all by getting up to dance. And over the course of the evening, Satyendra noticed that everyone of importance made sure to steal a few moments with him.

He rarely hunts now but retains his popularity. I must learn his secret if I am to survive.

When he looked at Lord Gada Sapphire, he found the other man already watching him. The two of them exchanged a respectful nod, but Satyendra did not like it one bit. *There is little trust in those eyes and no warmth in that smile. It is like looking at myself with all the guile stripped away.*

Gada's brother, Lord Vasin, seemed subdued, his mind elsewhere. Despite this, there were many attempts to draw him into discussions. The man was clearly popular, both in and out of the house, though it was hard to see why. In fact, Satyendra was disappointed. After hearing so much about the great hunter of House Sapphire, who had, among other things, faced down the Scuttling Corpseman and rescued him from the Wild as a baby, he had expected more. *They call him a hero though I think Mother played a much bigger part in my survival. Funny how she gets so little credit. Her part in Vasin's legend is forgotten as swiftly as my own is in Rochant's.*

Then there was Lady Yadva, who in Satyendra's opinion was by far the most dangerous. Yadavendra was the only one in the room that the monstrous Deathless deferred to, and then only to his face. Before he could ponder her further however, she was planting herself in front of him, and filling up his cup.

'Drink,' she said, clapping him on the arm. 'You've a lifecycle's pleasures to catch up on!'

'That I have,' he replied.

'You've been missed. Father fair tore up the place when they took you.' The beads in her hair clacked together as she shook her head. 'Dark times. We've been holding our

breaths all these years, waiting to see if you'd make it back.'
She met his eyes. 'But I knew you would.'

'Oh?'

Her finger prodded his chest. 'You're too damned clever
to go out like that. I knew you'd have another vessel tucked
away or some kind of plan. That's what I've always liked
about you, Rochant. You know which way the wind is
blowing before the Birdkin do.'

'I'm sure it has changed direction many times in my
absence.'

'Oh yes.' She raised her cup. 'To the future. May the winds
be ever at your back.'

He copied her gesture, but sipped where she drank deeply.
There was an energy to her that he found unnerving, and
he was glad when she left.

Aside from the Sapphire, two Tanzanite Deathless were
also in attendance, but they had been seated at the opposite
end of the table, and he caught only glimpses of them. Only
two things Satyendra saw for certain, that they were not
being made particularly welcome, and that neither seemed
excited by the food.

As each guest reached their limits, they came to pay their
respects. Again, Satyendra was glad for Rochant's reputation
for being reserved, it meant he didn't have to reach for much
enthusiasm. The low level tension had proved to be exhausting
and he was eager to spend some time alone.

However, when it was Yadavendra's turn to leave, he
beckoned for Satyendra to follow, a command dressed up
as invitation. They walked together in silence, until the High
Lord was ducking through the door into his chambers. He
immediately strode to the opposite side of the room and

leaned on the windowsill, while Satyendra waited by the door, keeping as much distance between them as possible.

'The house was in good spirits tonight,' said Yadavendra, 'did you see their faces, old friend?'

'Yes.'

'Our people are pleased to see you return and they are pleased to see us whole again. Too often, house business stops one of us from attending a rebirth, or one of us is between lives. It is auspicious that tonight was different, a sign that things will change for the better. Yes! I feel it.'

Yadavendra let out a sigh, and sagged a little, his enthusiasm flipping into plaintiveness. 'While you were gone I did everything you asked of me. Even Sorn. They begged us for help, you know? Raised tributes, made sacrifices . . . I stood by and let them be taken.' He lifted his head to gaze out of the window. 'The others don't understand. How could they? Do you think I could tell them now?'

I have no idea, thought Satyendra. 'A High Lord does not need to explain himself. Do so and they will think you weak. It will only invite more questions.'

Yadavendra nodded sadly. 'As always you speak the truth. Ah, but it is hard. My daughter hates me, and the others think I have gone mad. But you, old friend, you know the truth, don't you?'

'Yes, my High Lord.' Even as he was replying, Satyendra's mind worked furiously. *Sorn's destruction was by Rochant's design? But why? It was his own settlement. If he'd wished to punish the people there were a thousand ways he could have done so. Ahh, but all of them would have involved taking responsibility. Somehow, he had the High Lord carry out his dirty work for him.*

Yadavendra's shudder of relief was emphasized by the great crystal wings. 'That simple words can bring such pleasure. Know that I never doubted your brilliance, but, as the years went by I found it harder to hold onto. You were right, of course, my sister was poison, and I've seen how that poison seeped into the house, corrupting everything. It's easy to burn things away, but to rejuvenate them is beyond me. How to make things right again? That is the question driving everything I've tried to do since becoming High Lord. It's all I want, you know. To make things right.'

Satyendra fought to keep the sneer from his face. *He's trying to convince me of this rot and he's not even convincing himself.*

'And I began to worry. It was you who warned me that Nidra's soul was so evil, so warped by her compact with demons, so vile, that her Godpiece itself was corrupted. But what about Samarku Un-Sapphire's Godpiece? Could that not also have been corrupted?' He spun round, pointing his glaive directly at Satyendra's chest. 'I gave his Godpiece to you!'

He wanted to flee but forced himself to be still, to stay calm. *Rochant would stay calm.* 'You are wise to be vigilant, my High Lord. We must be most careful who we trust. Had I not come directly from the Bringers of Endless Order, I would advise you to test me as thoroughly as you must test the others. But you were there. You saw with your own eyes that I am no abomination.'

Yadavendra was nodding now. 'Yes, that is true.'

'And have I ever given you reason to doubt my loyalty?' Satyendra fervently hoped that Rochant had not.

'No.' Yadavendra banged the butt of his staff on the

ground. 'You have been a steadfast friend to the house and now you are back we can take decisive action. This pleases me . . . But still, sometimes I think about my sister and . . . did I go too far?'

'What other choice did you have?'

Yadavendra's mouth worked silently for a moment, making ghosts of words that he could not bring himself to say. 'I had to be strong.'

'Of course you did, you are the High Lord of House Sapphire. All of the others follow your lead because you are strong. The strongest of them all.'

'The strongest of them all,' whispered Yadavendra. As quickly as it had vanished, his confidence visibly returned. 'Now, enough of the past. Let us talk about the future. The other houses band together to challenge my rule. But what to do about them? They will make their demands tomorrow and I must answer, one way or another.' His eyes narrowed accusingly. 'You said they were all bluster, that they would never come if we looked ready to fight. I have armed my people and put them on the Godroad. I behave like I am hungry for war. My own people are scared of me, and it has not worked! All this,' he lifted his glaive, 'constant display of force. Years of it!' he brought it down again, hard. 'All for nothing!'

It soon became clear to Satyendra that he was expected to conjure up a solution, something brilliant. It was almost too funny to be true! He, who knew nothing of the higher level politics of the Deathless, was supposed to be Yadavendra's guide in the darkness. Out of his depth and only vaguely aware of the rules, Satyendra did what he had done his whole life in such situations: he bluffed.

'You were wise to make them wait until after the feasting. Whatever their authority, they are coming onto your lands. I say, keep them comfortable but give them nothing.'

'And when they invoke the authority of the Council of High Lords? What then? It is one thing to ignore a message, which, I tell you now, I have done many times. Quite another to refuse a Deathless to their face.'

'With what power do they remove you? They are two Deathless with a handful of loyal subjects. You are six, with a castle stuffed to the brim of the finest Sapphire. What can they possibly do to you here, in the very heart of your power?'

'Yes. Yes! You are right.' His smile was only brief however. 'But what if they make demands? What if they threaten me? I have already crossed so many lines . . . '

'If they are foolish enough to threaten you here, then let them suffer the consequences. Make an example of them and the other houses will not dare to cross you.' Yadavendra was nodding again so he decided to push his luck. 'And might I suggest receiving them out of your armour? It will show how little you respect their authority, and be far more comfortable.'

'Take it off?' Yadavendra looked down at himself, as if surprised to find the armour there. 'I could rest. It feels like so long since I just . . . stopped.' He raised an arm, twisting it so that the gemslight danced along the sapphire plates. 'I don't know. There are so many enemies.'

A perverse desire rose in Satyendra: to be there when the armour was removed, to know what was left of the man inside. *What does it smell like in there?*

The High Lord dismissed him with a gesture. 'I will consider it.'

Yes you will, he thought, bowing and slipping out of the room. *And sooner or later, you will become my puppet as surely as you were Rochant's. He wanted you to take the fall for Sorn, that much is obvious. And for Nidra Un-Sapphire too. He was as corrupt as I am. Perhaps worse!*

When the time came, did he intend the other High Lords to remove Yadavendra, or did he have some other plan? With a thrill, Satyendra realized it didn't matter either way. *It's up to me to decide his fate now.*

Pari had barely sat down on her bed when the old woman shuffled into her room. Though she hadn't sung for entrance, Pari didn't mind. She considered herself something of a patron for eccentrics.

'Here you go, Lady Pari, a little drink and some fresh baked biscuits for your nighttime snack. I know good Lord Rochant is very fond of his Lady Pari so I've come here myself to see these got to you in good time.'

'That's kind of you, my dear.' She didn't mention that she'd come straight from a feast and done nothing but eat or drink for the last four hours. 'Have we met before?'

'Not to talk proper, no. But I've seen you. Seen you many times, I have.' The cup and the saucer clinked as her shaking hands lowered them onto the table. 'Careful with the biscuits, my lady. I know you Tanzanite like things a bit spicy, so I added some fire to them, if you know what I mean.' She gave a yellowing smile.

'Lovely. And your name?'

'Oh, where are my manners? I'm just Roh, my lady. Served my whole life in the castle since I was a girl. Last time you were here, you looked even older than me and now you look more like my granddaughter. No matter how much I know, it still bakes my thinking parts every time I see it. Must be nice to go to bed all old and achy one day, and come back all fresh faced the next. Very nice.'

'Nice doesn't begin to describe it, believe me. But even this young face needs to rest.' She gestured to the door.

'Right you are. Good night, Lady Pari.'

Pari decided to enjoy a few moments peace before calling on the servants to help her undress. It was late, she was tired, and the day had been frustrating. They'd all but been seated with the Dogkin during the feast, and virtually ignored by High Lord Sapphire. At least it had eased Arkav back into things gently. He'd seemed quite overwhelmed by the spectacle of it all. *Tomorrow is going to be difficult for him.*

She idly picked up a biscuit and gave it a nibble. There was a pleasing kick of sweet warmth under her tongue. *Not a bad effort for a Sapphire.*

Then she saw the note hidden underneath. She recognized the style immediately; it was from the same mysterious sender that had written a warning about the assassination attempt on Rochant at his previous rebirth. Like the last one, this was short and to the point:

Your lover has not returned. A pretender claims his title and enjoys the trappings of his power. Once again, he needs you. Act swiftly.

Pari put the remains of the biscuit back on the plate. She went to the room next door and found her brother surrounded by servants in the process of removing his clothes. 'That may be a bit premature, my dear. The night isn't quite over yet.'

They quickly restored the paint on his face, and reattached his headdress of violet and gold leaf, before slipping away to leave Pari and Arkav in private. 'I'm going to see if Lord Rochant really has returned to us and I want you to come with me.'

'Isn't it a bit late for that?'

'No. I think it's the perfect time to pay a visit. We're more likely to see the real him if most of the castle is asleep.'

'I'm not agreeing with you, but I'll come.'

'Thank you.'

'How are we going to approach him?'

'Gently. I can handle Rochant, whoever he is, but I want you there just in case I handle him in the wrong way.' She had been aiming for a touch of humour to lighten the mood but the words came out flat, and Arkav looked concerned rather than amused.

She took Arkav through the castle via a secret passage, one that Rochant has showed her years ago to allow her to visit him discreetly. The passage was just as low and winding as she remembered, but this time her knees were more than up to the challenge.

When they'd crawled to the end she slid aside the panel – that was covered by a picture of a surprised young man – to admit them directly into Rochant's bedchamber.

She saw him sit up in surprise and spoke quickly. 'Well, you didn't expect me to use the door like everyone else?'

He recovered quickly. 'Of course not.'

It was strange to be in Rochant's room again. Familiar paintings covered the walls, each one was a portrait, and most were by different artists. Over the years, Rochant had told her about all of them, and she had forgotten almost every word. This was because she didn't really care about the subjects, she just enjoyed watching his face when it was moved by passion. In the weak gemslight, Pari has the horrible feeling they were all staring at her. Rochant himself was definitely staring at her. Or, at least, the one pretending to be Rochant. Unlike them, he had been prepared for sleep, the paint stripped from his face, and only a thin sleeping robe covered his slender shoulders. His new body, *assuming it is his body,* was smaller than the last one but he had that familiar poise and sense of calm she'd grown so fond of. And yet something was off. Her heart did not lift as quickly at the sight of him.

She climbed out of the passage and held out her hand to her brother as he did the same.

'Lady Pari Tanzanite,' said Rochant, rising. 'Lord Arkav Tanzanite. I must say, this is . . . unexpected.'

'Well, you know me, I hate to be predictable.'

'Of course.' He gave the slightest of smiles. 'No one could ever accuse you of being boring.'

'I wanted to see you.'

'We've just been at a feast together.'

'Hardly, you were at the other end of the room with your High Lord. I couldn't even get close.'

He tilted his head. 'Is that why you're here? To get close?'

'Maybe.'

He came forward and took her hand, bringing it to his lips. 'It is a pleasure to see you again, Lady Pari.'

Suns! Is he flirting with me? If so, he's out of practice. She wasn't sure how she'd been expecting Rochant to react to her. Anger, perhaps. After all, the last time she'd seen him, she'd abandoned him to Nidra's mercy. But if this was Rochant, that meant he'd escaped Nidra, escaped the Wild, and outsmarted them all. *This meeting could just be another part of his plan, but I can't shake the feeling that this man before me isn't Rochant.*

Her train of thought was interrupted by her brother, who had stepped forward to stand next to her. He was holding out his hand. 'It's been too long.'

Rochant took Arkav's hand and kissed it, and they stared at each other. There was something in the air between them, something she now realized had not been present a moment ago, when it was her turn. *Does Arkav have a complicated history with Rochant too? Impossible! I'd have known about it. One of them would have told me.* But looking at the two of them gazing into each other's eyes, she felt a stab of doubt.

To break the spell and nip the sudden growth of uncomfortable feelings in the bud, Pari spoke: 'It is so good to see you back, my dear, and in such rude health. House Sapphire has been in a terrible mess since you were gone.'

With what seemed like genuine reluctance, he released Arkav's hand. 'Things will be better now.'

'Regardless,' said Arkav, 'we still have to discharge our duty. High Lord Sapphire must come with us.'

'Is that why you're here? You hope to turn me against my High Lord?'

Pari ran her finger along one of the paintings as she replied, something Rochant normally couldn't abide, as it left a stain on the glass. 'Nothing so dramatic. We merely wished to see our dear friend once more. Tomorrow will be unpleasant, that doesn't mean tonight has to be. This isn't personal.'

'If you say so,' replied Rochant.

Nothing! Not a flicker. He didn't even care about the painting. She decided to test him further, letting her finger come to a rest under the subject's chin. A weathered-looking woman in her last years, with pale road-born features. It was an ugly painting, but one she remembered Rochant was particularly fond of. 'Oh,' she said, 'I haven't seen this one before. Are people sending gifts already?'

'Yes, you're not the first to surprise me today.'

It was strange. There was no sense of the lie in his features. He spoke with all of Rochant's calm, but she had him now. *This was what the Bringers wanted me to see. This proves that the note spoke true, and that the author is privy to my affair with Rochant, but knows nothing of my break from him.*

'Well,' she said, 'tomorrow is fast approaching, and promises to be both long and tiring. We must get what rest we can. Good night.'

They returned to Arkav's room in silence, neither speaking until the servants were dismissed again. 'That was interesting,' said Pari.

'Yes.'

'It isn't him.'

'No.'

'He's quick though. Could it be that their High Lord has raised him as a new Deathless to replace Rochant? It seems illogical but this is Yadavendra we're talking about.' She poked him on the arm. 'And what about you? What was going on between you two? I swear you'd have been teasing each other's tongues if I hadn't been there.'

'I . . . it's difficult to put into words.'

'Now I really have to know.'

'At first, I couldn't see him at all. His face was a mask and his words were . . . untethered.'

'I don't follow?'

'I couldn't link them to him, to his heart. I couldn't tell if his feelings were behind them or not. But then, when he was close, I saw him.' Arkav looked past her and his pupils dilated, as if he were reliving the moment. 'There is an emptiness inside him. A need that is constantly being held back. A hunger. Yes. I saw him, and he saw me. It was like looking into a mirror of the broken bits of myself.' He gave her a shy look. 'I like him.'

'Sometimes, Arkav, and I say this with great fondness, I am convinced you will be the final death of me. Putting aside your feelings, important as they no doubt are, we've agreed this man is not Lord Rochant Sapphire. He might be Deathless, he might not. Either way, we need to let Lord Vasin know without drawing attention to ourselves. Preferably before tomorrow's business.'

'I take it you have a plan?'

'No. But I will have by morning, count on it.'

The suns were only just starting to rise as Chandni finished her morning preparations. Tradition had been served and, as much as she knew she should probably wait, she could not bear it any longer. She would pay her respects to Lord Rochant, and then put her fate in his hands.

The last piece of the mosaic sat on her dressing table. It was a lower middle piece, and depicted the linked hands of the people in the picture. As she peered closer she could see that clasped between their fingers was a miniature version of the same mosaic, the picture partly replicated again inside itself. She wanted to get out the other pieces and finally complete the image but it seemed wrong to do so before she had seen her lord.

It took her longer than usual to get ready. Being nervous did not sit well with her perfectionism. A hand she couldn't feel didn't help either. Luckily she had planned for all of these things, and allowed plenty of time to cater for her foibles.

She was surprised to hear one of the young lads from the kitchens singing for entrance. She quickly hid the mosaic piece as he came in with some fruit and fish, and set in on her bedside table.

'What's this?'

'Cook wasn't sure if you'd be up for leaving your room today so she asked me to bring this up.'

Chandni couldn't recall the last time she'd eaten but her stomach was wound far too tight to even consider breakfast. 'Thank you,' she said. 'And please pass my thanks to Roh.'

'She asked for you to come down and see her, as soon as you were able.' He rubbed at his ear and pulled a face.

'Did you hurt yourself?'

'Oh,' he froze, and then unable to lie, looked at the floor. 'That was cook, she said it was important that I tell you to go down, and she clipped my ear so I wouldn't forget.'

'She clipped your ear preemptively?'

'Yes, Honoured Mother. Said it was a taste of what I'd get if I actually forgot.'

Chandni frowned, not exactly approving, but not wanting to challenge Roh's authority either. 'I see. Tell her I'll make time later, though I'm not sure when.'

'Yes, Honoured Mother.'

She checked her appearance one last time before setting out. The castle would be slow to wake today, she knew, which suited as there was not an ounce of smalltalk in her. The familiar twist and turn of the corridors took her to Lord

Rochant's chambers. She noted Zax and another of Yadavendra's hunters by the stairs and two of her guards by the door. All four looked tired, no doubt they had been there all night.

The morning shift are slow to arrive. I must have a word with the guard captain about that.

She ignored the hunters and asked the guards if she might enter. After a short discussion she was allowed inside. To her surprise, Lord Rochant was still in bed.

She bowed deeply. 'My apologies, my lord. I'll come back later.'

'M—Honoured Mother Chandni? No. Wait. I'm awake now. What did you want?'

'Two things, my lord. To see you with my own eyes and know you are returned to us. That is the most important thing of all.' He was back. He was truly back. In her heart, she rejoiced. *All of my sacrifice, and my Satyendra's sacrifice, was worth it to see this.*

'And the second?'

'There are things you must know, my lord. Things I did to protect your vessel and restore you to life.'

He sat up. For a moment she thought there was a glimmer of excitement in his eyes but no, it was just the sunslight reflecting through the window. 'I am listening.'

'When the assassins came at your last rebirth, Satyendra was the only Honoured Vessel to survive. I fled with him into the Wild, and to survive there, to make sure he survived, I . . . ' She forced herself to keep looking at him ' . . . broke your laws.'

'What did you do?'

'I made compact with the Wild. Once to keep myself alive,

and a second time to keep my son alive. I intended to confess when we returned, but my son was sick, and I feared that without me, he would die. He struggled sometimes, but I helped him, and in the end, he overcame the taint of the Wild and brought you back to us.'

'You made two deals with the Wild?'

She lowered her head. 'Yes, my lord.'

'What were they exactly?'

'The first was with a Hunger Tree. It saved me from the assassin's poison and in return it took the nails from my middle finger and thumb on my right hand. They've never grown back.' She showed him her gloved hands. 'I've kept them covered ever since.

'The second deal was for the Wild to protect Satyendra. I sacrificed the life of another in exchange for his. She was an exiled woman called Fiya, whose family had served our house long ago. She turned on us and I . . . did what I had to to protect your line. I don't know which demon accepted Fiya's body, but I know that one did.'

'You killed someone, gave them to the Wild, so that a demon would protect your son?'

'Yes, my lord.'

'Is that why he was sick?'

'I don't know. So much happened to us there. A Whispercage tried to steal him. Perhaps its touch infected him. Or perhaps he caught something in the Wild. Forgive me, my lord, I hate to think that it might have been my actions that made Satyendra sick, but it is possible.

'May I ask if you have felt strange since your return, my lord? Satyendra had an allergy to the castle's sapphires, and resonant crystal could blister his skin.'

'No. Any sickness your child had was purged when my soul returned.'

She put her hands to her chest. 'That is such good news. I had hoped but was concerned.'

'Does anyone else know of your crimes?'

She thought about Varg. He knew, and she doubted he would have told anyone else. But giving his name could place him in danger. She squeezed her hands together, aware that the nails on her left were digging into the skin on her right, but feeling nothing. 'No, my lord.' *In this one thing, I will fail my house. I owe Varg that much.*

'Honoured Mother, your actions have doubtless saved my life, and for that, I, and House Sapphire, will always be grateful.' When she looked up she found he was watching her, waiting to catch her eye. 'However, you have broken our sacred trust and that cannot be ignored. After all, my people look upon you as a bastion of the house. You are an example to them. Let you be so in death as you have been in life.'

The breath stopped in her throat. She had feared this, expected it even, but to hear it was something else. *I deserve this. I do. And yet I feel angry. Cheated. I must not let it show.*

'Deathless,' Rochant continued, 'Sky-born, and road-born, all can rise by their action, and all can fall. You will go from my castle and you will enter the Wild. There, you will bring your life to an end. You will make two deep cuts in your flesh, one for each transgression, and then you will walk until the demons take you.

'In recognition of your service, we will keep this between us. History will know only the good that you have done.

382

Like your son, they will remember what you achieved rather than the mistakes along the way.'

She felt dizzy, the blood rushing through her head, but she found the presence of mind to bow. 'Thank you.'

He got out of bed and crossed the room, putting his arms around her. It was an unexpected honour. She tried not to shed any tears on his shoulder as he whispered into her ear, 'I will not forget you, Honoured Mother.'

'When should I go?'

'Immediately.' He rang a small bell by his bed. 'I will have my guards escort you to the gates.'

She blinked. It was over. After all the years of worrying and hand wringing, of keeping secrets and telling lies, it was over. She bowed again, but he was already turning back to his bed. Her last sight of him as the guards led her away was of him gripping the headboard with both hands, his body softly shaking, and for the life of her, she could not tell if he were trying to suppress sobs or laughter.

CHAPTER TWENTY

Vasin stormed through the castle, his face storm-cloud dark. He'd been in a bad mood anyway, ever since Yadva had humiliated him, and he'd had to pretend to be cowed by her. *Again.* And he'd been unable to sleep when he'd needed all the sleep he could get. *Typical.* And that had been before Lady Pari had appeared like some Wild spirit in his room to tell him about Lord Rochant.

Her remembered words floated in his head, mostly drowned out by the internal roar of his anger. As always, she had sounded calm, as if everything were as it should be. As if she was in control. Perhaps that was what had made Vasin lose his temper. On some level he was extremely jealous of Pari's calm. On another, he began to wonder how much of it was bluff.

She'd told him that Lord Rochant's rebirth had not been successful. That the man at the feast was not him. She couldn't explain what *had* happened, or who knew about it, but if they were going to overcome the High Lord today, he needed to understand.

His mood radiated ahead of him, clearing a path without need for words. When he finally reached Rochant's room, the guards straightened in alarm. 'Give us privacy,' he said, and they quickly moved clear of the door.

It was dark inside the room, its occupant still in bed. Vasin ground his teeth. *Rochant is an early riser.* His loud footfalls as he crossed the room soon woke the imposter up.

'Who is it now? Can't I just have a couple of hours sleep without—'

Vasin reached the bed.

'—Lord Vasin?'

Vasin grabbed the soft silk sleeping robe and tipped its wearer onto the floor. 'Who are you?'

The man rolled to his feet, arms up, in a defensive stance . . . *He lacks Rochant's grace.* This only served to make Vasin angrier. He vaulted the bed and caught the man's hand even as it was swinging for his head, twisted the man's arm up hard against his back, and slammed him harder still against the wall. Vasin brought his middle and index finger to the side of the man's neck.

'I will ask you one more time, imposter, and if I do not like your answer, you are dead.'

The words were out of his mouth before he had time to think. The truth was he'd stopped thinking ever since Lady Pari started talking to him. But he started thinking now. His threat was empty. Nobody killed a Deathless in their own castle and got away with it. Especially not the child of Nidra Un-Sapphire. An act like this would destroy his hard-won reputation, not to mention usher in his last death.

While he was thinking this, the man in his grasp began to shake. Then he began to cry, his face folding in on itself like a child's. 'Satyendra,' he gasped. 'I am Satyendra.'

'The Vessel?'

'Yes.'

'How is this possible?'

'I don't know. Please stop hurting me.'

Vasin's fingers pressed deeper into Satyendra's neck, making him gag. Then he released the pressure but left them resting lightly against the skin. 'What happened?'

'The Bringers did the ritual and it didn't work. But everyone acted like it did. They were so happy I didn't know what to do. Please, my lord, I'll do anything, but please, don't kill me.'

He realized that he'd been digging his fingers in again. A part of him wanted to kill Satyendra. Everything was such a mess, he just wanted to lash out. *But this isn't Satyendra's fault. The ritual must have failed because Rochant's soul is still in this world. Until he dies, he can't be reborn. Satyendra is pathetic but he's no abomination, there would have been no demon for the Bringers to find.*

'How did you pass their test?'

'I used my knowledge of Lord Rochant and I . . . got lucky.'

'Lucky? By the Thrice Blessed Suns I should kill you.'

But he was starting to think this might be good news after all. If Lord Rochant were still in the Wild, there was a chance they could catch him before he returned. There was a chance Vasin's crimes against the house would stay secret! Moreover, Yadavendra was without support. *There is an opportunity here. One that my mother or Pari would not pass up.*

Satyendra's tears had started to dribble down his fingers. He released his grip and stepped back. 'Do you know what they would do to you if they found out?'

'I can guess. Are you going to tell them?'

'That depends on you.'

Satyendra fell to his knees at Vasin's feet. 'I am your servant! I'll do anything. Anything you wish, but don't tell them. I beg you!'

'Mark this moment, Satyendra. It is the one where your life became mine. Believe me when I tell you I know how unpleasant that is, so I make you this promise: Serve in the interests of the house, do not betray me, and I will keep your secret, at least until this mess can be fixed.'

'Thank you, oh thank you.'

'Swear it.'

He rubbed the snot and tears from his face, controlling himself so quickly that Vasin wondered how much of it had been an act. 'I, Satyendra, child of Chandni and Mohit, Honoured Vessel of Lord Rochant of House Sapphire, swear to obey you in all things.'

'Good. And if the oath isn't enough for you, remember the pain you've just experienced, and know it is only the barest hint of what you will suffer if you fail me.'

'Yes, my lord.'

'Less of that. It's time to stand up and pretend to be a Deathless. Now tell me, and tell me honestly, do you like High Lord Yadavendra?'

He looked at Vasin then, his eyes calculating, hard. 'No. I despise him.'

'Then this day may not turn out so badly for you after all.'

He did not warm to Satyendra, much less trust him. But given the timing, he was too good a tool not to employ. Vasin knew he would have to be careful if he was to survive the day, and he would have to be brilliant if he was to find victory amid the many chances for failure. And more than that, he knew he was going to have to be cruel. For what did Satyendra's happiness matter when held against the lives of everyone in House Ruby? Or those of all the houses? For that matter, what did his own?

'We do not have much time before the Sapphire gather. Are you ready?'

'I am.'

'Then listen very carefully to what I'm about to tell you.'

The night had been long and cold. Rochant constantly shivered while he slept. Despite his efforts, Sa-at could not keep him warm. The sunrise brought light but little heat. It also brought Tal, stumbling through the trees towards them, ushered along by Crowflies, who hopped and flapped behind him.

Sa-at stood up. 'You're back!'

Tal crashed down in front of them, his arms full of clothes. 'Yeah . . . Managed to grab some things . . . Got lost . . . Crowflies found me. Thought it was trying to kill me at first, then I realized it was guiding me back.' He put down the bundle to pat the Birdkin on the head. 'Thank you Cro—'

Crowflies' white beak snapped the air, and Tal snatched his hand back.

That's nice. My friends are becoming friends, thought Sa-at. *Very slowly.*

They dressed Rochant in new clothes, wrapping him in several layers. Everything was too big for his wasted frame, hanging oddly, and it wasn't enough, he still shivered, so they put the things Tal had stolen for Sa-at over the top, puffing him out so that his head and feet seemed far too small. When they were done, Rochant flopped asleep, exhausted. He didn't look any warmer. It was as if the cold had got inside him. *Inside his bones.*

'We need to get Lord Rochant back to his castle,' whispered Tal.

'How do we get him up in the sky? He's too big for Crowflies to carry.'

Tal chuckled. 'You don't need wings to go to a floating castle. There's roads that go up there. Not sure we can drag him that far though.' He rubbed his hands together for warmth. 'What we need is a way to carry him. Like a cart or one of those big Dogkin, and don't even think of asking me to go and steal one. I can't and I won't!'

'We carried him before.'

'But this is much further, and uphill. It'd take forever.'

No ideas came to them and Tal soon fell asleep, Rochant leaning on his shoulder. Even though they were wearing the same style of clothes, the two looked so different: Tal's face was pale, the veins a soft blue against his neck, Rochant's was dark, making the gold tattoo crisscrossing half of his face all the more striking. Though he could not say why, it brought him pleasure to see his friends resting against each other.

Crowflies came and went several times. The first trip brought Sa-at some scavenged meat, the second was heralded by the Birdkin's squawks of concern.

'Sa-aat!'

'What is it?'

Crowflies tapped at his knuckle, and he pressed it into the Birdkin's beak. The proboscis buried deep in its throat levered out, pressing just enough to slide beneath the skin. Sa-at closed his eyes. Sometimes, when they were connected this way, he saw the world as Crowflies saw it. This time, however, it was different. The forest seemed to move about him, and yet he knew he was standing still.

I'm flying!

But I'm not flying.

This isn't me. This isn't now. It's the past. I'm seeing Crowflies' thoughts. No. I'm seeing a memory.

Through its compound eyes, the forest was broken into tiny pieces, each a different window showing a slightly different vision. Shadows no longer matched the things that made them, the trees seemed to loom more, some openly hostile, others indifferent, still others shifting their branches, allowing easier progress.

A shape became visible, hulking, crimson-skinned, moving slowly, guiding himself by touch: Crunch! He was muttering to himself, a bitter, hateful monologue, and Sa-at knew he was the subject of the vitriol. Crowflies banked away and the memory took Sa-at all the way back to them. It was not a long flight. If they didn't move soon, the last Red Brother would find them.

Crowflies broke contact, pinching the wound shut, and Sa-at opened his eyes again. Crunch did not just linger in his mind, his scent lingered on his palm, carried by the wind, a sharp and bloody tang. He quickly woke his friends and explained the situation. 'We need to run!'

Tal dutifully sat up and put one of Rochant's arms over his shoulder.

'Wait,' said Rochant. 'Before we expend our energy, what is our plan?'

'I told you: running.'

'That isn't a plan. Are we going to run to the Godroad? To Sagan? All the way to my castle? Is running even the best approach here?'

Sa-at just stared at him.

'What do you know about your enemy?'

'He's scary.'

'Good. What else?'

'He's . . . big?' Rochant continued to watch him, patient. 'He's strong. He has sharp teeth. He's angry.'

'How angry?'

'Very.'

'Why?'

'Because his brothers are dead.'

'Good, continue.'

'He has big ears that hear everything, but he's blind and he can't smell.'

'Anything else?'

'He's good at hiding.'

'So you have an enemy that is enraged, not thinking clearly, and desperate for revenge. He is strong, and knows that is his advantage. He will favour a direct approach, but he has limited abilities to find you and he is slower. This means he will need to rely on his stealth. He will likely try to get as close as he can before making his attack. If he can get his hands on you, he wins.'

'Yes,' agreed Sa-at, and his bottom lip began to tremble. It was all too easy to imagine. 'My plan is to run.'

Tal gathered himself to stand again.

'Wait,' said Rochant. 'What about you. What are your strengths? How can you fight back?'

'I can't! I'm too small and I don't have any glowing glass, not like—' He put a hand over his mouth. He'd been about to talk about the lady with the golden lips. 'I don't have anything he's afraid of.'

'Listing things you don't have is a waste of time and energy. Forget them. Focus on what you do have.'

'Well,' he lowered his voice to whisper, 'Crunch,' then continued normally, 'is alone and I have you and Tal and Crowflies and . . . ' He stood up. 'I know what to do. Tal, you stay here and look after Rochant. I have to lead him away from here. If he hears you, he'll eat you.'

'Okay,' said Tal. 'What are you going to do?'

'I'm going to my friendly tree.'

Leaving the castle was a surprisingly brisk, mundane affair for Chandni. There was no fanfare, nothing to mark the moment. Most people were still eating breakfast as she was escorted to the main gates. It left her unsure of how to feel. There was a kind of dignity to this end, and though secret, it lent a quintessentially Sapphire shape to her life. Certainly, her mother would approve. But then again, her mother was dead and the only other family she knew was an aunt who she hadn't seen since she was a girl.

Lord Rochant's decision had been so swift, so immediate,

that she had only the clothes she'd dressed in. No cloak to protect her from the elements, no walking shoes, no food, nothing. Then it occurred to her that dead women didn't need to be warm or fed.

As she put the outer wall behind her and walked towards the Bridge of Friends and Fools, the guards stationed there saluted her. If they questioned her leaving, alone and unsuitably attired, they let none of it show on their faces. Silent and dignified, they passed each other with barely a glance. *Like the true Sapphire we are.*

She stepped out onto the bridge, resolutely refusing to look down. Through the slats it was possible to see the great chasm that yawned beneath Lord Rochant's castle. Heights didn't bother her particularly, but looking into that endless drop was like looking into despair, and she didn't want to lose her composure, especially with people watching.

The wind caused only a slight sway in the bridge, and she quite enjoyed being in the open, surrounded by sky and little else. It puts things into perspective. She was like a tiny cloud, blowing briefly across a vast expanse . . . Then the bridge jolted under her feet to the sound, behind her, of five paws and two wheels.

Glider!

Varg!

Struck by happiness, then sadness, then guilt, Chandni stopped, not quite able to turn herself to face them.

The thundering noise drew closer until Glider's three shadows fell over her and a long nose appeared by her shoulder. It sniffed delicately at her ear, like a very cold feather, and Chandni squealed.

'Yes, Glider, it's me.'

The Dogkin took her shoulder in her mouth and gently spun her round. Three human eyes and one canine one looked at her like disappointed parents.

'I'm sorry,' she said.

'You promised me, Chand,' said Varg. 'You gave your word.'

'When I told Lord Rochant what I'd done, he commanded me to leave, immediately. I haven't even been back to my room. It was all so sudden, I didn't have time to think.'

'I guess it's different for you,' Varg replied, his arms folded.

'What's that supposed to mean?'

'Forget it,' he muttered.

'I've apologized. What else do you want me to say?'

'Nothing. I just . . . I wouldn't have forgotten you, that's all.'

She sighed and walked over. He was too high for her to reach, so she put a hand on his ankle instead. 'It might be better if you do. Lord Rochant's decree was final. I'm not coming back.'

'We'll come with you.'

'Oh Varg, you don't even know where I'm going.'

'We don't care, do we, Glider?' Glider barked agreement. 'It don't matter if we're in a castle or in some village some-where, or just in the wagon! Don't you get it, Chand? I want to be with you. That's all I've wanted since we first met.'

'When we first met, you told me to—'

'Yeah,' he said quickly, 'but pretty soon after that, I got to caring for you.'

'And I care for you too, you know that.'

He leaned down and plucked her off the bridge and put her down beside him on the front of the wagon. The warmth of his thigh was pleasant against hers. He wanted her, she could see it in his eyes, feel it in the way his hands moved naturally to rest on her arm and hip.

She kissed him. Because it might be the last chance she'd get. Because in that instant, doing anything else seemed like madness. On another day, Glider's enthusiastic barking might have embarrassed her, but she did not care. Nobody could see them. *And what if they could? It won't matter soon either way.*

With that thought, she pulled back, only to find Varg following after, drawn along with her lips. His eyes were closed, an expression of absolute peace on his face. *After all this time, he is still adorable.*

She stopped his advance with a finger. 'I shouldn't have done that.'

'Bollocks. It was great. You should do it again.'

She felt the heat rise in her face. 'That's not what I meant.' Her finger pressed on his lips to stop him from getting any closer. 'Before we do anything . . . more, I need to tell you something.' He sat back and looked at her. 'We were wrong to hope, Varg. I've been sentenced to death.'

His eyes widened in horror. 'What?'

'I've been told to go into the Wild and sacrifice myself.'

'Kill yourself? Alone?'

'It's an honour, actually.' Somehow, telling Varg, it didn't seem like such an honour any more. She dipped her eyes, feeling oddly ashamed. 'Nobody will know, you see. So I'll be remembered well. In his wisdom, Lord Rochant has saved me from a traitor's death.'

'He sounds like a fucking monster to me.'

'Well . . . ' Some part of her started to automatically leap

395

to his defence, but she suddenly felt too tired to argue. Varg didn't seem tired at all.

'Yeah, a right fucking monster. And after all you did for him! They're all the same, these Deathless. They use us like a pair of fucking boots. Trample us into the shit and muck and then throw us away when we wear out. Well I say, fuck him. Why don't you come and live with me? He'll never know.'

'But . . . I'd know.'

'Fine. Then I'll take you to the Wild myself.'

'I can't ask you to do that.'

'You don't have to.'

'Varg, I . . . '

'Come on, Glider, let's go.' Glider gave a sad bark and the wagon began to rumble forward again, the wheels thudding over the slats on the bridge. 'We're with you all the way, Chand.'

'Even to the end?'

He put an arm around her and pulled her close. 'Yeah.'

She nestled in. It felt safe and warm, and she could hear his heart thudding merrily in his chest. *I'm happy,* she thought, *for the first time in so long, I'm happy.* There were tears running down Varg's cheeks. Hers too, she realized. It was very un-Sapphire, and it didn't matter, not one little bit.

Sa-at ran through the forest, his coat of feathers rippling at his back, and Crowflies gliding at his shoulder. He brushed the trees as he passed them, tagging leaves with his hands, tapping trunks, leaving a swirl of noise in his wake.

Each knock echoed in the canopy, passed from one tree to another, each footfall rippled outwards. Sa-at knew that somewhere nearby, Crunch would hear those sounds, and would come for him.

He was counting on it.

He held on to what Rochant had told him. *I am faster than him. I have eyes. I have friends.* But it was hard. He couldn't help think other things too: *I am weaker. I am scared. I—*

A stray root caught his foot and he stumbled, lost his balance, and fell. Momentum took him into a roll and back onto his feet. A few whirls of his arms and he was steady again, barely any time lost. After that, he stopped thinking and focused on where he was.

Without the others to slow him down, he soon reached a friendly looking tree – a marker of Murderkind's territory – and put his back to it, panting while Crowflies settled on a nearby branch. He caught his breath quickly but his heart continued to beat as if he were still running. 'Crowflies, go and tell Murderkind that I am ready to keep my promise.'

The Birdkin shuffled from one foot to the other. 'Sa-aat.'

'Don't worry about me. I'll be okay.'

Crowflies tilted its head, unconvinced.

'Fly fast, my friend.'

The white beak bobbed once, and then it was gone in a flutter of wing beats, leaving Sa-at with only the friendly tree for company. He gave the trunk a hug, letting his finger trace the gnarled lines of its bark, and then he climbed quickly into the sanctuary of its upper branches.

I must be like Rochant, he thought. *I must say one thing and feel another.*

He began to hum the song Crowflies sung to him when he was tiny, the one his mother had once sung. Sa-at didn't know how he knew this – he had no real memory of his mother beyond some vague sense of being held by her once – but he did. He tried to sound as happy as possible, repeating the song over and over, until the friendly tree began to rustle softly along with the tune.

It wasn't long before the knuckle where his little finger used to be began to itch. Sa-at ignored it and continued humming. He tried to appear calm, reclining against the branches as if he didn't have a care in the world, whilst at the same time stealing glances of the forest floor. There was no sign of Crunch, but he was close, Sa-at knew.

His heart hammered in his chest, and he was struck by the awful need to piss, to run, and to scream, all at the same time. But he kept humming the tune.

One moment, there was nobody, the next Crunch was there, as if he'd stepped through an invisible door. Parts of his face had been burned white from when Sa-at had hit him with the tanzanite, and others had puckered, no longer completely covering his teeth. 'Happy are we? Happy up there in your nest, Birdspawn? Come down to me and I'll make you sing a different song. A red song of screaming.' The vertical slit of his mouth opened wide and he licked his ragged lips. 'Hmm, yes, I'll chew the notes from your bones.'

'I'm not coming down,' said Sa-at, and started to hum the song again.

Crunch roared and put his huge hands either side of the friendly tree. 'I'll shake you down! I'll break you down! You don't have wings to save you, just arms that flap and legs that snap.' With a roar, the Red Brother shook the trunk. The tree made a terrible groaning noise, and a shower of old leaves came loose, to pat softly against Crunch's shoulders, arms and feet. It was all Sa-at could do not to tumble down after them.

When Crunch stopped, the world continued to rock back and forth for a few moments. Sa-at made sure he was well braced. 'I'm still here.'

'I'm just getting started!'

'You won't get me down.'

'I will! I'll get you down and grind you down. I'll pop out your eyes and twist off your ears!'

'You said that when Pits died. And when Eyesore died too.'

It turned out that Crunch *was* just getting started. He shook the friendly tree a second time, twice as long and twice as hard as the first. Sa-at clung to one of the thicker branches as his legs swung wildly back and forth. His teeth clacked together, and he bit the inside of his cheek by accident, hard enough to taste blood.

Somehow, he managed to hold on until Crunch stopped and doubled over, making ugly grunting noises.

The friendly tree's distress continued to echo around them, masking the whisper of wings as Crowflies returned. The Birdkin had not come alone. Others just as black, with grey beaks, and the same compound eyes, took up positions in the neighbouring trees, plugging the spaces where shafts of sunslight peeked through. Crunch could not see the dimming of light, but he must have felt something, for he straightened.

'What's this? Do we have a sneaker in the shadows?'

'I'm still here,' said Sa-at quickly, leaning down so that he could poke the top of Crunch's head.

'Raargh!' replied the giant. Sa-at had expected retaliation but he hadn't expected it quite so fast, the black-nailed fingers of Crunch's hand scraped painfully across his shin as he scrambled away. The Red Brother had marked him, but he didn't stop to gloat. Instead, he grabbed a handful of the friendly tree's upper branches and pulled, bending the trunk, and Sa-at, towards him.

Sa-at tried to pull his legs up but he was too late and one of Crunch's grasping hands wrapped around his ankle.

'Got you!'

Sa-at forgot he was supposed to be pretending and screamed.

'That song is much better.' One flex of Crunch's powerful arm was enough to dislodge Sa-at's hold on the friendly tree and leave him dangling upside down. 'I'm going to squeeze another from you.'

At the same moment, the assembled Birdkin screeched and dived from their perches, swooping downwards. They converged above Sa-at's head, crashing into one another to become a tangle of dark shapes, blotting out the suns entirely.

Sa-at couldn't see anything any more, but he felt the feathers brush his face and talons press at his shoulders, taking his weight, shifting him so that he was sitting rather than hanging.

'Murderkind,' he whispered.

'Murderkind?' asked Crunch, with a tinge of panic.

'Murderkind,' echoed the trees a third time, and then it was true.

'I too have come to hear a song,' said Murderkind, 'a secret song not squeezed or screamed; a telling, an understanding, a promise delivered.' The demon's voice came from all around them, issued from the throat of every Birdkin.

'You should not be alone Red Brotherless. You should not be harming that which is under my protection.'

Sa-at felt the buffeting of wings in the dark, and heard the movement of many beaks and many claws. Finger by finger, Crunch's hand was removed from his ankle.

'You should not be joining my enemies and walking my domain. You should not be here, Red Brotherless.'

It sounded like Crunch was trying to reply, but it was muffled, as if something were reaching deep into his throat.

'Red Brotherless, you should not be.'

There was more flapping, more strange gagging sounds, and then Crunch was moving away, moving up. His legs kicked as they went past Sa-at and into the canopy above. There was a glimpse of a foot, thick and twitching, the toes extended, as if trying to grasp a branch, then it too was whisked away. No longer close. Not above nor below.

Gone.

I am glad, very glad, that Murderkind is my friend and not my enemy, thought Sa-at.

He told Murderkind what he knew about the Corpseman, its plans and its vulnerabilities, leaving nothing out. *Better to not feel special than to break a promise.*

When he was done, the chorus of Birdkin cawed in a self-satisfied fashion. 'You have done well, bound friend. Much understanding, you have given, and an enemy to feast upon.'

Sa-at beamed. Murderkind was happy with him and the Red Brothers were gone! He felt lighter. And hungry. 'I'm hungry,' he said.

'I will share my bounty with you, bound friend.'

'Thank you.' The thought of food was comforting and he

decided to try really hard not to eat it all. *I must save some for the others.* 'I have a friend who can't walk. Could you help me move him?'

'Not that one. And beware who you call friend.'

'I will.'

'Then rest with me, and this stout-rooted ally. Be fed,' said Murderkind, and meat, raw and rich was brought from the shadows. 'Be calmed.' Sa-at's heart settled dutifully. 'Be still.'

He slept.

CHAPTER TWENTY-ONE

'Is everything to your satisfaction, my lady?'

Pari examined herself for the third time. If only her face wasn't swollen! She wasn't usually vain about her appearance, but it was one of the few things left about the day she could control. 'More jewellery, I think.'

Her servant added a second, longer necklace to compliment the first, and draped a string of mixed stones from the horns of her headdress. *It might break my neck, but by the Thrice Blessed Suns, they'll certainly see me coming.*

'Much better. Is Lord Arkav ready to go?'

'Yes, my lady. He's been asking after our progress for some time.'

'Then we had best not keep him waiting any longer.'

Two more servants took up position behind her, kneeling down ready to pick up her train when she moved. Normally she favoured the star-shaped gowns that required four servants, but today was for Arkav to shine, not her, and so she'd toned things down.

He was waiting for her in his own finery, a long violet robe that darkened towards the bottom, spilling out in seven directions at his feet. In one hand, he held a chain from which hung a triangular lantern to represent the three minor houses, with panes of ruby, opal and peridot. In the other he held a wand topped with another lantern, four sided, for the major houses: Sapphire, Tanzanite, Spinel and Jet. Both were lit by a diamond, deftly signalling that the Bringers were behind him as well. From head to toe, Arkav sparkled, the lantern lights dancing on his heavy hooped earrings, and the many tiny stones set like stars in his sash.

Seeing him like this, it was hard to remember how frail he was inside. She hoped the illusion would be enough to convince the others.

'You look marvellous, my dear.'

He inclined his head. 'As do you.'

'The lanterns are a nice touch.'

'High Lord Primyamvada gave them to me before we set out. They were made by the Bringers.'

'Well aren't you blessed? She only had words for me before I set out.' *And not especially nice ones at that.* 'Shall we go and teach the Sapphire a lesson in style?'

'It would be a shame to go to all this effort just to bring justice and stability to the land.'

'I couldn't agree more.'

It wasn't easy for the servants to carry both of their outfits in such close proximity, and Pari quickly took pity on them, allowing Arkav to walk in front, though she did mutter quietly about the corridors being too narrow. At least they were better than the ones in the House Ruby castles. The one time she had visited there, it had felt like being threaded through a succession of needles.

Many, many guards lined the walls as they walked, all armed and stony faced. 'I think they're trying to make a statement,' she said to Arkav.

'Really?' he replied. 'I hadn't noticed.'

She chuckled with delight at his sarcasm. *He sounds like his old self today. Perhaps he does have the strength to see this through.* Silently, she willed this to be true, firing every positive thought she could at her brother's back.

Heads held high, the two of them entered Lord Rochant's throne room at a stately pace. All evidence of the previous night's festivities had been cleared away. No longer packed full of revellers, and with the tables gone, the space appeared massive. Fresh new hangings divided the grey of the walls in blocks of rich blue, and the stone floors had been polished until they shone.

House Sapphire's Deathless were already in attendance. The one pretending to be Lord Rochant stood to one side, displaced from his throne by the Sapphire High Lord. In his winged armour, there was no way Yadavendra could sit in it comfortably, which meant not only could no one enjoy the throne, but all of the others were forced to stand as well.

If only they could see themselves.

It was obvious now that Rochant had not truly returned. There was something indefinably young about the imposter that no amount of paint and posing could hide. She wondered that the others could not see it too. *Perhaps they do, or perhaps they lack my intimate knowledge.*

The other Deathless were at least dressed appropriately,

each face aged up or down to make them ageless. They gave respectful nods, even Lady Yadva, though it took a prompting glance from Pari to get it. She and Lord Taraka Tanzanite had witnessed and recorded Yadva's humiliation in Pari's previous lifecycle, and she wanted to be clear that it had not been forgotten.

They stopped at a respectful distance, the servants laying their gowns artfully and retreating from the room. She knew that Arkav wanted to flee with them. When he glanced at her, as she knew he would, she turned her head to whisper, 'I am with you.'

He nodded, and when he addressed the Sapphire, his voice was clear. 'My sister and I come before you today on behalf of our High Lord, Primyamvada Tanzanite, and the High Lords of Jet, Spinel, Peridot, Opal and Ruby. We demand that Yadavendra, High Lord of the Sapphire, leave here with us to face the judgement of his peers for breaking our sacred laws and threatening the eternal order of the Deathless.'

Well, thought Pari, *that was direct.*

'You see?' replied Yadavendra, gesturing towards them with his golden glaive. 'This is the tone they take. Ordering me like some common criminal in front of my own family. Strutting about as if this were some Tanzanite hall. But we knew this day would come, didn't we? And we are ready for it.'

Arkav leant backwards as if blown by a breeze, and Pari sensed, as her brother did, the sudden threat of violence.

Yadavendra's Sky-legs halved the distance between them in a single bound. 'Nothing to say, have you! I will not be meekly led away to slaughter. I am High Lord here and I will defend our sovereignty with force if need be.'

Facing an armoured Deathless when not similarly elevated was shocking. It made Pari appreciate what it must be like for the road-born witnessing a hunt. Yadavendra's anger radiated outward like a physical force. It distressed her, and she dreaded to think what it was doing to Arkav. Her brother seemed rooted to the spot, his eyes wide, unable to do anything but drink in the vision before him.

Unwilling to allow the sapphire-bladed staff to get any closer and unable to retreat, Pari started talking, her mouth going into action before her brain. 'As my brother said, it is not us making the demands. This is not a Tanzanite matter. It is one for all the houses. We are but messengers doing our sworn duty, as we hope you will.'

'I see. Well, *messenger*, I will consider what has been said.' He brought the base of his staff to rest on the floor with a bang. 'You may go.'

'We are keen to do so, High Lord of the Sapphire, but Lord Arkav and I are bound to stay until you acquiesce to accompany us to the Hall of Seven Doors. Though I would not presume to make a demand of you, a demand that binds all of us has been made nonetheless.'

'You dare?' hissed Yadavendra.

And just when she thought he was going to attack, Lord Vasin hurried between them. She did not envy him his position in the front line. 'My High Lord, it is known that the road-born and sky-born serve the Deathless, and it is known that the Deathless serve their High Lords, who stand above all. But a High Lord must serve too, and are as bound by the traditions as any of us. They have to be. Even you must see this.'

'Even I? You forget your place, Lord Vasin.'

'If so, it is only because you have forgotten yours. Know that if you stand against the other houses, you do so alone.'

'Hardly! I have House Sapphire at my back. For your past services I give you this one chance to stand aside. Do so now or be counted with the enemy.'

'I am standing exactly where I should be. I only wish I had stood here sooner.'

'For once,' said Yadavendra, raising his glaive, 'we are in agreement.'

Pari took in the scene. The High Lord towering over them, the other Sapphire Deathless seemingly as stunned as they were. Lady Yadva was the only one moving, though whether that was to her father's or Vasin's aid was unclear.

It doesn't matter much either way. None of us are exalted. The whole room could turn on Yadavendra and he'd kill us all without breaking a sweat.

For a moment the glaive hovered above Vasin's head, and it seemed that despite his bluster, Yadavendra was genuinely reluctant to kill his nephew. The moment passed however. She saw it in Yadavendra's eyes, the twitch of a muscle, the slight narrowing of the iris, little heralds of the death-stroke to come.

On instinct, she moved first, taking two fistfuls of Vasin's robe and pulling him backwards.

The sapphire blade stabbed the place where he'd just been, and Yadavendra came with it, closing the gap easily, raising the glaive a second time. Pari had long enough to wonder if Vasin's body would be enough to stop the point killing her or whether he would skewer them both, when Arkav stepped in front of them.

'No!' she shouted, too late.

As the Sapphire High Lord lunged, Lady Yadva grabbed the end of the shaft. Unlike the others, her robe was sleeveless, to better show off her arms. One bicep was inked in gold, a many-limbed demon depicted in two pieces to celebrate the time she ripped it in half. Pari watched the image of the monster bloat and shake as Yadva's muscles rippled with the strain. She had surprise and a good angle, but even with all of this, it took everything she had to twist the glaive from her father's hands.

'Traitor!' he yelled, whirling round. His wing smacked solidly into Yadva, hurling her back across the room as if she were no more than a child. Vasin tried to take advantage of the High Lord's confusion but, before he could act, Yadavendra had him by the throat and three feet off the ground.

Pari tried to think of what to do. She was unarmed, and there were no real weak spots in the armour she could exploit barehanded, at least none that would allow her to end the fight. She wanted to help Vasin but knew she could not hope to break the crystal gauntlet's grip.

She put a hand on Arkav's arm instead. 'Run,' she said. 'Tell the others.' She would buy him time. If Arkav could escape, he might be able to persuade the Tanzanite High Lord to have her reborn into a decent body.

But Arkav shook his head. 'No, Pari. No more running.'

He set his jaw and began whirling the lantern on its chain like a weapon. Its light blurred, the trail getting longer until it met itself, becoming a multicoloured disc. Then he let go, and it flew towards Yadavendra, shattering on his chest plate.

There came a sound like thunder, that Pari felt through her teeth as much as in her ears. Yadavendra looked round in surprise just as Arkav brought the second lantern down on his head.

In the aftermath of the second boom, the room was deathly silent. Pari wasn't really paying attention to the others, she was looking at the way Yadavendra's arm was shaking. The sapphire vambrace was no longer glowing, and that sense of presence, of him filling the room, was gone. One by one, the plates of his armour began to fall away. They clinked dully as they struck the floor, followed, with a soft thud, by Vasin. The armour on Yadavendra's chest and back detached next, the wings shattering with the impact, then his helmet, which started to fragment so fast it became a cloud of blue glitter about his head.

Yadavendra remained on his Sky-legs, giving him the look of some strange featherless Birdkin, scrawny, hollowed out, and covered in tattered silks. Pari gasped as the sight of him. The skin was paper thin on his bones, his hair like a faded memory rendered in straw, the paint around his eyes no longer able to maintain the facade of sanity.

Even the ever-stoic Deathless of House Sapphire struggled to contain their shock. Yadavendra turned slowly, seeing himself in their eyes. Pari saw he was looking for support, but got nothing back. When at last he was facing her, she said: 'It is time.'

Arkav nodded in agreement. He was still carrying the wand the lantern had been mounted on, somehow he made it look like a badge of office.

With something akin to pleading, Yadavendra looked into their eyes. 'No,' he said, 'no, I cannot, I have things that . . . '

'It is time,' she repeated.

With a wail, Yadavendra sprang away. Though it surprised

her that he still moved with such agility, it did not surprise her that he was springing towards one of the tall windows that looked out to the horizon.

'Stop him!' shouted Arkav.

But the Sapphire made no move to intervene, each lowering their gaze as Yadavendra gathered speed. There was a crash that seemed trivial compared to the sounds they'd recently heard, an anticlimactic breaking of glass, a last sight of him sailing through the air, trailing blood from a hundred tiny cuts, and Yadavendra was gone.

Stunned silence followed.

Then, to her surprise, Arkav started to cry.

This seemed to prompt Lady Yadva to stand and collect herself. 'Lord Arkav. Lady Pari. I am sure you will respect our need for privacy at this time.

'Of course,' said Pari, taking her brother's arm and guiding him from the room.

Satyendra was glad of all the distractions. He didn't know if he was coming or going. When the lanterns shattered it had felt like someone were placing hot metal under his fingernails, but when Yadavendra's armour had broken . . . When they'd met eyes and he'd tasted the depths of the other man's despair, there had come a high he had not known possible. It was if all the other times he'd indulged the hunger had merely been sniffing at pain rather than tasting it. Yadavendra's final emotions were a rich broth he'd drunk down, and now his body thrummed with power, his mind working so fast everyone else seemed to be moving in slow motion. The only shame of it all was that Yadavendra had thrown away his life too quickly, leaving only the briefest taste of perfection.

It had been so pure, so potent, it tingled in his bones, making him aware of them in a way he'd never been before. It was as if they longed to stretch. *To grow. To change.* A thread of fear came with that thought and what it might do to him if they did, but it was hard to hear against the roar of joy and blood in his ears.

The two Tanzanites had left, the guards dismissed, the great doors closed behind them. Only the Sapphire Deathless and he remained. Lady Yadva hauled Lord Vasin onto his feet. She was trying to appear sombre but he could see the delight in her. *Surely the others see it too.*

'This is a sad day for House Sapphire,' she said, 'but we have to move forward.'

'Can we not even catch our breath?' asked Lord Umed. Though his face was composed, Satyendra sensed he was profoundly troubled by what he'd seen, and quietly despairing over Lady Yadva's obvious greed for power. Umed's emotions were softer and more controlled that Yadavendra's had been, but there was a sorrow there, aged like a fine wine, that Satyendra longed to savour. He couldn't help but move closer to him.

Lady Yadva pointed towards the doors. 'The Tanzanites are inside our walls. They have seen . . . ' She scowled in distaste, then flicked a hand towards the broken window, 'That. We cannot let this be the last image in their minds. House Sapphire needs direction.' She looked at Lord Vasin, expectant, but he did not meet her gaze because he was looking at Satyendra.

It was all unfolding as Vasin had predicted. Yadavendra had gone, his daughter was making her bid to succeed him, and that meant it was time for Satyendra to step in. 'Lady

Yadva speaks true,' he said. 'There will be time to grieve later but first we must put ourselves in order.' He looked at Yadva long enough to make her think he was on her side, just because he could. *What is the use of having this power if I can't enjoy it.* 'Therefore I propose we pick a new High Lord, here and now, and I say it should be . . . Lord Vasin.'

She'd been so convinced he was going to say her name that she was halfway through a nod when the meaning of his words got through. Immediately, her eyes went to the others to see how they had reacted. Lords Umed and Gada had not reacted, however, they remained on the sidelines, watching. *They want to make sure they're on the winning side and they don't know which it is yet.*

Satyendra was ready to push the issue. 'What say you, Lady Yadva?'

'Much as I am fond of my little cousin, I do not think he is suitable for High Lord. I'd say more, but I'm sure he doesn't want me to elaborate, especially in company such as this.' She gave a cold smile. 'That is the case, isn't it, Lord Vasin?'

What's this? Satyendra was all ears. *She has something on him. If I could learn what it is, I could control him. But it is of no use to me if Yadva takes power, or if she shares that information now.*

'It doesn't matter what you think,' he said.

Yadva snapped her head back to glare at him, and he added, 'It doesn't matter what any of us think. What matters is who is strongest here.'

'I am,' replied Yadva, 'and you all know it.'

'Prove it.'

She laughed. 'Very well. I state my claim to be High Lord. Do any dare challenge it?'

Umed shook his head. 'I have seen enough violence today.'

Gada was conspicuous by his silence.

I have never felt so powerful as I am in this moment, thought Satyendra. *Could I face her down myself?* It was tempting to try and take her alone, but such a gamble. He remembered how easily Vasin had humbled him and decided against it.

'I challenge,' said Vasin, though there was a resignation in his voice that did not inspire confidence.

'Just you then,' replied Yadva. She lifted a fist, weighing it before her as if it were a hammer.

Vasin did not take on a fighting stance. 'There are many types of strength, cousin. Not everything is about being bigger or stronger.'

'You only say that because you are smaller and weaker. Give up.'

'I have Lord Rochant's support. The others haven't spoken yet. That places me in the position of strength.'

Her lips curled down as she considered his words, and then she hit him. Vasin bent double over her fist, then fell to his knees. 'Do you see now, little cousin? I am the one in the position of strength, not you.'

Satyendra walked away from the empty throne and towards Yadva. However bad it would be serving Vasin, he knew serving her would be worse.

When Vasin was able to speak again, his words came out in a wheeze. 'I do not see it.'

'You need me to hit you again?' She shrugged. 'I don't mind.'

If she attacked Vasin again, he would have to try and stop

her. A part of him delighted in the thought. He wanted to test his strength, to enjoy it before it faded. He wanted them all to see.

Very slowly, Vasin pushed himself to his feet, and met Yadva's gaze.

'Alright then,' she said, and swung for him.

Satyendra caught her fist before it reached Vasin. It made a meaty thwack against his palm. She snarled and pushed against him, but though his hand shook, it did not budge. An impulsive smile split his face. It was very un-Rochant of him but he couldn't help it. *I'm at least as strong as her!*

'Get off me!' she snapped, but there was a hint of panic there, panic that tipped the odds even more in his favour.

Satyendra's smile turned vicious, and he began to push back, forcing her arm down, one inch at a time. Perhaps he had been too hasty in his support of Vasin. A new road was revealing itself. *I could take down Yadva in front of them all and become High Lord myself!*

He pushed down on her and was rewarded with the sight of her knees buckling. *Just a little more . . .*

Suddenly, there was no resistance and she was falling backwards, pulling rather than pushing to take him with her. Her feet came up under his chest, lodged there, and kicked. The next thing he knew he was in the air, then spreadeagled on the floor, face down.

No! I am stronger! How is this happening?

Yadva was above him, one knee pressed hard into his back, and her hands clamped down either side of his head. 'Withdraw your support.'

He flailed uselessly, unable to bring his strength to bear.

The surging unnatural confidence evaporated, leaving him scared and in pain. He wanted to withdraw. In that moment, he wanted to very much. But Vasin knew the truth about him. If it came out, he was done for.

'Wait,' he gasped.

He felt the flex of her muscles, and his head hit the stone floor so hard he couldn't see.

'Withdraw your support,' she repeated, raising his head again.

'Hold!' said Vasin. 'Don't kill him.'

Yadva paused. Satyendra lay insensate beneath her, his head a ripe piece of fruit between her hands, ready to be pulped.

'Are you prepared to accept that I am stronger?'

It was a good question. Doing so would put Yadva in charge, no doubt doom his mother to final death, and lead to all kinds of personal misery. And for what? To save one life? The truth was he didn't even like Satyendra. But to stand by and let him die like this was too much.

'Will you promise to help House Ruby? And to never abandon our people?'

'That depends. Do you agree to serve me as High Lord?'

He closed his eyes. *I cannot win, but at least I can make House Sapphire do the right thing.* He tried to speak but pride closed his throat. Why couldn't he say the words? Was it because of his mother? Did he dare try and bargain for her life too?

'I have reached a decision.'

It was Gada who spoke. He scooped up Yadavendra's sapphire bladed staff and held it out to Yadva, who smiled and let go of Satyendra's head with one hand to grasp it.

At the last second Gada pulled it back. Vasin wondered if he were just being petty but then he saw Gada had raised it to swing. The glaive connected with Yadva's face with an almighty crack, breaking something, her nose at least, maybe her cheekbone, and she crashed to the floor. With a slight nod, Gada turned and held out the glaive. 'I stand with Lord Rochant in support of my brother.'

'You'd better not be about to do the same thing to me,' said Vasin as he took it.

Gada gave him a weak smile and stepped well back as Yadva started to groan.

'Then it is settled,' said Umed. 'I support you also, and recognize your authority above all others.' He walked over to where Yadva lay. 'That just leaves you. I implore you, end this ridiculous display and fall into line.'

'But Uncle,' she spluttered, sitting up to spit blood. 'It should be me. You know it.'

'Nonsense. You'd make a terrible High Lord. Strength has nothing to do with our current body's condition, it has to do with the power to move others. Should Lord Gada rule because he knocked you down?'

'No,' she muttered, giving Gada a hate-filled look.

'And should you rule because you knocked Lord Vasin down?'

'Fine,' she growled. 'You've made your point. I give my support to Lord Vasin.'

Vasin held out a hand to her. 'You mean it? We have to go forward together or not at all.'

She took it and hauled herself upright. 'I swear it as child of the Sapphire Everlasting.' Then, in a lower voice, she added: 'At least you can hunt properly.'

'Good. Now help me get Lord Rochant off the floor.'

'Yes, my High Lord,' she said.

She was talking to him. High Lord Sapphire. That was his title now. He felt dizzy with the truth of it.

Umed cleared his throat. 'High Lord, your name must grow with your stature. What should we call you?'

The name came to his lips instantly: 'Vasinidra.'

There was a pause. This was his first statement as High Lord, an honouring of his mother, an implicit criticism of what had been done to her.

Yadva looked shocked, Gada more so, and Umed, nodding, blinking hard to stop the tears from forming, said, 'Then, from this day forth, Lord Vasin shall become High Lord Vasinidra. All hail Vasinidra!'

'Vasinidra!' shouted the others.

He took this in, noting that Satyendra, back on his feet, seemed dazed. Standing next to Yadva, it was incredible to think that one so small had been able to hold his own against her at all. Though, now he came to think of it, perhaps he wasn't as short as all that.

'I feared we'd have to get you a matching tattoo on the other side of your head.' He put a hand on Satyendra's shoulder. 'Thank you. I won't forget what you did here today.'

He guided Satyendra to Rochant's throne. 'Sit. Rest. You've earned it.'

'What about the rest of us, High Lord?' asked Umed. 'Have we earned the right to rest too?'

Vasinidra favoured his uncle with a grim smile. 'For today, yes. But not for long. We must prepare to hunt.'

'Hunt where? I have heard of no sacrifices being made.'

'That is because they were made long ago and ignored, much to our shame. We go to Sorn. It is time to clean out that old wound and let it heal.'

Despite her rapidly swelling face, Yadva perked up. 'You mean to hunt the Scuttling Corpseman?'

'I do.'

She laughed and wiped the blood from her cheek. 'Maybe you won't be such a bad High Lord after all.'

CHAPTER TWENTY-TWO

Refreshed and free of the burden of the Red Brothers, Sa-at had made good time catching up the others. They carried Rochant between them, travelling in short bursts. Crowflies flew ahead, keeping out a compound eye for trouble. Now they were in the shadow of a huge mountain range, and beyond it, he could see a great block of grey in the sky. It was Rochant's castle. The base of it looked like natural rock but on the top it had smooth walls and pointed towers, and Sa-at had never seen anything like it before and was so excited he immediately started to jump up and down. 'You live up there? In the clouds?'

'Yes,' said Rochant. 'I wasn't exaggerating.'

Sa-at had lots of questions he wanted to ask Rochant, but it was hard to talk and carry him at the same time, so he focused on the important ones. 'How does it fly when it doesn't have wings?'

'It doesn't fly,' replied Rochant. 'It floats. There's sapphire growing in the stone that is lifted by the essence currents.'

'What's an ess-ss-ense current?'

'Imagine a wind that only blows certain things. If you dropped a leaf it would fall straight down, but the right kind of crystal would be carried by it.'

They walked on for a while as he digested this. 'Who carried the rocks up there?'

'A good question. The truth is we know far too little about how it was done. The castles were constructed at the end of the Unbroken Age, and predate all of the Deathless in House Sapphire. Only the very oldest of us know anything about that time, as the castles and the Godroads came before we did. The High Lord of House Spinel is said to have been born at the end of that era, but he lives a long way away from here and doesn't travel, so I haven't ever had the chance to ask him. Perhaps, when things are calmer, I'll ask for permission to visit.'

'If you go, can I come with you?'

'We'll see. One journey at a time.'

The morning moved into afternoon, the three suns pale discs behind a curtain of cloud. They were walking alongside the Godroad, keeping to the edge of the trees. Though Tal was nowhere near as fast as Sa-at, and clumsy, there was no doubting his tenacity. He bore the brunt of Rochant's weight without complaint, his pace unchanging, steady.

Crowflies screeched in the distance.

'Is someone coming?' asked Tal.

'Yes,' Sa-at replied, frowning. 'But . . . '

'But what?'

'I don't know. Crowflies sounds odd. I can't tell if its excited or worried.'

'We shouldn't take any chances,' said Rochant. 'My enemies

won't brave the Godroad, but they have agents who will.'

Tal started dragging him towards the trees, leaving Sa-at standing alone. He scratched at the scar on his knuckle, frowning at the shape materializing on the Godroad. It was an old wagon, drawn by a giant five-legged Dogkin, with fur as white as the snow on the mountaintops.

Crowflies came down to land at Sa-at's side. It looked from him, to the wagon and back again. 'Sa-aat.'

'What is it?'

The Birdkin began to sing a lullaby, one of his favourites. A strange sensation began to rise in his chest, as if too many feelings were coming all at once, and had got stuck trying to get out.

As the wagon got closer, he could see people sitting on it. One of them was a man, pale and broad shouldered, his eyes intent on the road. The other was a woman, with long dark hair. She was looking at him.

He took a step towards her as if it was the most natural thing in the world, his foot sinking into the thick mulch of dead leaves and bark that formed the dead zone between Wild and Godroad.

Crowflies continued to sing.

He would run to her. If he were quick, he could reach the wagon before it went past.

The woman on the wagon raised a tentative hand.

Sa-at went to do the same, just as Tal returned and grabbed his shoulders.

'Get down!' he hissed.

Before Sa-at could reply, he was pushed face first into the thick muddy dirt.

*   *   *

It was the strangest sight. Her Satyendra was standing there. Right there! He was wrapped in black feathers like the one that grew from the back of her head, and his long hair was blowing in the wind.

'Varg, we have to stop.'

'What's up?'

'Look, it's my Satyendra. Look!' Varg turned to her, concern written into his lined face. 'No, not at me, over there.' She pointed, and Varg dutifully followed her finger.

'There's nothing there.'

'Yes there is, there's—' She stopped talking. Varg was right, there was nothing but trees as far as the eye could see. 'But he was right there.'

'He can't be, Chand. He's dead.'

For a moment, she fought the truth of what he was saying, so strong was the feeling in her heart. The facts were relentless, however: Satyendra was dead, and that long hair that she loved so much had been cut away by her own hand. *It could not be him. This is the Wild's doing. It is playing tricks on me.* The last time she had come here, it had been the Whispercage that lurked on the periphery of her vision. Now it seemed the ghost of her son had taken its place.

The Godroad was quiet and calm. She'd been bracing herself for the black feather to turn to ash or burst into flames, taking her hair with it, but nothing had happened. She didn't understand how the taint had caused Satyendra so much pain and yet done nothing to her. *Surely I am just as corrupted as he was?*

They travelled on for a time. It occurred to her that she'd never specified exactly where she wanted to go, and Varg hadn't asked. The truth was, she didn't know, but hoped she would when she saw it.

One of Varg's arms was over her shoulder, and one of hers around his waist, clamping them together by mutual assent. He was solid, something she could hold onto. During Lord Rochant's absence, she had been the one to keep order, and she had done so alone.

It is so good to be held. I wish I could stay this way forever.

'The suns'll go down before we get anywhere useful,' said Varg. 'Do you want to set up a camp or go on through the night?'

'When the suns go down, I have to go too.'

'Why not wait one night? We've only just found each other again.'

'Because if I wait one night, I might never have the strength to go.'

'I'm okay with that.'

She reached up to touch his face. 'I . . . I can't, Varg. Please don't make this any harder for me.'

'I don't understand you Sapphire, an' I don't get why you're following such a stupid order. If Pari told me to do something like this, I'd tell her to piss off.'

Chandni didn't say anything about this being more to do with the nature of true authority, or that Lord Rochant Sapphire could hardly be compared to Lady Pari Tanzanite. 'I made a deal with the Wild and now I have to pay the price. That's just the way it is.'

He set his jaw in a way she didn't like. 'Then I'm going to pay it with you.'

'Don't be ridiculous.'

'I made a deal too, with Fiya, so I could stay in that tree, remember? I'm just as bad as you.'

Chandni had made that same deal. With horror, she realized that she'd never mentioned it to Lord Rochant. *How lost must I be that a deal with the Wild becomes trivial? Forgettable?* But then, compared to the others, it was trivial. A little hair was nothing, compared to giving up her own blood and nails, or the blood of another . . .

'I don't think you're as bad as me, Varg. Believe it or not, in some ways, I think you're better.' She sighed. 'But you must make your own choices.' He squeezed her closer to him and she added: 'I wish you were somewhere else, with someone else, where you could be happy, but . . . I am glad you're here.'

'Yeah?'

'Yes.'

If she could have stopped time and stayed on the wagon, she would have. However, the suns continued to cross the sky, preparing to set in all their inexorable cruelty.

'Here,' she said.

Varg brought the wagon to a stop. 'You wait on the Godroad,' he said to Glider.

Glider barked back, making it clear she was not happy about the situation.

'Let her out,' said Chandni. 'We won't be coming back and she should be allowed to make her own choices too.'

He nodded and unstrapped the Dogkin. 'There. You're free now.'

Glider watched them with her mismatched eyes as they climbed down the side of the Godroad. She barked at them several times as they walked away, then jumped off to pad alongside.

Chandni stroked her muzzle. 'Thank you.'

Varg had taken her right hand. Though she couldn't feel the contact, she forced her fingers to curl around his.

'Can I borrow your knife? I didn't have time to pack one of my own.'

'Uh, yeah. Sure.' He passed it over and she took it in her left hand. There were fresh tears glistening in his beard.

The suns hadn't fully set, but it was dark inside the forest. Any self-respecting Gatherer would be well on their way home, for in the depths of the Wild, things were already stirring.

With the tip of the knife, Chandni drew back the sleeve on her right arm and made two shallow cuts. Then, because there had been a third deal that she'd forgotten to tell Lord Rochant about, she made another. It was small consolation, but there was no pain, and she had to rely on her eyes to be sure she'd broken the skin enough to bring her blood to the surface.

Together, they walked into the Wild. They hadn't gone far when Glider began to growl softly. 'Here we go,' said Varg. 'Can I have my knife back.'

She passed it to him without comment. He knew as well as she did that a knife wasn't going to make any difference here.

A Birdkin settled in the trees above. It had the same black feathers as the one in her hair, and multifaceted eyes, that it took turns to study them with, jerking its head from left to right in sudden movements. Another Birdkin came, of the same breed as the first. Then another, then another. They lined up on either side of Chandni, marking out a path through the shadowy trees.

She took it. Sooner or later something would be lured by her blood. She might as well not draw out the agony.

More Birdkin came. The ones further back hopping from tree to tree, gliding after her as new ones appeared ahead. Every so often, one would drop down to peck at the blood that had dripped from her arm into the dirt. They were eerily quiet, and Chandni was reminded of the time she'd called out to the powers of the Wild, and they had stopped to listen.

They're listening now, she thought, and shivered.

She heard barking from somewhere far away, and recognized Glider's voice. Whirling round, she found the Dogkin was nowhere to be seen, and that Varg had gone too, her fingers curled around empty air.

'Varg?' she called. 'Glider?'

There was more barking, and perhaps the faintest sound of Varg's voice, shouting her name, but it was being rolled between distant trees, making it impossible to discern where they were.

Perhaps this is a good thing. They don't need to die for me. Please, Glider, keep him safe.

It was getting harder to see, but she thought she could make out a larger shape, some confection of feathers and darkness that stood tall and majestic. She fancied that its arms were open, and that is was waiting for her.

Chandni raised her head and the Birdkin watched, intense and silent, as she walked towards it.

They'd put it off for as long as they could, but eventually they had to get Rochant onto the Godroad. Tal scrambled up first, using Sa-at's shoulder as a stepping stone, and then between them, they lifted Rochant up the ten feet of sheer crystal.

'Your turn,' said Tal, holding out a hand.

Sa-at backed off so that he could get a good run at it. He was good at jumping and climbing, and was pleased that Tal would get to see. With practised ease, he sprinted forward, then sprung into the air. Tal caught his hands and pulled, adding to his momentum, and the two of them stumbled into the middle of the Godroad, both immensely pleased with themselves.

By the time Sa-at had realized that his right palm was itching, the sensation had already escalated to a searing hot pain. He called out, clutching his wrist so that he could hold his hand steady and look at it. The pain intensified, and within the darkness of the oval pit in the centre of his palm, he saw a light. Not blue nor silver like that of the Godroad itself, but yellow and red, flickering.

It is fire.

It is fire!

I am on fire!

He fell to his knees, unable to scream, unable to do anything but watch the skin hiss and the smoke belch from his palm, a prisoner to his pain.

Tal picked him up under the shoulders.

'No,' said Rochant.

'But, my lord, look at him! I have to get him off the Godroad.'

'Leave him be. He needs to be purged if he is to come with us.'

Tal let go and stepped back. 'I'm sorry.'

Sa-at didn't react, couldn't react. The fire brightened but

did not spread, building until his eyes hurt with the sight of it. Worst of all was the smell, seeping into him.

In the end it was too much. His eyes blurred with tears, the light fragmenting into a dozen spots of burning brightness, and then he was falling sideways.

It felt as though he fell for a long time, and it was some surprise to find that when he came to, much, much later, that he was still on the Godroad. His hand ached and when he looked at it, there was an oval of skin, puffy, featureless and white, where the nostril in his palm had been.

'It's gone,' he said. And though it stung every time the air brushed against it, he felt better somehow, lighter.

'Can you walk?' asked Rochant.

'I think so.'

'Shouldn't we wait, my lord?' asked Tal. 'Let him rest a bit.'

'Do you think my enemy will rest?'

Tal lowered his head. 'No, my lord.'

'Do you think they will take pity on us if they find us in this state?'

'No, my lord.'

'Then help him up and save your breath for the climb ahead. Trust me, you'll need it.'

Sa-at shared a sympathetic look with his friend. What Rochant had said was true . . .

But I don't like it. It feels wrong.

He couldn't say why, and the thought soon floated away, replaced by the demands of travel.

They trudged along the Godroad, using its light to guide them. Rochant kept driving them on, determined to make the most of the darkness. Sa-at was more concerned about

Crowflies however. The Birdkin refused to join them, flying about fifty metres parallel, and calling his name again and again, clearly distressed.

Eventually it landed, crowing but refusing to come any further.

'We must keep going,' said Rochant.

'But Crowflies!'

'Cannot go where we are going. It cannot use the Godroad.'

'But I saw that big Dogkin use it.'

'That's different.'

'Why?'

'A Dogkin's soul is part human, but Crowflies is as much demon as it is bird or fly. The energies of the Godroad would destroy it as surely as they purged your hand.'

'But Crowflies is always with me.'

'Not here,' said Rochant. 'You need to choose: stay with your demon or help me get back to my castle.'

Sa-at looked up. The castle looked even more beautiful up close. Gemslight glowed blue in the night from the battlements and windows. It softened the hard edges of the building, making it seem warm and magical. There would be people up there, all waiting to meet him as Rochant had promised. More than he could count. More than he could even imagine. *Tal can't manage on his own. Rochant's need is greater than Crowflies.*

'I'll come back soon!' he shouted.

'Sa-aat!' protested the Birdkin.

'I promise!'

'Sa-aaaaat!'

He'd never heard Crowflies sound so sad before, and wiped a tear as he went away. He thought about the Birdkin many times as the road got steeper and steeper. Of course, it had left him to forage, but this felt different. Now there was a barrier between them, one only he could cross.

He also thought about the woman he'd seen.

I felt like I knew her.

I felt like I liked her.

I felt like she knew me!

If it hadn't been for Tal, he would have said hello. He knew it wasn't Tal's fault but he couldn't help but feel annoyed.

After a while Crowflies was too far away to hear, which made Sa-at feel really bad. He had this horrible feeling he would not be back soon. It felt like they were not just travelling in miles, they were going into a different world. He was still excited by that, but also sad to be leaving his friend so far behind.

When they came level with the rocky base of the castle, Rochant told them where to find a side path.

'I'm sorry, my lord,' said Tal. 'There's not much path left.'

'That's as it should be. It's a secret path. The going will be hard from here on, so rest if you need to.'

They did, but Sa-at had hardly closed his eyes when Rochant was ordering them up again. It seemed that the higher they got, the more he seemed to tell rather than suggest. It made Sa-at uncomfortable.

Slowly, they scrambled around the side of the castle until they came to some loose bricks. Under Rochant's supervision, they removed them, revealing a small gap in the wall. Sa-at was able to squeeze through easily enough, but Tal and Rochant had to strip off their outer layers of padding to get through, and both were shivering by the time they'd got to the other side.

431

They were in a walled courtyard full of tents. Though the corner they'd arrived in was dark, there were lots of lit areas, and the sounds of people's voices. Sa-at could hear talking and laughter, and something that sounded like talking but was more melodic. There were smells too, of food and fragrances that he had no name for. It took all of his self-control not to go and investigate further.

They hurriedly dressed Rochant again and carried him towards the side of the keep where a couple of steps led to a small door. 'Keep your heads down and my hood up,' Rochant instructed. 'If anyone speaks to us, ignore them. If they insist, let me answer.'

'Why are we hiding? Isn't all this yours?' asked Sa-at.

'Not now,' replied Rochant.

He bid them wait on the edge of the darkness. It seemed to Sa-at as if he were listening to something, and then, seemingly at random, told them to continue. They crossed the patch of light to get to the door and as they reached it, there was a loud roar from the tents, followed by lots of clapping.

Sa-at flinched from the sound but managed to stop from calling out. He'd learned long ago that staying small and quiet was the best way to survive. Suddenly, meeting all of those people seemed less appealing. They dragged Rochant up the stairs, but the door was locked.

'Should I knock, my lord?'

'Yes. Three short knocks, three slow ones, then one more.'

Tal did as instructed. After a while they heard slow footsteps on the other side of the door, and a heavy key being turned in a lock. The door opened to reveal a large kitchen that promised both delicious things to eat and a place to rest their tired limbs. Between them and it however, was a stern-looking woman, the oldest Sa-at had ever seen. Her teeth were yellow and her eyes sunk deep in a lined face. 'Go away,' she said.

'Are you the cook?' asked Rochant.

'Aye.'

'I was hoping for something to eat. Food fit for a lord.'

She scratched the side of her cheek thoughtfully. 'I've a castle full of hungry lords to feed and I've only some scraps left to spare. What you after?'

'A snack for the ages.'

Her body went rigid and she gripped the side of the door for support. 'Might be I have what you want. But I warn you, it's bitter.'

'As it should be. All things that do not die . . . '

'All things that do not die . . . ' she repeated in a whisper.

'Are bitter,' they finished together.

With a creak, the old woman dropped to her knees. 'It's you! Good Lord Rochant, back from the dead. I knew that other one wasn't you. Knew it soon as I looked at him. He didn't even know the proper words.'

She ushered them inside and they put Rochant into a comfortable chair while the old cook fussed about with all kinds of tools Sa-at had never seen before. He wanted to know what every one of them was called. And why everything was shaped the way it was. And how did they capture the stars and put them in their windows? He had so many questions!

He was also incredibly tired. He and Tal squeezed onto another chair together. It was hot in the room, a large shelf of sapphire casting blue light onto the ceiling and warmth to the walls.

'To answer your earlier question,' said Rochant. 'This is all mine, but my enemies think they have taken it from me.'

'Nasty people, they are, my lord,' added the cook.

'Now I'm here,' continued Rochant, 'I intend to take it back, and I'd like your help. What say you?'

Tal agreed instantly but Sa-at hesitated. 'I'm not sure. Your enemies aren't my enemies. They might even be my friends.'

'Trust me, they're not. It's not just my life they've taken away, Sa-at. It's yours too.'

'What do you mean?'

'Oooo!' said the cook. 'I see it now. He's got his father's eyes and his mother's face.'

He looked at the old woman. 'Do you know me?'

'Saw you born, I did. Pretty little thing you were, we all said so.'

'Help me,' said Rochant, 'and you'll be reclaiming your own life too. They took you from your home and left you to die in the Wild.'

'They did?'

The cook nodded sadly. 'Killed your cousins and your father, would have killed you as well if old Roh hadn't stopped them.'

It struck him then: this place should have been his home. He should have grown up surrounded by lovely smells and warm places to sit. He should have had a father and a mother, cousins, friends, people to watch out for him, people to hold him in the dark.

Sa-at didn't often feel angry, but he felt angry now. 'Okay,' he said. 'I'll help you.'

Rochant met his eyes, approving, and all of his tiredness fell away in a rush of pride.

The cook clapped her hands together. 'I'll go dig out some biscuits and a little of your favourite cheese, my lord. I can see it's going to be a long night.'

Pari and Arkav bounded beneath the bulk of Lord Rochant's floating castle, their armour glowing in the night. In great loping strides they came to the crest of rock at the edge of the great chasm. Waiting there were the Bringers of Endless Order, seven robed silhouettes. One of them broke away from the others to approach, the one who had agreed to help them, Pari was sure of it. In her armour, she felt sharper, more confident in her intuitions.

'Good evening,' said Pari.

'Are you ready to begin?'

'Not quite. Those lanterns you made for High Lord Tanzanite, the ones she gave to Lord Arkav. You designed them to work against the armour, didn't you?'

'We made what was asked of us.'

'She knew Yadavendra wouldn't go without a fight and so did you.' She looked at Arkav. 'But how did you know to use them as a weapon?'

'High Lord Primyamvada told me before we left,' Arkav replied. 'She said they were a last resort.'

'Why didn't you tell me? No, let me guess, she told you not to.'

'Yes.'

'Did she say why?'

'She said I could be trusted to show proper restraint in their use.' He shrugged, his wings glinting in the dark. 'I agreed with her.'

'After all this, you didn't trust me?'

'I trust you with my life, Pari.' A hint of humour showed in his eyes behind the helmet. 'I just don't trust you to show restraint.'

'Believe me when I tell you I'm showing a lot of restraint right now.'

A lone howl sounded in the dark. The first of the predators setting out from the Wild. She turned back to the lead Bringer. 'Was it really necessary to do this at night?'

'Yes. The place you are going to is closer now than in the day.'

'I don't follow.'

'No,' agreed the Bringer. 'You will need this.' She pointed to a large chunk of stone that had been wrapped several times in chain. There was a loop of links that formed a handle on the top.

'Why?'

'For its weight. You will be flying down, the currents will be pushing up. Let yourself be dragged deep. Lord Arkav's presence will draw out the demons. When you have retrieved the lost piece of his soul, release the weight, and come back to us. We will light the way for you.'

Pari put on her best sarcasm. 'Sounds simple enough.'

'How do we find my . . . the . . . piece of me?' asked Arkav.

'It will find you but the demons will come with it. Separate them and we believe the rest will take care of itself.'

'Believe?' asked Pari.

'It has been a thousand years since the last attempt.'

Attempt. They failed last time. 'Do you mean demons like those in the Wild?'

The Bringer shook her head in a way Pari did not find encouraging.

'Can you elaborate?'

The Bringer looked at her but said nothing.

'Then I suppose we should get on with it.'

As she went to take the chain, Arkav took her arm. 'You don't have to do this. I could go alone.'

'What and miss the chance to see what's down there? I think not. Besides, you won't last ten minutes without me.'

There was more she could say but she didn't need to. Arkav could see it in her eyes. He nodded, and they picked up the chain. Between them it presented little challenge, though Pari wondered how the Bringers managed to drag it here. Maybe they too were stronger than they looked.

'Watch for our lights,' said the lead Bringer. 'There will be seven, no more, no less. Only they will guide you home.'

In her last lifecycle, when Pari had leapt from Lord Rochant's castle, she had done everything she could to avoid falling down this chasm. *And now look at me.*

They hefted the great chunk of stone out over the edge. It was unmoved by the essence currents and hung straight down. Their wings were another matter, and Pari had to fight to stop from being blown backwards.

'Ready?' she called to Arkav.

'On three,' he called back. They bent their legs in preparation, their Sky-legs coiling, building power. 'One . . . Two . . . '

'Three!' she shouted, determined to get the last word.

And together, they jumped.

Acknowledgements

It feels strange to be writing this now. There's a big gap between drafting a book and writing the acknowledgements, and in that gap for *The Ruthless* my life has changed radically. If you'll forgive the pretension, I feel a little like a Deathless who wrote a book in one lifecycle and is reflecting on it from another.

Given how certain aspects of my existence have shifted I feel especially lucky to have a team of people around me that are tried and true, and that I can rely on. Big thanks to my agent, Juliet, who gives great advice and has a way of making me feel better even in tough times. It's taken me a while to learn that she is always right, but I think I've got it now.

We should probably all thank Natasha, for general editing awesomeness and for crushing a certain section of the book for the sake of your reading pleasure. Thanks too, for additional edits from Jack, copy edits from Joy, and general fabulosity from the Harper Voyager team of ninjas that continue to work from the shadows. And thanks to Chris Tulloch McCabe for the wonderful cover.

I'd also like to give a special mention to Emma for coming to the book's rescue at one point with colour-coded post-its, an objective eye and a warm drink.

Lastly, thanks to you for picking up *The Ruthless*. I'm not always sure why people read the strange things I write, but it means the world that they do.